PREFACE

BODY LANGUAGE

He closed the door very gently and then Gallagher's staring, accusing eyes. Covering his own with trembling hands he sank to his knees on the floor in front of the corpse. There was no remorse. But there was fear . Of being caught. He had to move fast. Think fast . Somebody might come in at any moment. Hospitals were busy places.

*

Danny Hagan glared at P.J. and Plum and spat on the pavement.
"Ah'm telling' ye'se fur the last time. It's fuck a' tae dae wi' ye. Ah don't care who he's connected tae. He's gettin' it the night. If anybuddy's gonnae beat the shit oot ma faither it's me. He goes doon the night."
Danny drew the immaculately tailored gaberdine coat closer, and buttoned the middle button against the freezing wind. His right hand raised the Prussian collar and his left closed round the handle of the axe in the left hand coat pocket. Turning abruptly, he crossed Sauchiehall street and headed for the pub near Jamaica Street.
"Fuck's sake," said P.J. "we cannae let him go himsel' Plum. He'll get fuckin' slaughtered!"
"Wait tae he's oot o' sight. You go up tae the Locarno an' get the team. Ah'll go intae the Bay Horse an' see who's in there."

*

Lassiter moved politely through the crowd surrounding his boss at the office night out.
" I know it's not about business tonight Daniel but if I could just have a quick word if you don't mind. It won't take a second honestly."
Daniel Taylor turned round smiling and ever so slightly drunk. Just at the right time to catch Lassiter's perfectly timed head butt.

*

Sarah's eyes searched her mother's face for some sign that this was all some horrible nightmare and that the news from the hospital wasn't true. She'd arrived home from school to find the priest holding her weeping mother's hand in both of his. A policeman sat at the other end of the worn old couch. A policewoman sat next to her mother, on the arm of her mother's chair.
"Your daddy's gone to heaven pet. He went this afternoon."

"No he hasn't. No he hasn't. He's still just sick isn't he? I don't want him in heaven. I've got a picture to show him. I drew it tod..." Sarah's mother drew her hand from the priest's and held both her arms out to her. Sobbing hysterically Sarah knew at last this was no nightmare."

*****

CHAPTER ONE

OLD TIMES

"Nothing changes much does it Maggie? Over thirty years and we're still doing the same old double act. I buy you a double and you tell me you don't know where he is. I buy you another and you tell me you've always fancied me. After the third you suddenly remember where I might find him. I mean, I could just take you next door to the off-sales and buy you a couple of bottles if I thought it would help, but you and I both know you'd only tell me a lot of shit. And stop calling it sherry. It's wine Maggie, cheap fortified wine. Tastes like camel's piss. I should know. Remember?"

"Didnae know you'd tasted it. Camel's piss I mean."

Lassiter grinned, lifted her glass from the table, and went to the bar to get her a re-fill. He'd always liked Maggie. He hadn't met too many women who could make him laugh but she was one of them. Things might have been different with him and Maggie back then. But it had ALL been different back then.

When he returned with her drink she was slipping the hand mirror back in her handbag on the pretence of getting her cigarettes. She'd done that back then too. Never really believed how attractive she was. And she was still very attractive. A real enigma into the bargain.

"How do you manage it?"

"Manage what?"

"You drink that stuff like water and never seem to get drunk."

"Ah've always liked the taste and the smell. That's why I drink it. Ma auld granny used to say. Some people kin drink an' some cannae. Ah must be wan o' the wans who kin an' you're the ither type."

"You make everything sound so simple. Life's not like that."

"Mine is."

" Maybe yours is, but mine isn't and neither is Danny's. I want you to give him a message for me. The Gallagher case has come up again. I'll need to speak to him."
"Shit! No' again!"

****

"What are you trying to tell me? That someone murdered my father in that hospital ward all those years ago? That my mother and I have spent the last thirty odd years believing that he died because of complications, and all the time his murderer's been walking about scot free. Someone first attempted to murder him in a pub! And then came back to finish the job. In a bloody hospital! Is that what you're saying Inspector? By God, somebody's going to pay for this. My husband will crucify you all in the press. You'll all lose everything. He'll see to that. Now get out of this bloody house and don't come back! Don't any of you ever come back here!"
Sarah collapsed behind the closed front door. Her knees gave way, and she fell to the floor sobbing uncontrollably. Suddenly she was a frightened little girl once more. She banged her fist on the door and let out a terrifying scream . It was a long drawn out, child's scream.
"Daaaddy!"

****

"I want everything you can get on him on my desk by tomorrow morning. Everything! We're going after this bastard big time. Gangster? We'll see. Now, I've got to go. My wife's not well. Wonder what's wrong with the stupid bitch this time. She phones her doctor for valium if the window cleaner misses a bit on the window pane. Neurotic cow. Still, her doctor's pretty fit. I wonder if she'll still be there when I get home? She said she's put my wife to bed. Wonder if she'd do the same for me."
Taylor's assembled reporters and his chief crime journalist sniggered dutifully as he rose from his desk buttoning the middle button of his immaculate designer suit and headed for the door.
"Remember, everything you can get on Horner on my desk first thing. Anything really juicy about him phone me at home."
"Tosser!" said Gil the chief crime journalist as Taylor left, slamming the door as he always did. " I don't think our boy knows what he's fucking about with here. Our Mr. Horner's a very bad man. Mega, mega bad!"

****

Dr. Jeffries was just slipping her long , shapely legs behind the wheel of her Mondeo when Taylor's Merc. screamed to a halt, inches from her rear bumper.

He strode up to the offside just as she started to wind down the nearside window and opening the door, leaned inside

"Good afternoon Doctor. Looking your usual ravishing self I see. Why is somebody as beautiful as you are,still content to be tending neurotic women, screaming brats and smelly old people who should have been dead years ago? Mystery to me I must say. What's wrong with the stupid bitch this time?"

Patricia stared straight ahead, gripping the steering wheel tightly to control the urge to slap him.

"Your wife, MISTER Taylor has had a very traumatic experience this morning, which she will no doubt relate to you as soon as she feels a little better. She is under sedation at the moment, and resting in her bedroom. Now if you'll excuse me I have a very sick child to attend to. That little girl is very beautiful and has been very ill. Quite far removed from a screaming brat. In the meantime I would suggest that if you cannot be more supportive of your wife, at least leave her alone. And me too for that matter. You really should see someone about that

halitosis. Preferably not me of course. Good day MISTER Taylor!"

Patricia leant over, slammed the door and put the car in gear. Leaving the driveway of the impressive house in the well to do Newton Mearns area of Glasgow, she pointed the car in the general direction of the West End of the city still very angry both at Taylor and herself.

"You're supposed to be above these feelings you silly bitch. Objective. You're a practising G.P. for God's sake , woman."

Taylor stood in the driveway for a few moments after she'd gone and wondered why she was still playing hard to get. She must be aware of how much he was worth, and how most women found him irresistible.Doctor Jeffries drove on towards the Partick area of Glasgow unable to get Daniel Taylor out of her head.

****

Taylor poured himself a very stiff vodka, loosening his expensive silk tie with the other as he did so. He glanced briefly at the morning's mail Sarah had left on top of the drinks cabinet as she always did. Removing his jacket he dropped it deliberately on the floor knowing Philippa their housekeeper - cum - maid would pick it up, brush it and hang it carefully back in his wardrobe beside his others.

"Where are you Phil?", he shouted, "what the fuck's wrong with her now?"

Phillippa Jarvie hated being called Phil. Taylor had learned this shortly after he employed her, and therefore refused to call her anything else. If Daniel Taylor found a way to annoy someone he considered inferior, and that applied to most people, it made his day.

.

"Phil!" he roared again. "I asked you a bloody question. Where are you woman?"

Philippa appeared meekly from the huge kitchen where she had been trying to tidy up the mess Sarah had left. When Taylor's wife was hurting she tended to throw things, and she had been hurting a great deal.

"I'm sorry Mr. Taylor. Miss Sarah...."

"How many times do I have to tell you her name is Mrs. Taylor. Not Miss Sarah, not Miss anything. She is married to me so therefore she is a Mrs.. But then you wouldn't understand the difference would you Phil? Nobody ever asked you to marry them, did they Phil? Maybe you're an old dyke. Now what's wrong this time? I won't ask you again."

Philippa Jarvie swallowed hard, counted to ten, and stooped to pick his suit jacket off the floor. "The doctor only told me that Miss, sorry Mrs. Taylor, had a visit from the police this morning Mr. Taylor and it disturbed her a great deal. She has given her a sedative and she is not to be disturbed further. They must have been here very early because..."

"No, you were here very late as usual. I've been meaning to speak to you about that. This is not a fucking holiday camp. I pay you a lot of money. Above the minimum wage I seem to recall, and for what? A bit of tidying up here and there, and the opportunity to drink endless cups of tea with a madwoman. There are going to be big changes round here. Just you wait and see. Now hang that up, but make sure you press it first."

Phillippa picked the jacket up and silently left the room closing the door very quietly behind her. Once in the hallway she searched through the pockets for anything of value or interest and smiled the very evil little smile that Taylor had never seen.

"Won't be long now Mr. bloody Taylor. Your times just about due you bastard." she said softly patting her hair into place as she passed the hall mirror. She started to hum to herself as she climbed the stairs. She had a lot to look forward to.

****

John Horner didn't look like his hero. What he did have in common with him, was the ability to strike terror in some people's hearts at the mere mention of his name, while appearing to live a fairly innocuous life as a grandfather and family man. Horner had learned a lot from the lifestyle of Carlo Gambino, the legendary New York crime boss. He'd read everything he could find about the man. Horner could be a good friend if he liked you. The strain of remaining friendly with John however could be unbearable at times. The alternative was not really an option for those who knew him well enough.

In common with many who had been teenagers in late sixties and early seventies Glasgow, Johnny Horner had been heavily involved in the city's gang culture. Most people grew out of it, but Johnny grew with it, and had loved every minute of it. Never stupid, he realised remarkably quickly that there wasn't much point in being loyal to any one gang. However if he appeared to be on good terms with most of them, he could then walk the streets in comparative safety thus reducing the risk of being seriously injured or even killed in some totally pointless street confrontation. A very regular occurrence. But Johnny was no soft mark.

No coward, his easygoing manner, concealed an explosive temper and something else. A photographic memory. Do Johnny Horner a bad turn and it would never be forgotten. It was selective too. Sometimes he had to be reminded of a good turn someone had done him in the past This selective memory procedure could also be unfair. Any wrong done Johnny, real or imagined, had to be paid for and this applied directly to the perpetrator's relatives. In later life John Horner changed his view on that. Partly because he had mellowed a little, but principally because he simply realised it was bad for business. And by that time he had quite a number of them. Horner's lifelong hero, old Carlo, had had the appearance of a gentle, elderly grandfather which , to some people, he may very well just have been . Gambino had shunned publicity. John Horner ,on the other hand, loved it! A slim, good looking man with impeccable dress sense, he loved to be seen, heard and talked about. Whatever was said or written about him interested him greatly and it made no difference to him whether he was loved or hated. As long as he was noticed. His name, depending on how well those using it knew him, was either whispered or bragged about as being a close friend of whoever did so, and was enough to settle virtually any dispute instantly. This fear driven behaviour applied to all but a handful of people in the city . Horner knew who all of these people were and, more importantly where, they were most of the time. He kept a very close eye on them. He was no coward but neither was he a fool. In his fifty odd years

spent steeped in the Glasgow crime scene he had only met four people who had impressed him as very dangerous, and , as far as he was aware, all four were all still alive and well , and also well capable of organising any attempt to remove him from the scene. Permanently! Daniel Taylor, with his rag of a newspaper, however, was not one of those people. He was going to have to be dealt with and soon! He would have to use one or both of the Jamiesons again. They would know the answer. One of them always did and had done since he first started using them in the late sixties.

Maggie lifted the receiver and dialled the number Danny had told her to use only in an emergency

"Hello."

"It's me. Lassiter wants to see you. It's about you know what again."

"Fuck. Whitd'ye tell him?"

"Nothing"

"Good. Keep it that wiy. Ah know how tae git tae him. Ye huvnae spoke tae me and you don't know nuthin' aboot where Ah'm ur. Awright hen? Thanks."

"Who was that?"

"Maggie, jist."

"Come back to bed then."

"Right Doactor"

Patricia Jeffries drew back the covers, exposing her nakedness, and Danny Hagan followed doctor's orders.

END CHAPTER

CHAPTER TWO

OLD FRIENDS AND OLD FEUDS

As usual the mangy, half-starved Alsatian attempted to garrotte itself on the thirty foot length of rope which restrained it, as Horner's Jaguar turned into the car park at the rear of the Jamieson's dingy pub in Glasgow's East End. It's furious barking brought Phil Jamieson to the open cellar door where he had been engaged in filling recognised, reputable brand name whisky bottles with the cheap rubbish he bought either from the cash and carry, the local supermarket or the Pakistani shop some blocks away.

"If you don't shut that fucker up, I swear I'll shoot it wan ae these days!" screamed Horner, opening the Jag. door after first making sure that Jamieson had the beast firmly under control. Horner didn't like

dogs or cats or any pets for that matter. They contributed nothing and cost money. "Ugly bastard!"
"Better lookin' than some o' thae wimmen that drink in here. Fuckin' hell!" Jamieson shouted back from the doorway.
Horner smiled grudgingly, and entered the pub. With less than an hour to go till official opening time, it was still a mess. Upended chairs, tables and a broken pool cue
littered the unswept floor. Dried blood adorned the pillar which stood in the centre of the pub.
"Whit the fuck happened here?" said Horner lighting one of his small cigars.
"Wan o' thae young team got ambitious last night. Sorted it oot nae problem." said Jamieson with a dismissive shrug.
"Watch yur back then. Evil wee bastards some ae them, an' they a' use the blades. Gie's a hauf An' none o' yir shit mind. Black Label fae the same bottle you drink fae. You shouldnae be drinkin' onywiy. Fuckin' bammy enough as it is.
"Whaurs yir brither?"
"Coort. Witness jist."
"Ah swear tae tell the truth, the whale truth, an' nuthin' like the fuckin' truth." Horner laughed . Jamieson didn't. Neither of the Jamieson's were known much as laughers.

****

On the other side of the city Phillippa Jarvie closed the bedroom door on the still sleeping Sarah but only after she'd sent the text message on Sarah's mobile phone that lay on the bedside table.

....

Lassiter was very, very good at what he did. It was just unfortunate that a lot of the time he didn't enjoy doing it. In his line of work he seemed to be forced to meet and mix with a disproportionate amount of prats. Daniel Taylor was right up there with the best of them. As a freelance journalist, Lassiter was forced to look on Taylor and his newspaper, The Glasgow Voice, as a possible outlet for his work. He consoled himself with the fact that now and again he could take Taylor's money. It would never make up for what Taylor had taken from him years previously, but it was some consolation. Taylor's wife, Sarah, had been Lassiter's one and only true love and he had never forgotten her. A good ten years younger than him, she had fallen for his rough and ready lifestyle back then ,but had later opted for the safer, more predictable future that life with Daniel Taylor had offered. Taylor was nearer her own age, good looking, a snappy dresser and had a lot of money provided by, and still largely being provided by, his father. His father had made a fortune in the non-ferrous and semi-precious metals industry. Lassiter still felt the pain of losing Sarah to Taylor but was no longer bitter. Some thirty years later however, he knew he was still in love with her. He very much doubted if the feelings were mutual. He still remembered the irate phone call he received from her the morning after he had head butted her future husband some thirty years earlier.

■■

"How did this all come about then? The poor bastard's been dead for all this time and they couldn't find a motive then. What's changed?"
"Apparently some woman phoned somebody at the "News", and told him her mother told her before she died, that somebody had helped Gallagher on his way. Pulled some of the drips out and the poor sod was nearly dead anyway. As people tend to do when their throat's been slashed from ear to ear. It seems the mother had been a nurse on the ward at the time. She had a bit of a problem with the sauce and was told by one of the doctors that it was her imagination and to forget all about it. Gallagher had died from his wounds and the resultant complications that had set in, and that was that. But the woman who phoned said the nurse maintained on her deathbed that it was no accident. Seemingly she never forgot about it. Never got over it. Mentioned it every time she was drunk it seems. Never got over that habit either. Not like you my old son."
"Shut up a minute Gil, I'm trying to remember something. I'll need to speak to Danny Hagan first."
Lassiter put the phone down on the chief crime journalist at "The Glasgow Voice". That was a very big drink he owed Gil. Pity he couldn't join him. He still missed drinking sometimes. Even after all these years. But if he'd carried on he would certainly have killed himself, and maybe one or two others as well. He frowned, trying hard to remember everything Sarah had told him about her father on the few occasions she had been able to speak about him, back in the days when she and Lassiter had been close. She had loved her father very much and had tried as hard as she knew how to blank it all out. That was it! The one thing she had always said about him. A decent, "hard working" man who worked "all the hours God sent." He must have had money worries. Maybe he went to the wrong people to solve them. Why hadn't anybody thought of that back in 1968. Especially him. Too pissed probably. It had usually been the case back then.

****

There was no doubt who the text message had come from. Previously the blackmailer had always used different ways to get in touch. Now , whoever it was, was simply phoning newspapers. That was upsetting. Most upsetting. Something would have to be done. Bit of a nuisance really. Three decades later, and still no real peace of mind. Mind you it was obvious they still weren't really sure who they were blackmailing. As long as it stayed that way the money was incidental. Nothing , really.

****

Taylor left Sarah to sleep as instructed. The doctor hadn't said what the "traumatic experience" had been, but knowing his wife it could have been anything from her aged mother having caught the cold , to one of her stupid friends having marriage problems. He knew his wife.

The problem with Daniel Taylor was he had never got remotely close to knowing his wife. He poured himself another stiff vodka and kicking his shoes off , pressed the remote to watch the lunchtime news. The main reason for doing so was to ogle the extremely sexy young presenter he had reason to believe he could entice away from her current boyfriend. He was wrong about that as well. He glanced up now and again from reading his mail, as it was only a report about some fire somewhere , and even that was being brought to the nation's attention by the other presenter who was male and annoyed Taylor intensely. The presenter was very professional, articulate and handsome. He was also of Asian origin. All of these were reason enough to annoy Taylor, or D.T. as he liked his staff to call him. Behind his back the same staff delighted in adding the apostrophe "s."

Taylor's inability to drink and behave himself at the same time was well known in press circles.

The presenter glanced up from the sheaf of papers on his desk and Taylor could have sworn he was looking directly at HIM.

"Strathclyde Police are refusing either to confirm or deny at the moment, if investigations have indeed been re-opened into the death some thirty years ago of Thomas Gallagher in a Glasgow hospital. Mr. Gallagher was the victim of............"

Taylor stared blankly at the screen seeing and hearing nothing except Thomas Gallagher's last words to him all those years ago. He had to wake her up. He had to know EVERYTHING she knew.

****

He had changed very little over the years, except for the eyes. Gone was the chilling coldness to be replaced by something slightly softer, more world weary . But that was the only difference. Danny Hagan was obviously still a very dangerous man. His whole body language seemed to scream it somehow. Those same eyes had terrified a lot of people over the years, and Lassiter knew that the same chilling stare could still be turned on if required. He had seen some of the hardest reputations in Glasgow back down because of that stare. Hagan had always liked Lassiter however , and although it was never discussed they both knew why. Lassiter had stood shoulder to shoulder with him many times all those years ago and Hagan hadn't forgotten. Lassiter, on the other hand, had tried very hard to, and had , to a large extent, almost totally changed his lifestyle. Now he was going to have to resurrect some of it. He felt both embarassed and strangely guilty about it all. Odd that.

"Still gettin' paid a fortune fur writin' a loat o' shit?" Danny grinned, punched Lassiter playfully on the shoulder and slid along the bench seat, at the rear of the Gorbals pub.

"Better writin' it than talkin' it. Lager?" Lassiter stood up to go to the bar. No waitress service in this pub. Only hard, capable looking men behind the bar. And in front of it.

"Ye know, you're wan ae the very few I would let talk to me like that." Danny wagged a reproachful finger, still grinning widely. He was still impeccably dressed in a charcoal gray suit and black woolen casual shirt. "Aye, an' a wee sherry as well, seein' that the press is piyin'."

"Bloody hell. You an' Maggie both. Sherry my arse."

"You're jist crabbit because you cannae drink it any mair. Noo get yir arse up tae the bar an' then tell me whit this is a' aboot THIS time. An' whitever it is keep Maggie right oot it a' this or you an' me will fa' oot. Ah mean that Tommy."

"Nae problem. She means a lot tae me an' a' Danny." It even felt strange to use the Glasgow dialect again after all the years of improving his speaking voice to try and impress editors and the like. Stand up the real Tommy Lassiter. "D'ye need fags?"

"No' really, but if the press is piyin..."

Lassiter grinned and made his way to the bar, shaking his head.

****

"We really don't know how to thank you Doctor. If you hadn't acted so promptly in getting Sally to the hospital, God knows what might have happened. That other doctor that came out to see her the first time, just didn't seem to listen to what we were saying to him. He just said it was a tummy upset probably from too many sweets, but you seemed to know right away it was more than that. Appendicitis. The operation was a complete success and....."

"There is no need to thank me Mrs. Greenlee. Really there isn't. I'm just delighted to see her looking so well and so quickly too. Bet you can't spell that big long word Sally, can you?"

The six year old looked up from the comic book her mother had

brought her and smiled shyly at the doctor.
"Applendy...."
The two women laughed and Patricia Jeffries stood up to leave the hospital bedside ruffling the little girl's hair as she did so.
"Now you be a good girl Sally, and do what your mum and the nice nurses tell you, and you'll soon be back at school telling all your friends how brave you've been. Because that's what you have been. A very brave little girl.
"Doctor I'm not little any more. I'm seven, nearly eight."
"Of course you are. I'm sorry pet. It's because I'm so old, everybody's little to me. Now I really must go. Your mummy will bring you to see me when you come home, won't you mummy. Would you like that Sally?"
The little girl nodded her head, and patting her mother on the shoulder as she passed, Patricia Jeffries made her way down the ward. Sometimes it was just so good to be alive, and able to help people.

****

"I've seen it." Taylor barked down the telephone. "Get hold of that dolly bird from the television and get me on her programme as soon as you can. And I'll only speak to her mind. As soon you possibly can. Do it now!"
"Sure thing D.T. I'll get right on it immediately." Gil put the phone down and muttered to himself. "Dolly bird? What fucking decade does the clown think he's living in?"

END CHAPTER

CHAPTER THREE

OLD SCORES

"Right then Danny, we both know the police tried very hard to prove the Gallagher wounding -because that's all it was when you were arrested- was down to you. We both also know why. They wanted you, and it didn't really matter whether you were guilty or not. Gallagher didn't really matter too much to them then at all. Just another Friday night slashing to them. But it's not that way now."
"Where the fuck did the posh accent come fae all ae a sudden? Forget your auld arse Tommy boy, an' ah might no' tell you anythin'"
"It' my investigative reporter's voice, and I forgot who I was talking to. Anyway I'll talk fuckin' Chinese if I want to, when I'm trying to keep you out of the shit."
"O.K. pal. Sorry. Jist takin' the piss." Hagan grinned his likeable grin

again, and took a long swig of his pint , taking the opportunity to have a quick look round to see if any of the pub's customers could be a source of unexpected trouble. He'd lived that way for years and Lassiter felt strangely sorry for him. It hadn't all been his fault.

"Right. Gallagher was found in the lane at the rear of the pub, with his throat slashed. He was a good guy. He didn't deserve that. Tell me again how the whole thing started. Reasons. Everything. Remember I was in London when all this happened."

"That's right. Forgoat aboot a' that. You were still doon in the Smoke win't ye? Tae teach a' thae Krays an' Richardsons an a' them, aboot bein' real gangsters. You an' wee Bingo." Hagan smiled at the memory and Lassiter shuddered at it. "Well, you know ma auld faither haunded ower a loat o' money tae the bookies? Well nane ae it was his. First it wis ma' mither's an' then he goat worse an' it wis somebody else's. Morton's. Remember him? Fuckin' clown."

Lassiter remembered him. A thin faced youth with a stammer who was related to Glasgow's most feared name of the time, Ally "Scrap" Turner. Turner had never been known to back down from anybody regardless of size, weight or fighting ability. A small, slightly built man himself, his awesome reputation for never starting trouble but always finishing it, was legendary. His nickname had been earned both by his trade as a scrap metal merchant, and what he could do very , very well if challenged. He had been a real fighting man. He also made no secret of the fact that he had killed at least four people, and had never been convicted of one murder. Turner had survived countless attempts on his life including two stabbings, a shooting and a razor slashing. Both he and all his gang were quite prepared to kill under the slightest provocation, but in Ally Turner's case he preferred to leave that side of it to one of his boys. He preferred to fight and would often help his opponent to his feet, after beating him to a pulp. It was common knowledge however, that if he ever thought it necessary he was quite prepared to kill, using any weapon or "tool" to hand. He hadn't been young then and was now long dead. Morton had lived on his great uncle's reputation. The rumour at the time was that even Turner couldn't stand this particular relative but few were prepared to gamble on it. Except Danny Hagan! Danny had, at one time, been a quiet, shy child. At school he was well liked by pupils, including Lassiter, and teachers alike. At the age of twelve, coming home from school, he had been chased, attacked and almost killed by a gang of older youths for no reason whatsoever. At the time one of the youths had commented to the press that they had been bored, or to quote his exact words "fed up. We'd fuck a' else tae dae. There's nuthin' tae dae aboot here." The powers that be decided, in their wisdom, that what they needed therefore, was a youth club, and later duly presented them with one. The youths, in their turn, had presented Danny with something.

A totally new outlook on life! Years later Lassiter and Danny Hagan had met again in Glasgow's George Square one warm summer night.

****

Lassiter saw them long before they spotted HIM. At least twenty of them, impeccably dressed to maintain their image as the best dressed "team" in Glasgow. They were still some distance away, but he knew which of the bus stops they were heading for, and it wasn't because they wanted to catch a bus. As they drew nearer, four of the youths at the head of the crowd, detached themselves from the others and strolled slowly through the queue awaiting the midnight bus, staring icily at every male in it.
"Shit," thought Lassiter, " Reggie's at the back of them!" He had had a number of previous run-ins with this guy and in each of them, the small, pimply faced youth bringing up the rear had come off second best. But each time that had happened they had both been on their own. That was quite definitely not the case this time. Lassiter knew it was pointless trying to run. He would be caught and severely beaten or worse. He had to face it down now, or "brass it" as they would refer to it, with a bravado he was far from feeling. His heart pounding, and the familiar icy fear in the pit of his stomach he cooly stared back at each of the youths in turn. Then it was Reggie's turn. Lassiter took the biggest gamble of his life. He had spotted Danny Hagan in the main body of the gang, and knew Danny was now the main man for this particular outfit. Hagan had changed dramatically since Tommy Lassiter had last seen him, but hopefully not that much. He had never had any problem with Danny. Time to put it to the test.
"Whit are you fuckin' starin' it ya fuckin' wee shite. You shouldnae even be oot at this time o' night. Fuckin' midget." Reggie's face went white with fury and then bright red with embarassment as first Danny Hagan, then his second man "Adjie" Gilmour , then their fellow, would be gangsters and finally almost the entire bus queue burst into peals of laughter.
"Awright Tam? How ye daein' ya wee bampot?"
"Ah'm o.k. Danny. Yirsel'?"
"Ah'm awright as well wee man. But ye'll need tae watch yirsel' buddy. Ah' might no' be here the nixt time. Fuckin' leave it Reggie. Pal o' mine. Went tae school thegither." Lassiter knew he had made a good friend, and an even better enemy that night!
Lassiter watched Reggie's hand come out of his inside jacket pocket empty, but Reggie clearly was not in the least bit happy about that.

****

"Ye were really chancin' yir arm that night Tam. Dangerous wee bastard wi' a razor that wee Reggie. Ah wonder where he is noo? Either inside or deid probably. Never heard any mair aboot him, efter he did time fur that Govan caper."
"If you would come back up memory lane we could maybe talk about what happened that night in the boozer in Jamaica Street?"
"Did there no' used tae be a boozer ca'd that? Memory Lane? Ah..."
"Fuck's sake Danny. Now tell me everything you can remember about that night. Because you're going to be asked a lot more times when they re-open this case . Stand on me about that
"It wisnae anythin' special.. Jist the yasual. There were six or seven ae them when ah went in, givin' it mouth tae some older guy in the corner. Turned oot later it wis yir man Gallagher. Recognised him fae the picture in the newspaper. He wis fuckin' gemme ah'll tell ye that. Jist sat there starin' at them. Somebody told Morton ah'd come in, an' he started laughin' when he saw ah wis jist masel'. But he nearly shit himsel' when ah took the aixe oot. Least ah thought it wis that till ah heard the noise behind me an' there wis P.J. an' Plum an' aboot fifteen o' the boays fae the dancin'. Some team we hid in thae days. Nae good at daein' whit they were telt right enough. Ah'd already telt the ither P.J. an' Plum tae let me handle it masel'. That wee Reggie wis there an a' that night. We fuckin' wrecked the place. An that's it. Yi've read a' the rest. If ye mind that place there wis a back door an' they went oot it fast. Gallagher must huv tae, because the next time ah seen 'im wis when he's photie wis in the paper. That's when they started tryin' tae blame me fur it. The polis' ah mean. Ah'd never seen the guy afore in ma life."
"I knew him alright. He didn't want me to have anything to do with his daughter, but he was an O.K. guy. That's why I went to London. That and to sort out their gangsters." Lassiter smiled wryly at the memory of how stupid he had been back then and briefly, very briefly, felt like going up to the bar and ordering a drink.

CHAPTER FOUR

VOICES OLD AND NEW

"What you do, is exactly what I tell you to do. You leave her sleeping, and you wait till I get there. I've got one phone call to make, and then I'm leaving. Daniel, just relax. Everything is alright and Sarah's going to be just fine too. You know she always listens to what I have to say. She looks to me for the support most girls would get from their real father. I'm very good at that, as YOU should know. I'm really very fond of her as you should also know. Somebody has to be. You're no bloody good at it!"
"Thanks dad. I feel a lot better just having spoken to you."
Charles "C.J." Taylor drained the last of his gin and tonic from

the special glass they kept behind the bar for him, made the phone call, and giving Andy , the bar manager, his customary over generous tip, hurriedly left the golf club.

****

"Who the fuck did ye steal that fae?" Phil Jamieson growled at the pub drunk-or the first of the many who frequented his pub each day to be exact- and filled Horner another whisky."An' nane o' yir bein' sick in here again. Ah'm fuckin' pissed aff cleanin' up eftir ye. It's that Buckfast breakfast ye huv before ye come in here that dis it. Fuckin' waster."

"Ah never stole it. It wis a present fae ma' sister. She likes to keep in touch wi' me tae make sure ah'm a' right wi' me no' keepin' well an' that."

"Ye'd keep a loat better if ye'd gie that mornin' Buckfast a fuckin' bye!"

"Nane o' yir cheek noo. Ah spend a loat ae money in here mind. If ah wis thirty years younger..."

"Aye right. Heard it. Heavy? Ah know ye spend a lot. Normally somebuddy else's fuckin' giro. An' ah meant whit ah said aboot you bein' sick Reggie. Last fuckin' warnin'!"

With trembling hands Reggie grasped his pint, but not before making sure the mobile phone message he had received earlier from his sister had been deleted first. Better get it done before he got drunk She'd better still be sober enough to make the phone call. She'd need tae use the public phone at the shopping centre. "Shouldnae have left her ony wine" he thought briefly.

"Ah'll no' be lang. Mind an' no' let onybuddy near ma pint"

"Who'd want tae drink it eftir your gub bein' fuckin' roon it?"

Jamieson lifted Reggie's pint and put it on the shelf beneath the bar, and Reggie left to give his wife, Jean, her instructions.

"Watch him Phil, ah'm tellin' ye. He might be an auld eejit noo right enuff, but he wis a right evil wee bastard when he wis younger."

Phil Jamieson looked up at Horner, surprised and then nodded his head. Horner never joked about things like that.

****

"But C.J....."

"No buts Sarah. The doctor told you to stay in bed and that's exactly what you're going to do. You won't change a damn thing, by not following her orders. I'll be here to look after you and to make sure that you do just that. Daniel will have to go back into the office by tomorrow. He's as much use as a chocolate watch round here anyway. I can do what I like with regard to my time . Companies

virtually run themselves nowadays , anyway. I employ a lot of good people and pay them plenty of money to make sure of that. He can get into "The Voice" and start trying to get to the bottom of all this. There, that's the lecture over."
"Phillippa...."
"Phillippa can't do everything my dear. She's got the housework and Daniel to look after. After a couple of days when you're better you'll see that I'm right and then we'll start getting to the bottom of all this. You've suffered enough. How's your mum by the way? In a way it's a blessing she's the way she is. Shock of all this would probably kill her. O.K. is she?"
"Just the same. Barely knows people sometimes . . At other times she's as sharp as a tack"
"God help you love. You've had some time of it over the years and that fool of a son of mine's been very little help. I blame myself totally. Spoiled him rotten."
"You're a lovely man C.J. He's not so bad sometimes you know. Never had to grow up, that's all. I envy him most of the time."
"He doesn't deserve you, and that's a fact"
"I really am still very tired. I think I'll just close my eyes for a while."
"That's exactly what you're supposed to be doing. Now remember I'll be downstairs at all times."
C.J. Taylor kissed his daughter-in-law lightly on the cheek and went downstairs to confront his son.

****

Meanwhile, upstairs in her bedroom Sarah lay back, and closed her eyes. C.J. was such a dear. Always gentle and understanding. But she needed somebody tougher now. Somebody who'd both lived on, and also knew the streets well. Lassiter! She groped over for to the far side of the bed for the telephone. Lassiter! He'd know what to do.

****

Gil took the call in Taylor's office indicating to the other assembled staff that it was personal. They watched through the glass partition, as though lip reading.
"Of course Sarah. I know how to get hold of him. He's never changed. Trusts very few people still, does our Tommy, but he'll listen to me. Especially when he knows it's for you. He's never changed about that either. You take care of yourself and we'll talk later."

END CHAPTER

CHAPTER FIVE

" THE VOICE"

"He won't be any problem. As far as he knows you'll simply be working with us on the Gallagher case. He will know nothing about the fact that his wife requested it. Unless you want to tell him that is. He certainly won't hear it from me, and nobody else knows about it."
"How did she sound Gil? She never got over it happening in the first place , and now this."
"Not too bad , surprisingly. I don't think she's as fragile as you seem to think Lassiter. She'd need to have some kind of strength to put up with Taylor for all these years after all. Oh dear, am I being disrespectful to my boss again:? How very disloyal of me."
Lassiter chuckled down the phone delighted that Sarah had even thought about contacting him, after all the years that had passed since they had been close.
"I'll meet you in the usual place after your weekly conference. When is it? Tomorrow?"
"Sure is. The boy Daniel phoned me this afternoon with his instructions. He's on television tomorrow night about it all, with that gorgeous looking presenter on the six o'clock spot. Earth shattering stuff that'll be. Fucking prat! Still, I can just turn the sound down, and content myself with looking at her."
"No you can't. You'll be watching it with me in "The Grapes" and the regulars will lynch you if you go anywhere near the remote."
"Shit. Am I never to get peace"
Lassiter chuckled drily and put the phone down.

****

"Any chance ah could huv a wee word wi' ye Mr. Horner? Ah know somethin' ye'd mebbe be interested in. It's aboot the Gallagher thingmae. Ye know what ah mean. Ah wis there tae that night. Mind?"
"Fuck's sake Reggie. If ye mean the Gallagher murder, say the fuckin' Gallagher murder. Ah've goat nuthin' tae hide aboot that. Whit the fuck happened tae you? You used tae be somethin' at wan time. Look at the fuckin' state o' ye. Right, through the back then. Awright Phil? We're goin' intae the cellar fur two minutes. Ah mean it Reggie. Two minutes an' then ah'm fur the off. Tell "Adjie" tae phone me the night, Phil. Ah need tae know whit happened tae that grassin' bastard he's at court aboot."
Phil Jamieson nodded his assent and continued to pour the pint for the battle scarred, ex booth fighter who'd just come in, swinging punches at imaginary opponents, as he always did.
"Fuck's sake Sanny. Wan o' these days ye'll fuckin' knock yirsel oot

wi' that shite. Full o' heidbangers this pub." Phil Jamieson muttered to himself.
Jamieson regularly spoke to himself in the morning. The sane and relatively sober punters didn't come in till later.

****

Gil was in his usual seat facing the television above, and to the right, of the bar in the "Grapes". In his scruffy old sports jacket, and even scruffier cavalry twill trousers and suede shoes, he looked exactly what he was trying hard to look like.. A throwback to the late sixties or early seventies. With his unlit pipe- he had never smoked nor wanted to - and thick horn rimmed glasses he was, or so he fondly imagined, the stereotypical newsman of that era. The image was completed by a battered old trilby to cover his almost total baldness. The unshockable and cynical newshawk. Yet Lassiter had always felt comfortable with Gil on the few occasions they'd met previously.. As though he had known him all his life somehow.
"What'll you have me old son? Ginger beer and lime or have you changed your poison?"
"That'll do. He's definitely on , is he?"
"More's the fucking pity, but yes, he's definitely on. The question is will anybody get a bloody word of sense out of him. His stupidity constantly astounds me and can only ever be equalled by his vanity. Prat!"
Lassiter chuckled and made his way to the gents before the six o' clock news bulletin started."
"One man who has sworn to leave no stone unturned until he gets to the bottom of this thirty year old case is Mr. Daniel Taylor , the proprietor of Glasow's weekly newspaper "The Glasgow Voice." Mr. Taylor, with your family's close involvement in this case down the years, what will be your next step be now that Strathclyde Police have officially stated that enquiries have been re-opened into it?"
"Let me say first and foremost, that my dear wife's peace of mind will be uppermost in my mind as I do my utmost to pursue the ends of justice here. Anyone who knows us both well enough , also knows how happy we are together, and how I share, and have shared for many years, her grief at the untimely and brutal slaying of her dear father. However justice must be done, and more importantly, seen to be done."
"I fully understand Mr. Taylor. And what will your next step be, however?"
Looking slightly put off by the very pretty young interviewer's dogged professionalism, Taylor adjusted his already perfectly knotted silk tie and smiled condescendingly.
"That, Sally, if I may make so bold my dear, must remain confidential for now. But let me say this. Mr. Gallagher's family WILL know exactly what happened both before and after his arrival in that

hospital. They have been silent for thirty years. The Glasow Voice intends to change all that. We will give them a voice."
"Bloody prat" said Gil draining his whisky. Lassiter stared thoughtfully at the television set as the interview reached it's conclusion.

****

Horner parked the Jag outside his garishly decorated, ex-council house, home and sat thoughtfully behind the wheel for quite some time, turning over in his mind everything Reggie had told him in the cellar of the Jamiesons' pub. So he had a sister who worked for that bastard who was in charge of The Voice, did he? And Reggie believed that his sister knew something that could do damage to the bastard, if made public. Horner was very much looking forward to helping her, as much as he could , to achieve that.

Less messy than just having him sorted!

Gil didn't go home when he and Lassiter left the pub. He went back to his office to check if any messages of importance had been left for him. Jill, the most promising of the trainee journalists employed by The Voice, had left a scribbled note to tell him there was a message for him on voice mail. After playing it over a couple of times Gil sat alone in his office and realised he wasn't the only one out to do Daniel Taylor some damage. He smiled to himself in the dimly lit office.
"The more the merrier," he whispered to himself in the darkness. "The m fucking merrier."
Gil lifted his car keys and left his office whistling. It amused him greatly that Lassiter still didn't know who he was. He would find out before all this was over. So much for his investigative reporting. Gil hoped he wouldn't have to tell him himself. See if he could figure it out on his own. Or as much as Gil wanted him to figure out, to be precise.

END CHAPTER

CHAPTER SIX

STREET TALK

"I was only a raw recruit back then ,but even I could see that Hagan and his outfit had nothing to do with it. Nor, I believe, did Morton and his pals. They were too busy trying to get out the back door of the pub. They must have been shitting themselves. If the powers that be had taken the time to listen to the young barman on duty that night he would have told them exactly what happened. Apparently Gallagher virtually ignored Hagan and his crew, finished his pint and left the pub the same way he always did. Out the back door and down the lane. Somebody was waiting for him. Someone with a motive and a sharp knife. Hagan had neither. He did have an axe, admittedly, but was still inside using it to smash the pub to smithereens."

Lassiter had always liked Hegarty. On the few previous occasions that they had collaborated on cases, he had been impressed both by the C.I.D. man's common sense approach to them, and also his world weary acceptance of things. That crime, and therefore criminals, existed and would always exist. It was his job to stop them. But that did not involve taking the convenient route. Either taking money for favours done for some of the major crime figures, or worse still, sending someone down for something he didn't do.

"So it's not a problem for you if Gil and I do a bit of nosing around. See what we come up with?"

"Be my guest."

"Who's this Horner guy I hear about on the street? I've been around a long time and I've never heard much about him until recently. Strange that because I hear he's about my age."

"Watch yourself there Tommy boy. Be very careful. Very careful indeed. Career criminal. Very dangerous, or certainly used to be, but slippery with it. I hear his ambition is to be like old Mafia Carlo. But he acts more like John Gotti. Looks a bit like him too strangely enough. Snappy dresser and loves publicity"

"He won't like what Daniel Taylor's planning for him then. Assuming he knows that is."

"He'll know. Horner will know alright. He hears everything. Why do you think we have such a fucking problem nailing him?"

....

"I'll make a deal with you Mr. Horner. Everybody else now knows me as Gil. Just Gil. Now if you don't use that name again I, in turn, won't call you Jack. You don't like being called Jack do you Mr. Horner?"

There was a long silence at the other end of the telephone.

"Right. Where d'ye want tae meet?"

"Somewhere very public. Very public indeed Mr. Horner."

....

Phillippa Jarvie loved her twin brother with a passion, and hated his wife Jean with equal passion, blaming her totally for Reggie's slide into a life where all he did was await his giro, or hers, and proceed to spend the entire amount in the off-sales. But she had one thing to thank Jean for. Making the phone calls that always had the same result. Five crisp, twenty pound notes being delivered to the post office box no. specified. She'd got the idea from a film. Based on the premise that every human being has something to hide, she'd decided to try her luck. Having known the nurse in question, on duty in casualty at the hospital that night, personally, had helped of course. The nurse had always claimed that Gallagher had been murdered in the hospital that night by means of someone simply removing the drips he needed to keep him alive. Whenever Phillippa thought that sufficient time had passed between phone calls she would instruct Reggie to get Jean to make another one. Always from a different location and always the same message. Jean neither knew nor cared why she was asked to leave the messages for Daniel Taylor at his office at "The Glasgow Voice." All she cared about was the bottle of sherry she got for doing it. The message was very simple and always the same.

"There are drips and drips Mr. Taylor!"

****

" I never said I was a patient of Dr. Jeffries. I asked if you would give her this telephone number and ask her to call me back."

"Dr. Jeffries is extremely busy and..."

"Just give her the bloody number. She's not too busy to phone me."

"What name did you say?"

"Hagan. Maggie Hagan. We go back a long way."

Maggie Hagan replaced the receiver, stubbed her cigarette out and stared thoughtfully into her half-empty tumbler.

"Right P.J. It's time you an' me had a wee chat." Maggie said quietly to herself, drained her glass, and then dialled Lassiter's number."

****

Gil opened the passenger door of Horner's Jaguar, parked very publicly in the Kelvingrove area of Glasgow, and removed his hat and glasses.

"Fuckin' hell. You've changed." said Horner mouth wide in amazement.

"The word is you haven't. I need to know a lot of things. Your pal Phil Jamieson? You've known him since the sixties right? Him and his daft brother. Were they there the night somebody decided to open Gallagher's neck?"

Still slightly taken aback by Gil's change in appearance, Horner lit one of his small cigars before replying.

"One of them might have been."

"Stop fucking about Johnny. I don't have the time. Taylor doesn't have the brains or the bottle to do you real damage, but I could, and you know it. And the other two are still kicking about somewhere aren't they? Thought so. So save your crime boss shit for those it impresses. The other thing I need to know is did Phil Jamieson ever have the nickname P.J.? Most of us had stupid nicknames in those

days. I know of at least two other P.J.'s from back then. And they were both fairly dangerous. One of them's definitely dead though."
"Ah've heard people call him that. Whit dae ye need tae know fur?"
"Something an old woman in a nursing home keeps repeating. And something Gallagher might have said to the young barman in the boozer, before it all went down that night. Right we're about to go down memory lane together. What happened to that wee shite Reggie?"

****

Reggie Jarvie was in his element. He had spent the morning in the company of the local young team who had supplied him with copious amounts of cheap wine. Two or three of them had fathers who remembered
Reggie from the late sixties and early seventies. All Reggie had to do in way of payment for his drink , was regale the youngsters with tales of how violent everyone connected to the gangs of that era had been. It worked admirably, and had been doing since he had first ingratiated himself with them. In truth , Reggie really had been a particularly vicious type in those days, and several people in the Greater Glasgow area still had the scars to prove it. He had long been a spent force however, and nobody of importance took him seriously anymore. The would be gangsters of tomorrow did, though, and that was all that mattered to Reggie. He was amongst his intellectual peers when he drank with them.
When the youngsters left to collect their giros, and subsequently their drugs, Reggie sat for a while reflecting on how clever he'd been. Anybody who really knew him, would have known that his story about the mix-up at the Social resulting in him being temporarily without the price of a "swally", was patently untrue. It was rumoured that when Reggie's giro arrived each Thursday, the envelope regularly hit him on the back of the neck because of the blinding speed involved as he bent down to pick it up, and rip it open. Almost certainly physically impossible, but it got a laugh in the pub.
For now he was content to sit alone on the park bench, the dregs of his wine bottle at his feet, continually feeling to make sure his own , unopened giro was still in his pocket.
If Reggie had been sober enough and observant enough , he might have noticed the Jaguar parked on the other side of the public park football
pitch. Reggie liked to drink in parks. He might also have recognised Alistair Jamieson, Phil's physcotic brother. Alistair was receiving clear cut instructions from his boss , on how to dispose of Reggie's body once he had killed him, if it indeed proved necessary to do so. Then they would deal with his sister! But not unless it was absolutely

necessary. Only then. Timing was important.

END CHAPTER

CHAPTER SEVEN

BACKTALK

"I don't know if I approve of all this Sarah. I mean have you considered Daniel's reaction to it. You say you and this Lassiter chap used to be close. Before you met Daniel , admittedly, but I still don't think he would approve. And to let him take you to see your mother. She's used to me taking you. And you're still not strong enough. Oh, I just don't know. I...."

"You're such an old fusspot C.J. But you are a dear and I don't know what I'd do without you most of the time, but I've got to do this. Anyway Daniel knows all about it. Gil squared it all with him. And Lassiter is an investigative journalist now. It's all about a name or a nickname or something that my father had mentioned to mum a week or so before that awful night when...."

"O.K. pet I understand. As long as you think you're strong enough, and you don't need me for anything,or want me to come, I think I'll pop into town then and see if I'm still making money out of metal. Not that they need, or even want, me around nowadays. Bet they call me a bloody old nuisance behind my back, same as you probably do. I know I would, if I were in their shoes."

"Never." Sarah offered her right cheek for C.J.'s customary peck, and continued brushing her beautiful auburn hair at the dressing table mirror. "Drive carefully. All these different businesses and different cars. Which one have you got with you today?"

"D'you know. I can't remember. I'd need to check the car keys and they're downstairs on the table."

They both laughed. C.J. went downstairs and Sarah tried to calm her excitement at the thought of seeing Lassiter again. "Wonder if he's changed much? Hope not." She started applying her make-up.

****

"A Miss Maggie Hagan called earlier asking to see you Dr. Jeffries"

"Thank you Rose. Have a nice week-end and look after that cold. I'll see you on Monday"

"Thank you Doctor. You too."

****

Sarah tried very hard but but the urge was overwhelming. She threw her arms round Lassiter's neck, kissed him briefly on the cheek and ,

swallowing hard, just as quickly released him.
"How have you been? You've lost weight , but it suits you."
"It's an old suit I dug out for the occasion. Does he treat you alright? Because if he does, you're the only one apparently. If he doesn't......"
"I think he thinks he does. I thought about calling it all off you know. Coming down to London to look for you. But you know how my father thought and..."
"You're not making this any easier, Sarah. I've been o.k., I suppose, in my own half-arsed way. Gave up the drink a long time ago. I liked you're dad you know. And I think he liked me. Just didn't think I was right for you. Maybe he was right, but it didn't help. I think you're even more beautiful now than I remember"
"Lassiter I..."
"Let's leave it for now. Any decent coffee? I wonder if you're mother will remember me."
"Now she really did like you. Used to say to me if she had been younger she might have fancied you herself. We were great pals. Her memory is pretty good sometimes for things that took place years ago. It's what happens today, yesterday, last week. That sort of thing she struggles with."
"I know what you mean. Feel a bit like that myself sometimes."
Sarah smiled the same smile that had made him fall in love with her all those years ago.
"I'll get you that coffee."
"Good. We've got some names to go over first. The we'll go and see your mum."

....

The surgery was closed for the week-end and it was a security guard on duty at the desk in the the reception area, not any of the receptionists. The doctor had obviously told him to expect the arrival of a Miss Maggie Hagan, and she was directed , without any fuss, to the room where Dr. Jeffries would see her straightaway. Maggie tapped lightly on the door.
"Come in Maggie." the doctor's soft, cultured voice came from within. Maggie closed the door firmly behind her and took the proffered chair adjacent to Dr. Jeffries large desk
"Hello P.J. It's been a long time. I'm here aboot Danny. You an' oor Danny actually. If you screw him up again ye're gonnae huv tae answer tae me. Dae the medical profession know aboot you P.J.? How fur years ye ran aboot wi' wan o' the best teams in Glesca tae get yir kicks? Aboot how ye kerried their tools fur them in yir handbag P.J., an' wir jist as bammy as any wan o' them? An' how ye did the dirty oan ma brither when ye ran aff wi' his best pal "Adjie? Gilmour wan time? Ah think masel' they might be interested in

that kind o' background. Whit dae you think P.J.?"
Patricia Jeffries permitted herself one very brief blink and rose to her feet, smoothing her skirt over her shapely hips as she did so.
"Would you like some coffee Maggie? I'm afraid we don't run to Buckfast but you could have a twelve year old single malt if you prefer?"
Simultaneously they collapsed in fits of giggles. The ice was well and truly broken. Impulsively they gave each other a brief hug and then stood apart a little embarassed. It really had been a lot of years.

****

Theresa Gallagher was still a beautiful woman. In her early seventies now, the family resemblance to her daughter was still very evident. Apart from the angina attacks and the dizzy spells there wasn't too much wrong with her physical health either. She was in the nursing home because she had become increasingly afraid of living alone, and her son-in-law point blank refused to let her come to stay with her only daughter. Sarah had pleaded with him, C.J. had tried to reason with him- it had even caused a rift for a time between father and son - but Daniel Taylor was adamant. He had to entertain important people, and had no place for an old fool sitting knitting in the corner of the lounge, as he and his friends set the world to rights. Theresa had never knitted in her life. And she was certainly no fool. She couldn't stand the sight of Taylor but to her eternal credit had never once told Sarah that. If she had, she may well have been surprised to find that her daughter fully understood. And sometimes even agreed. Not many people could. There was nothing wrong with old Theresa's memory sometimes either.
"Oh Sarah you've brought Tommy! Tommy, you rascal. Where have you been all these years. Sarah's dad always used to say you'd be dead before you saw thirty and you're still here and he's...."
"How are you Mrs. Gallagher?"
"Always so polite too. Not like..., oh never mind, come and sit beside me and tell me all about yourself. Sarah, Cathy will bring us tea if you ask her nicely. I like Cathy" she said to Lassiter, "she's always nice to me." It was a statement more expected from a young child, and suddenly Lassiter felt immensely sorry for her. He bent down and kissed her lightly on the cheek and to his amazement her eyes shone and she blushed. Lassiter was pleased he'd done it. She was a lovely old lady.
After they'd all had tea, cakes and small talk Lassiter decided it was time to get down to business.
"Now Mrs. Gallagher I'm going to have to talk about Mr. Gallagher and what happened. Please tell me if I'm upsetting you and we'll stop the whole thing, O.K.?"

"It's alright Tom. I've told mum. She knows what you've got to ask about. Her memory's very good long term sometimes, isn't it mum?" The old lady nodded. Sarah and her mother sat holding hands on the slightly worn sofa and once more Lassiter felt sadness, this time for both of them.
"Must be if she remembers me. Most people try to forget me." The older woman laughed but Sarah just said poignantly,
"I know that feeling."
Lassiter experienced something approaching elation at her words, and got down to business.

****

As is often the case with identical twins they not only looked alike, but thought alike, and seemed to know things about each other, even when apart. Phillippa and Reggie had had an almost telepathic understanding of each other since childhood days. Their natures were not attractive, both possessing a natural cunning, a vicious streak and a desire to get even with the world at large. All of these characteristics were capped by a profound stupidity which made them both very dangerous people in slightly differing ways. There were enough character defects there to dispense with both of them.

"This might be fun after all!"

The sentence was underlined, the diary was closed and then replaced lovingly in the safe.

****

The Jamiesons had also had quite a reputation dating back to the late sixties, which was when Horner had first met them. Phil, the slightly older of the two, had been afraid of no one, and was still pretty much the same thirty years later. Alistair or "Adjie" as his older brother had nicknamed him, had been pretty much afraid of everyone in his early teens, and had relied on his older brother's growing reputation as a hard man for years. Until he himself, discovered how to use a knife in his late teens that was. All of a sudden things became a bit different. The street gangs were still wary of Phil's explosive temper, but everybody knew "Adjie" was now the one you never turned your back on. Never! The streets carried the word that even Phil never did it. They were right in that assumption. "Adjie" Jamieson had a habit of staring at a total stranger with pale, expressionless eyes which somehow said that he was seriously turning it over in his mind whether it was a good idea to kill him or not. The eyes were telling the truth. "Adjie" Jamieson had become very, very dangerous indeed. They both arrived in Phil's car to meet Horner in the same public park they always met in , unaware of the conversation Horner had had there with Gil from the "Glasgow Voice", sometime earlier. Horner liked to keep all his options open at all times. Horner got out of the dark blue Jaguar and strolled over to Phil's second hand BMW, lighting one of his small cigars as he did so.

lighting one of his small cigars as he did so.

"Whit's the down?" Phil enquired as his electric window slid down.

"Couple o' things. First of all what did that grassin' bastard Mc Intosh say in the coort "Adjie? Ah telt Phil tae tell ye to phone me."

"Ah'd sombuudy tae see first Mr. Horner. Fuck all. He's no gonnae say anythin' wi' me sittin' starin' it him is he? Gutless shite!"

Horner chuckled and and stood on the cigar he'd only taken a couple of puffs from.

"There's a guy gonnae be comin' intae yir boozer tae ask you an' Phil some questions "Adjie", so try tae answer them withoot lookin' it him wi' that mad stare ae yours wid ye? It's aboot this Gallagher thing. If he asks aboot me yes've heard aboot me right enuff, an' how ah'm a great guy an' a' that shite. Dae a loat fur charity an' a' that. Name's Lassiter an' he'll be comin' in aboot two the morra' efternin. Tell him everythin' he asks aboot, withoot tellin' him anythin', awright?" Horner signalled the conversation was at an end and returned to his Jaguar.

****

Danny Hagan had appointed himself guardian to his young sister long before the death of their parents. Their father from a life of dissolution, and later on their mother from a life of desperation. Their mother- who had never once complained about her difficult life- had simply worked herself to death and was greatly missed by both of them. Danny , in particular, had always had a soft spot for his father although he tried to hide it as much as possible. It had not been unusual for Danny to stick a couple of pounds, or even the odd fiver, in his father's jacket pocket when he wasn't looking , just to see the look of delight on the "old bastard's" face when he discovered money he never knew he had. Nor did he ever enlighten him as to where it had come from. Far from upsetting his mother- who Danny really gave the bulk of his money too as a youth- these acts of kindness only served to endear her son further to her, and she already thought the world of him anyway. Deeply religious, she would thank God for having blessed her with such a wonderful son. And daughter she would add, almost as an afterthought . Maggie knew Danny was her mother's favourite, and it had never really bothered her to any great extent. Irritate her yes. But that was all.

She, too, idolised her older brother. They had been strangely blissful days back then, even although sometimes very hard. Although Maggie was well aware of Danny's reputation when he left the house and onto the Glasgow streets she had never once played on it. Conversely she had tried to hide it. It tended to affect her boyfriend count. Or , at the very least , make them a bit nervous. Not that Danny ever did anything to deliberately further his image. He was what he was, and that was that. A real product of late sixties' , early seventies, Glasgow. The aura of danger that surrounded Danny Hagan, ensured that he never had any problem attracting women. They fell over themselves just to be seen in his company. It had also had a mushrooming effect on the amount of female friends Maggie had dropping in unexpectedly to see her in their tenement home, on the off chance that they would be introduced to Danny. It was round about this time too, that Maggie had two serious boyfriends within a short space of time. One was Tommy Lassiter , and the other was Alistair Gilmour, Danny's right hand man in the Glasgow team with the particularly ferocious reputation that they both headed up. Alistair was also nicknamed "Adjie" but he was a different proposition to "Adjie" Jamieson. THIS "Adjie" could really fight, and was completely without fear of rival gangs or gang members. Maggie had kept in touch with Lassiter but had often- until comparatively recently that is - wondered where "Adjie" Gilmour had disappeared to. Nobody had seemed to know his whereabouts. But something had always told Maggie that he wasn't dead. "Adjie" was just too stubborn to be dead. It was obvious her brother didn't know either. Or if he did he certainly wasn't saying.

****

Lassiter phoned Gil immediately after the phone call from Danny Hagan . Gil seemed strangely relaxed even cheerful.
"Tommy. Alright kid? How did you get on with Sarah's mother and Sarah herself come to that?"
"I'll tell you all about it when I see you. We have to meet but it'll have to be sometime after tomorrow. I'm going to see a couple of fairly dangerous people if you remember. You should do. You arranged it, after all. But I'll be alright. I've just had a phone call from Danny Hagan and he wants to come with me for some reason. What I want to know is, how he got to know I'm going to see the Jamiesons in the first place. Did you tell him?"
"Not me kid. But don't worry too much about it. Word about things like that spreads very fast. You ought to remember that. These kind of people can't sneeze without certain other people getting to hear about it. And from what I know about Danny Hagan, he'll be one of the very first somebodys. What are you worried about anyway?

Thought he was an old friend of yours. Keep him one. You're in dangerous waters now kid."
"Suppose you're right. Maybe I'm getting paranoid."
"That won't do you an ounce of harm either. I've been writing about some very dangerous people for years now. I still ge t nervous if I answer the door to a new postman, or even a new paperboy , come to that. You don't have to be too old to be a hitman these days. Must be the drugs, or maybe it's just another equal opportunities load of shit from the council."
Lassiter laughed and hung up after arranging to meet Gil in "The Grapes" a couple of days later.

END CHAPTER

CHAPTER EIGHT

SIXTIES TALK

"Ah told ye ah might huv tae put the Scotstoun team on tae that. That fucking clown needs sortin' oot an' they're the very boys tae dae it. D'ye no' listen tae a word ah say?"
Horner was in a foul mood. He was always in a foul mood when people owed him money and didn't pay on time. And he didn't give them a lot of time in the first place.
"But that's no' whit ah'm phoning ye aboot. He'll get sorted oot a'right. That guy that's comin' in tae see ye the day? Lassiter, or some fuckin' name like that . Remember whit ah told ye. Tell him fuck all. Ah'm a pillar ae society if he mentions me. An' tell Adjie tae behave himsel'. Ah'll" be ower tae the pub sometime this week."
Phil Jamieson put the phone down-he'd been holding it well away from his ear in the first place- and turned to serve the well dressed stranger who'd just entered the dilapidated pub. The stranger looked extremely out of place, simply because he was well dressed.
"Right, boss. Whit'll it be"
"A half-pint of lager, please"
Confused on two counts- very few people had ever said please to him in his pub, and even fewer drank half pints- he tried to remember where the half pint tumblers were located. Then he remembered about the journalist guy Lassiter.
"Right. You'll be that guy Lassiter then."
"Sorry? Lassiter did you say? No, I'm afraid you must have me mixed up with someone else. No, no, I'm just passing through on a business trip, and thought I'd have a break for half an hour or so. I don't suppose you do food do you?" In addition to being well dressed the stranger was well spoken. Phil was really confused now. He finally located the half pint tumblers and proceeded to fill one without cleaning it.

"Well jist crisps an' that."
"No thank you. I'll snatch a bite later on. Stop somewhere later. Full of character these old pubs aren't they?"
"Gie it a couple o' hoors pal. You'll see some fucking characters a' right." Jamieson kept his thoughts to himself and took the ten pound note.
"Have one yourself barman. It's expenses money anyway."

Phil accepted the offer and poured himself a glass of whisky.
"Dae yirsel' a big favour pal. Don't tell anybuddy else in here that. They'll end up askin' ye tae stiy the night wi' them."
Looking slightly startled, the extremely well dressed stranger sipped his half pint and smiled appreciatively.
"I'm trying to locate an old friend of the family. I'm told he sometimes drinks in here. Goes by the name of Reggie. Reggie Jarvie?"
Phil was no longer confused. He'd given up totally.

****

The talk with P.J. had had a strangely unsettling effect on Maggie Hagan. Too many memories. About Lassiter, Adjie Gilmour and P.J. herself. It had all been so different back then. Parties, gangs, fights. Now P.J. was Patricia Jeffries M.D. and the good Doctor had been even more amazed to learn what Maggie did for a living nowadays.

****

"Askin' aboot me? Whit did he look like? Fuck's sake. He must hae been fae the Social. Ye didnae tell him anythin' did ye Phil? Ah widnae shop you. Ah widnae shop onybuddy. Everybuddy knows that daen't they Phil? He's no comin back is he Phil?"
"This guy wisnae fae the Social. Too fuckin' polite fur a start. Use yir fuckin' heid fur wanst Reggie. Wid he leave a drink fur ye if he wis fae the fuckin' Social.?. Sorry ah gie'd ye it noo. The only reason ah gave ye it in the first place, wis because he left anither wan fur me, an' told me tae tell ye ye'd be hearin' fae him. Ah'm sure he said his name wis sumthin' like Gadgie . or sumthin' like that. Mebbe ah'm gettin' mixed up because ae oor "Adjie". Ye'd know if HE wis lookin fur ye awright. Jis thank fuck it wisnae him wee man. Ye've went a' white Reggie. Better drink up yir free drink cos it's yir fuckin' last. If oor "Adjie" wis lookin' fur ye, it wid be yir fuckin' last"
Reggie had indeed gone very pale and started to shake, but strangely enough not because of "Adjie" Jamieson. The visitor had

not said his name was Gadgie, he didn't think. But he might have said something very similar. Very similar indeed. Maybe Reggie's violent past , with which he loved to regale the local young team, had finally begun to catch up with him at last. He fervently hoped the visitor hadn't been who he thought it might be. Reggie was concerned about another " Adjie" altogether. Naebuddy knew where THAT wan hud went tae.

****

Maggie Hagan loved her chosen career with a passion. She had been one of the first women to do it in the Glasgow area, and no one was more surprised than Maggie when , first of all, she got offered a future in it in the first place and secondly how quickly she had became accepted by her peers who were, at that time, predominantly male. Things had changed a lot in the twenty two years or so that she had been doing it, and now there were any number of women doing the same thing, but Maggie was still out there knocking seven bells out the opposition. She had been selling metal for so long now she could do it with her eyes shut. Her only problem at the moment was that she still loved what she was doing, but was unhappy with the firm she was doing it for. She had been instrumental in securing the business of a number of new accounts for her new employers in the six months or so she had been with them, and felt that this had gone largely unrecognised and , more importantly, unrewarded. The promises made to Maggie when she had first agreed to take the job with them had not been fulfilled, and she was extremely unhappy about that. She was already on the hunt for a new and more reliable employer. One who would put the money where the mouth was. In this respect Maggie Hagan was totally mercenary, and that's what this morning's meeting with one of her biggest new accounts was really all about. On the face of it she was there to sell metal, but Maggie was really there to sell herself. She was very good at that too. Her sporty, if definitely second or even third hand, little MG was shining brightly in the car park of Meredith Metals, and Miss Maggie Hagan was shining even more brightly in the plush reception area.
"Maggie Hagan to see Mr. Meredith. I'm afraid I'm a little early due to the cancellation of an earlier appointment, but it will give me a chance to go over some figures if I could....."
"Oh Miss Hagan, Mr. Meredith said to bring you straight through the moment you arrive. Apparently Mr. C.J.'s here at the moment and wishes to meet you. Would you like to just come through?"
Maggie smiled sweetly, and followed the still handsome, and very capable secretary through to Meredith's even plusher office. C.J. Taylor! The emperor! And he wanted to meet HER. Maggie wondered if he liked strong, forceful women, or the slightly fluffy and demure

type. It didn't matter. She could do either equally well. She took a deep breath, broadened her smile, and entered Meredith's office.

****

"Right, let me oot here an' ah'll go in first. Go an' park somewhere's an' then come in as if yir oan yir ain."
"What's this all about Danny. I'm a big boy now remember. I'm allowed out on my own"
"Better bein' safe Tommy boy. Always check yir back, ma man. There's two or three o' ma boays already in there. Don't say ah'm no' good tae ye."
"Still a bloody nutter eh Danny?"
"Dinnae you be ungrateful noo Tommy. Ah'm only tryin' tae look eftir an auld pal."
"Go on. Get out of here. Hey, and thanks anyway."

"Nae bother sojer. Nae bother. Gie me a couple ae minutes tae get in an' get a pint up an' that, an then you come in. Right?"
"O.K. pal. I won't forget this Danny. But I don't need it, and didn't ask for it."
"Who said Ah'm gonnae let ye. Couple ae minutes mind."

....

"Good morning Mr. Meredith. Thank you for seeing me. Oh Mr. Taylor. A privelige to meet such a famous man."
"Now, now none of that nonsense my dear. Everyone round here just calls me C.J. Those that know who I am that is, or even care come to that."
Maggie tittered dutifully and struck the correct pose. Slightly unsure of herself, but still seemingly confident. She had started to relax ever so slightly.
"Edith will you bring us coffee please my dear? Oh sorry James I'm taking over again. Throw me out the next time I start giving orders."
It was James Meredith's turn to titter dutifully.
"C.J.'s right as always. Edith. Coffee would be nice. Coffee o.k. with you Maggie?"
"Coffee would be very welcome Mr. Meredith thank you" Maggie knew the form. Meredith hadn't given her permission to use HIS first name yet.
"Sit down my dear. Sit down. Take a load off. There I go again James. Sorry."
Maggie was now quite relaxed, but still alert. What a lovely man she thought. Still very good looking for his age, and beautifully dressed in very expensive casual wear. However she also noticed that Meredith

was every bit as respectful of C.J. as she herself was. At this point Taylor seemed quite content to leave Meredith and Maggie to it , and appeared to be absorbed in the goings on in the firm's car park and the surrounding area. Meredith made small talk about golf handicaps and rising club fees while they awaited Edith's return with the coffee.

****

"My, my Miss Sarah you look so much better now, since that Mr. Lassiter came and took you across to see your mum. What an improvement. Almost back to your old self. Not quite, mark you, but a whole lot better. What an improvement!"
"Thanks Phillippa. You're a treasure. I do feel a good bit better, as a matter of fact. Tom's an old friend from way back. Yes, seeing him again has cheered me up. We had a good chat about the old days. Things were all so different back then. Exciting and even a bit dangerous, but uncomplicated somehow. D'you know what I mean?"
"Of course I do. I know exactly what you mean. Everyone's out for what they can get these days. No nice people any more. Present company excepted of course ma'am. You've been so good to me. So kind."
"Now, now Phillippa. I've told you before not to call me ma'am, or anything like that. I'm not royalty. Plain Sarah will do."
"You're anything but plain, Miss Sarah. This job means so much to me. It really makes my day coming here to see you. The little chats we have and so on. It's not like a job at all really. And Mr. C.J.'s always so pleasant to me when he comes round too. It's just....."
"I know, I know. Don't say it. I'll have a word with my husband again about the way he speaks to you. Try and make allowances for him, will you? For me? I know it's hard at times, but he is under a lot of pressure at the moment. What with the newspaper and my dad's..."
"Now, now Miss Sarah. Try not to think about that , or you'll make yourself ill again. I've just made a nice pot of tea. Or do you want coffee? We'll have one of our chats and you can tell me all about how you got on when Mr. Lassiter took you to see your mum. Did she remember him? You certainly look as if you do?" They both giggled like schoolgirls and Sarah sat down at the kitchen table.
"Bloody Hell" thought Phillippa Jarvie. "Her bloody man's right about one thing. She is one stupid bitch!"

****

The first thing Lassiter noticed about the Jamieson pub was that it had no name. In his experience that meant only one thing. There was no sign outside , or anywhere else for that matter, to indicate that it even had one. He knew that that normally meant trouble, but he had known that all along anyway. This was not going to be easy. He cast both his mind and his demeanour back thirty or so years, and entered.

Loud, repetitive and boring described the rap music blasting from the the beer splattered juke box at one end of the bar. It also applied to the five youths standing round it. For the umpteenth time he asked himself why the modern day Glasgow hoodlums all spoke in that irritating, nasal whine that apparently classed them as really hard. However four genuinely hard cases WERE leaning against the equally beer stained counter at the opposite end of the small, filthy saloon bar. They glanced once in his direction. Once was enough. The message was clear. They were not the type to indulge in small talk. The only other three occupants were a very capable looking big guy behind the bar, Danny Hagan quietly sitting reading his newspaper near the door he had just come in, and one other very thin man also sitting alone. The look he got from this one didn't simply indicate that he was dangerous. It indicated that he was evil! He was deathly pale, and this was made all the more striking by the coal black crew cut hair and the even blacker goatee beard. HE didn't glance at Lassiter. His glittering eyes followed Lassiter all the way up to the bar. He had to crane his neck round the corner seat he was sitting in, to do so. Because Lassiter now had his back to him , he didn't notice him now starting to stare at Danny who appeared engrossed in his newspaper, and seemingly blissfully unaware of him doing it. A lot of people had fallen for that trick. Hagan knew he was being stared at alright. He chose to ignore it. That was all. He also knew instinctively that the thin man wasn't the type to let it go at that. That was the precise moment when the three, fairly drunk salesmen types came out of the gent's toilet laughing loudly. All of a sudden the little pub seemed crowded. What the bloody hell were they doing in a pub like this? That was when Lassiter noticed the pool table round the top corner of the pub and the three men in paint spattered overalls, playing pool. They'd be Danny's boys. He relaxed ever so slightly. At the same time as one of the drunken salesmen staggered over to the pool table, and another decided to play the jukebox, leaving one, the one who looked like an accountant with his old fashioned horn rim spectacles alone at the bar.

■■

Gallie and The Wee Man still found it hard to take in. Now high on smack and cheap wine they were in awe of the fact that he had even spoken to them earlier in the day, much less given them money and a job to do for him. "Adjie" Jamieson had actually considered them wide enough, and big time enough to trust them to do something for him. They would have done it for nothing, but he had insisted they take the money. Real gangsters didn't do anything unless they got paid for it he'd told them. He'd got paid for his first job he'd insisted.

"Ah waant tae dae it. You'll fuck it up. Go ower the score. Jist a jawmark "Adjie" said. We take the kerry-oot up tae he's hoose, get the two ae them steamin', dae it an' leave the knife beside her. Awright?"

"Wonder whit it's fur. Whit he's done ah mean. Ah mean he's been awright wi' us an' that." The Wee Man spat on the pavement and took another swig of the wine before passing the bottle back to Gallie.

"He's aye oan aboot how mental he wis back in the sixties. Must be sumthin' tae dae wi' him openin' his mooth at the wrang time or sumthin.' "Adjie" fuckin' Jamieson! Imagine us gittin' asked tae help "Adjie" Jamieson oot wi' sumthin. Wait tae we tell the rest ae the team this wan. Fuckin' mental man intit?"

The Wee Man nodded, pulled the hood up on his casual jacket and watched Gallie do the same. The fact that it was neither raining nor cold had nothing to do with it. The image had to be right at all times. Especially now! Gallie smashed the empty wine bottle next to the swings where he knew the younger children played, and they made their way deeper into the park. The Young East End Team were really big time now! "Adjie" fuckin' Jamieson! Nobody was gonnae mess wi' them now. Clapping their hands in unison they started to shout their gang slogans

****

"Just a glass of coke. I'm looking for a Mr. Jamieson. Phil Jamieson?"

"Found him then, bud. Ah take it you're this guy Lassiter ah've heard wis comin' in. Somethin about that Gallagher case way back. Ye work fur wan ae the papers. That right? Don't know if ah can help bud. Ah wis only a daft boay back then. Shut it you'se four. Ah heard that." Jamieson grinned at Lassiter and inclined his head in the direction of the four hard cases at the end of the bar. One of them had muttered something about him being only a daft old bastard now.

"Should bar the four ae them. But ah'll jist keep takin' their money. At least they spend some. Every other fucker's oan the slate in here. It's only thae four that knows whit money looks like. The rest ae them are in the land of the bouncin' giro." The four men at the end of the bar guffawed loudly. Lassiter smiled at the joke and paid for the coke which was of that detestable, draught variety. He had no

intention of drinking it anyway because of the filthy glass it was in.
"Thanks. It's really just some background information I'm looking for. Anything that might be helpful to the newspaper. As you've probably heard on television the police have re-opened investigations into the case and our editor has a personal interest in it."
"It'll no' be the first time he's hud tae help the polis wi' their enquiries. That right big man?" This remark came from the tallest of the four men propping up the end of the bar. The one with the broken nose and the long-healed white scar on his left cheek.
"Shut the fuck up Malky. Naebody wis talkin' tae you." The sudden flash of anger in Jamieson's narrowed eyes didn't go unnoticed by Lassiter. This man was unpredictable.
"We're not really concerned so much with you Mr. Jamieson. More what you can remember from back then. And about your boss. The gentleman who does a lot for charity. Mr. Horner?"
"Well the night that Gallagher got it , ah think ah wis in the Locarno wi' some ae the team ah ran aboot wi' back then. Whit ah dae know is that ah wisnae in that boozer that night. But ah heard there wis a riot near enough. Some Maryhill team came in lookin' fur that eejit that used tae lend he's auld uncle's money oot . Whit wis his fuckin' name again?" Jamieson's frowned and scratched the back of his head genuinely trying to remember the name.
"Morton?" said Lassiter and saw the surprise register on Phil Jamieson's face. The sudden realisation that he wasn't dealing with a fool. This guy knew the script whoever he was.
"That's the bastard. Naebody liked him. Heard some guy came in himsel' wi' jist an aixe furst, an' then his back up team showed up. Story ah heard back then wis that he didnae know they were comin' in tae back him up neither. Must've hid some fuckin' bottle tae go' up against a team ae six or seven. Jist himsel' tae. Forgoat HE'S name an' a' . Other side ae the city fae me. Mebbe ah knew him. Mebbe no'. Should've by the sounds ae it. Some bottle." This, admiringly.
Lassiter said nothing about Danny's part in it.
"Well he was interviewed and cleared at the time. Could you tell me about somebody called Reggie? Might have been a nickname. Somebody said he was handy with a knife in those days. Would that be right? I know he was in the pub that night.
"Sorry pal. Cannae help ye there. Disnae ring a bell." This time it was obvious that Jamieson was lying. "See in thae days we a' drank in wur ain areas. Case we goat jumped or that. Know whit ah mean?"
"Strange that. Somebody told me he drinks in here."
"Wee Reggie that comes in here drunk, so that he kin get drunker? You tellin' me he used tae be a blade man? Ah wid never huv thought that. Jist goes tae show ye eh? Come tae think ae it. Somebuddy else wis in here lookin' fur im no sae long ago. Said he

knew his mither or somethin' like that. Mebbe's a wee bit aulder than you. Awfy well dressed. Wis he fae your paper an a'?"
"No. Might have been the police."
"Dinnae think so. Ah kin normally tell. A wee bit too auld tae ah think. Onywiys, they widnae come in here unless they wur mob handed. Said his name wis Gadgie or sumthin. Sounded like that onywiys. But mebbe ah'm gettin' mixed up. See, ma brither's nickname's "Adjie". Everybuddy knows him. That's him ower there."
"Mind if I have a word with him later?"
"Ah don't, but he might. He's a bit-whit's the word?- aye, unpredictable, oor "Adjie". Aye that's it Unpredictable "
"Just some background. Same as with you. Now could you tell me about your business relationship with a Mr. Horner the well known Glasgow gangster?"
The question was so sudden and unexpected that the effect was electric. Jamieson's eyes narrowed and the and easy, even affable manner of speaking changed immediately.
"You're talkin' aboot a friend ae mine pal. A respectable businessman. Dis a loat fur charity an' that."
"I heard that. Been quite charitable to you hasn't he? Smoothed the path with the licensing board to get you in here didn't he? When you previously wouldn't have been considered for a TV licence? Your brother does lots of little favours for Mr. Horner too I heard. Smooths HIS path in various ways. Would I be correct in that assumption Mr. Jamieson?"
"Look ah'm no' listenin' tae this shit pal. It's shuttin' time fur YOU. Right noo. Just fur you. Adjie's gonnae show ye the wiy oot. A different wiy fae the wiy ye came in. Ye kin write aboot him in yir paper Wanst ye're oot the fuckin' hospital that is"
Lassiter always knew instinctively when someone was standing behind him. A sixth sense told him "Adjie" Jamieson was directly behind him. What "Adjie" didn't know was that Danny Hagan was directly behind HIM.

END CHAPTER

CHAPTER NINE

SWEET TALKING

"So therefore, Maggie, what I'm saying is this. I believe your talent and skill at what you do, is being wasted where you are at present. I think what we're offering is only fair, in the light of what you have achieved in this industry over the years. I believe the package we are offering reflects that. And the future, should you decide to join us, would reflect it even more. You have seen our success over the years, and both C.J. and myself would be delighted should you

decide to join us. We have achieved a great deal to date, but we are going to achieve a great deal more, and we would like you to be part of that. There is no need to give me your answer right away. Take whatever time necessary to decide. We are so impressed, the offer is open-ended. Care to add anything C.J.?"

James Meredith smiled at Maggie and turned to C.J. Taylor who still appeared to be more interested in whatever he had been watching in the car park. It soon became apparent that he had been listening very carefully however

"Not really James. You've covered everything admirably, as usual. You can see why they don't really need me around at all, can't you Maggie? Good thing they still put up with me anyway. But those rising golf club fees have made you stingy James. How about sticking another couple of grand on that salary? And you forgot about the expenses for business suits and the like. Pretty ladies deserve pretty clothes."

Maggie had to resist the impulse to run over and throw her arms round C.J. What a lovely man! A real charmer. She knew instinctively that Meredith would do exactly what C.J. suggested and the original offer had been irresistable anyway.

Resisting the impulse , Maggie smiled demurely at them both and broke her respectful silence.

"At the risk of giving you both the impression I act on impulse, can I say yes now? It would be an absolute joy to work here, and I can assure you both now that I would be a tireless member of staff. Thank you both so, so much for even considering me for the post."

Meredith smiled broadly and rose to shake her hand while C.J. beamed equally broadly in the background. Looking strangely embarassed C.J. also shook her hand and lifted his very expensive ,beautifully tailored raincoat from the sofa.

"Well that's that then. Absolutely delighted to have you on board my dear. Now I really must be somewhere else, where I'm sure they can do without me equally well."

Maggie gave both her new employers her best smile and moved respectfully aside, to let him past.

"I'll leave you two to sort out the details then and I look forward to meeting you again very soon Maggie. I've heard so much about your past triumphs. I'll be off then.. Bye for now."

Maggie smiled again and watched as the undisputed local king of the metals business made his exit.

****

Phillippa Jarvie had had the feeling of impending trouble for days now and it wasn't going away. Her intuition told her that something, somewhere was not quite right and , as always, her thoughts immediately turned to Reggie. Fiercely protective of her twin brother since childhood she liked to think she had been instrumental in teaching him how to look after himself in his formative years. What she totally overlooked, was that looking after oneself was not quite the same thing as winning at all cost. Particularly when it involved the use of anything sharp or blunt you could lay your hands on. She also thought it permissible that the win at all costs rule applied whether the opponent was male or female. The Jarvie twins had been a pretty fearsome little partnership in the late sixties also. She wouldn't be able to rest until she knew Reggie was o.k It never occurred to her for one moment that maybe her concern was for the wrong twin. It should have done!

****

The staff at "The Glasow Voice" could sense that there was something wrong with Daniel Taylor. He hadn't been just as obnoxious since the Gallagher business had been resurrected by the police. He seemed pre-occupied, even worried, most of the time. The cruel sarcasm wasn't quite so cruel, and the ridiculously bad manners not quite so ridiculously bad. It didn't make any difference to them. Gil ran the office anyway. Everybody knew that. It just wasn't a very good idea to tell Taylor that.

The involvement of Lassiter didn't help matters. Quite a few people knew the story about the head butt at the Christmas do all those years previously , and the reason for it too, but only Gil knew the real reason for Taylor's troubled air. The anonymous phone calls about the supposed removal of drips from a hospital patient. Only Gil had witnessed the effect that the very first call had had on Taylor. It certainly had not been the normal reaction of a would be newspaper mogul, hungry for news. It had been very far from that! Gil had been witness to the fleeting sign of panic in the eyes and the subsequent attempt to conceal it. It was very obvious Taylor was hiding something.

But then, so was Gil.

****

Phillippa felt a lot more relaxed about things after she had phoned her brother. She knew he was o.k when she got the usual response asking her if she'd any spare money. She said she'd see what she could do before the end of the week, and told him as usual that he'd be able to look after his money better if he got rid of that stupid, drunken slut he was married to.

"Aye an' she wis askin' fur you an' a'. Ah'll need tae go hen, there's somebuddy at the door. Sounds like a couple ae that young team. Ah hope they've goat fuckin' drink oan them."

****

Immediately Reggie told him about his sister and the fact that she knew something about Taylor, Horner sensed his opportunity to kill two birds with the one stone. This was not the time for anybody to go digging around in Johnny Horner's past. Particularly his whereabouts on the evening of the Gallagher attack. Most people didn't remember. But Horner did.
Together with a lot of his contemparies including Hagan. Especially Hagan!

****

"I'm embarassed Miss Sarah. You know I hate asking you for money before my wages are due, but I just can't seem to make ends meet sometimes. What with looking after my poor, sick brother. You remember I told you he lives alone? And at the other end of the city. Not a nice area either."
"Not another word about it Phil. It's our little secret. It's my fault anyway for having such a stingy husband. Are you sure that will be enough now? And if you try to give me it back when you get your wages, I won't take it . You should know that by this time. After everything you've done for me!"
Phillippa smiled sweetly and put the twenty pound note in her purse. She put the purse back in her worn handbag beside the ten pound note she'd stolen from Taylor's jacket pocket earlier. Never take too much. It would almost certainly be noticed. Her mother's advice rang in her ears and her mind drifted.
Unmarried parents had not been so common in those days and the twins' mother had done her best in the only way she knew how. The money from occasional prostitution had supplemented her meagre wages as a chambermaid in one of Glasgow's posher hotels of the time. Jessie, their mother, had been a likeable enough girl from the Maryhill area of Glasgow. Her only real fault was that she lived a life divorced from reality. Because she saw a lot of people with a lot of money in the hotel she worked in, she decided she should have some of it. Somewhere along the way she became convinced she originated from monied people and wouldn't answer to anything else but Jessica. The twins were the result of an ongoing affair with a travelling salesman based in Didsbury in Manchester called Charlie. Jessie decided in her own mind he was really Sir Charles somebody or other from one of the wealthiest families in Scotland- Charlie was a native Scot - and had named her children as she thought befitted them. Reginald and Phillippa! In truth Jessie's only real fault was her liking for other people's money, and she was basically a good enough sort

of person. The darker side of the twins nature obviously came from the travelling salesman. Reggie's name was not a nickname, as most people thought, a tribute to his idol, Reggie Kray, but Phillippa brother's real name. The names had caused them both problems from the off. There hadn't been too many Reginald's or Phillippa's in Maryhill, one of Glasgow's toughest areas. Phillippa forced herself from her childhood memories and back to the job in hand.
"But I feel such a cheat when you don't take it back and you know I would never cheat you or Mr. Taylor. Much as he doesn't seem to like me too much. I don't know what I'd do without this job. I really don't"
"Now then Philippa. It's not that he doesn't like you. Sometimes I wonder if he really likes anybody very much, apart from his father. Even me."
"Not like that Mr. Lassiter I bet. He'll get to the bottom of all this terrible, dreadful business. I bet he does." If Phillippa Jarvie had known of Lassiter's treatment and humiliation of her dear Reggie all those years ago in George Square there was no doubt she would have tried to even the score back then. Maybe even now. But she didn't. Reggie had never told anyone about THAT incident. Nobody!
"He's got a real soft spot for you that one. Women can tell these things. You know that."
Sarah's face took on a wistful look and she took another ten pound note from her own purse.
"Here take this as well Phil. Buy him some more whisky, or something, to cheer him up. Your brother I mean. Off you go now and take care on the way home. You're a really good friend Philippa. Apart from you and Lassiter and Gil at Daniel's office, I don't think I have too many friends you know."
"Nonsense Miss Sarah. I'm sure you've got loads. Everybody loves you. And what about Mr. C.J.?"
"You're right as always . How could I forget dear old C.J.. I'm really very lucky I suppose."
"Thanks again Miss Sarah. I'd better go right enough or I'll miss that bus again."
"Thanks again you stupid bitch." whispered Phillippa softly to herself as she made her way down the hall.

****

As promised Patricia Jarvie kept in touch and rang Maggie the week-end after her interview with Meredith's Metals.
"You didn't, did you? Congratulations Maggie. What kind of car are they offering you? A what? Bloody Hell girl! Well done! Want to swap for a third hand Mondeo? No I can't. I've got all sorts of paperwork to catch up with, honestly but we'll definitely do something in the next couple of weeks. Once you've actually started

working there, then you can tell me all about it. No you tell him. He's your brother. He'll be really chuffed for you. I promise. Next couple of weeks."
Replacing the receiver, Dr. Patricia J arvie M.D. lifted the her briefcase from the side of the sofa and took out the shiny surgical blade.
"Right then. Time to make use of you isn't it?"
Dr. Patricia Jarvie M.D. giggled softly to herself, and rose from the sofa running her thumb the length of the wickedly sharp blade.

****

Gil crossed the street to Horner's waiting Jaguar.
The front passenger seat was already occupied. Gil opened the rear nearside and got in.
"Hello Adjie. Long time no see."
"Told you he'd chinged, din't Ah?"
"Hello Maggie. Miss me?"
Maggie Hagan put her mobile phone back in her handbag and turned to have a closer look at her old boyfriend.
"Adjie Gilmour! What happened to all that beautiful hair then? No wonder Lassiter has never recognised you. I don't know if I would have either, unless Johnny had told me first. I think it's the glasses. They change your face somehow. Take them off, till I see if you've still got the killer eyes. Yeah, still got them. God Adjie it's good to see you again after all these years. And you've never really been away have you? You and Tommy Lassiter. And working together now too."
"Only he still doesn't know it. There's a lot of things our Tommy boy doesn't know. Good to see you again too kid. How's Danny?"
Gil settled into the back seat of the Jaguar and gave his old girlfriend the time to absorb the shock. The chemotherapy treatment all those years ago had taken it's toll, but the main thing was it had worked.
The dark blue Jaguar moved off towards the city centre.

END CHAPTER

CHAPTER TEN

THE TALK OF THE TOWN

If Reggie Jarvie had had any misgivings about opening his door to comparative strangers, they disappeared the moment he saw what it was that both the youths were carrying. Gally and the Wee Man's arms were filled with cans of beer, and obviously full bottles of cheap wine protruded from the plastic carry-out bags. Christmas, New Year and the Glasgow Fair Fortnight all rolled into one.
"C'moan in boays. Ah'm chokin' fur a drink. Where did ye'se get a'

the bevvy?"
"Gally hud a 60-1 shot come up at the bookie's." said the Wee Man in the same peculiar nasal whine Lassiter had already heard from the would be gangsters in the Jamieson pub.
"Jean. Move yir erse. Two wee pals ae mine ur here an' they've brought some amount ae swally wi' them."
Jean wakened from the already half drunken sleep she'd been having on the worn three seater couch.
"Oh hullo. My you'se ur nice lookin' boays int ye'se." she slurred leering, and adjusting the one earring she had in , while looking for the other which had fallen out somewhere.
"Shut the fuck up an' turn that telly aff. We're gonnae huv a party."
"Every day's a bloody party fur you." Jean muttered before remembering their guests. "Ah' awfy pleased tae meet ye'se both. Sit doon the pair o' ye'se."
If Reggie had looked out of the window before opening it to give the neighbours the benefit of the sectarian music he was about to play, he might just have noticed the shiny Jaguar parked further down his street.

****

At precisely the same moment Reggie was opening his window and failing to notice the Jaguar, events in the Jamieson pub were taking place that would be whispered about in certain Glasgow pubs for weeks to come.
"I think you should remember that an awful lot of people know where I am at the moment. Like the press, the police and so on. I merely asked you about your association with Mr. Horner. That was all." Lassiter spoke calmly and cooly which was a million miles from the way he was feeling.
"Business. An' it's nane o' yours. Now fuck off oot ae here, before yir kerried oot." Jamieson slung the filthy dish towel over his shoulder to indicate that their conversation was at an end. At that precise moment a significant number of other things took place. First of all "Adjie" Jamieson attempted to put his hand on Lassiter's shoulder. One of the drunken salesmen types miraculously sobered up and walked quickly back over to the blaring jukebox and, with astonishing speed, stooped and yanked the plug for it from the wall. And then then came the biggest shock of all. The taller of the other two salesmen- the one who looked like an accountant- opened his raincoat to reveal a sawn-off shotgun and the smaller, fatter, one suddenly hit his pool opponent, one of the three men in paint-spattered overalls, with the pool cue, raising a pudgy finger in warning at the same time.
"Fuck's sake." growled Malky from behind Lassiter. "Don't fuckin'

move for fuck's sake "Adjie", bastard behind ye's goat a fuckin' shooter!"
That was when Danny Hagan spoke for the first and only time.
"In case ye'se wur a wee bit mixed up aboot things, ma pal Tommy here's gonnae be leavin' noo. If he his tae come back tae ask ye'se anythin', be a wee bit mair civil tae him fur fuck's sake. We widnae waant tae huv tae come back. Ah'm Danny Hagan by the wiy "Adjie." Ur ye gonnae tell Plum ah wis askin' fur 'im? C'moan boays. Right Tommy boy. Wuv made wir point!"
Lassiter had never been so pleased to leave anywhere in his life.

****

"I'm telling you Gil, I've never seen anything like it, and I've seen a few things in my time. The bastard's mad, not to mention the three he had with him. God help him. I can't help liking him, although he frightens the life out of me now. I'm lucky not to be in Barlinnie right now."
"Danny knew what he was doing , although I agree with you , he is half-mad. He just wanted to make sure you didn't get in out of your depth kid."
"Who the bloody hell's Plum incidentally?"
"I'll tell you all about in "The Grapes." There's still quite a lot you don't know kid. There's a hell of a lot more to this. Probably a lot that you found out from Sarah's mother too. Is there?"
Lassiter put the phone to his other ear to light a cigarette.
"That's right. I'd forgotten about Theresa, and something she told me. No bloody wonder after this afternoon. Right "The Grapes" it is. When?"
"This is what Wednesday? Friday O.K.?
"Wis I knew who this Plum was, but you're not going to tell me are you?"

"Oh, you know him alright. At least of him, anyway. And I've got one or two other surprises for you. Keep you on your toes kid. See you Friday."
"Cheers Gil."
Lassiter put the receiver down and drew thoughtfully on his cigarette.

END CHAPTER

CHAPTER ELEVEN

ALL TALK AND NO ACTING

Lassiter couldn't quite get his head round it at first. And then discovered it was only the first surprise.

"You're bloody taking the piss , Gil. You? You're "Adjie" Gilmour. Danny's right hand man from all those years ago? "Adjie" with the long hair and the dark, tinted glasses? Afraid of nothing. Some people said, not even Danny. What happened to the long hair? I mean not that I would have expected you still to have long hair, but I would have expected you to have some more left than you have. We were roughly the same age for God's sake."
"Illness I'm afraid kid. Came out and never came back."
"Oh, I'm sorry Gil. Let me take my foot out my mouth ,please. Sorry once again. Bloody hell, I don't know what to call you now."
"Gil will be just fine. Never could stand that bloody nickname, but then we all had them in those days. It's okay-about me having been ill I mean- I've never really been up nor down since. Pretty fit really."
"Alistair, that's Jamieson's real name too I think. You know the one they call "Adjie." He looks a real nutter incidentally. Never got a chance to prove it though. That your real name too?"
"Well my father used to call me that, so I suppose must be." Lassiter chuckled.
"Who'd have thought it, and yet when I first met you at "The Voice" I remember I did have that feeling. You know the one where you think it's all happened before."
"Well it had kid. But I'm perfectly happy being who I am nowadays. There's only one or two others who know, so count yourself priveliged. I know you'll keep it to yourself. You'll understand. There's a lot you don't want to remember either, isn't there?"
"There's a lot I can't fucking remember Gil. But that's life I suppose." Gil chuckled heartily.
"Right kid. Just because you don't drink anymore doesn't mean I don't" He shoved his empty glass across the quiet table they were seated at in the quieter of the two lounge bars in "The Grapes." Same again's just fine. Now that's what I call an apology. We've got a lot to talk about."

****

Who he was , or where the car suddenly appeared from, Phillippa Jarvie had no idea, but he had an immediate and profound effect. At first she assumed he was simply looking for directions. An extremely well dressed gentleman, in his late fifties or thereabouts, got out of a shiny Jaguar car, which had just screeched to a halt on the opposite side of the street from the bus stop she was standing at outside the Taylor's home. She knew it was a Jaguar because Mr. C.J. had one very similar. Mr. C.J. had three or four different cars. Rich bastard.
The businessman type crossed the street leaving the door open and the keys in the ignition, as toffs like to do and enquired politely
"You're the lady who works for a Mr. And Mrs. Taylor I believe? In

that case I have a message for you, and it is simply this. If you ever get your drunken brother's equally drunken wife to make another stupid phone call to any newspaper, anywhere , about anything, you WILL be found and you WILL be killed. Is that understood? I hope I've made myself clear."
The statement was all the more earth shatteringly effective because of the extremely friendly smile which accompanied it.

****

At the same time approximately that Phillippa Jarvie was receiving the warning that would ultimately save her life, something else was taking place that would perhaps do the same thing for her twin brother's. There was a piercing, insistent ringing of his front door bell and Reggie answered the door to "Adjie" Jamieson.

****

Danny Hagan's decision to help an old friend had affected a lot more people than the amazed onlookers in the Jamieson pub that afternoon. Somewhere in the Greater Glasgow area a diary was closed, returned to it's safe and it's owner sat alone in the dark deciding the next move. Everything could be turned round now. Looked at from a different angle. It may well prove unnecessary to kill anyone else at all. Pity! Two or three phone calls may well suffice. For the moment, at any rate.

****

"Right you'se two. Leave the bevvy fur ma pal Reggie an' he's missus. Ther' must be somebuddy oot there ye'se could be oot chibbin' or at least annoyin'"
"Aye but Adjie. Ah thought...."
"Did ah hear you say BUT tae me ya wee shite? Get tae fuck the pair o' ye'se. Ah waant tae talk tae Reggie. Gaun noo! Fuck off!"
Gally and the Wee Man did not dare to ask any more questions. He was allowed to change his mind. HE was "Adjie" Jamieson after all. Before this morning he hadn't even acknowledged their existence.
"Aye, dae whit ye'se ur telt ya pair o' bastarts." said Jean helpfully, eyeing the huge amount of drink she had suddenly fallen heiress to.
Reggie said nothing. He was still in shock because "Adjie" had referred to him as his pal.

****

If Reggie Jarvie was astounded by "Adjie" Jamieson's old pals act it was nothing to the astonishment "Adjie's" brother Phil experienced

when he phoned Horner.
"Ah told ye tae be nice tae him. Did ah no' tell ye'se tae be nice tae him? Answer his questions an' be nice tae him. Is that no' whit ah said? Noo look whit's happened. Danny, fuckin' Hagan! That's whit's happened!"
"But we didnae know who the guy wis. Ah've no seen him fur years. He wis jist sittin' there it the back near the door.. An' these other three. They looked like fuckin' tossers at first. Drunk an a'. Naebuddy wis botherin' their erse wi' them at a'. An then...."
"Aye, Ah don't suppose it wis a' your fault right enough. Hagan's aye been aff he's fuckin' heid. Dinnae worry aboot it the noo. Ah'll git it a' sorted oot. It's awright. "Adjie" already knows whit tae dae."
If Jamieson hadn't known Horner better he could have sworn his boss was mildly amused by the entire incident. But he knew him better than that. At least he thought he did.

****

Phillippa Jarvie had been absolutely terrified by the incident at the bus stop, and after she had locked her back and front doors and shut the blinds, collapsed on to her sofa to trying vainly to stop her stomach churning and her heart from pounding. The one thing she knew with certainty was that her budding career as a blackmailer was over. The man in the Jaguar car had made certain of that. His smiling, polite manner when he delivered his chilling message only served to make it all the more effective. She had been left in no doubt whatsoever that he had meant every word he uttered. When her phone suddenly rang, she jumped and had to stop herself from running from the room. At the same time she knew she had to answer it. She had to! What if it was him again? She had to try to make them understand somehow. She hadn't meant any harm. Not really. It was just a joke on Mr. Taylor. She would leave Glasgow and never come back. She picked the phone up with both hands to try to stop them from trembling. That was when she got her second shock of the evening.
"Hello Phillippa? Ah you're home. Good. Daniel Taylor here. Listen I'll tell you what it is, Phillippa. I've been thinking things over of late, and because of the pressure I've been under at work lately, my behaviour toward you recently has been nothing short of abominable. Especially in view of the help you have been to my poor wife. Please accept my apology. Come and see me tomorrow before I leave for work, and we'll see about raising your wages. And we're not talking buttons here O.K.? Enjoy the rest of your evening, and I'll speak with you tomorrow. Goodnight Phillippa."
Phillippa collapsed back onto the sofa and buried her face in her

trembling hands. What was going on? Was he trying to drive her off her head?
Surely he wouldn't harm her with his wife there? She wouldn't let him. Not Miss Sarah. But what if she went there and she wasn't there? Oh God what should she do?

****

Daniel Taylor replaced the receiver and turned round to speak to the other two occupants of his spacious living room.
"Satisfied now?"
"And about bloody time too. Where would Sarah be without the woman at times like these? And see you do it too. D'you hear me Daniel? Alright Sarah?"
"Thanks C.J. She's been a good friend to me." Sarah leaned over and gave C.J. his customary peck, which always made him blush.
"I'll do it dad. I promise. First thing. I will Sarah. Let's all have a drink."
"Not for me" said C.J. getting to his feet very smartly for a man of his years. "I really do feel my age sometimes. I'm really quite tired, and I've still got one or two things to deal with when I get home. Did I tell you we've got a very bright new lady starting with us at Meredith Metals Sarah? Very bright indeed. Very pretty also. Just about your age too. G'night m'dear. 'Night Daniel. I'm off."
C.J. made for the door patting Sarah on the shoulder in passing.
"Now remember Daniel. See to it first thing. Sarah's peace of mind is paramount just now."
"Thanks again C.J." said Sarah patting his hand , as it touched her shoulder.

C.J. left the room whistling.

END CHAPTER

CHAPTER TWELVE

"VOICE" TALK

Daniel Taylor seemed very much more relaxed than he had been of late. Even cheerful. He draped his expensive suit jacket over his desk chair and sat on the edge of his large desk. It would be very wrong to class Taylor as stupid. You didn't get where he was by being that. Stupidly, perhaps even stupendously, boring and predictable maybe, but that was a different matter. This morning, however, he was strangely businesslike and alert.
"Morning everyone. Right Gil. What have we got? Start with Horner."

“O.K. But you’ll be disappointed I’m afraid. He openly associates with criminal types yes,but then an awful lot of business people do. It very much depends on what type of business you happen to be in. And John Horner happens to be in an awful lot of businesses. I know that he has been capable of violence in his past and on one or two occasions, and that is a matter of police record. But that is the point. IN HIS PAST.” Gil emphasised the last three words heavily.
“But he openly consorts with criminals. Meets them on a regular basis. Find the link.”
“I, too, have openly met HIM Daniel. Find the link there. Not easy.”
“You’re a crime reporter for God’s sake. It’s your job to meet the likes of him.”
“He’s a successful businessman. His job is to meet anybody who can help him in business. Most of the people I know from that era, late sixties, early seventies had some kind of brush with the law. Most of us grew out of it. I suspect John Horner grew because of it , but that’s going to be very difficult to prove.”
“I didn’t have any brushes with the law.”
“Didn’t you? I certainly did. Daniel you still break the law on a daily basis. You know it, and I know it. Do you want me to tell Tommy about your hobby?”
“That’s an oversight.”
“That you continue to oversee although you know it’s a criminal offence and a very serious one at that.”
Daniel Taylor, an expert shot, had two valuable shotguns and a pistol at home which were neither licensed , nor securely housed. He was just too tight fisted to meet the necessary expense. Taylor looked very uncomfortable suddenly, and turned to Lassiter.
“Have you come up with anything? Because I’m only going to pay YOU on results. You know that.”
Lassiter tried not to look curious about whatever it was that Taylor had to hide- he knew Gil would tell him later anyway- and spoke for the first time.
“Mr. Taylor. I would advise you to be more civil in the manner in which you address me. For two reasons really. One, I am here at the express wishes of your wife, and two, I haven’t changed that fucking much and I might just fucking hit you again. Shall we all start all over again? Pretend I’ve just come in perhaps?”
Gil coughed loudly to conceal the chuckle and Taylor reddened. He rose from the edge of his desk , moved nervously to the rear of it and putting his jacket on, sat down in his leather desk chair.
“Yeah you’re right Tommy. We’re all in this together after all. And what happened to Daniel eh? What’s this Mr. Taylor stuff? Sod that. It’s just the stress of all this business. It being Sarah’s father and all that. I had to apologise about my manners towards one of our household staff this morning too . Not too big to apologise.” He

neglected to mention he only employed one member of household staff.
"Apology accepted , Danny."
This time Gil tried to hide the chuckle and failed miserably Taylor chose to ignore the familiarity.
"Right then Tommy. We're all ears."
Lassiter opened his briefcase.

****

The Glasgow Voice had a small team of hard working journalists and office staff , quite a number of whom only stayed on because of Gil. This hard core would really only answer to him anyway, and they knew that whatever was being discussed between Taylor, Lassiter and Gil in private in Taylor's office, would be passed on to them later, if need be. They did not feel left out in any way, and to be truthful, were slightly relieved not to be invited in the first place. The other, more junior members never were anyway.
Tony Pearson, Gil's right hand man in the office, was curious as to why Gil was choosing to remain quiet regarding some events rumoured to have taken place in a certain East End pub. He assumed that, as usual, Gil would have a very good reason for doing so. He always had done in the past, and in any event that's all they were at the moment. Rumours. It happened all the time. At that precise moment he was more interested in another rumour he'd heard that the "Grapes" was closing temporarily for renovation. Now THAT was a rumour that needed urgent attention paid to it. Where would he go at lunch-time every day? In fact where would he go most of the time? Tony headed for the door, struggling into his jacket as he went.
"Ten minutes" he roared to the rest of the office. No one even looked up. They knew that meant half an hour, at least. And that was on a good day. But he was a bloody good reporter, so it didn't matter.

****

"I've heard lot's of stories about Horner," began Lassiter "but strangely enough none of them from the people I would expect to know him. MY criminal associates. If he's the gangster you seem to think he is, they certainly would know him, or at least of him, and believe me these people would not be afraid of him. Gil?"
"They know him alright. Leave him just now. How did you get on with Sarah's mother? Make any sense"
"A fair bit actually. I'm very fond of her. Always have been. Strangely enough, it seems to be mutual." Taylor studiously ignored the

inference.
"What , exactly?"
"Well, painful as it was for her, and Daniel's wife of course, we went back over the week before the murder and she came up with quite a bit actually. Some of it may be relevant. Some not."
"Well?"
"Well apparently he hadn't been happy at his job for some time, for some reason or other. Now the reason she remembers that so well, was that he always had been before. Lorry driver. Loved the job. Worked as many hours as he could. He was also more nervy than usual. You know. Jumpy. That sort of thing. And he was also doing a bit of muttering in his sleep. None of which made any sense to her. But there was one thing she remembers clearly. She overheard him talking to someone on the phone about a week or so before he died, and could have sworn she overheard the words "death certificate". She was so positive she remembers asking him about it, and apparently he laughed at her and told her she was either going deaf, or daft, or both. But she's adamant. Swear to it on a stack of bibles. Did he know he was in danger? You tell me." Lassiter turned to Taylor.
"No, you tell me. You're the one who spoke to her. Daft old bat anyway. Remember she's living in a nursing home and she was having memory lapses before she went in. Wouldn't be there otherwise."
"Oh really? Not according to your wife. I repeat. She was adamant about it and I, for one, believe her. Your mother-in-law is as bright as you or I.. Well, me anyway."
Gil had to stop this. It was getting out of hand and Lassiter was winning hands down.
"Let's go down the "Grapes" and have a break and a bite. Tony'll be there by now probably. Did I actually say probably there? Bloody certainly!"

****

If John Horner had had any inkling of how much time had been spent in Glasgow pubs NOT talking about him recently, but about a certain Danny Hagan's sudden resurrection on to the streets of the city, he could have been understandably upset, even jealous, but he certainly didn't look it. He looked almost carefree as he strolled into the Jamieson's pub. He did ,however, have the latest copy of "The Voice" under his immaculately suited arm which he threw carelessly down on the bar.
"Nuthin' in there aboot yir cabaret yisterday efternin!"
"Jist as well. We've only hud wan real customer this moarnin. Wan fuckin' customer! Apart fae you that is. An' you an "Adjie"- he's jist

away by the way- urnae customers. Wan disnae need tae piy fur drink, an' the other wulnae."
"Who wis the other wan?"
"That well dressed fucker ah told ye aboot that came in the ither day day an' asked aboot wee Reggie. He wis readin' a copy ae that fuckin' rag, that guy Lassiter works fur. Asked aboot Reggie again. Says he's goat business aboot here. Dae you know him?"
"Ah might. Leave him the noo. Right. "The Gunfight it the O.K. fuckin' asylum" yisturday. Tell me aboot it!"
"Ah've telt ye everythin'. Thae guys wurnae fur fuckin' aboot. Even "Adjie" looked impressed, an' ye huv tae be a class act tae impress him. So that wis Hagan wis it? Ah never rec'nised him comin' in.. Jist looked like a wee, skinny, middle-aged guy it furst. Turns oot tae be "Al Ca-fuckin'-pone" Horner gave his wry smile that wasn't really a smile at all.
"Hagan's always been a real class act. Huvnae seen him fur years masel' though. But ah knew he wisnae deid. Ah WID huv known aboot that.!"
"This guy Lassiter? Whit's he askin' aboot you fur onywiy? Whit huv ye done tae him?"
"Nuthin'. Yit! It's no' him that's stirrin' the shit, it's that flash bastirt that runs this fuckin' rag. Taylor. Aye it's Taylor ah need tae fuckin' shut up. An' yir wee cabaret yisturday, ah'll start wi' that. Right this other auld bastard that's been nosin' aboot. Whit dis he look like?"
"By the wiy. Afore ah tell ye aboot him. This guy Hagan, he mentioned another name special like. Wan YOU'LL no' like. He said tae make sure tae tell " Plum" he'd been in."
This time Horner didn't smile? Hagan had just let him know all bets were off. Their live and let live agreement of the last thirty years or so could be coming to an abrupt end. So it wis back tae Plum wis it?

****

Hagan knew better than to react. She would reach a stage where she either ran out of temper, or crockery, or both. Her reaction was understandable. His behavour was, in her mind, unforgiveable. But he knew she would have to do both probably, before she calmed down. But he had to GET her to calm down quickly, and he knew that at the moment she wasn't ready to do that. For a doctor, especially one who knew a lot about hypertension, depression and how to deal with excess stress in one's life she wasn't very good at following her own advice. "Fuckin' Hell, P.J." he thought to himself, "calm fuckin' doon , hen It wis bound tae happen sooner or later. Ah couldnae let anythin' happen tae an auld mate noo, could Ah? Ye know that. . Fuck's sake girl. Even Plum wid fuckin' know that. It's jist the wiy things ur. Ayewis been that wiy wi' me."

****

Gil watched Taylor at the bar. There had been a very definite change in his behaviour again over the last couple of days. As though some sort of pressure had been lifted recently. As if something he had been very concerned about was no longer a matter for such concern. He wondered what it was.

"Thank fuck! He's going back to the office. Good old Tony. He can always be relied on to come up trumps when needed. Never really gets drunk you know, Tommy boy. Just loves to talk to people and where better to do it than in his favourite boozer. Taylor can't understand that. Tony's popular with everybody. Taylor's popular with nobody. D'you think maybe that's why Taylor dislikes him so? Surely not eh kid?"

They both laughed as Taylor ushered Tony Pearson towards the door, Tony walking backward and delivering the punch line to a joke he had been telling the bar staff, as he did so. The girls collapsed in fits of laughter, Tony waved to Gil and Lassiter and followed his boss out the front door.

"Character." said Lassiter.

"He's certainly that alright. Been around a long time has Tony. A little bit older than us. Seen it all, done it all kind of guy. I'd trust him with my life."

"Dangerous thing to do Gil. I don't know if there's anybody in my life, or ever has been come to that, I could say that about."

"Some day you may have to. What about old Danny boy yesterday. Wasn't that trusting somebody with your life?"

"Different thing entirely. Nobody asked him to do it. Not that I'm not grateful of course. I am. Of course I am"

"Got to trust people some time Tommy boy. This tough guy attitude's alright for teaching you how to survive, but if you want to live, I mean really live, you've got to trust people sometime. Take it from one who knows."

"So you're not cynical, world weary and all the things you'd like the world to think you are then? What's that then, if not a different kind of image? You're a fraud Gil. Just like me."

"Now we're getting somewhere. You're admitting you're living an image. We all do kid. What I've always been interested in is not the fact that we do it, because we all do, more the reasons why we do it. Some sort of protection mechanism going back to childhood probably."

"You're a deep thinker Gil me old son."

"You've got no idea how deep Tommy boy. No idea. Talking about deep thinking, it's about time I let you into some more trade secrets.

Things I know about people. Who they are, and maybe much more importantly, who they were. Or shall we shall we settle once more for who they thought they were?"
"Fuck's sake. Not all that shit again."
They both laughed and began to put their cards on the table. Lassiter, in particular was about to learn some astonishing things about some people.

END CHAPTER

CHAPTER THIRTEEN

TALKING IT ALL OUT

" Maggie? It's me P.J. We've got to talk. I take it you already know that Danny's suddenly decided to let Glasow, particularly the East End of it, know that he's still around. Bloody maniac. Honestly I could kill him. What possessed him to bring all this shit back into our lives, I just cannot imagine."
"I can. I know my brother. Calm down. Let me make one phone call and I'll call you back. I don't think it's as bad as it first sounds. Something's not ringing quite true here. This is all meant to impress someone, but I'm not sure if that someone is who you and I think it is. God help us all if I'm wrong because, if I am, we're all going right back thirty years or so!"

****

"Ah've already telt ye. A good wee bit aulder than you an' me mebbe. Well dressed an' talks as if he's goat a bool in his mooth. Whit the fuck he wid waant wi' the like's ae Reggie , ah've goat nae idea. But he dis. That's twice'st he's been in here lookin' fur 'im"
"How much aulder? Did ye see his motor? Whit wis he drivin?"
"Ah dunno, dae Ah? He didnae bring it in wi' 'im?"
"Dinnae be fuckin' smart you." Horner smiled in spite of himself. "Ye see if ye'd bothered tae ask yir brither, ye wid know that there's other motors like mine oan the road, an' if this guy wis drivin' wan ae them , an' he's who ah think he is, auld or no', he's fuckin' trouble. Time wis he might huv driven he's motor right intae yir daft fuckin' pub. Afore he blew the place up that is! Big fuckin' trouble. "Adjie's" bringin' wee Reggie here eftir shuttin' time so mind nae hingers oan the night. Just us four. Goat it? Ah'll be back jist eftir ye shut. An' keep that mangy fuckin' dug oot ae ma sight, or Ah will fuckin' shoot it this time. Flea ridden fucker that it is."

....

Lassiter had initially only gone to London to forget all about Sarah , but ended up staying there just short of a year. In subsequent years he had spent a lot more time in the capital honing his skills in journalism , but he was astonished to learn from Gil just how many things-and people- had changed over the years. Hardly surprising really, given the number of years involved. Nevertheless some of them still astounded him. He knew who Horner was now alright and also who Plum was.

It occurred to him to that he hadn't asked Maggie what she was doing now, or what had happened to that other, rather strange, P.J.girl. The journalist in him had taken over and he had forgotten that they were all just people. Some of them old and close friends. Strange how he had forgotten , and somehow divorced himself from all that. Danny Hagan in particular. Hagan had saved him from himself, and numerous other dangerous people come to that, on countless occasions. Lassiter felt guilty and strangely sad about it all. He would try to make it up to him somehow. It would appear that Danny might well have now put himself in a very dangerous position with someone. Someone, perhaps, who could be more dangerous than all the rest put together. He and Gil headed back to the "VOICE" both hoping that Daniel Taylor had decided to piss off home. Unfortunately he hadn't.

....

After making her phone call Maggie felt much better about things and immediately phoned P.J. back. Friends during their teen-age years, she'd always been able to calm her down back then and talk her out of her temper fits. Even now prone to violent moodswings , P.J. had been a real handful in those days. Only Danny and Maggie had been able to handle her. Nowadays Patricia Jeffries M.D. was much, much better at keeping her violent temper fits in check. Danny was her mainstay there. Her rock. As a G.P. she now avoided prescribing strong sedatory drugs to others as much as she possibly could. Long term usage could have very harmful side effects. Not many doctors had the first hand knowledge of that piece of information that Patricia Jeffries had. Neither of the senior partners in the practice could have had an inkling about her teen-age drug habit. Or they wouldn't have taken her on in the first place would they?

....

"Right Reggie. Settle doon noo. Naebuddy's gonnae work ye ower or anythin' like that. Ah jist waanted tae know a couple ae things. Whit exactly is it yir sister's goat oan that eejit Taylor?"
"Ah don't know Mr. Horner. Honest ah don't. An' neither dis she really. She jist knows that her pal that died seen 'im up in the hoaspital the night that Gallagher died."
"Aye but he wis winchin' Gallagher's daughter then. They'd a' huv been there visitin'. The three ae them. The mither, the daughter, an'

him."
"Ah know that. But the wumman, she wis a nurse then, said that he came back later. She seen 'im talkin' tae a doactor. An aulder man in a white coat. She thought it wis funny, because she didnae know the doactor too well. Only seen 'im a couple ae times in the hoaspital. At first she thought they were arguin' aboot somethin. An then Taylor went back intae the room that Gallagher wis in. Himsel'."
"Ur you sure aboot this noo? Supposed tae be that nurse hid a right problem wi' the bevvy. Never aff it, it seems."
"Mebbe's she did right enough, but ma sister says she never waanst chinged her story. Right up tae the day that she died. Used tae tell her daughter it tae. The exact same story. Right up tae the day she died. Honest Mr. Horner. Wid ah lie tae YOU?"
"Naw. Ah don't think ye wid. Phil gie Reggie a drink. An gie him somethin tae take up the road wi' him an a'. Fur him an' he's wife fur a wee drink the night."
"Goad bliss ye Mr. Horner."
"Ah doubt it Reggie. Ah doubt HE'll dae that. Ah'll mebbe git a turn aff the ither fella' but, right enuff. "Adjie" see him up the road. Make sure thae bad boays don't take his swally aff him. He's no' the man he used tae be. See ye Reggie."

****

"Right let's re-cap then. Theresa Gallagher maintains her husband was not himself for about a week before he died. Maybe even longer than that? Correct?"
"Correct."
"She's adamant he was talking about a death certificate to someone? Life insurance?"
"Possibly. The bit I really don't understand is why would he would be discussing the other stuff she says he was talking about. She's just as adamant about that Gil. Guns? Medals? She says he never had anything to with guns or anything like that. And he'd never been in the forces either. Don't forget I knew him too. He was half-Irish. Not too fond of the British Army, as I remember. But no terrorist either. Religious man."
"Glasgow gangsters forcing him to do it?"
"Could be. Using his truck. Bit far fetched mind you. There were guns in those days, sure, but nothing like today's level. And I don't remember the Glasgow teams handing out medals to each other. Second prizes , yes. Medals, no."
Gil gave a tired smile, removed his thick, horn rimmed spectacles and rubbed his tired eyes. Lassiter was suddenly aware of how startlingly blue they were. Startlingly pale blue, and every bit as chilling as Danny Hagan's. Dangerous eyes. They must have made

some team Hagan and Gil. He still couldn't quite get his head round the fact that Gil was "Adjie" Gilmour. The eyes helped.
"Fuck it Tommy boy. "Grapes" time, and you're buying. Wonder how many Pearson has had down his neck by now. Hard to tell with him. Let's go kid."

END CHAPTER

CHAPTER FOURTEEN

GIRL TALK

"You never really knew Tommy Lassiter too well P.J., did you? If you had known him like I did, you would understand better. Tommy had a heart of gold. Help anybody. Good looking too. And very brave. The guys used to call it "game" in those days.Remember? So he was a bit unusual. The girls fancied him, and the guys trusted and liked him. Good company too. Dry sense of humour. Do you see why Danny would want to back him up?"
"Suppose so. But we don't belong there anymore Maggie. That life. It's long gone. For all of us. You as much as anybody. All our lives have changed"
"I know. So's Lassiter's, believe me. I've met him very recently. Danny's always been the one who found change the hardest. You know that P.J. He's tried very hard. But people wouldn't let him because of who he was. They didn't change. So they wouldn't let HIM. The result is, a lot of the time he thinks the old way. He thought Lassiter needed his help. Tommy never let HIM down in the old days. Lassiter didn't need it, or even want it, but Danny thought he had to help. He's never let anybody down that way. You ,of all people, should know that I don't remember him letting you down either. Do you?"
Suddenly P.J. felt incredibly guilty. After all, it was Danny who had finally got her off drugs and away from Plum once and for all. He hadn't needed to do it but he had done it anyway. And the way he had looked after his old , fiercely Irish mother and Maggie , too for that matter, until she was able to look after herself.
"I've been a selfish bitch again haven't I?"
"Well, maybe not entirely. Plum still is one dangerous bastard to know. The one thing in Danny's favour is that Plum now knows that he does not impress my brother one little bit. The problem is that Danny doesn't know that that feeling is mutual. Plum respects Danny , but that's as far as it goes. He's certainly not scared of him. Not one little bit. I don't think he ever was, come to that"
"Bloody Hell! What a mess."

****

"Are you sure you're alright now Phillippa? I know Daniel has treated you abominably in the past, but he really does seem to be trying hard to mend his ways. The chat C.J. had with him, between you and I it was more of a lecture really, seems to have made him think. I was actually here when he phoned you. Did he talk to you about that increase in your wages yet? I didn't see him before he left this morning. I slept very late as you know. It's just that you still don't seem your old self. Worried looking or something. I don't know."
"Oh I'm alright Miss Sarah. I...., I.... had a bit of a funny turn the other day and of course there's my brother,I'm still worrying about him too, but yes Mr. Taylor has spoken to me about my wages. Starting next week. And very welcome it will be too. I'll be able to help my poor brother more. This week his giro thing didn't come again and...."
"Here. Take this just now to tide you over. Not another word. Poor old soul."
"God bless you. I'll pay it back without fail next week. And Mr. Taylor can be really nice , when he wants to be, can't he?"
Phillippa was trying her best to change her ways too, but the silly bitch was making it really hard. The well dressed man in the Jaguar HAD really terrified her, however, and there would be no more phone calls made by Jean. That was definite. That game was well and truly over now. What Phillippa didn't make allowances for was the fact that Jean wasn't the only woman in Glasgow who could make phone calls.

****

"I've left my mobile downstairs in the car P.J. and I've got one more important phone call to make about all this. I could use your phone, but I can't remember the bloody number and I know I keyed it in to my mobile. Two minutes. Anyway I hate leaving mobiles in cars. Wide open invitation."
"Oh we don't have many car thefts round here Maggie. But convertibles are more tempting , I suppose Anyway you'll soon have your new car. You'll have to tell me all about it when you come back upstairs. The job sounds out of this world. Maybe Danny'll be home by then. I'm worried about him."
"Don't be. He'll be alright. I know my brother. What was that rubbish about no break-ins round here. This is bloody Partick my dear. Not Palm Beach.. I'll be lucky if I've still got four wheels to drive home. Get the coffee on. No drink for me tonight . More's the pity."
As Maggie went downstairs she checked that her mobile was indeed still in her shoulder bag, where it always was, and then headed for the corner shop where she knew there was a public telephone.

****

Jill, the trainee journalist, answered the phone, automatically switching on the voice mail at the same time. She wasn't sure how it did that, but she knew it did.

"Glasgow Voice. Jill Butler speaking."

The woman's voice was muffled but somehow Jill didn't think it was the same voice as before. But the message was definitely the same message.

"Ah.ve goat a wee message fur Mr. Taylor. There are drips and then there are the other drips, Mr. Taylor. Wid ye make sure he gets that wee message hen? Drips and drips."

END CHAPTER

CHAPTER FIFTEEN
TALK'S CHEAP

"Talk's cheap. It's time you started coming up with some sensible contribution to what it is that "The Voice" is trying to trying to find out in this investigation. Our main aim is to assist the police in whatever way we can. I've got a meeting with Hegarty from C.I.D. later in the week. What do I tell him? I can't think of anything new that you two have come up?"

Daniel Taylor's last words to Lassiter and Gil rang in Lassiter's ears. The annoying thing was that the bastard was right for once in his life. He sat alone at the kitchen table in his comfortable little flat, drinking endless cups of coffee and staring at what he had written. The ashtray was overflowing with cigarette stubs. What really astonished Lassiter was the sheer number of people this one death had had some sort of effect on. What was even more astonishing was , that in one way or another, they all seemed to know each other. Some of them maybe weren't even aware of that fact, but they either knew one another, or were mutually acquainted. Gil had helped him see that. Now all Lassiter had to do was find the one, important connection. Fucking hell! They hadn't bothered to tell Taylor about all the possible connections. He'd never have got his brain round it.

"Cheers Gil. Thanks a lot." Lassiter said softly to himself and lit another cigarette.

****

"Hello Lassiter. I do remember you now. Maggie Hagan thought it important we should meet. Patricia Jeffries. No, nothing for me, thank you. I haven't a lot of time. Both my senior partners in the practice are attending a medical conference in Leeds and I'm rushed off my feet at the moment. I believe we have a number of mutual acquaintances."

Lassiter found it hard to believe that this cool, self assured woman could possibly be the same person he remembered.

"I'm sorry. I'm struggling to get my head round a lot of this at the moment. You're sure I can't get you anything. Coffee?"

"No thanks. You've changed from the guy I remember. I only met you once or twice, but from what I remember of those days, both of us needed drastic changes in our lives anyway."

"You're very direct and honest Doctor. I'm sorry, but I can't help remembering you as you were then , rather than as you are now and probably have been for the last thirty years. I'm very pleased things worked out for you."

"The feeling's mutual. I take it you know about Danny and me. I owe him everything"

"Maggie did tell me on the phone. He's been a good friend to me too. Never turned his back on me at any time."

"He only does that for people he can depend on. Now, Maggie said you needed help with some information."

"You've got that right. Because I've spent a lot of years down south and lost touch, I'm looking for information about some old names from those days. Nicknames and the like. And one person's maiden name, if you know it. That O.K.? I'm going to have to do the same with a lot of people."

"Sure. If I know them. I'll have more free time after tomorrow when Dr. Meredith and his wife come back from Leeds."

She didn't notice Lassiter's very slight narrowing of the eyes. Another connection. Possibly.

****

"Thanks for phoning James. I'm really looking forward to tomorrow. I only hope I live up to your expectations. Yours and Mr. Taylor's"

"You will Maggie. You will. We have every confidence in you. C.J. Taylor can spot talent with his eyes closed, and I'm not too bad at it either. You'll be a sensation. Till tomorrow then Maggie."

"I probably won't sleep a wink James but I'll be fine when I get there. Good night then and thanks again.

James Meredith replaced the receiver and sat in his darkened office.

"Till tomorrow, Maggie my dear. Tomorrow. It shouldn't take too long to establish just how much you really do know."

He went over to the wall safe and swiftly dialled the combination. He had to check his diary. His diary was very, very important to him. He had been unaware that Maggie Hagan knew Patricia Jeffries, until he got the phone call from his older brother in Leeds. The senior partner in Dr. Jeffries practice relied very heavily on his longest serving receptionist to keep him informed about Patricia Jeffries when he was out of town. Dr. Patrick John Meredith and his wife had been very selective as to how much information they thought their junior partner should be privy to. James Meredith's older brother's professional ethics had been called into question on more than one occasion over the years. Accurate record keeping, or lack of it to be more exact, together with an arrogance and lack of concern , verging on professional misconduct, with regard to his patients general wellbeing had continually dogged his career. But the really important factor now was that he had been Thomas Gallagher's family doctor at the time of Gallagher's murder.

****

Lassiter had arranged with Maggie that he would give her a call to let her know once P.J. had been to see him.
"Maggie? Lassiter. All the best for your new job tomorrow incidentally. Sounds like a dream come true. Yes, she has been to see me and and believe it or not remembers me. That's a bit of a miracle for both of us." Maggie chuckled. "You know the more I talk to people from back then, the more I'm amazed at how we're all connected to each other in some way or another."
"It's not really , you know, according to some book I once read. This guy claimed that if two people -total strangers- talked long enough about people they both knew they would have any number of mutual acquaintances."
"Law of averages eh? Suppose he could have a point. It's certainly happening with astonishing regularity at the moment. Once I talk to some more people can we all get together do you think? You know, you, me, Danny and P.J. and Gil of course. At least we're all certain of our connection to each other. Good idea?"
"I think it's a must. I think there's somebody else that should be there as well. But that could be a big problem. Anyway you carry on just now and when you're ready we'll get it all arranged, somehow or other."
"Great. Good luck again for tomorrow. How's Danny by the way? Have you seen him yet?"
"Nobody's bloody seen him! But I know he's alright. He phoned me earlier. P.J.'ll know where he is by now. But she won't tell you. Not if he doesn't want anyone to know. Not even me. I know him Lassiter. He's O.K. Trust me."
"Take your word for it. If anybody does talk to him, tell him I said thanks again. I really mean that."
"You tell him whenever we all meet."

****

"Sarah called me this morning kid. Apparently her mother would like to see you again. Maybe it's Sarah who really wants to see you again. I said I'd speak to you, and get back to her. How're things anyway? Getting anywhere?

"So far, no. All I seem to be doing is coming up with a lot of people who know each other even if they aren't aware of it. Too many co-incidences. Maggie Hagan started a new job this week working for a company owned by the golden boy's father. Run by some guy called Meredith apparently"

"Could be the reason it's called Meredith Metals then. What do you think? Some co-incidence kid. You'll have to do better than that."

Lassiter smiled to himself , and moved the phone, searching for his cigarettes.

"Listen to me Gil. The senior partner in P.J. Jeffries practice is also called Meredith. Meredith was also the name of the Gallagher family doctor all those years ago. I checked. Now if these two are related we've got something. Don't ask me what, but we've got something."

"Fucking hell kid. You could be on to something there you know, because I'm convinced I've met this guy. The doctor I mean. Arrogant bastard he is too, if it's the same one I'm thinking of. Met him at some poxy dinner party Taylor forced me to go to with him. Spent the whole evening telling me how much money he could make. And guess how he was going to make it? Wait for it kid. Are you ready for this?

"Go on then."

"Running nursing homes for the elderly. I'll phone Sarah now if you're finished. I'm coming too. To the nursing home. Thanks for the invite."

"What invite? They might keep you in."

"Fuck off."

END CHAPTER

CHAPTER SIXTEEN

MONEY TALKS

"Adjie" Jamieson nodded that he understood, and opened the passenger door of the Jaguar. The man driving it sat behind the wheel staring straight ahead.

"Remember. Nothing happens to him. Nothing happens to anybody for the moment. Make sure of that."

"Adjie" nodded again and closed the passenger door. He shivered although it was a fairly warm night.

****

"Aye but ah thought ye waanted us tae....."
"See if you fuckin' "but" me waanst mair son. Reggie disnae get touched. Nae buddy gets touched, or ye'sll answer tae me. Understood? See if ah hear he's even caught the fuckin' cauld, ah'll come lookin' fur the pair o' ye'se"
Gally and the Wee Man stared at "Adjie" Jamieson's retreating back and then at each other mystified. It was going to be hard work learning how to be a gangster.

****

"The only thing I remember about him now was that I didn't like him. I was very young Lassiter but I do remember I was frightened of him. He wasn't a nice man. I do know my mother never liked him. She gave him his place, as he was the family doctor , but she never liked him. I didn't even know he was still alive. And I don't remember if Daniel or C.J. ever mentioned this other Mr. Meredith who works for C.J. C.J. never talks about business to me. And Daniel sometimes doesn't talk to me at all. He's a strange man. But his father is a dear. Money? C.J.? Apparently he's worth an absolute fortune but he never discusses it and you would never dream that he's a very wealthy man , because he's so unassuming. Well you know it was him who put Daniel where he is."
"I sometimes wonder exactly WHERE Daniel is. He certainly doesn't seem to come from the same planet as me, thank God." Lassiter was delighted to hear Sarah giggling on the other end of the line.
"I'll pick you up tomorrow then and we'll go to see your mum. Did Gil tell you he's coming too. Spoilsport." The giggle again.
"Till tomorrow then Be careful Lassiter."

****

Maggie Hagan returned to her window to gaze at it in amazement for the umpteenth time. She still couldn't believe it was really hers. Well , hers to use for the foreseeable future, at least. To drive for as long as she was an employee of Meredith Metals. It meant she could now afford to get rid of the MG sports car she had bought on the promises from her previous employer. Promises that had never materialised. It's quality and comfort spoke for itself. By God would that snooty bitch two doors up be jealous. The MG had been bad enough for her. Green with envy she'd been. But both C.J. and James Meredith had insisted that she drive something more befitting her position with the company. Slightly more responsible looking, was how CJ had put it. A bloody Jaguar! It sparkled and shone amongst all the modest other, common as muck, saloons and company vans in her street. So what if it was an old one of C.J.'s that he didn't need? Only she knew that. She made for the phone to make sure P.J. was still coming over to see it .

****

"Yir man phoned me earlier. Ye goat that wee eejit Reggie up the road the other night? Horner disnae waant anythin' happenin' tae him noo. Him or he's sister. Somethin' tae dae wi' whit they know aboot this Taylor guy at the paper. "Adjie?" You fuckin' listenin' tae me?"
Phil Jamieson looked up from the pub sink, from where he was making a half-hearted attempt to clean the pub's filthy tumblers. His brother looked pre-occupied by something.
"Aye. Ah'm listenin'. Safe an' sound. Ah jist wonder why the wee shite's so fuckin' important all of a sudden, that's a' Dae you know?"
"Horner knows whit he's daein'. He always knows whit he's daein"
"Adjie" still looked pre-occupied with his own thoughts.

****

Since his father had spoken to Daniel Taylor about his treatment of Phillippa Jarvie, the change had been quite amazing. And her promised pay rise had been astonishing too. A lot more than she had expected. Phillippa being Phillippa , she immediately started to ask herself why. Money certainly talked alright. But old habits died hard too!

****

Theresa Gallagher made a face and took her daughter's hand in her's.
"Never liked him from the moment I clapped eyes on him. Too big for his boots. But Tommy always thought he owed him something because he got him that job driving for his younger brother's company."
"When did you last see him Mrs. Gallagher?" enquired Gil suddenly. It was the first time he had spoken since he had arrived with Sarah and Lassiter. Looking slightly taken aback Theresa Gallagher turned to answer him furrowing her brows in concentration.
"Oh, it was years ago, Mr., sorry Gill? Was that your name?"
"Just Gil. That'll do fine."
"I can't even remember too well what he looked like exactly. Quite good looking I think. You know distinguished. But I remember the way he spoke. Quite cheeky. Talking down to you sort of thing. I

remember that." Gil nodded and looked thoughtful.

"Never mind about him Theresa. I believe you told Sarah you wanted to speak to me again." Lassiter had moved onto the sofa beside Sarah and her mother.

"But what's Dr. Meredith got to do with everything?"

"Very probably nothing. Now what did you want to see me about?"

" Oh that. It's just that I had two other visitors the other day. Well they didn't really come to see me, they said. Just to look the nursing home over for a relative of theirs. But they were asking a lot of questions. About what I knew about the doctors who run or own this place. And about the old times. How good my memory was for years back. That sort of thing. I just thought you might need to know Tommy. You know? For your investigation? I know you're trying hard to help Sarah and me get to the bottom of all this. God bless you son."

"What did they look like Theresa?"

"Oh one looked like a businessman. Not young. The other one had a very pale face and a beard. He looked horrible. Frightening. The businessman asked all the questions. I think he said his name was Horner. Well, I think that was it. Yes Horner. And you could tell he had money by the clothes he was wearing. Money talks doesn't it.?"

"If you were talking to who I think you were talking to , it would be screaming Mrs. Gallagher."said Gil.

He nodded as if to himself, and looked thoughtful again.

END CHAPTER

CHAPTER SEVENTEEN

THE TALKING HAS TO STOP

"Wid you say ah'm fuckin' stupit "Adjie"? Ah mean wid ye? How long huv you fuckin' known me? Hus it ever been known fur me tae dae anythin' as fuckin' stupit as that? Tae go an' see an auld wumman whose man's murder they're tryin' tae connect me wi', an' whit's mair, tell her ma fuckin' name? Gie's a break Gilmour."

"That's twice you've used names that I'm no longer known by. Would you like me to start using yours?"

"Awright. Ah wis angry. But that's an insult tae ma intelligence that."

"Settle down Johnny. I believe you. But the other one certainly sounds like "Adjie" Jamieson." Gil had been certain from the start that Theresa Gallagher's visitor had not been Horner. He just wanted to hear him say it. "YOU don't know where he is all the time do you?"

"Naw but ah dinnae think it wid be him either. He knows aboot the paper tryin' tae tie me in wi' it. An anywiy he's no' the only ugly, frightenin' lookin' bastart in Glesca wi' a beard is he? Place is

hoachin' wi them!"
Gil chuckled. "Suppose you've got a point there. Listen would you be prepared to come to a meeting next week with some faces from the past. It could help you. Because if we don't all talk we might all end up back where we were thirty years ago. And I for one don't fancy that. And I don't really think you do either. Do you?"
"Depends on who the faces ur. Name names."
"One of them could be Hagan."
"Noo Ah know yir aff yir fuckin' heid. You serious?
"Deadly."
"Ah'll phone ye back."
"Do that."

****

"How's the new job?"
"It's out of this world Lassiter. They're paying me loads of monry and they've given me a Jaguar to drive."
"Danny would say you've sold out. Driving Jaguars. Talking polite. Told me that."
"Ma big bree lives in the bluddy past. Eejit! You see my dear Lassiter, I pride myself I can communicate in any manner of speech. I change as and when required. No matter the company involved I change as the situation changes. An' if ah huv tae chinge ma accent noo an' again Ah'll dae it. Awright?"

"You're an amazing lady Maggie. Maybe I should have married you. Could have been fun not knowing which Maggie I was waking up with."
"In thae days ye widnae huv known onywiys. Ye'd huv been steamin' drunk"

Lassiter laughed outright and automatically lowered his voice as he spoke into the phone.
"Listen. I want you to ask Danny if he'll do me a really big favour. It's a big one."
"Is that why you're whispering my dear Lassiter? Ah cannae bluddy hear ye! An' neither kin anybuddy else. We're oan the 'phone mind. Nae need fur ye tae whisper."
He chuckled again. She really was amazing. Some lady.

****

"And you're sure you and Daniel are getting on a lot better now Phillippa? He's still treating you alright. I know he increased your wages."
"Yes, honestly Miss Sarah. He's been very nice to me recently. Really. Are you alright? You're very quiet Something wrong Miss?"
"Oh probably my imagination. Thought I caught him looking at you funny a couple of times that's all."
Immediately fear clutched at Phillippa Jarvie's heart again. What was going on?

****

"I don't know why the phone calls upset him so much. But there is definitely a link to the woman's phone calls and his change in behaviour. I mean we all know how Gallagher died. It doesn't affect any of us. But it definitely seems to unsettle him. Doesn't really surprise me. He's a strange bugger at the best of times. Nothing Daniel Taylor does or says, would ever surprise me. Mind you, I suppose when all's said and done, we are talking about his wife's father here. He's very deep and maybe the woman's phone calls do upset him. Who knows."
Gil looked thoughtfully at Tony Pearson. There were only the three of them left in the office. Jill, Tony and himself. The others were either all on breaks, or out on assignments.
"Do you really think so Tony? As far as I'm concerned , he's just a shallow bastard and nothing like that would get to him, unless somebody was getting too close to home about something else more important."
"Maybe you're right."
"I know I am."

Just then the phone rang.

****

Reggie Jarvie had once been what HE thought was something and now after all these years he was being treated like something again. The word had spread that he was under Horner's protection for some unexplained reason, and the effect had been immediate.
"Awright Reggie? Waant a drink?" Malky stood in his normal position at the end of the bar, his back to the wall, hands in both pockets. "Gie wee Reggie a drink Phil wid ye? Oan me."
"Thanks Malky. Mooth like a Turkish wrestlers jockstrap. Wee bevvy last night. Me an' the wife."
"Must huv made a nice change fur ye'se." Phil Jamieson's sarcasm showed how impressed HE was by Reggie's new found status.
"Aye. Mr. Horner gie'd me money tae take hur oot if she wanted, but she couldnae be bothered. So we stiyed in an' jist hid a wee drink in the hoose."
"Couldnae be bothered? Couldnae staun up mair like."
"Haw you. That's ma wife yir talkin' aboot. But yir right enough by the way."
All three sniggered. Reggie still had money left over from the money Horner had given him, and the still uncashed Giro in his hip pocket. But no one needed to know that.
"Thanks Malky. Ah'll need tae shoot the craw efter this. That fuckin' Social's no' sent ma Giro again. Ah'll need tae go doon the broo an' see aboot it."
The only problem Reggie had now was to first find, and then go, to another post office where no one he knew could see him cashing the Giro.
"Ye better hing aboot wee man. Here's that auld guy comin' in that's been in here twice't lookin' fur ye."
Reggie turned, and then turned chalk white, when he saw who had come in the door.

****

"Right if ah decide ah'm gonnae go- an' ah've no' made ma mind up yit- it's jist me an' him by the way. He disnae bring onybuddy wi' him an' ah don't bring onybuddy wi' me'. Clear?"
"If he goes in the first place, he would want it that way anyway. You know that. You know him. Or you used to. There'll be others there but nobody that would do the dirty on either of you."
" Fuck's sake!This is Glesga yir talkin' aboot. Naebuddy tae dae the

dirty oan me or him? Where ur a' the ithers comin' fae then? The Vatican?"
Gil chuckled and put the phone down on Horner. Now to see how Lassiter had got on about approaching Danny Hagan.
"I've asked Maggie if she can swing it. If he'll do it for anybody, he'll do it for her. Who is this Horner guy nowadays? All I know about him is what you've told me and a bit from Hegerty at C.I.D. I've seen photographs. He doesn't look particularly dangerous to me. Then or now."
"They never do kid. They never do. Just take my word for it. He is not to be fucked about with. Ask Hagan."
"What happened between you and Danny. You were like brothers once."
"Nothing. Not a thing. I chose to change and move on. Danny chose to stay where he was and try to change other people. Guess who succeeded. If you can call working for Daniel Taylor succeeding that is."
"So you're still friends?"
"You don't need to see much of someone to be that Tommy boy. Sometimes it can strengthen any friendship. Let's just say we wouldn't be a disappointment to each other if the need arose. Which it hasn't up till now."
"And Maggie?"
"Same goes. But she didn't know about that until recently."
"She's a class act Maggie. She could be in any company and fit right in. Adapt to any situation. I honestly believe that."
"She might have to very soon. Things are starting to take some sort of direction in all of this fucking mess. Some sort of crazy logic. And at the root of it there is someone who is precisely that. Crazy!"
Lassiter put the phone down after speaking to Gil and sat for a long time just thinking and smoking. He puzzled for a long time over why the last word Gil had used seemed so very, very apt.
It was time to get the show on the road. The talking had to stop. He lifted the phone and dialled Dr. Patricia Jeffries home number.

****

"P. J.? Lassiter. Sorry to bother you at home but you did tell me to, if necessary. Maybe this could be a bit awkward for you. Two things. One, would you be prepared to have a chat me with me about your employer and colleague Doctor Patrick John Meredith? And two, would you be prepared, always providing I can arrange it first, to

attend a meeting with some of your old friends. I've already asked Maggie if she can try and persuade Danny. I'm asking you individually as it's your strictly your own choice whether you want to attend or not. Also to protect you and your relationship with Danny. That's nobody's business but yours', and whoever else you two have chosen to tell"
"I like your style Lassiter. Lessons on how to sell things from Maggie? Let me think it over . Strangely enough, the second invitation is the one that poses the lesser problem. Doctor Meredith can be a very strange man. Just a little bit scary at times."
Lassiter put the phone down once more and again sat thinking and smoking. He had to find out more about Meredith. And his brother. Who were these people, and why had their connection to so many other people involved in the Gallagher case never been spotted by anyone before? Time to talk to Hegarty at C.I.D. again. Without Taylor, or even Gil's, knowledge.

END CHAPTER

CHAPTER EIGHTEEN

ON AND OFF THE RECORD

Lassiter met Hegarty outside. He'd always loved this building , and the story about the architect throwing himself from it when he discovered it had been constructed facing the wrong way round. Utter rubbish of course. Or was it? HE'D never met anyone personally who could either prove or disprove it. The Glasow Art Galleries. Lassiter loved the place, and the general public who visited it. From all walks of life, backgrounds, countries and continents. They were a bit special to him. All of them.
" I used to come here a lot on my own when I was a lot younger and this really was a mean city. Real hard men to deal with every day. It was like coming to a different world then." Hegarty looked tired.
"Aye, Anderston, Partick, Govan, Whiteinch all within spitting distance and this stuck right in the middle. And over the back of it there you could very quickly be in Hillhead and Kelvingrove , where the toffs stayed. And just back of that Maryhill where they didn't. I still love this city but they've changed it. Too much."
"Let's go inside. I think you'll have me in tears before long. Hard bitten policeman my arse." Lassiter grinned and they went up the steps.

****

"Who said ah wis gonnae let him away wi' it? Whit ah said wis ye

dae nuthin' aboot it the noo. Noo shut the fuck up, an' listen tae me. Ah've goat bigger fish tae fry than Hagan. He's yisterday's news. An' he'll be the morra's an a' if he fucks wi' us again. If ye'd brains ye'se wid be dangerous you'se two. Tell "Adjie" this fae me. Ah know a loat ae ither people who're jist dyin' tae huv a go it HIM , never mind Hagan. So you tell him fae me he dis nuthin' withoot ma' say-so. Goat that Phil? Ah'll sort Hagan oot in ma' ain good time. Naebuuddy fucks John Horner aboot mair than waanst.. Naebuddy!"
Horner slammed the phone down on Phil Jamieson and stubbed out his cigar in the ash tray.
"Ah meant everythin' ah said there by the way. Everythin'!"
Gil nodded and held his gaze. Now was not the time to disagree with anything Horner said. He'd seen the results of people making that mistake before. Gil was not afraid however, only cautious.
"I know that John. And so does Hagan. The difference between him and I is that he doesn't care."
"He will eftir he's seen me. That's a fucking promise! Ah'm no pittin' up wi' any mair ae his shite."

This time Gil decided to stay totally silent.

****

They sat quietly for a while before the Dali painting portraying Jesus on the cross.
"Do you know what happened to the young barman who told you all this? Not that he'd be a youngster now"
"Not only do I know what happened to him, I know where he's working now. And he's still a barman. His name's Andy Lynch and he's the bar manager in a plush golf club in Bearsden." said Hegarty sounding pleased with himself. He liked Lassiter. Liked his style.
"Thanks Jim. You're a miracle. Which golf club?"

****

"There's a difference between being brave and being bloody suicidal Danny. When will you bloody come to terms with that? What you did in the Jamiesons' pub was just stupid. Tommy didn't want anything like that." Maggie Hagan reached across the kitchen table and took her brother's hand. "He appreciates it, but he didn't want it. Bloody Hell Danny you can't go around watching your back for ever."
"Who said I need to watch my back? Ah've still goat back-up. Too much fur thae tossers. An' that cardboard gangster Horner an' a'. We'll see whit he tells them tae dae noo. Ah'll tell ye'se whit. Fuck all! That's whit. Fuck all!"
Behind his back P.J. put her finger to her lips for Maggie's benefit,

but Maggie knew her brother better than P.J. did.
"Tommy needs another favour Danny. Maybe next week?"
"Name it."
"You haven't heard what he's asking you to do yet. It's definitely not your style. Time you changed your style anyway. Bloody brassin' yir case a' ower the place! And me a high-powered sales executive wi' an image tae maintain"
Danny Hagan chuckled. He was very proud of Maggie and everything she'd achieved.
"Stick the kettle oan P.J., tae ma wee sister tells me whit it is ma pal Tommy needs."

"Not for me if you don't mind Doctor , really, because whit ah really waant the night is a wee swally. Because ah'm no drivin' ma big Jagyooar the night. Ah hid tae come in the doactor's wee , stupit motor the night ye see Danny.. A glass or two of the house red would be ever so welcome. If the good doctor could run to that I'd be ever so, terribly, grateful."
P.J. and Danny both visibly relaxed at Maggie's antics. The speed at which she could almost change her entire personality was astonishing. No wonder she was successful. She could have had a career on the stage, if she hadn't opted for selling metal. She knew almost as much about metal as some qualified metallurgists did into the bargain . Tommy Lassiter didn't know about that either.

****

Lassiter and Gil arranged to meet Andy Lynch , on one of his few nights off, in his local in the Clydebank area of Glasgow. Andy was Glasgow through and through. A small, still good looking , dapper man in his late forties or early fifties with a street-wise sense of humour , he was obviously well liked and well respected by the staff and customers alike judging by the complimentary drinks that kept arriving before him where he sat in the end corner of the busy, well-run pub. It was also obvious that he wanted a degree of privacy with his two guests , so that's precisely what he got.
"Thanks for seeing us Mr. Lynch. Good of you. I'm Lassiter and this is Gil."
"Andy, Mr. Lassiter. Just, Andy. Only people who don't like me call me Mister."
"Fine Andy. I'm just Lassiter and he's just Gil. Never went for that mister crap either. Seem to have lost our first names along the way somewhere, anyway."
"Fine by me. No thanks. I've got enough drink here. Look at it all. You'd only have to carry me home, and I live in Drumchapel. Never

moved out of it, though I've felt like it once or twice. Nowhere's the same nowadays. Grew up there though, and I know I'd miss it. Only drink in here because of the amount of free drink I get. Just joking Betty, you know it's because of the affair I keep hoping you'll let me have with you."

"I keep telling you it's o.k, but it's you that's feart of your wife. Glesga men! Aw mooth!"

The extremely pretty young barmaid was ideal for a Glasow pub. Pretty, capable, and always ready with an answer. Glasgow men liked that. Lassiter had no doubt the customers would be fiercely protective of her, and genuinely upset when the day inevitably came that she decided to move on. For now she was THEIR barmaid.

"Married to my mate's nephew. Great wee lassie." said Pat lifting one of the drinks spread out before him. "Now, you wanted to talk to me about this Gallagher thing. And about something else, Jimmy Hegarty said. About the golf club? Jimmy's a great guy. Don't see him much now, but even now I remember him as one of the good cops that night. We'd better sit over here in the corner. Betty's an awfy nosy lassie fur her age. Oh sorry Betty. Nae gossip fur ye the night hen."

"Who'd waant tae listen tae anythin' you've got tae say Andy Lynch. Aw lies anywiy."

All three chuckled and made their way to a secluded table in the corner.

****

The diary had not been written in the first place, nor subsequently meticulously added to, for any vicarious thrill seeking. It was purely and simply a simply coded form of record keeping to remind it's author precisely what had been said to any given individual, with regard to the Gallagher case, on any given date for the last three decades or so. Only mad people would have done it for any other reason. And for it's author that was something inconceivable; not even a remote possibility. It was purely and simply a safeguard.

After consulting it's entries for some specific dates the desk light was switched off and it was returned to the safe. At least family knew how to keep their mouth shut. And it helped when they didn't know the whole truth to begin with. What to do next? The darkness always helped the thought process.

****

"No, he certainly wasn't his usual self that night. Hadn't been for a while. He had always been the sort of customer I liked. The kind of guy who would tell you to take one for yourself , now and again. Not all the time, just to be flash. Not that type. Just a good guy. When I asked if he was alright he told me he only come in that night on the off chance. To see if someone else might show up. He said something about his doctor and his boss and tests for something. I was pretty busy checking the gantry for the brewers' visit the next day, at the time, and to be honest, I wasn't really listening too well. but I could have sworn he mentioned something about boats and sailors as well. The only other thing I can tell you is about the words he had with Morton and his crew. There was one of them who was doing most of the mouthing off. Never liked him. A dangerous wee shite back then. Not the kind to turn your back on either. Blade merchant. That type. Went by the name of Reggie. Apparently they knew each other from work. Some argument they'd had through that, about something or other."

Lassiter stared at Andy Lynch.

"You sure that was the name, Andy? Quite definitely? Reggie?"

"Positive. I can visualise the wee shite now. I was always wary when he was about. Help?"

"Maybe a lot more than you know Andy. Maybe a lot more. Can we give you a lift home? And , please, make sure all your friends have a drink on me if you're staying."

Lassiter placed a twenty pound note on the table and nodded his head in the direction of the door to indicate to Gil that it was time they talked alone.

"They've seen the money now Lassiter. I've got no option! Good to meet you both. Cheers. Those golf club punters wouldn't have done that."

"You're welcome Andy. Maybe I could talk to you again. About the golf club and it's members?"

"No problem Lassiter. Stingy bastards most of them. Mind you there are one or two exceptions. Well, three actually. Just you let me know. I liked that man Gallagher."

"Cheers Andy. Thanks a bunch. We'll be in touch."

"Wait till I tell Taylor you're throwing his money about Tommy boy."

"Shut up a minute Gil. The Reggie thing is important. So he was with the Morton team that night was he? And he knew Gallagher from work did he? Why did Danny Hagan tell me he was with him that night then?"

END CHAPTER

CHAPTER NINETEEN

CARDS ON THE TABLE

The meeting had been arranged by Daniel Taylor, and he had insisted that he himself be present at it. The Meredith brothers themselves had asked for it. Not Gil or Lassiter. They met in Taylor's office at "The Voice"

"Lassiter, Gil, these two gentlemen are close friends and business associates of both my father and myself, and have asked to have a word with you both with regard to some things. Allow me to introduce Mr. James and Doctor Patrick John Meredith M.D."

"Charmed, I'm fucking sure." muttered Gil under his breath nudging Lassiter under the table.

"Paddy John, would you like to start? Gil and Lassiter by the way will treat everything you have to say with the utmost confidence."

"Who told you that one Danny boy?" Gil was enjoying himself, keeping his voice at the perfect pitch so Lassiter alone could hear him. The doctor turned and looked up from the copy sheet lying on the ornamental table in the far corner of the room.

"Shit that's the second time he's had that effect on me and I've only met him twice." Gil kept his voice really low this time. "A bit spooky."

"What?" whispered Lassiter.

"Tell you later."

"Good afternoon gentlemen. I won't take up much of your time. I will put our cards on the table here and would ask you to listen carefully. I hate having to repeat myself"

"You arrogant bastard! I don't bloody like you at all." thought Lassiter.

****

"Cards on the table time," said Tony Pearson in the other office, "either you tell me what this is all about now, or the police become involved big time. No more silly messages that no one understands, least of all Mr. Taylor. I would remind you that the police are investigating a very serious matter with all this and they will track you down. Believe it! If you have anything constructive to say, say it, and it will be duly acted upon. If not clear this line immediately for anyone else who may have. Mr. Daniel Taylor knows nothing about the Gallagher case, other than the effect it has had on him and his wife. You're being extremely cruel to both of them"

"Who said Mr. Taylor knew anythin' aboot the drips in the hoaspital? Ah never said that. He's a different type ae drip. But he dis know somebuddy that dis know aboot the hoaspital kind. And how tae pull them oot!"

The line went dead.

"I am well aware that there has been renewed interest-though God alone knows why- in what I believe was simply a particularly nasty street brawl of some thirty years ago. I believe it to have been simply that. My friend Daniel here, I am a golfing chum of his father's by the way, is directly involved through no fault of his own, but my brother and I are concerned that your investigation may now be taking you into areas of our lives where we really don't want you to be. I , for one..."

"Maybe you're making sense to yourself Doctor Meredith, or Billy Joe, or whatever the fuck it was he called you, but I'll stop you right there if I can. You can tell his father all about me on the golf course when you see him next. First and foremost, - I'm Lassiter by the way- , I do not give a toss how concerned you and your brother are. A man died in that street brawl, or later, to be exact, in a hospital. This is now a matter of great concern for Strathclyde Police , amongst others, due to a rumour that is spreading and refuses to go away. I will conduct my research into this very serious matter as I see fit. Please go on."

Lassiter's interruption, and language, took the doctor totally by surprise. He was older than his brother and still good looking and well dressed. Impressive but with a hard glint to the eyes. Just for a second Lassiter saw something else in them as he glared back at him. Whatever it was, it was more than surprise. Fury? Recognition? Embarassment? No none of these. And then it dawned on him. Fear! Definitely fear. This bastard had something to hide.

"Just a moment Mr. Lassiter. We appear to have got off to a bad start here. I think all my brother was trying to make clear here is that we are both, he and I that is, in a difficult position through no fault of our own. He, as this unfortunate man's family doctor all those years ago and myself, simply because I gave him a job back then."

James Meredith was not only a good deal younger than his brother, but a good deal smoother. Every inch the successful businessman. His eyes were wary.

"We are guilty of nothing that would warrant any undue attention. That's all."

"I don't believe either myself or anyone else has suggested , at any time, that you are Mr. Meredith. However your concern is noted. Whether I understand what is concerning you or not, is another matter altogether, however. And just for the record. At the moment I am working with this newspaper and Mr. Taylor here. Not FOR him. Or any of his friends, come to that. I would ask you both to remember that.

Daniel, I have to go. I've someone else to meet. I'll be in touch Gil."

Lassiter made for the door. Even Gil was impressed.

"Do that kid."

Maggie had arranged for them to meet in the same Gorbals pub.

"Thanks for coming. Alone? That's a relief. I could do without the live entertainment today. Who were those guys? By God I'll remember them. I think a number of people will. Danny, I've got something I have to ask you."

"Is this aboot meetin' the Mafia man? Fuckin' Mafia my arse. Ah...."

"Sorry to interrupt you, but no it's not about that. Well not only that. It's something else. When I last met you in here you mentioned that you had backup that night, that you didn't expect. You mentioned some names. But I don't remember you mentioning "Adjie". "Adjie" Gilmour I mean. Was he there? He was your second man"

"Noo that's somethin' ah never did find oot. Somebuddy told me he wis. But ah never saw him. Oot the back wi' a wee message in his pocket fur any smart bastard mebbe's, but they a' ran like fuck the ither wiy onywiy. Ye see me an "Adjie" hid hid a wee stramash the week afore. Aboot Maggie it wis. Nuthin' serious. Wimmen always cause problems fur pals. Ah'm sure oor Maggie knows where he is ye know. Ah'll tell ye wan thing ah dae know though. If he wisnae there wi' the rest ae them, then he must huv hid a good reason. Or else he didnae know anythin' aboot it. He widnae huv let a daft argument like that stoap him. No "Adjie"

Once again Lassiter felt strangely sorry for him. He looked forward to the possibility of putting them back in touch with each other. But there was something else first. He had to be tactful.

"You definitely said Reggie was there though?"

"Yir wee pal? Aye."

"Danny I've got to be honest here. Somebody told me that Reggie was already there, and mouthing off to Gallagher before you came in. Which is it?"

"That's whit ah've always liked aboot you Lassiter. Bottle. Ye nearly ca'd me a liar there. No' quite, but nearly. Aye ye're right but. Ah did say he wis there din't ah? Aye ah did right enuff. Yir educations no' done ye much good his it? Ah did say he wis there right enuff. Ah jist didnae say he wis wi' us. Always wis a treacherous wee bastard. You know that."

Lassiter didn't know what to say. He hadn't listened properly and made an assumption. The wrong one.

"I'm sorry Danny. You're right of course. Gil thinks..."

"Who the fuck's Gil?"

This time Lassiter had a brainwave. And it might just work.

"Danny. This meeting possibility with this guy Horner. I take it Maggie spoke to you about it?"

"Tommy, it's a big favour. Me an' this guy go back a while."

"I know nothing about him other than what I've heard."

"Mebbe ye dae. Know him ah mean. He wis awright at wan time. People chinge."

Lassiter overlooked the unintentional irony.

"Listen Danny. This is not a promise, because I'm not sure if I can swing it yet. I don't know if Maggie knows or not. But I think I might know where your old pal "Adjie" Gilmour is. In fact I think there's a chance I could get him to come to this meeting. Just a chance."

Hagan was genuinely astonished.

"Ye mean it? The real "Adjie?" Ma auld pal? No' that tosser Jamieson?"

"The real McCoy."

"Ye're oan Tommy ma man. Ye're fuckin', definitely oan."

Lassiter felt good about himself mixed with that strange, slightly sad feeling again. Danny was caught in a thirty year time warp. Lassiter really did feel sorry for him. Grow up Danny, for fuck's sake!

Now all he had to do was persuade Gil to tell him ,Danny, who he really was.

And what he did for a living nowadays.

"It was a chance meeting. I knew him years ago. We all knew each other back then. You know that. Some years ago I went to see a customer who was buying metal from the firm I was working for at the time. A real dodgy bunch they were too. Somewhere in the East End it was. I went into the office to collect a cheque they had been promising. It was a glorified scrapyard really. They'd virtually threatened the other sales rep. who was working with me at the time, when he'd been sent to collect the money from them . He was an older man, with grandchildren. Never tell Danny this, promise? I phoned them, and in the course of our conversation, let it slip who my brother was. They told me to collect the cheque that Friday."

"He would not be pleased. Probably not so much because you used his name, but that you went there on your own." Lassiter lit another cigarette.

"I know. I know. Anyway when I went in the cheque was waiting. And it was the first one that didn't bounce."

"I'll bet it didn't."
"I think they both found it quite funny actually-they were a father and son operation- but when I went in, there he was sitting in the corner handsome and smartly dressed as ever. To this day I've never figured out whether it was some kind of return warning, or whether he just wanted to see me again. Johnny Horner! After all those years. Back then the girls either swooned over Johnny, "Adjie" Gilmour and yourself Lassiter, or our Danny. It was a close thing at one time. Did you know he and Danny were also pretty close back then. Life's really strange isn't it?" Maggie took a sip from her wine. She looked relaxed and happy.
"I got the first hint of that from Danny today. What happened?"
"I'm not sure. A lot of things started to change after the Gallagher thing. I don't know if that was the main reason, or whether it all just happened that way. I really don't. Our Danny's the only one who hasn't"
"I wish he would. He'd be a lot happier. I know that."
"Are you?"
"Most of the time. I'm really looking forward to meeting this guy Horner. He can't be all bad, if Taylor doesn't like him. I think Gil said he can swing it."
"I can tell you now. He'll be there. And I'll tell you something Danny doesn't know about him. He won't put up with any more of Danny's shit. There is one thing that Johnny Horner is not , and that's a coward. I've known him for too long. And you're right, he's really not all bad. Not all good. But not all bad either."

END CHAPTER

CHAPTER TWENTY

FAMILY CONVERSATIONS

"There's never been anything drastically wrong with my mum's memory Lassiter. Especially for faces. If she says that's not the man who came to the nursing home with the one who scared her, then it's not. She can still look at photographs from thirty years ago and remember who everyone is, can't you mum?"
Sarah sat on the old fashioned sofa holding her mother's hand, as she always did. It was late afternoon. The lounge in the nursing home was quiet. Only one other old lady in the far corner , and she was fast asleep.
Lassiter felt more confused than ever. He had taken it for granted. Again!
He put the newspaper clipping back in his wallet. Whoever had

thought it important enough to ask some questions of Theresa Gallagher, one thing was now pretty clear. It hadn't been John Horner!

****

"We're no' tae make any mair phone calls tae the paper. Ur ye listenin' Jean? Ah've telt Mr. Horner everythin. That well dressed bastard frightened the life oot ma sister, whoever the fuck he wis. She wishes she'd never tried anythin' at a' noo. It wis a good enuff wee scam fur a while. We wur only chancin' wur arm wi' it onwiy. It worked fur a wee while but it's scrubbed noo. SHE didnae really know onythin' onywiy, but somebuddy dis. Sumthin' must've happened in that hoaspital right enough. Wid ye credit it?"
"Awright, awright. Ah heard ye the furst time. It's a' that sister ae your's fault. Fuckin' chancer that she is"
"Didnae notice ye knockin' her money back. Knocked her fuckin drink back right enough ."
"Don't you bluddy swear at me. Ony drink left by the wiy?"

****

"Ah'm tellin ye Adjie. Make sure nuthin' happens tae that wee shite Reggie noo. Ah don't know why an' neither dae you but Horner dis, an' that's a' we need tae know the noo. Ur ye listenin' tae me noo. Nuthin' happens tae him. Nuthin!"
"Ah heard ye the furst time. Ah've telt them a'. He'll no' be touched. Gie's a hauf. Whit aboot that Hagan bastard?"
"He's no' said another thing aboot that. It's awright. He'll no' let'm git away wi' that. Nae chance! He'll be bidin' his time. It must a' be tied in thegither somehow. If he didnae sort it a' oot right away, there's a reason fur it. We jist might huv tae wur two selves. But no' tae he tells us. Awright?"
It was the first time Phil Jamieson had seen his brother smiling for days. It was not a pretty sight!

****

"I just don't like her. Never have, and never will. I've never managed to catch her at anything but I will. One of these days I will. And neither you nor Sarah will prevent me from personally booting her through that front door. Sarah hangs on every word she says. I can't stand the sight of her. And you've got me not only being pleasant to her but increasing her bloody wages! In God's name, why? Dad?"
"Do you ever consider your wife Daniel? I mean ever. So what if she relies on the woman too much. You're never here. I blame your mother for the way you've turned out. You were always her blind spot. Her one blind spot. You could have committed murder, and she

would have forgiven you. And that's the truth!"

If Daniel Taylor had not had his back to C.J. as he made for the door, the older man might have noticed the sudden, concerned look on Daniel's face. Lassiter would have done!

****

"I don't see her as any kind of threat if that's what you mean. It remains to be seen how much she really knows. She certainly knows something. She's smart and street-wise. Give me time. If she's going to be troublesome in any way then C.J. or not, she will have to be dealt with. If I were you, my dear brother, I would be much more concerned that perhaps my own junior staff may know a little bit more than might be healthy for them. Give it some consideration."

James Meredith exhaled a plume of cigar smoke and settled back in the leather armchair in the golf club.

Dr. Patrick John Meredith smiled. Only his mouth. The eyes showed no emotion whatsoever.

"When will you learn, my dear brother, that I possess the brains in this family. I know a great deal more about Dr. Patricia Jeffries than she does of me. Do you honestly think she would be in our practice if I didn't?"

Just then C.J. Taylor swept in and the younger Meredith rose to greet him in the lounge doorway. Even after all these years the likeness to his older brother could sometimes be quite astounding.

"Over here C.J. What can I get you?"

****

Theresa Gallagher smiled fondly at her daughter and offered her cheek for the goodbye kiss.

"Get her off home now Tommy please. She spends too much time here as it is. She doesn't look well enough to me to be out yet. I keep telling her to take up other interests to occupy her. Remember her amateur dramatics back all those years ago Tommy?"

Lassiter gave Theresa a peck on the cheek and escorted Sarah to the door. As they both turned to wave goodbye he nudged Sarah for all the world as though it were thirty years previously.

"I'd forgotten all about that. You were bloody good too."

Sarah looked pleased he remembered. She hugged herself and her eyes shone.

END CHAPTER

CHAPTER TWENTY ONE

SALES TALK

"I'll handle Horner. You Danny. Alright?"

Lassiter nodded and lit another one up.

"Right, we know quite a number of things now that we didn't before. We'll go over them later." Gil suddenly looked every inch the excellent newsman he really was.

"Why do I have the feeling that they make more sense to you than they do me?" enquired Lassiter.

"Maybe they do, maybe they don't. I do know that I still know a couple of things about a couple of people that you don't, but it won't stay like that. You'll find out everything shortly. You would anyway. You're good enough. You haven't met our golden boy's father yet have you? The metals magnate? I know you haven't, but I'll tell you something. You'll swear blind you have. Fun this isn't it??

****

"The only way to get rid of any problem is to face it dead on. I don't need to tell YOU that."

"Horner's no' a problem tae me."

"I never said he was , Danny. And the best way to prove that to everybody is to go to this meeting, once we decide where to have it. And don't forget, if everything works out, you're old pal "Adjie" Gilmour will also be there. I think I know how to get in touch with him now. Think about it Danny. If he does, that makes him, P.J., me and Maggie there. And Horner of course. Nobody else. Who would have the most friends among that lot, between you and Horner."

"Ye've goat a point there. Naebuddy else?"

"Nobody you'd know. Or maybe just one, but he's harmless to my knowledge."

"Right. Ye're oan. But if anythin' happens tae Maggie, or P.J. ower the heid o' this Tommy..."

"I know, I know but let me ask you to think about something. You're the one who pulled the gun in HIS pub. I know you were only looking out for me when you did it. But it wasn't really mannerly, was it?"

Hagan chuckled over the phone.

"Never wis ma strong point. Arrange it, and let me know."

Hagan put the phone down at his end. Lassiter lit a cigarette.

....

"You tell him fae me. Things huv chinged. Ah'm no gonnae pit up wi' that kind ae shite fae him. People in this toon know who ah um, an' whit they kin git away wi'. He's the only wan who disnae seem tae know."
"Point taken. But think about this. What if those same people got to hear that he wanted to have a meeting with you to apologise, and you refused to go. Not very good for business. Thought you were a businessman?"
Horner stared long and hard at Gil and threw the cigar butt threw the open window of the Jag.
"Ye're a clever bastard right enuff, uren't ye? Right set it up. But ah'm no stupit either. Fuckin' remember that!"
Gil opened the passenger door and got out.
"I'll let you know as soon as possible."
"An' remember this. This is wan ye owe me. Ye know who it is ah'm really eftir!"
Gil nodded and closed the door.

****

Lassiter left it to Maggie and P.J. to deal with Danny now that he had finally agreed to go. He still had other people to see. To talk with. Sarah for one. And for some reason or another, Gil thought it important that he meet her father-in-law C.J. By all accounts, he and his son were like chalk and cheese. That had to be good news. And if Maggie had been happy to go and work for him, then the guy couldn't be at all bad. It was the younger Meredith brother she hadn't quite made her mind up about yet. He remembered her saying that. Well, she was half right anyway.
Lassiter hadn't liked either of the Meredith brothers.

****

"Of course I'll speak with him my dear. Only too glad to help in any way I can. We've got to get to bottom of all this now. For you and your mother's sake of course. And don't tell him I said this, but Daniel's too. He's been very uptight of late. More so than usual and that's saying something. When do you suggest? Any time suits me. You know that. Don't seem to be needed much anywhere, anymore. Be nice to talk to someone who's prepared to listen. Eh, Phillippa?"
"Oh everybody always listens to everything YOU say Mr.C.J. You're so relaxed about everything. Always seem to know the right thing to

say and do. Isn't that right Miss?"
"An absolute treasure. So I'll tell Lassiter it's o.k. then. What about the golf club? Some day next week? When it's nice and quiet."
"Fine by me Sarah. Does he play?"
"I don't know. There are a lot of things I should know about Lassiter, and don't. Daniel must have told you that I went out with him at one time. Before I met Daniel."
"Oh yes, it's that one. I remember now. He certainly has. Didn't see eye to eye then, and don't still. Nothing unusual in that. Where did I go wrong with that boy? No don't tell me. Never mind my dear. Won't make any difference to me. Look foward to meeting him. Best regards to your mum when you see her next. Let me know when I've to meet what's-his-name."
Sarah offered her cheek for C.J.'s parting peck absent-mindedly. She had suddenly remembered the night when not seeing eye-to-eye with Lassiter had ended head to head.
"Gosh Miss Sarah. Haven't you got the nicest smile." said Phillippa Jarvie.
"That's more like it," said C.J. turning at the kitchen door on his way out "smile and the world smiles with you."
Sarah waved goodbye to him and felt guilty. None of this was his fault. None of it.

****

"Oh he get's on with everyone. Most popular man at the golf club. And it's not just because of who he is. It's what he is. He's just a nice guy. Everybody likes C.J. Taylor. Tips like you do Mr. Lassiter. Very generous man."
"The difference between me and him is that he uses his own money probably. I prefer to use his son's."
They both laughed and Lassiter put the phone down on Andy Lynch He'd made sure he'd phoned him at home and not the golf club. Never know who might be there, listening. Now was not the time to start making silly mistakes.

****

"I decided to change my entire lifestyle. And in order to do that I had to change the people I chose to associate with. I made a very good job of it. My appearance had changed quite dramatically because of my illness so therefore it was easier to do than it might have been. You didn't know me as well as you knew the others. I did a lot of stupid things in my youth, but I was never stupid. Moderately intelligent as a matter of fact. When the doctors saw fit, and I WAS fit, I started thinking about what I was going to do with my life from there on in. My own G.P. was of enormous help there. He had a brother in this industry who pulled some strings and got me my first job in newspapers. The rest is history. I started at the bottom and my rise to somewhere just above it was meteoric. I've been there ever since."

"Don't give me that shit. You're a superb newsman. That's why I need you to be there. I honestly trust the other three. I know them all, like them all, and believe they're telling me the truth. But I don't know Horner. You do. I value your opinion that he had nothing to do with it either, probably, but I don't know that because I don't know HIM. And you say he knows who you are now anyway. How did that come about?"

"He had to find out because I had to let him know that he was dealing with someone who might just know the real answer to the questions I was putting to him, before he answered me. Not some half-arsed reporter who knew nothing about the streets. Maggie Hagan knows too."

"Well she obviously hasn't told Danny. Do you really think that's fair Gil? Not that she knows and he doesn't, but that Horner knows and he doesn't. What harm could it do? Not that he would anyway. Cause harm, I mean. I mean, does he even know about your illness? It would explain a lot of things to him. I think he's mystified by your disappearance off the scene altogether. Betrayed somehow. He thinks like that still."

"It was all so different back then , kid. You and I know that, Maggie knows t Even bloody Horner knows that! I made my decision then and I've never ha reason to regret it. It's my life, Tommy boy. It was back then, and last time looked, it still was. Most people respect that. With the exception of the Dan Taylor type of course. What right has he got to know? Danny I mean."

"None really I suppose. I just feel strangely sorry for him, that's all. He still lives in a world that he's oddly out of place in. Danny always had standards. Cockeyed standards, sure, but standards just the same. No liberty taking. That sort of thing. Try getting today's weasels to understand that one."

"Lassiter, I've made my mind up. He doesn't need to know, so therefore he won't."

"Pity that. Look's like we'll have to call it all off then."

"Explain!"

"Oh just that I told him I'd tracked his old pal " Adjie" Gilmour down and this "Adjie" Gilmour had expressly asked to see his old mate Danny Hagan once again. One of his conditions for coming. Main one actually."

"You bastard Lassiter! Remind me to kill you when this is all over."

Lassiter smiled innocently. Now they could go ahead and arrange a suitable time and place.

END CHAPTER

CHAPTER TWENTY-TWO

MEETINGS TALK

"Delighted you've settled in so quickly Maggie. And you're making an impact already judging by the fresh enquiries , and one firm order, we've had already from companies who previously didn't buy from us. Magnificent stuff! Magnificent! And you're pleased with the car? I'll be letting C.J. know when I speak to him. I think my brother and myself are having a round of golf with him tomorrow, if my memory serves me correctly. He's a superb golfer as well as a superb judge of who can do a job for this company. And the other staff have all taken to you. Apparently you're quite a mimic. Hope you don't do me. Just joking. Do what you want as long as the business keeps coming in. Terrific! Really."

James Meredith shrugged himself into his beautifully, cut casual jacket and searched his desk for his car keys and mobile phone.

"Anything else you wanted to ask me? Only I've got to meet my brother and his wife for dinner. They're both doctors you know. His wife really had to struggle to qualify Tough upbringing. You know the sort of thing. I really admire people who do that, don't you?"

Maggie ignored the possibility that the question might be a leading one, and handed Meredith his mobile phone.

"Yes. Apparently my sister-in-law's father had even been involved in the Glasgow underworld at one time. She told me all about him one night. Violent man apparently. Had a nickname. Forgotten it now. Thanks Maggie. It just goes to show you though doesn't it? Remarkable what people can achieve with their lives isn't it?"

"Good evening James. Hope you have a nice dinner. Yes it is isn't it?"

Maggie smiled her sweetest smile and escorted him to the door of his office where they'd just had their first, impromptu sales meeting.

"Really remarkable. Clever people come from everywhere though don't you think?"

Now she knew it had been a leading question. The question was where had it been leading? Maggie knew whose practice P.J. Jeffries surgery was part of. Or had it been directed at her because of Danny?

James Meredith was worth the watching already. And she'd only been there three days. Lassiter would want to know about this.

****

"Listen to me carefully, both of you. I'm the head honcho around here and what I say goes."

"Head honcho?"muttered Gil to Lassiter. "I'm telling you. This guy's from another dimension altogether."
Lassiter nudged Gil under the desk as Daniel Taylor turned round from inspecting himself in the fell length wall mirror at the end of his office.
"Paddy John Meredith and James Meredith are both business associates of my father and , as such, will be treated with both respect and courtesy. The first thing you can do Lassiter , is apologise to both of them."
Gil just about fell off his chair and even Taylor looked taken aback at Lassiter's meek response.
"I've been thinking about my behaviour yesterday Daniel and, yes, you're right I'm sorry. I was rude and out of order. If you would care to arrange it I will apologise to them both personally. If you can't , or they won't, please do so on my behalf. It was unforgiveable."
"Eh? What did you say? That's more like it. Very important people, you know. Well, I'll try and arrange it for you if I can. I'll see what they say."
"I really wasn't feeling very well yesterday. Tired, frustrated, I don't know. I would welcome the chance to offer my apologies though. I really would."
"Should be easy enough to arrange I suppose." said Taylor looking slightly mollified "They'll listen to me of course. Right. Meeting over"
"Can I just ask Daniel? I know the tie up with your dad and James Meredith. Metals of course. Does your dad's empire extend into the medical profession too?"
"Must do. Mind you, I'm not sure if it's medical or not. But there is some business concern or other. Must be"
"Thanks Daniel. I'll bear that in mind when I'm apologising."
For the second time that day Gil swore under his breath at Lassiter. This time in admiration. Clever bastard! Don't get too clever, kid!

****

"Right Reggie. This wee wumman that's deid noo. Tell me exactly whut yer sister says she telt her. Take yer time noo. Ah need tae huv it right. Thur's tae be a big meetin' aboot a' this. "Adjie!" Sit oan yir fuckin' arse wull ye! Gie HIM a drink Phil. Paddin' aboot there like that. Gettin' oan ma fuckin' wick, so he is!"
"She says the auld nurse ayeways said they wur awright when she checked them earlier oan , but they wur definitely a' pulled oot when she checked them eftir an' fun 'im deid. An' she says the doactor telt hur she'd imagined it. The same doactor she seen talkin' tae young Taylor earlier oan. They wur kinna arguin' like, she said. An' pointin' tae the wee room Gallagher wis in. That's a' Mr. Horner. Gospel truth. Ask ma sister if ye don't believe me."

"Ah believe ye Reggie. Ah believe ye. Tell yer sister no' tae worry noo. She'll no' be gittin' any mair frights. "Adjie!" Wull ye sit oan yer fuckin' arse! Fuck's sake!"
The mangy, half-starved Alsatian barely gave them a second glance as they left the pub and bundled the now fully drunk Reggie into the Jaguar idling in the car park. It moved smoothly into gear and onto the main street.

He didn't turn round, speaking into the rear view mirror.
"I have no alternative now. You both know exactly what you have to do. There will be no slip-ups. Understood?"
"Adjie" Jamieson and the other back seat occupant both nodded. The meeting had been brief and the message crystal clear.
They would now pick up Reggie's wife and then his sister. All three knew part of the thirty year old secret. All three now knew more than was good for them.
Someone else did too. A frail old lady in a nursing home!

....

"That's marvellous Mr. Taylor. I'll be able to speak to all three of you at the golf club then? Sorry? Oh alright, if you insist . C.J. it is then. Thanks. I really do owe the other two gentlemen an apology Mr T..... sorry, C.J. I was way out of order. I really was About three o' clock? Sure , that's fine by me. Looking forward to it. What's that? No, I don't play. Never have done. Too strenuous for me. Gave up darts when they became too heavy for me. Till tomorrow then?"
Lassiter put the receiver down on C.J. Taylor's hearty chuckling at the other end. After lighting another cigarette he quickly dialled Maggie's number.
"Hello Maggie. You left a message. Oh good. I wanted a word with you, P.J., and Danny before tomorrow anyway. I've got an important meeting with some people tomorrow afternoon and I want to make sure of some facts first. Is Danny there? Good. I've got some good news for him, tell him. And Gil says to thank you for not telling him. You know. Yeah.? Gil has agreed he's got to know now. But don't you tell him mind! I'll do that .. Make sure he comes to the meeting with Horner. Around eight be o.k.? Fine. See you all then."
His final phone call before having a quick shower, prior to going to meet the others, was to Gil. He wasn't at the office, so he tried his home number. Eventually he answered.
"He did? So Sarah managed to arrange it did she? You're honoured Tommy boy. Tell me what you think. You're in for a shock. And who? At the same time? Bloody Hell, kid! Are you ever in for a shock! Watch you don't feel the need for a medicinal whisky when you go to that meeting. Don't say I didn't warn you. You're off where? Oh right. What? Yeah, yeah it's o.k.. I've been doing a lot of

thinking about that too. Do me another favour when you see him will you? Tell the stupid old git I've missed him all these years. Make sure you tell him that"

Lassiter felt really good, and yet strangely sad again when he put the phone down for that last time.

"Snap out of it you stupid old bastard Lassiter!" he grunted to himself and headed for the shower.

****

He parked his car behind Maggie's gleaming new Jaguar outside P.J.'s smart but modest flat. P.J.'s nice, but also modest, Mondeo was parked in front of the Jag. Lassiter had never been one to crave after possessions of any kind, but the Jaguar was always a car he had admired since childhood. This one was a beauty. That fairly rare thing. A mechanical, man - made thing, of real grace and elegance. All the differing models seemed to be like that too. They all had that class look about them. Maggie's new job was either the opportunity of a lifetime or something else.

It was the something else that puzzled him. The Meredith brothers had suddenly started to figure very heavily in the lives of a lot of people recently. A few days earlier he hadn't heard of either of them. Perhaps P.J. would be able to enlighten him before he met them again tomorrow afternoon

****

Gil poured himself another whisky and pushed the bottle across the coffee table in his untidy, but comfortable, flat.

"I really don't know how much he knows. He's a bit of a loner in some respects. Keeps a lot of things to himself. But one thing I do know. He's in for a massive surprise when he meets YOUR father-in-law and YOUR husband tomorrow."

His guests both nodded their heads in agreement about the surprise, and then shook them at the offer of the whisky.

Both Sarah Taylor and Doctor. Ellen Meredith M.D. had been slightly nervous about that meeting also, but for vastly different reasons. Gil had also invited them both to his flat that night for vastly different reasons . He had also had to keep from both of them in advance the fact that the other would be there. He knew they were not friendly Far from it. Very far from it.

****

"Right P.J. let me see if I've got this straight. Once you got yourself straightened out and then qualified, you obviously did training and all

that sort of thing. Where?"
"Oh junior doctors end up all over the place. Hospitals, filling in here and there. All that sort of thing. That's how I met up with Ellen Meredith again. She had always tried to help me. Encourage me. She hadn't had it easy either. Of course I first knew her as Ellen Turner of course."
"You've lost me. Again? Turner?"
"I first knew her back in the old days. Her family were famous where I stayed. Well, her father was anyway. Ally Turner? "Scrap" Turner?"
"Fucking Hell! Was that who her father was? That old bastard? Danny, why didn't you tell me that for God's sake? Another bloody connection! Shit!"
Danny, P.J. and Maggie all looked suitably mystified at Lassiter's jubilation.
Still very much fragmented, certain parts of a possible jig-saw were starting to emerge. Still very obscure, but a jig-saw nevertheless!

END CHAPTER

CHAPTER TWENTY- THREE

THE NINETEENTH HOLE MEETINGS

As previously arranged, neither Lassiter nor Andy Lynch acknowledged the fact that they had ever met anywhere before.
"Good afternoon. My name's Lassiter. I have a meeting here today with three of your club members. A Mr. C.J. Taylor and a Doctor and Mr. James Meredith? They said they'd square everything with you when I arrived?"
"Oh yes Mr. Lassiter. That's perfectly alright sir. You are expected. What can I get you? And then, please make yourself comfortable. The three gentlemen concerned are out on the course at the moment. Should be here anytime now, though. Fresh orange did you say? Coming right up."
Lassiter thanked Lynch and took his drink over to a table in the far corner, facing the door. Quite a place. Very select. The two or three other occupants of the room ignored him the way sufficiently wealthy people do. Lassiter was pleased about that. He was not in any mood for idle chit chat. No distractions. Mentally he was still concentrating on his jig-saw.

****

Phil Jamieson had never liked doing it, but Horner seemed to expect it of him now. Phil found it demeaning but expressed his feelings in a manner he was more used to.

"Fuckin' embarassin' this. Kerryin' a bag like a wean sent fur the messages."

Horner grinned and adjusted his cashmere golf sweater.

"Yir no' a wean! Yir a caddy. A' the best golfers huv wan in here. An' ah've no' goat a real wan. So you'll dae. C'moan. That's me loused onywiy. Ah'll buy ye a swally in ma' clubhoose. Behave yersel' mind. Nae battlin' wi' onybuddy. This is ma' relaxation. Golf Did ye see tae that thing fur me last night? Ye know?"

"Oh aye. Nae bother. It's a' sorted."

Horner opened the Jaguar's boot for Jamieson to put his golf clubs in.

****

Gil had been right. The shock was immediate and stunning. He blinked, but nothing was any different. The handsome and extremely well dressed figure was still there, and still insisting he was who he said he was.

"Good day Mr. Lassiter. A pleasure to meet you. C.J. Taylor. Sarah's told me how much help you've been to her and her mother. Greatly appreciated. Greatly. Are you alright? You look as if you've seen a ghost. Don't worry. Happens all the time with us. He'll be in directly. No, you're not going mad."

Lassiter sat down again and tried furiously to recover. He knew it happened. It had just never happened to him before. Gil had definitely got his own back. The resemblance was astonishing. It was only the mannerisms-or manners to be more exact - that really set them apart. That and the expensive horn rimmed spectacles and the perfectly clipped and trimmed moustache. A very slight difference in height,- Taylor was a couple of inches taller-, and other than that he was looking at Doctor Patrick John Meredith M.D.

He completely forgot all about his mental jig-saw.

C.J. Taylor had just scattered the pieces all over the place.

****

"Listen. Ah'm worried aboot your "Adjie." He's gettin' a wee bit too unreliable fur ma' likin' the noo. Nervous like. Disnae seem tae like takin' orders the noo. Huv a word. Or AH will. He'll no' like it. Forgettin' his fuckin' place again. Believin' a' his ain fuckin' publicity again. Tell him Phil. Tell him. Ah'm no gonnae mention it again. Nae mair warnins'! Sort it!"

"Calm doon. Calm doon. Ah'll sort it a' oot. It's that Hagan bastard an' whit he done in the pub. "Adjie" loast face that day. In oor pub!

An' he thinks you're no' botherin' aboot it. He's beelin.' At that bastard Hagan ah mean. No' you. Knows better than that."
"He better know better than that. Ah don't care how many faces he's loast. He kin aye lose another wan. Sort it! Ah'll deal wi' Hagan"
It had been a long time since either Phil Jamieson or his brother had seen Horner lose his temper. A long time but neither of them had forgotten it.
"Ah'll sort it. Forget it noo. Ah'll speak tae him the night."
"Naw ye'll no.' Ye'll finish that pint an' go an' sort him oot this efternin' Right noo!"
Jamieson drained the pint. The old Johnny Horner had suddenly reappeared.

What the fuck had caused that?

****

"Quite recovered Mr. Lassiter? I really should have warned you. Entirely my fault. The problem is all my family and friends are well aware of it by now. The physical resemblance between my old friend and myself, that is. I forgot all about it myself a long, long time ago. Not even aware of it most of the time. Nor are they. And it is after all no more than that. A resemblance. They can tell us apart quite easily. The problem only arises when we meet people for the first time. Slipped my mind to warn you. I do apologise."
"Quite a shock, I must admit Mr......., sorry C.J. Don't apologise, please. My colleague should have warned me. His idea of a joke I suppose. Getting his own back for something. Not important. But the likeness IS remarkable. You could be twins."
"Hardly that. But it does cause a bit of a stir with some people. Not related in any way either. They say everyone probably has one somewhere in the world, you know. Just never meet, most of them. We met a long time ago. He was a company doctor at the time, and I was a humble sales rep. We met by chance when I called on his company. More years ago than I care to remember frankly. Now enough of that. Let me buy you a real drink. What'll it be?"
"I'm fine thanks. Orange juice is fine then, if you insist. Yes, really."
"Orange juice it is. Thanks Andy. Ah, here they are. What'll it be boys?"

Lassiter stood and extended his hand.

"Gentlemen. I owe you both an apology. My behaviour the other day was rude and unforgiveable."
"Yes. It was." Patrick John Meredith M.D. stood as though addressing some medical conference. "I thought long and hard about this before coming at all. I do not allow people a second chance, under normal

circumstances."
The moment he opened his mouth Lassiter's dislike for the man re-appeared. C.J. Taylor he was not.
The strange thing was, that seeing them both together, Taylor and he didn't seem so alike. He could see differences close up. But the initial shock on meeting Taylor for the first time was what was important.
Other people could have got these two mixed up before. People like the police, maybe.

****

The reason for Horner's annoyance soon became apparent. He had his own seat, at his own table, in the clubhouse. No one else was allowed to sit there, unless invited. The beermats on each table in the clubhouse were individually dedicated to famous golfers. Nicklaus, Palmer, Player and so on. On his table there was one dedicated to Ben Hogan. Somebody had altered it to read Danny Hagan!

****

"Now then, Paddy John, I'm quite sure it was no more than a misunderstanding. Mr. Lassiter has a job to do and I'm quite sure he does it admirably. You're far too pompous for you're own good, you know. Always have been. Mr. Lassiter's help has been invaluable to my family in this unfortunate matter, and you and your stuffed shirt are not going to stand in his way. I won't have it. That right James?"
James Meredith smiled his oily smile and his brother looked suitably crushed. It was immediately and abundantly clear who ran the show among these three. C.J. had spoken. All four made their way back from the bar to a secluded corner table.
"Now then, Mr. Lassiter here's going to ask some questions and we're all going to answer them truthfully and civilly. Fire away Mr. Lassiter."
"Thank you very much C.J. Just Lassiter'll do fine."

****

"Right noo, listen tae me because ah'm only gonnae say this wanst. If it wisnae fur this Gallagher thing an' a' the other shite that's goin' doon right noo, ah'd huv phoned the Scotstoun team an' hud Hagan melted long before noo. But ah cannae noo. So go an' find yer physco brother an' tell him tae calm doon, or ah'll gie HIM tae the Scotstoun boays, jist tae be goin' on wi' the noo. Tell him that fae me. Noo, beat it. Gaun. Fuck off!"

The beer mat had really upset Horner!

****

"My thanks gentlemen. You've all been extremely helpful . I just wanted confirmation of what I knew already, to be honest with you. And that was that Mr. Gallagher knew all three of you in some way or other. Either through work, or his health care or in your case C.J. because of the friendship between your son and his daughter. All very normal and simple really. Straightforward. Now, I've taken up enough of your valuable time. This really is a lovely place. Thanks for having me." C.J. Taylor rose as Lassiter prepared to make his his way to the door.
"You come back any time, son. Just let Sarah or Daniel know. Makes a change from talking about sales figures or flu epidemics with these two. Welcome change. 'Bye then Lassiter."
Really nice guy, thought Lassiter. How did he father Danny boy he wondered to himself making his way past the bar on his way out.
He briefly thought of remonstrating with Andy Lynch for not forewarning him about the lookalike business with C.J. and the older Meredith brother.
The he remembered they weren't supposed to know each other. He was losing it. Getting old.
"Bye then."
"Good afternoon sir. Pleasure to meet you."

END CHAPTER

CHAPTER TWENTY FOUR

THE JIGSAW MEETING

Lassiter had spent a good part of the
last twenty four hours alone in his flat. The evidence was in every ashtray. He had to go out for some air. Get out of the flat for a while. To walk and think
He headed for Glasgow's dock area. His normal walk was always the same. Through Scotstoun and along South Street. Past Yarrow Shipbuilders and then back home to the flat. The shipyards had figured greatly in the Lassiter family at one time. His father and uncles had all worked there. The area brought back fond memories from his childhood, and helped him think.
If he had been less pre-occupied with thoughts of tomorrow's meeting, and something Andy Lynch had said, he would probably have noticed the Jaguar with it's three occupants cruising slowly

past.
And he would certainly have recognised at least one of those occupants too.

****

The upstairs lounge of "The Grapes" was the chosen venue for the meeting. It was indeed closed for re- furbishing but both Gil and Tony Pearson knew the owner well enough to secure it for their exclusive use that evening. Total privacy was guaranteed. Entry would be through the owner's own living quarters at the rear of the premises. Lassiter would bring Hagan, and Gil, Horner. P. J. and Maggie would come separately and alone

One more occupant would already be upstairs in the lounge. Andy Lynch would be serving drinks, if required, as he had done some thirty years earlier in another Glasgow pub.

****

"The brother and sister act have been left in no doubt as to what will happen to them if one more phone call is made to "The Voice" or anywhere else concerning the Gallagher affair?"

"Adjie" Jamieson nodded. The smart clothes and the cultured manner of speaking in no way disguised the fact that the man in the driving seat of the Jaguar meant every word of the instructions. Emphasised them somehow. This was a man who always meant every word he said.

"They are , both of them, stupid and relatively harmless. But that does not mean I will not have them both killed. Make that crystal clear to both of them."

He switched on the engine, the signal that the conversation was at an end.

"Adjie" Jamieson smiled his evil smile.

****

"So you're the same barman? The one serving in the pub that night? I'm Maggie Hagan, Danny's sister."

"Pleased to meet you Miss Hagan. Andy Lynch. Mr. Lassiter brought me in earlier to introduce me to the landlord and his wife. All very secretive this isn't it?"

"I know George and Rose anyway. They know my brother and myself. Have done since childhood. Good people. Call me Maggie please."

"What'll it be Maggie?"
"Give me something that you would serve in your golf club, please. Something that my new employers would have. I feel I might need it. Lassiter was there the other day I believe? Isn't C.J. a dear?"
"You know I've never met anyone who doesn't like him. See what you think of that. It's my own concoction. People seem to like it."
"Mmm. Lovely. Probably expensive, is it?"
"It is in the golf club, but it's all on the house tonight. Mr. Lassiter's footing the bill."
"I think you might have it slightly wrong there Andy. Somebody will be footing it, but it won't be Lassiter. Take my word for it."
They both laughed and Maggie took her coat off to await the others.

******************8

"It's just that it's so unlike her C.J. She hasn't turned up for work for the last two days. And there's no answer when I phone her flat. The last time I saw her she still seemed a bit edgy. I know her brother doesn't keep well, and I put it down to that at first."
"Her and Daniel still getting on O.K.?"
"Seem to be."
"Well look, if she doesn't turn up again tomorrow, I'll organize something. From what you tell me, it's not like her. And we are paying her well enough now to keep you company. Particularly just now with Daniel in London, or wherever the hell he is. Has HE even bothered to phone you? No? I despair of him, I really do. Look I'll come round. She knows the arrangement. When Daniel's away on business she's supposed to stay over. Especially just now with all this nonsense going on. Damn the woman"
"Don't be silly C.J. I'm perfectly alright, honestly. It's Phillippa I'm worried about. Now don't you dare bother to come round. I'll phone you tomorrow. Promise"
"Make sure you do. You're quite sure?"
"Positive."
That was when Sarah started to think about Lassiter. Trust him to have an important meeting or something tonight.

****

"George and Rose not on tonight Mary? I was going to ask George about his upstairs lounge. These gentlemen heard that he's going to be re-decorating and were wondering if he'd be interested in an alternative quote. They're in that business apparently. We just got talking and..."
"Sorry Mr. Pearson. He gave me strict instructions. Apparently there's some sort of very private do on up there tonight. Very hush-hush.

Nobody else allowed upstairs . Bloody cheek! I thought they had their own halls for their all their meetings." Pearson had no idea who she was referring to, and wondered briefly whether she herself did.

The four very different looking men sitting next to Tony Pearson at the side of the bar had one thing in common. Not one of them looked the type to be remotely interested in painting or decorating. Tony Pearson shrugged his shoulders to his new found friends.

"Sorry, lads. You heard the lady."

It didn't stop him accepting another drink from them. He'd tried after all, but had already known what the answer would be.

Lassiter had got there first with Danny and a few minutes later P.J. had arrived alone. Danny looked strangely nervous . Andy Lynch looked at him, and immediately was back in sixties Glasgow. It was an odd feeling. Even Danny's style of dress hadn't changed. The suit was still very, very smart, the hair still short and the stance exactly the same as he remembered. It was like some sort of time warp. A thirty year black hole or something. Weird.

"Star turn no' fuckin here yit? Awright, Maggie hen?"

"What'll it be Danny? Long time."

"Zat you Andy? Fuck's sake. How ye daein son? Wife an' everybuddy daein o.k? By fuck, it's been years, wee man . They wur the days son, eh? No' like noo. Good tae see ye, wee man. Mean that."

"Same here. What can I get you?"

"Listen tae him Tommy. Talks a' posh like you dae. Disnae matter wee man. Ye were ayeways a gemme wee guy. Ah remember that. Gie's a hauf pal."

Lassiter was pleased to see Danny relax a bit. In the car he had been like a coiled spring P.J. didn't look much better, now she'd arrived.

"And for the lady? White wine? Coming right up. Lassiter?"

Lassiter shook his head at Andy's enquiring look and lit a cigarette.

"Is that coffee machine working? Good. I drink gallons of the bloody stuff. Let's all relax a bit shall we. Danny, sit down will you. You're making me nervous."

Danny grinned. He and P.J. took their drinks over to where Maggie was sitting and he gave his sister a brotherly punch on the side of her arm.

"O.k. pal? How's the new joab?"

"Fine thank you my dear brother. Any job would be a new one for you, wouldn't it?"

Danny chuckled heartily and visibly relaxed. He tensed up again, however, whe he heard the voices on the stairs

So did Lassiter.

****

Dr. Ellen Meredith rang Sarah's number on the pretext of asking how she and her mother had been bearing up, during all this dreadful business. Dr. Jeffries was not there? Where HAD she said she was going this morning? The doctor paused from talking aloud to herself on the line, presumably to see if Sarah had any knowledge and then spoke once more

"Sorry to bother you Mrs. Taylor. It was just a long shot really. She's not at home, and there were some figures I needed for the practice. Thought I'd kill two birds with the one stone, so to speak."

She gave a strange little nervous laugh, as though she'd made some sort of joke.

"Sorry if I've bothered you, ringing so late, but I'm trying to trace her. It's quite important I find out where she is. I must have picked her up wrong earlier when she said she had to see you about something."

Sarah thought about ringing C.J. She had never liked Ellen Meredith or her husband. The phone call had unsettled her.

****

He was impressive. He came in first and alone. The suit was impeccable, the camel coat was not worn as normal, simply draped over both shoulders. The silk scarf was not folded or knotted but slung casually over the coat shoulders. This was a man who knew how gangsters were SUPPOSED to look. He did it very well. To his rear, Lassiter could see Gil standing in the hallway, still out of sight of the others. They were seated, Lassiter stood alone at the bar with Andy Lynch behind him. Was it only the photographs he'd already seen of him, or was Horner vaguely familiar too. He knew the answer to that one the moment Hagan opened his mouth.

"If you're still alive there's a loat ae fuckin' people in Glesga that cannae shoot straight "

"Danny."

"Plum."

Two things were immediately apparent to Lassiter. One, that he did indeed know Horner from back in the sixties, and , two, the narrowing of the eyes told them all he did not relish being referred to by his old nickname. Obviously why Danny had used it.

It would appear that Horner too had changed . Horner's entrance was the penultimate, so it was clear to everyone who it had to be coming through the doorway next. Hagan only uttered two words

"Fuck's sake!"

"Alright Danny? Missed me, you old bastard?" said Gil.

....

C.J.'s easygoing manner had disappeared. It was obvious to both Patrick John and Ellen Meredith that dinner at the golf club was cancelled as of that moment.
"Listen to me both of you. I will not repeat myself. Daniel's in London or somewhere, and that bloody woman's disappeared. Anything could happen. Everyone knows the frame of mind Sarah's in at the moment. I don't know if she knows it, but there are two shotguns in that house that my half-wit son thinks nobody knows about. My daughter-in-law's a danger both to herself and other people right now. You're the bloody doctors! Attend to it! Be careful when you get there both of you, but do your bloody jobs for once."
This C.J. Taylor was not the C.J. the other golf club diners knew. This was the one who'd made all his money knowing when to stop being nice to people.
As the Merediths both left hurriedly, he turned to those diners who'd overheard.
"Please accept my apologies everyone. My daughter-in-law is very, very dear to me. They need to be discussing her health, not the bloody golf club menu. Honestly. The arrogance of it!"

****

His face contorted with fury. The Scotstoun team and "Adjie" Jamieson had seen it before, and were slightly more prepared for it than the other three. It had, however, a profound effect on Reggie and Phillippa Jarvie, and to a slightly lesser degree Phil Jamieson. This man was terrifying. He turned to repeat himself and to indicate to the Scotstoun boys that it was time to leave.
"If I ever have to return to this cesspit it will be for one of two reasons. Either to blow it up or to burn it down. I haven't decided which yet. But as all four of you would already be dead by that time, it would therefore be immaterial to you. You have your instructions. Come gentlemen."
The Jamiesons were impressed. The Jarvies, just terrified.
The Jamiesons looked at each other. This guy was in a different league from Horner, or even Hagan.

****

"I'm going downstairs to make a couple of phone calls. Some things I need to check on. It'll give you all a chance to get re-acqainted anyway. Everything is on "The Voice" Andy, remember. Give me twenty minutes or so. Thanks."
Lassiter went downstairs. He hadn't mentioned to Horner that they'd

met before but he knew Horner remembered.
Lassiter too had been a very different man back then. Horner remembered alright!
"Thanks Mary. Tony Pearson gone home? Gentlemen, a word please if you don't mind. This is Gil's idea, not mine. No one upstairs knows you are here. I have Hegarty's word that it will remain that way. The purpose of the upstairs get together is to establish , if we can, some hitherto unknown details concerning Thomas Gallagher's suspicious death. That is all. The present day standing of anyone at that meeting upstairs, is not the reason you have been asked here. I have Hegarty's word on that. Agreed?"
The four very capable looking men shrugged their agreement. These plain clothes police officers supplied by Hegarty looked more dangerous than anyone Lassiter had seen in the Jamiesons' pub, or anywhere else for that matter. With the possible exception of Danny's salesmen friends.
"Thanks. I can assure you both men are here alone. They were good enough to keep their word. I ask the same thing of you. Or Hegarty's word to to be precise"
They nodded again and Lassiter immediately felt more relaxed about their presence. They WERE Hegarty's men after all.

.

END CHAPTER

CHAPTER TWENTY FIVE

TEAM TALKS

Lassiter had no idea how it had been achieved, but achieve it he had. Somehow or other the ice had been broken, or a little melted at least, between Horner and Danny Hagan. It had to be Gil's influence. Horner not so keen to impress, and Danny not quite so determined to be unimpressed. How the bloody hell had he done that? The atmosphere in the room was still far from friendly, just not so charged with dislike. Perhaps it was the shock of seeing his old friend after all those years but Hagan seemed happy to disregard Horner for the moment. Horner seemed oddly peeved about that, but settled for being left alone to have another drink at the bar and play his gangster role. The girls were chatting to each other. Gil and Danny were deep in a muttered conversation and Andy Lynch was trying to do the same with Horner but getting nowhere.
As far as he could see, the incident in the Jamieson pub had so far gone unmentioned. It was possibly too much to hope for, that it would stay that way.
"Right ladies and gentlemen. If there's any air to be cleared, I hope it can be put off till a later date because I need all of your help.

Everybody's."
Neither Horner nor Hagan were the type to instigate trouble until they'd sussed out the situation first anyway.

Neither of them was that stupid!

****

Daniel Taylor had been nowhere remotely near London for the last couple of days. He had been doing what he did best. Cheating. In this case, with an accomodating young lady who worked for James Meredith at Meredith Metals, as a part-time receptionist. Diane was easily impressed, easily persuaded but not quite so easily fooled. As he was having a shower, she checked his wallet, found out who he really was and suddenly realised that some of the things he had said over the last couple of days when he had been under the influence of either drink or drugs, or both, might be of interest to some people she knew, who lived in Scotstoun. They were very, very dangerous people and she liked to keep on the right side of them.

****

"Ah know ye noo. Ah never connected the name efter a' these years. Ye wur a gemme boay then. Still the same? Mebbe's ah could put some work your wiy. Improve ma image."
Horner laughed at his little joke, and carelessly flicked ash from his small cigar onto the floor, pointedly ignoring the ashtray on the bar. Hagan and Gil were still deep in their quiet conversation. Lassiter took the chance to massage his ego. He needed everybody's help in this case.
"I remember you well now. When I got back and everybody was whispering your name I thought, "Who is this guy they're all talking about?" I only ever knew you by your nickname. Everybody knew that then. Plum? How'd you get that?"
"Stupid fuckin' nickname fae school. Ye know. Johnny Horner. Jack Horner fae the nursery rhyme. An auld teacher startit it up, an' it stuck. Ah've wantit tae shoot the bastard ever since. He'll be lang deid noo onywiy, an' ah don't dae things like that noo. Ah'm respectable." Lassiter thought of telling him respectable people use ashtrays but decided to leave it.

****

There was going to be quite enough confrontation in this meeting without his contribution.
He sat in the darkness. The diary had been returned to the safe. The powerfully built and incredibly fit young man from Scotstoun , hadn't wasted any time coming to see him. He had been thanked, rewarded

and dismissed

Loose mouths had started to loosen the screws on a coffin lid nameplate. The nameplate read Gallagher and they had to be tightened again. NOW!

****

When they left the golf club they left in opposite directions. Both the Doctors Meredith had urgent house calls to make. Both on matters of extreme urgency, both for very different reasons, and both in very different areas of Glasgow. Two doctors. Two Jaguars. One East. One West.
Neither of them had the Hippocratic oath on their minds.

****

Lassiter stood at the bar. He felt like a drink but he often felt that way when he was tired.
"Give me another coffee please, Andy, and then I'll run you home. You were a great help tonight. I mean that. Thanks."
"I was just pleased to see some old faces after all these years. You must be pleased. I could see you were worried earlier."
"Tell me about it."
"If you want my opinion, which you probably don't, from what I saw and heard, I don't think anybody in that room tonight knows the reason why Mr. Gallagher was killed or who did it either."
"I could have told you that before it started, I think. But they all knew a bit that I didn't know before. And I'll tell you something else. A few of them knew some people who couldn't have done it. That was a help. It's been worthwhile. Gil and I have a lot of talking to do. I'm glad the brothers grim made no attempt to kill each other."
"Horner and Danny Hagan? I never thought they would. They were close friends at one time you know. Or so some people say, at any rate"
"I remember that, you remember that, but did they?"
"You know something Lassiter? I think they did at that As a matter of fact I'm sure of it."

END CHAPTER

CHAPTER TWENTY SIX

BODY TALK

"Right Tommy boy, let's start with what we already knew and what we learned last night that we didn't. Gallagher was first assaulted outside a pub where he had had words with some rather dangerous young people. In that pub were Andy Lynch, Danny Hagan by this time, one other unnamed middle aged customer, Morton and his crew from wherever and our friend Reggie who by this time was a Morton supporter. Ran about with more teams than a footballer."

"Fuck off Gil." Even Gil grimaced at his own awful joke making reference to Greenock Morton F.C.

Lassiter unwrapped his fresh packet of cigarettes. His third that day.

"Danny didn't do it, because he never left the pub. Neither did any of his back up who had arrived by that time-including P.J., Horner or Plum or whatever- because neither did they. That leaves Morton etc. The assumption is made that they all left in too much of a hurry to do it including our little friend Reggie. Wrong. They-or one of them anyway- could either have waited or come back to wait for Gallagher leaving the pub."

"Would you have, knowing who was still inside and no longer on his own?"

"Point taken. We'll never know from Morton now anyway. According to Horner he died in jail in the late seventies. Stabbed by another inmate. What about Reggie now. Where is he?"

"Disappeared, according to Horner. Remember?"

"And so has his sister according to what Sarah told me on the phone before you arrived. Did you know her in the sixties? Reggie's sister?"

"Think I saw her once with him. Almost identical., but she was uglier."

"But that wasn't the reason Sarah phoned. Apparently she had a phone call and then a late night visit from her doctor. Unnerved her and she phoned my mobile but I was running Andy home. I switch it off when driving. Got her later though."

"Not P.J. She was here."

"No and not the arrogant one. His wife.

So not him. Her. Very interested in finding out where P.J. was incidentally. Sarah didn't tell her because she simply didn't know. Odd,eh? Why does this always come back to one or other of the Merediths, Gil?"

"Now you're talking."

****

"Ah'm fuckin' tellin' ye Phil. Horner's fucked. Finished. First Hagan comes in an' treats this pub as if it's fuckin' his. Makes you an' me look like fuckin' eejits in wur ain pub. An' noo this posh maniac bastard. Did ye see his fuckin' eyes? Horner mouths aff aboot the Scotstoun team. He only fuckin' brought them wi' him!"

"Aye. Handy lookin' bastards tae right enough. An' ye're right, that posh bastard looked fuckin' cuckoo. Right mental. Ah think ah've seen his photie afore somewhere. Ah cannae mind where. Some newspaper or ither Ah think. Wish Ah could mind. It a' started that day that other posh git came in lookin' fur that wee shite Reggie. He knows somethin' he's no' telt us or Horner. Mebbe he disnae know he knows it right enough. Swears he's telt Horner everythin' Where is he onywiy?"

"In he's ain hoose. Wi' that stupit sister an' that slag ae a wife ae his."

"Mebbe's we should huv a wee word wi' him."

"Naw, naw. Nae chance. Dae somethin' behind that posh bastard's back? Nae wiy Phil."

"Aye ye're right enough. Mental bastard. But dinnae you be daein' anythin' behind Horner's back neither. He's mental an' a'. Believe it. An' then there's fuckin Hagan! Whit a toon!"

Neither of the Jamiesons considered for one moment that they could be just slightly out whack themselves. Just normal, everyday hoodlums. Nothing wrong with that.

Unknown to Phil, "Adjie" knew quite a bit more about the "posh bastard " than he had told his brother. They'd first met in the physciatric hospital where they'd both been guests for a while. And quite often since , in the comparative luxury of the latter's Jaguar. Or somebody's Jaguar. And he also knew which newspaper his brother had seen the "posh bastard's" face in.

****

The only way the Jarvie family had survived the last couple of days had been with medical help. These four strange men who now occupied their house were terrifying. Each seemed more terrifying than the other. They seldom spoke, but they stared a lot. When they did speak it was only to give an order, like soldiers . They did not approve of Reggie's fondness for the grape so therefore they didn't allow him any. Neither him nor his wife. A doctor had arrived and administered drugs to both of them, when they suddenly took ill because their liquid drug supply had been denied them so abruptly. Phillippa was administered sedatives too, by the same doctor. Being less disorientated than her brother and his wife, she recognised him immediately for two reasons. He was one of the doctors from the health centre. Married to the older lady doctor. Not the young one who came nowadays to see Mrs. Taylor. She'd thought he was Mr. C.J. the first time she'd met him. They were like twins, they were so alike. Now what was his name again?

....

"I'm truly sorry if I frightened you my dear. You know I wouldn't do that for the world. But you were on your own, and I had a prior engagement and I simply thought it for the best that she look in on you. After all she is one of your doctors. Remind me to play hell with that son of mine. And Phillippa. No word from her either I don't suppose?"

"Now don't apologise C.J. You're a treasure for thinking about me and I do appreciate it. Really I do. It was just that Doctor Meredith appeared so late, knocking at the door, and I have to admit I got into a bit of a state and I wasn't too polite to her. The sudden loud knocking on a door has always frightened me. Since childhood. And I prefer the younger lady doctor. Dr. Jeffries. I can talk to her. But it wasn't anybody's fault. I can see that now. You were only trying to help, and so was Doctor Meredith. I'll apologise to her."

"You'll do no such thing. Should have been looking after you much better in the first place. It's their bloody practice after all, although Doctor Jeffries works for them. I'll speak to Paddy John at the golf club. Make sure they send the other lady doctor the next time. That do?"

"Well I'm more comfortable with her. I'm afraid I still associate Dr. Meredith's husband with my father's death somehow. I know it's wrong of me, but I can't help it."

"Perfectly understandable my dear. His manners aren't the best either. I'll sort it all out for you. It won't happen again."

"Bless you."

....

Maggie had only listened to the tape once since Gil and Lassiter had given it to her. She put it in her handbag so she could play it while driving. It shouldn't take more than a couple of days.

After that no one would be able to tell the difference. Then she could start on the phone numbers!

....

The frequency with which the Meredith name cropped up had concerned Lassiter from fairly early on.

"What do we know about the other one Gil, the one Maggie works for? Slimy sort of bastard I thought."

"Doesn't make him involved in anything, although I agree with your assessment of him. Anybody as friendly as he seems to be with Daniel Taylor would automatically be a slimy bastard, I would have thought. Job requirement."

Lassiter chuckled. "You really don't like him, do you?"

"I've worked with him too long. But I don't think he's capable of any real involvement in anything as heavy as this might turn out to be. Do you?"

"If I thought there was even a chance of that he might be dead by now."
Gil took a long, hard look at Lassiter.
"D'you know. I think you might just mean that."
"Oh I mean it Gil. Believe me, I mean it. Now let's concentrate on the people who just might be capable of it. This business about guns and medals and ships and all that shit, that Gallagher was reputedly talking about before he died. What's all that about then, eh?"
"And death certificates. Don't forget that. Who deals with death certificates on a regular basis?"
"Oh, give me some bloody credit. First thing I thought of. I'll deal with Doctor Doom and his wife. You handle Metal Micky. I think we've agreed Daniel Taylor's a non starter."
"Agreed. Doesn't have the brains."
"But his father does, doesn't he?"
"Bloody Hell Lassiter. You can't be serious."
"I'm deadly serious. Everybody's a suspect as far as I'm concerned. And I still don't know where you were that night come to that, do I?"
"I was with Maggie. Ask her."
"That time I really was joking Gil. No fucking sense of humour that's your problem. Right, we've got death certificates, drips, hospitals, and two family doctors old enough to be involved."
"Wrong. You've got three. P.J. She's old enough too don't forget. Everybody's a suspect. Your words I believe"
"But I thought we'd agreed..."
"No fucking sense of humour. That's your problem."
"Bastard!"

****

Lassiter had decided after the "Grapes" meeting that for this to have any chance of being successful, he needed the co-operation of both Horner and Hagan. He didn't have time for the various ways in which he could have perhaps achieved this. He needed their co-operation very quickly, because he had started to have a feeling that something was in the air on the streets of Glasgow. He knew the city. He understood what it meant when comparative, or more importantly, total strangers knew who you were and you didn't know who they were. The messages were being passed from pub to pub and somebody, somewhere, knew what they all meant. Time was not on Lassiter's side so he opted for route one.

That night Hegarty arrested both Danny Hagan and John Horner on suspicion of being involved in the unsolved suspicious death of one Thomas Gallagher some thirty years earlier!

END CHAPTER

CHAPTER TWENTY-SEVEN

LIMBS AND LAMBS

"Calm down P.J.. They haven't really been arrested. Either of them. They're not even helping the police with whatever it is people help the police with. They ARE probably sitting in the same room trying to impress each other with how hard they both are, but that's about the size of it. Promise."

"But "The Voice"..

"Don't believe anything you read in that rag," shouted Gil down the phone as he brought Lassiter's coffee. "I know the editor personally."

"I had to do this. It is very important that somebody thinks the police are focussing their attention on somebody. Anybody. Trust me, and tell Maggie the same thing before she phones me too."

"She's here"

"Put her on."

"Lassiter?"

"Hi Maggie. Have you done what I asked you?"

"Word perfect."

"Get the phone numbers ready, but wait till I give you the shout. Alright?

By the way. On the night Danny was on his mission all those years ago can you account for the whereabouts of one..."

"Eh?"

Gil grabbed the phone from Lassiter.

"Gil here, Maggie, ignore this idiot. Investigative journalist my arse. Tell P.J. something from us both will you? Be very careful around the Merediths. That goes for you too. Try to be normal but careful. That goes for both of them. YOUR new boss too. James Meredith. Maybe even specially him. Here's Lassiter again"

"Believe it Maggie."

Lassiter put the phone down.

****

"I don't care what either of you think about it. That's the way it has to be. Therefore that's the way it's going to be. My daughter-in-law only wants visits from Dr. Jeffries and I want someone she trusts keeping an eye on her. Her nerves are bad. Daniel is of no help to

her and still isn't there anyway, and the only other person , outside of myself, she normally has to talk to in that household has gone walkabout apparently. She wants Dr. Jeffries and Dr. Jeffries only. Otherwise she might do something very silly. And remember there are guns in that house. Understood? Have I made myself clear?"
"Perfectly clear C.J.. As crystal. Ellen thought perhaps the female approach as young P.J. Jeffries wasn't..."
"Who told Ellen she was a female? Get it sorted!"
Patrick John Meredith had never seen C.J. Taylor so upset. It was clear his daughter-in-law meant a great deal to him.

They would have to remember that.

"You're here because a good friend of mine asked a favour of me. Both of you. Personally I wish it was because I really had something on you. Especially you." Hegarty ponted a finger at Horner. "Not that I don't dislike you as much as him," the finger switched to Hagan, "but I never did believe you had anything to do with this case. It made a change for you not to be involved, but that's what I always believed. But I'll get you both for something someday. Especially you ,you slippery bastard."
The finger moved back to Horner. Hegarty was tired and going through the motions to impress the pretty young WPC more than anything else. Lassiter knew it and tried not to show it. The shrug from Horner he expected, the reaction from Hagan he didn't.
"That's fuckin' harassment Plum, so it is!"
Maybe this was going to work after all. He hoped so.

....

Reggie was very scared now. He wasn't so sure anymore that the scary guy, the doctor and the four tough looking men in his house now, had anything to do with Mr. Horner at all. They hadn't said they weren't from Mr. Horner, but then they hadn't really said anything at all. Just ate the food that his sister had made for them, told them what they could do and what they couldn't, and stared at them. In the two days they had been there. It had actually been four but Reggie had lost two somewhere. The scary guy hadn't been there again. Reggie was glad about that. These four were bad enough.
"Mr. Horner coming today? Or "Adjie?" They know Ah'm a good guy. Mr. Horner always buys me an' Jean a drink. Ma sister..."
"Ah told you before. Keep yir fuckin' trap shut!"
That was when it really hit Reggie. These men had nothing to do with Mr. Horner. Maybe even nothing to do with "Adjie"

"Oh fuck!" They wur fae that ither lunatic. The wan in the pub thoan night.

****

Hegarty was now content to listen. Strangely enough so were Horner and Hagan. They were not going to volunteer any information, but sat impassively while Lassiter spoke and Hegarty listened. Most of what Lassiter was saying was sheer conjecture, but Horner didn't know that. Lassiter was pretty sure of a couple of things from the body language of both Hagan and Horner, however. Maybe they hadn't heard of the Meredith family. But certainly both of them knew of a small team of enforcers from the Scotstoun area of Glasgow.
And neither of them knew the whereabouts of one Phillippa Jarvie. Of that Lassiter was convinced. But Horner did know Reggie, and therefore possibly where he lived.
"Look ah'll tell ye this much. This bastard Taylor's been eftir me fur some reason. Everybuddy knows that. Reggie's sister knew somethin' aboot him. Aboot that wumman that died. How she used tae get drunk an' talk aboot the drips bein' ripped oot an' a' that. An' seein' Taylor up at the hoaspital an' a' that. Talkin' tae a doactir. An aulder man. An' they wur arguin' or some fuckin' thing. That's a' ah know. Telt "Adjie" an' Phil Jamieson tae look eftir 'im. That's a'. Ah never knew anythin' aboot her . He's sister ah mean. Hus she shot the craw right enough? "Adjie" Jamieson knows where Reggie stiys. Talk tae him. Better take me wi' ye." Horner was telling the truth.
"If ye're gaun' tae his boozer wi' him, ah'm gaun' tae." said Danny Hagan very quietly.
Lassiter remembered much later that that was the first sign of co-operation between Horner and Hagan. Thirty years or so for that first sign. It was much later too that he realised how much it had meant.

****

Maggie played the tape Lassiter had given her first. Then the one she had made herself with her voice repeating the exact same words. "There are drips and drips. Mr. Taylor knows that."
Then she used the blank tape to add the bit on that Gil and Lassiter had told her to.
Pity. She'd loved the job. Perhaps the car even more. Out on a limb again Maggie.

****

Daniel Taylor didn't bother to phone his wife. He went straight to to the chemist with the prescription Meredith had given him. The combination of drink and drugs had now worn off and he had badly needed something to calm him down. If he had been a little less hung over, he might have been a little bit more observant. And if he had been a little bit more observant, he might have noticed a Jaguar following his Merc. all the way from Meredith's surgery to the chemists. And another member of the Meredith family parking it quite a distance behind him as he left his Merc. and entered the chemists.

****

"So if it's all the same to you Dr. Jeffries I would appreciate if you would allow me to decide which of my patients I will see, and when I will see them. I don't give a twopenny damn what she says, or what her father-in-law says come to that. She is a deeply neurotic woman, and regardless of what they both think, they do not have any say in the running of this practice. And may I remind you, nor do you really. Do you really think my wife and I did not know of your sordid past when you were taken on as a partner. Grow up my dear. Grow up. Nothing of this discussion is to go further than this room.

My wife and I will continue to oversee this practice as we see fit. And it will be our decision who goes to visit her the next time she has one of her little panic attacks, and needs her little sweets to calm her down. Have I made myself clear?

"Abundantly so Dr. Meredith. Abundantly so."

P.J. left Meredith's office. She had to get out of here. She could feel the rage building up inside her again. Only Danny could calm her down when she was as bad as this. Deep breaths. Deep, deep breaths.

Neurosis? The bastard didn't know the meaning of the word!

END CHAPTER

CHAPTER TWENTY-EIGHT

TALK -DOWN

Ellen Meredith entered the chemists just as Taylor was leaving it.

"Hello Daniel. When did you get back? I thought you were in London? On a business trip? Or something of that nature."

Taylor was never sure about Ellen Meredith. Only Taylor himself could have possibly failed to recognise how decidedly strange that was, considering her connection to him. Whether her husband-or her brother-in-law for that matter- told her some things about him, anything about him, or nothing at all. He had no idea. He knew that if he asked either of them, they simply wouldn't tell him. Consequently

he never knew what to say to her.
"Oh hello Dr. Meredith. I've just been to see your husband."
"Not for three days I hope. Relax Daniel. That was a joke. You do look a bit under the weather. Been sleeping alright?"
"A-A- touch of flu or something. Dr. Paddy John gave me something for it."
"Good. I'm glad. Can't have you catching anything now can we? You have to be there for Sarah now don't you? Poor girl. I went to see her the other night. But of course you were away on business at the time."
Taylor's paranoia was at fever pitch by this time. She knew something. Or was he imagining it? The next question floored him, and it really didn't matter any more whether she did or not. Ellen Meredith smiled her sweetest smile.
"Where do you hide the two guns Daniel , and do you really think it's a good idea? With the state of mind your wife's in at the moment? I really do think you should tell me so one of us can remove them from the house, don't you?"
The only thing she did right was lower her voice so the young girl behind the counter heard nothing!

****

"Look," said Horner, "ah'm no fuckin' daft. Everybuddy's heard aboot the team fae Scotstoun. But ah've never used them. Never needed tae. Ah've heard they're ex-sojers or somethin'. Supposed tae be fuckin' nuts, tae. Ah've mebbe drapped the name a couple ae times, tae pit the frighteners oan somebuddy. We a' dae that, but ah've never needed them. Ah've never needed onybuddy else. Ah've goat ma ain people."
Again Lassiter believed him. He didn't even ask Hagan. Hagan hated any kind of authority. It would have been against his street credibility to use authority figures of any kind. Ex, or otherwise. Besides, he'd already met some of Danny's friends. So all these stories about this dangerous little band of brothers circulating round Glasgow had nothing to do with these two.
Who then? His mind immediately thought of a family with medical connections and a brother in the non-ferrous metals business.
Lassiter realised that he was starting to think of Horner and Hagan as allies he could use against some kind of murky common enemy. Somebody who knew all about the events of some thirty years previous.

****

Both Lassiter and Gil were tired but they knew they had to talk and

compare notes on what they had. Gil had been meticulous. Press files, medical files, employment records and criminal records had been unearthed and pored over by him, and him alone. And not only for those directly involved in the Gallagher case, but for anybody else remotely connected to it. If Lassiter was good at what he did, he had nothing on Gil. It became apparent very quickly to Lassiter that it was Gil, and Gil alone, who was responsible for the success of "The Voice". The man was incredible.
"Right, so what you're telling me is that all the Meredith family were in some way connected to the hospital that Gallagher died in. The husband and wife both in a medical capacity, and the other one supplied some of the metal requirements? How do you mean? For surgical instruments or what?"
"Perhaps. I'm not really sure yet. But certainly stainless steel, brass, copper and the like to a fabrication firm and a shopfitting firm-seperate firms incidentally-who were involved in major renovation work going on at the hospital at the time. Huge contract seemingly. Other firms involved in structural work at the time too. Lorries going in and out of the place all of the time apparently. Patients were incidental at the time. Even your little friend Reggie was employed there at one stage. Notice I say employed. I very much doubt if he worked. So Gallagher would have been driving in and out too. Working for Meredith Metals. Before somebody used some metal on him, I mean. It would have been his job."
"And at the same time as friend Reggie. Explains them having words in the pub. And the other two as Doctors?"
"Well more so her than him. But he may well have been in and out. Both to see her, and as a G.P. for consultation. Who knows. Possible isn't it?"
"I'd say more likely probable. And from what you tell me, it was a busy place at the time."
"Extremely busy. People in and out all the time. Nobody quite sure who's who. Security probably lax?"
"Why didn't you tell me all this before?"
"For the simple reason, I didn't know before."
"You were in Glasgow at the time. You should have remembered. At least I have an excuse. I was in London. Newspaperman my arse!"
"You were in London pretending you were a gangster and I was doing the same up here. We weren't interested in anything normal going on round about us. Especially you, if my memory serves me well."
"Point taken. I was joking anyway. We might just make some sense of all this yet Gil. Some more pieces in the jigsaw!"

****

"Lassiter? It's PJ. Jeffries. I think we should talk. Is Danny alright? I want to see him."
"Danny's fine P.J. He's..."
"Lassiter, I want to bloody see him. They tried to fit him up before for this and...."
"Nobody's fitting anybody up for anything P.J. It's important both he and Horner appear to be released through proper procedures that's all. It's vital that everybody in Glasgow thinks that they are serious contenders for this. Trust me. I promise you, Danny's fine. They both are. Take my word for it . Now, I know Danny's fine. But you're obviously not. What's wrong?"
"I'm not sure. I think you're right about this Doctor Meredith thing. There's something very odd going on. Very odd. And it concerns Sarah Taylor. I know you're a friend of her's. This sounds silly, I know. But he's trying to stop me from seeing her. I know it sounds silly, as I said, but I think she might be in some sort of danger or something. Oh, I don't know if it's all in my imagination or what. I can't seem to think straight."
"Listen PJ.. It doesn't sound silly at all. Far from it. Now you calm down. Gil and I will go and see her right now. I was just about to phone her anyway. She might well be in some sort of danger. Maybe her mother too. And don't feel a bit silly. Thanks for ringing me."
Lassiter replaced the receiver thoughtfully.
"Off to see who? Was that P.J.? I heard some of that. We're going to see Sarah I gather. Fine but slow down a bit. Maybe a pinch of salt required here?"
"What do you mean?"
"Oh probably nothing. Just remember who she works for that's all. And who got her the job, because they knew each other from childhood. And didn't she work at that same hospital too for a while?"
"Bloody hell Gil. What was that illness of yours? Paranoia"
"Why must you continually try to undermine me?"

Lassiter chuckled.

****

"Look, I did it for your sake Sarah. I had a long hard think about it, and it's not right they should be in the house at all. But they are expensive guns. Collector's pieces someday, maybe. Paddy John Meredith has a pal who knows about these things apparently. But he's abroad this week. Can't collect them till early next week. Paddy John or his wife is coming to collect them then. I'm damned if I'm going to let them go without getting the correct price for them.

Surely you can see that, love."
Daniel Taylor was in appeasing mode. For a number of reasons.
"Well, I suppose you're right. It would be silly if they're worth money, I suppose. It's just that I hate that man being in the house. Gives me the creeps. He really does."
"Oh, Paddy John's alright. It's because of you're father I know. My dad wouldn't have anything to do with him if he wasn't alright , would he now?"
That's strange, thought Sarah, I never looked at it that way before. He must be O.K., or C.J. wouldn't have anything to do with him. Would he?
"Oh alright then. He can come for them."
"It might not be him anyway. Might be his wife. Look, I'm locking them in the cabinet and putting the key in my pocket. Out of harms way till next week. No bullets in the chambers anyway. Alright?"
"Mmm. I suppose so, then"
Might be her. If he was trying to reassure her then he'd failed miserably.

■■

"Now listen to both of us Sarah. There is something very peculiar going on. I can't say for definite who's involved in this, and who's not. But you're going to have to be on your guard. I don't think you're neurotic at all. Never have done. But I do think you've been conditioned to believe you are. If there is anything suspicious about what happened to your dad you'd want that to come out now wouldn't you? For your mum too?"
Sarah looked up at Lassiter from the couch and nodded tearfully. The sodden handkerchief was still being twisted slowly between slender fingers.
"It's very important that everything appears to be as it normally is Sarah. Everything. But I can tell you this. No harm will come to you or your mother . You have too many people trying to help you . The problem is, that it may not always be obvious to you who those people are. Some of them will be police and some won't. Gil and I have a lot of friends." Gil winked at Sarah.
Lassiter sat down beside her and took both her hands in his.
"I always knew you were beautiful. I didn't know you were brave too. And you are. Very."

END CHAPTER

CHAPTER TWENTY-NINE
THAT'S FIGHTING TALK

FOUR NETTED IN DAWN DRUG BUST IN EAST END

The headline in "The Voice" came as a shock to the drug barons in Glasgow. None of their dealers, suppliers or even small time peddlers, had been "netted" as far as they were aware, and their respective mobile phone networks were alive with frantic phone calls as they confirmed this with their own people, and eventually, grudgingly each other. Pretty pointless really, as they never told each other the truth in any case.

Hegarty's boys had done well. The Scotstoun team were fit, hard and very capable. The problem was that three of them were asleep and the fourth watching breakfast television, when the hall door collapsed under the power of the police drug busting ram and Hegarty's boys charged into the bedrooms , guns at the ready, and shouting like maniacs. A stun grenade was thrown in first for good measure and simultaneously two officers appeared, guns drawn and aimed, in marksman stance, at the balcony window of Reggie's top floor flat. The neighbour next door had never liked Reggie or his family, being just as bitterly religiously bigoted as he was. Unfortunately for the Scotstoun team, he kicked with a different foot from his neighbour and anyone from Glasgow would understand his co-operation in assisting the police in removing a noisy neighbour of the wrong religious persuasion. He perhaps thought the guns were a trifle unnecessary, but serve the bastard right. Him and he's fuckin' record player.

The Scotstoun boys surrendered like lambs and Reggie, Jean and Phillippa had individual kittens.

They were all terrified but they were also all safe.

****

It was a distinctly unpleasant sound, even worse, somehow, over the telephone. A sort of hissing sound rather like a snake or what he imagined the sound of a snake to be. Evil, repellant. And it was intended to be evil and repellant. It was also meant to be the sound of someone laughing.

"What do you mean you don't know what to do? Oh I think you know what to do alright. I think you know very well what to do. Don't you? And it's not phone your daddy. Not this bloody time"

Daniel Taylor put the phone down and tried vainly to stop shivering.

****

"Oh Adjie, Adjie. When ur ye gonnae learn? When ur ye gonnae learn, ya fuckin' eejit? Ye're no' mentally equipped fur it son. Tryin' tae play wi' the big boays. Ye're an eejit son. Jist be content wi' that."

Horner turned away from the table where "Adjie" Jamieson was sitting.

"Phil, gie's a boattle ae beer fur yir brother. Thoan German pish he likes. Aye that stuff yir haun's oan. That's it "Adjie" intit?

"Adjie" Jamieson nodded furiously.

"Ah didnae know you hudnae sent them Mr. Horner. Honest. They a' said the same thing. That they wur tae take ower the joab ae lookin' eftir Reggie an' he'se wife an' sister" Jamieson adjusted his bomber jacket and felt for the Stanley knife in the rear pocket of the faded jeans.

"It's awright son. Easy mistake tae make intit?. Eftir a', ah've drapped their name a couple ae times huvn't ah? The Scotstoun Team. Whit wur ye' supposed tae think? How wur you tae know ah didnae send them? It's awright. Here's yir boattle ae muck"

Jamieson reached to take the beer. A split second later he was sprawled over the pub table, the jagged end of the broken bottle precisely half an inch from his right eye, his throat held in a vicelike grip by Horner's other hand. The pillar next to the table ran with strong German lager.

"Noo whit's the name ae the bastart that really sent them, ya fuckin' tosser!"

Even Danny Hagan admired the move. Phil Jamieson hadn't noticed him and Lassiter coming in through the off-sales door at his back. He'd heard the bell tinkle, and yelled that he'd be there in a second. A second too late. Not that it would have mattered.

Hagan had looked out his axe before he came!

****

Hegarty leaned over the over the table in the interview room and smiled a good natured smile at Rankin, ex corporal Rankin, of the British Army .

"You've already met Dawson here with some of his pals this morning. You'll be familiar with some interrogation techniques perhaps, being ex-military?"

Rankin stared straight ahead saying nothing. He looked to be well in control of both himself and the situation. A born leader type.

"Quick to learn were you? A good listener? Good, because I'm not going to repeat this. See Dawson here? Dawson was never in the army but he was in special forces. Lot's of forces. Dawson has the distinction of being moved from every police force in the West of Scotland , for not being a good listener. Way, way too violent , our Dawson. And his three mates are just as bad if not worse. Dirty, dirty, sneaky fighters all of them. And they're with your three pals right now. As we speak. I wanted to give you a fighting chance, but

Dawson said no.

He thinks you should keep the handcuffs on. Just on the off chance –no chance believe me- that you'd overpower him and make good your escape. Wouldn't look good on his record. And his record's already very bad. Very bad indeed. Maltreatment of people in custody. You should see it Right I'll be off home now.

Have a beer and put my feet up."

....

"He's done bloody what? Don't worry Sarah. The boy's a fool. He knows you don't want Meredith anywhere near the house. I know he does, because I told him you don't. And I also told Meredith and his wife in no uncertain terms. Don't worry my dear. You're not upsetting anybody. They're not really friends of mine in any case. Golfing acquaintances, yes. Friends, no. There is a difference Sarah. And even his brother is merely an employee of mine, when all's said and done. A bit brutal, perhaps, but the truth nevertheless. Put it out of your head. Damn things should never have been in the house in the first place. Guns! I'll tell you what. If you don't mind, I'll dispose of the bloody things myself, with Daniel."

"It's alright C.J. Really it is. I've said it's alright just to get rid of them. And after all Daniel will be here anyway, when he comes. It has to be Doctor Meredith himself apparently, because he's the one who knows this gun dealer man or whatever he is. An expert of some kind anyway who can value them. And Daniel thinks they're worth a lot of money. One of them anyway. It'll be alright, really."

"Alright Sarah. I'll stay out of it then. But let me tell you this, I'm only doing this to improve your relationship with Daniel. Put a bit of trust back in it. He doesn't deserve it. But you do!

"Bless you C.J."

****

Lassiter and Hagan were now seated. The accountant and the salesmen were not. Neither was Horner. It was his show. The fact that Hagan was prepared to take a back seat, both figuratively and literally, indicated this immediately to the salesmen types, so therefore they were automatically on Horner's team.

Until Hagan indicated otherwise that was!

"Ye see "Adjie" ye've left me wi' a big problem noo. Whit dae ah dae wi' ye. Ah know whit ah waant tae dae. It's a long time since ah've bottled onybuddy, but ah'm sure it'll a' come back tae me. Like drivin', eh? Or ridin' a bike. Ye never forget." Horner's face was now inches from "Adjie's" which was now a very deep purple because Horner had tightened his grip on his neck.

"Mr. Horner, honest..."

"Honest, is it? Right son, ah'll be honest wi' ye. Ah'll rip baith yer fuckin' eyes oot right noo, if ye dinnae tell me the name ae that bastart whose money ye've been takin' oan tap ae mine. Then we'll start oan yer brither if we huv tae. That honest enought fur ye "Adjie?" Ah'm bein' as honest as ah kin, son!"

"Mr. Horner. Remember him that died. That scrapman Turner. Well, there's some ae that team that isnae deid Mr. Horner. Honest Mr. Horner. They were aye mental that skwad win't they? Well, it's some ae them that isnae deid Mr. Horner. They said they'd kill me an' Phil if ah didnae work fur them. Phil disnae know anythin' aboot it. It's the same wans Mr. Horner. Honest it is. Said they'd kill us if we said anythin'. Ah never telt Phil. He disnae know anythin. Wan ae them wis in the hoaspital wi' me thoan time ah wisnae well. Fuckin' scared the shit oot me then, an' he still dis."

"Oh aye, ah forgoat aboot yir wee hoaliday. Wis that the time ye stabbed the cat tae death? Or the time ye stabbed the coo in the field? Fuckin' nutter. Ah forgoat how fuckin' daft ye wur!

Right. Fuckin names! Noo!"

****

Rankin was neither a coward nor a fool. Rankin was a realist. Dawson had that strange detached look in his eyes that really dangerous people have. Came from looking real danger in the eyes once too often. Rankin knew that look because Rankin had done that too. And he did have handcuffs on.

"Got a fag?"

Dawson lit a cigarette and put it in Rankin's mouth. Dawson knew that Rankin wasn't afraid, and admired him for it

"Ur ye as bad as he says?"

"It's been known. Just gie me some names an' ye'll never huv tae find oot.."

"Ah could gie ye yer money's worth if ah didnae huv these oan ye know. Fit as fuck."

"Ah don't doubt it. But ye HUV goat them oan huvn't ye Rankin?."

"Aye fuck it. Ye're right enough. Ah don't owe the bastards fuck all."

"Jist gie me the names an' ye'se walk. The lot o' ye'se"

"Deal?"

"Deal"

"Whit aboot the guns we hud. Ye chargin' us wi' that?"
"We found some guns secreted on the premises later, when a more thorough search was made. Could have been anybody's. My own opinion is that they belonged to the same people whose names you are about to give me. You four didn't even have the drugs we thought you had. That's what my report will say. See I'm even using my report voice. More polite."
Rankin laughed. "Right. Ah'm yer man. It'll serve the auld bastards right. There's two or three ae them , ye know."
"Get ready tae walk."

****

It was late. Lack of funds meant that both Gallie and the Wee Man were sober, and also free of any other chemical influence as they sauntered by the Jamiesons pub.
"It's no. See. Different wheel trims tae. Telt ye."
"Ur they?"
"Aye. Some fuckin' machines a' the same thae Jaguars. Naw the wan "Adjie" wis in that night wis black. This wan's daurk blue. Must be Mr. Horner's this wan. The lights ur still oan in the pub. He'll be in there gie'in "Adjie" and Phil their instructions fur the morra."

Gallie had no idea how right he was.

****

James Meredith arrived in his usual manner. It was difficult to get too much engine noise from a superbly engineered machine like the Jaguar, but Meredith would do his best , braking fast on the gravel outside the golf club and sounding the horn to announce his arrival for good measure, simply to annoy the other patrons before finally slamming the driver's door as noisily as he could. He did his best to upset the committee at all times. James Meredith was very aware of his own importance, even if no one else was. He liked to show the world how infinitely more important he was than his brother. Needless to say his opinion was not shared by his sibling. And nobody else really cared very much.
Studiously ignoring Andy Lynch's polite "Good Evening Mr. Meredith" he marched importantly over to the secluded table where his brother and his wife
were already seated.
"You phoned?"
"Of course."

"Will he bear up?"
"How do I know? Remember you're dealing with Daniel Taylor, not his father."

END CHAPTER

CHAPTER THIRTY

MEDICAL AND METAL TALK

"Now we're really starting to get somewhere , Gil. Exactly where I'm not sure yet, but we now have it confirmed from two sources that it's the Merediths. I'm having a hard job holding Hegarty back from arresting all three of them right now, on suspicion."
"He's not that stupid. He knows they'd walk. We've got a lot more digging to do yet. We can't prove anything. How did you get on with your walk down memory lane with Burke and Hare. I trust they didn't disappoint?"
"You know they're pretty scary guys, both of them. Suffice it to say Hagan had his axe , and Horner acquired a broken bottle at some point. Oh and Danny's three salesmen friends were there again too. You know, just to make sure nobody got bored. Fucking hell! But they were effective. I'll give them that. Very effective."
"So "Adjie" Jamieson's been doing the dirty on Horner, and taking his money while doing it. That is not advisable. There was a time when Horner would have have used that broken bottle. When our friend "Plum" lost it back in the old days, he tended to lose it big time. Must have mellowed. What about Phil Jamieson?"
"I honestly don't think he knew much about it all. Said he didn't anyway and the atmosphere in that pub was not the kind where lies would sound convincing. He DID think that Horner had sent those guys for Reggie and co. Convinced me at any rate."
"So as far as the Meredith crew are concerned then, their Scotstoun boys are under arrest for this bogus drug bust thing, Reggie and family are in protective custody or banged up on drugs offences as well, and our slimy friend "Adjie" wasn't there at the time and can still be used by them. Have I got it right?"
"Right. And don't forget that Jamieson also told Horner that James Meredith had supplied him with the drugs that the local "Young Team" bought. So this drugs bust story will have our Meredith friends nervous. The two doctors in particular, hopefully. Your move Gil. What do you think?"
"I think it's time to make some phone calls."
"Who first?"

"Oh ladies first, I think. O.K?"
"Sounds perfectly in order to me. You're a gentleman."

....

Ellen Meredith continued scribbling her notes with one hand, and lifted the receiver with the other.
"There ur drips and drips Dr. Meredith. Hoaspitals ur busy places in't they? Wunner how many death certificates ur wrote oot every day."
Ellen Meredith had heard that voice before. However the message was slightly changed.
Her expensive pen rolled over the edge of the desk and onto the carpet.

....

They sat on the same seat outside Glasgow Art Galleries. Hegarty leaned back, puffed on his pipe, and after a long silence answered Lassiter.
"It's possible, I suppose. Highly improbable, but possible just the same. He ran this city for a very long time. There would certainly be a lot of money involved. Even from the scrap business alone. And then the criminal activities. That was where the real money came from. You really think so? Like father, like daughter? It reads like a bloody Hollywood script, but I've got to admit it could be possible. All these years? You really think so?"
"Gil does. And don't forget her husband, and ever so slightly physcotic brother-in-law."
"The Meredith Mafia. The Godmother! Oh I don't know Lassiter."
"Neither do I. But I definitely believe the brothers are up to their necks in some heavy shit of some kind. Maybe they take their orders from her. She publicly disowned her father certainly, but that goes for nothing. Old Turner never said a word against her. Would've killed anyone who did. Gil thinks it has possibilities."
"Right. Go ahead. I'll let you know what she has to say about this phone call she says she got concerning drips and death certificates. She seemed genuinely mystified on the phone though. If she was acting it was a good act."
"Don't blame me. Gil wrote the script."
"As long as he realises it's not going to end in a bloodbath. Make your phone calls. Hope you know what you're doing because I'm buggared if I do."

****

"But why?"said Lassiter looking mystified
"Why what?" said Gil looking equally mystified. "Because maybe she was on duty at the hospital the night Gallagher's drips mysteriously fell out is why. I should have thought it was obvious."

"Hang on a minute Gil. She was in the pub with Danny, Horner and the rest. It was P.J. and Plum, as he was then, who arrived with the backup for Danny. That was why she was at the meeting in the "Grapes." The only real reason I invited her. Maggie told me she got her kicks carrying weapons for the boys in those days."

"Ah! So that was the reason. I thought she was there purely and simply because she knew everyone back then, and also as a bit of a calming influence on Danny and Horner. I was slightly confused at the time about it and so , I remember, was Andy Lynch but it didn't seem to bother you as she and Danny are now an item. But it wasn't her, kid."

"What wasn't her for God's sake?"

"She wasn't the P.J. who arrived at the pub to give Danny Hagan a hand if needed. She wasn't that fucking mad! She was with Plum earlier in the evening sure, but all she did was go for Danny's back-up. Organize the troops. No, kiddo, it was Phil Jamieson. He was known as P.J. at the time also. We all had stupid nicknames back then.."

"Sit down Gil. This is now pretty serious stuff. I've been talking to her quite openly about all this simply because I assumed she had nothing to do with the Gallagher case, and now you tell me she might? Why didn't you fucking tell me? And why did Phil Jamieson make out he didn't know Danny Hagan that first day in the pub?"

"I didn't tell you because I thought you knew. Simple as that. And the reason Phil Jamieson played dumb about Hagan that first day in the pub is equally simple. He's a career criminal, and that's what career criminals do. They make out they don't know anybody. He knew Hagan from back then alright. Everybody knew Danny boy. You've been making assumptions again Tommy. No real harm done though.

But she gets a phone call too. I think it unlikely she's involved but our Dr. Jeffries gets a call too. I don't give a fuck who's girlfriend she is!

"Tell me about Danny and Jamieson."

"Not a lot to tell really. In those days Horner, Plum, was a floater. Mixed with all the gangs. I never trusted him because of that. He and Jamieson-only Phil mind, not that shit of a brother of his-started to hang around with us quite suddenly. Danny seemed to trust them. I didn't. Not happy about turning my back on either of them. Maybe I'd heard about the other Jamieson, I can't remember now. The upshot was that Danny and I fell out and that's why I wasn't backing him up that night. But I WAS with Maggie. Ask her"

"I'm beginning to wish I'd never met any of you again"

"WE thought that about you thirty years ago."

****

"When did you start paying any attention to my husband Patricia? You know what he's like. His feelings have been hurt by his idol C.J. Taylor, and he's taking it out on you that's all. You know how important you are to this practice, and how much I appreciate it. It'll all blow over. I think it's starting to already. I think C.J. is coming round a little. He thinks the world of Sarah Taylor you know, and that's what this is really all about. It's all very involved. But it has nothing to do with you or your contribution to this practice. You and I go back a long way, and I'm happy to have helped with your career. I see so much of myself in you with what you've had to overcome. Pay no attention to Paddy John and his outburst."
Ellen Meredith opened the door of her Jaguar and smiled at her junior partner as they both prepared to leave for the night.
"Oh by the way, remind me to tell you about the strange woman who phoned me about that Gallagher thing that's been in Daniel Taylor's newspaper. Very strange. I've informed the police of course. I'll tell you all about it tomorrow. Goodnight Patricia."
"Good night Ellen and thanks. You've certainly put my mind at rest"
Until you mentioned the Gallagher case again that is, thought P.J. Jeffries as she started the Mondeo. She often thought her violent moodswings had taken a turn for the worse after the Gallagher case. Thirty years later, and that night was still coming back to haunt her. She had tried so hard to make it up to Sarah Taylor. None of it had been her fault. She'd only been starting out back then. A mere novice.

****

"Oh back then they tried introducing various different alloys. Leaded brass for bearings for armaments, that sort of thing. Various trade names too, I seem to remember. Don't quote me on this because it's only off the top of my head, but I think there was a Scandinavian company, Johnson Metaal or something, and they had a trade name for it. JM1, I think they named theirs.

But it wasn't Naval or Admiralty specification. Let me check it all out and I'll get back to you. Not at all. My pleasure. Five minutes please and I'll be straight back. I want to check it all out first, that's all. As quickly as I can. Bye for now."
"By God you're good my girl! Isn't she James? Maggie Hagan of Meredith Metals. They won't know what's hit them, eh James?"
"Thank you C.J. Only doing what you're paying me for."
Maggie smiled her best shy smile and reached for the various

specification books in the filing cabinet to the right of her desk.
"A God send C.J.. How did we manage without her, one wonders."

If Maggie's smile was shy James Meredith's was decidedly dry. And C.J wasn't really smiling at all. Quite the reverse. His mind was in overdrive.

***********************8

"Hello, Mrs. Taylor? Good afternoon. Ellen Meredith here. And how is your dear mother? Grand. Tell you what it is. I understand from my husband and Dr. Jeffries that there's been some sort of misunderstanding. Oh good. All cleared up then? Because the last thing my husband or I would wish is to upset either you or your husband's father. C.J.'s a very dear friend of ours and the only time I've really seen him annoyed was when he thought my husband and I were interfering in the doctor/patient relationship you have with our Doctor Jeffries . He dotes on you , does C.J., and he's a very dear friend of my husband's as you know." At the other end of the line Sarah smiled. It wasn't exactly how C.J. viewed their relationship. Serve the arrogant bastard right. Merely a golfing companion was how C.J looked on Dr. Patrick John Meredith.
"Oh it's alright really, Doctor Meredith. My father-in-law and I have discussed this, and yes, it's alright for your husband to come round and remove the guns for my husband. Beastly things. Glad to get them out of the house once and for all, frankly."
"That's fine then. I'll let him know. Thank you so much. Men and guns! Children! Someone could have a serious accident couldn't they? But do THEY think of that? I'll let him know it's alright then."
"Yes, but if I could have Dr. Jeffries as my doctor on any subsequent visit?"
"No problem Mrs. Taylor. None whatever. Must keep you and your father-in-law happy. Bye then. My regards to your husband. Or is he away on business again? Such a busy man."
Sarah Taylor did not know what to make of the closing comment to the phone conversation.

But then she never knew what to make of Ellen Meredith either!

END CHAPTER

CHAPTER THIRTY ONE

IN CAMERA

"The first thing we have to do is establish if there's even a case to answer here. All you have at present are rumours. There will be wars and rumours of wars. Well, not on my bloody patch there won't! If you have anything concrete you come to me before you go off half-cocked upsetting all sorts of people. And why am I not dealing with the chief editor. Why are you not dealing with the editor-in-chief Hegarty? Oh yes, I remember now. My apologies gentlemen. Great sensitivity required here. Gallagher was Taylor's wife's father. Sorry"

The Chief Superintendent was in a foul mood. But then the Chief Superintendent was always in a foul mood on a Monday morning when his beloved football team had been beaten on the Saturday. What made it worse was that his team was one half of the Old Firm and a Chief Super had to be more impartial than anyone else. The truth of the matter was that he was an excellent Chief Superintendent, and really was impartial. Nevertheless he had to go on with the charade that he had no football allegiance. Political correctness shit! Impartality was alright as far as it went. Hegarty knew what team he supported though.

"Apparently there is also a remote possibility, very remote Chief, that Mr. Taylor may have been involved in some way."

"What? In his wife's father's death? Oh come now Hegarty. You don't expect me to take that seriously? Do you? Ludicrous!"

"I'll tell you what's not a remote possibility and what I would ask you to seriously take into consideration Chief Superintendent. The man is a prat! I accept it is highly unlikely that he was involved in any way, however minor, in the demise of his wife's father. However he IS extremely friendly with some people who may very well have been. I would ask you to take my word for it on the extent of his gullibility. I have worked with him-perhaps "worked" him would be a better description- for the past twenty years or more."

Chief Superintendent Bradford stroked his perfectly trimmed military style moustache to hide the little smile at Gil's remarks, and opened the file Gil and Lassiter had placed on his desk. He gave them both the benefit of his best icy stare.

"This had better be bloody good!"

He started to read.

****

"You have to make allowances for the fact that he's old, drinks far too much for his own good-or anybody else's come to that- and commits virtually everything to memory . Anything really important he jots down longhand in his notebook or diary or whatever. Doesn't like or trust computers, mobile phones or fax machines. He's still the best damn journalist it's ever been my privelige to meet. And I've met some bloody good uns I can tell you. This meeting we are about to have, never took place Lassiter. If you see what I mean. They kept

him on at the "News" because, even in his late seventies, he's still invaluable to them. Unpredictable, unreliable, unbearable at times yes. But still invaluable. He's met them all in his time. Bill Crombie's a REAL crime reporter. Friends on both sides of the street, if you know what I mean. In the sixties the story was that he could either have got you killed or jailed with equal alacrity. Still could, according to some people. Tony's bringing him here after six. What time is it?" Gil squinted to see his watch. They were sitting at the rear of the dingy South Side pub that was Crombie's chosen meeting place. The sort of place where Crombie could certainly have arranged to have you killed, if he so desired, by the look of it.
"Ten to. I"m really looking forward to meeting this old guy. He's the one who got the original phone call about the yanked out drips at the hospital?" Lassiter removed the cellophane from a fresh pack of cigarettes.. "Why aren't the "News" more active about this then?"
"He owed me a favour. And it wasn't him who took the original call, no. But he thought I should know about it. He knew me when I just started out in this game. Helped me then, and he's still doing it."
"What was the favour?"
"Taylor tried to employ him at one time. Offered him lots of money to leave the "News." I think Bill was tempted, although very loyal. I put him wise. Told him to stay where he was . He knew I wouldn't give him a bum steer."
"I'm going to the gent's to splash some cold water on my face before he arrives. Make myself presentable ."
"I said he could have you killed. Not fucking kissed."
"Piss off."

....

Maggie had now played the tape to all the telephone numbers Lassiter had told her to . What surprised her most of all was that of the two numbers that had actually been answered by the recipient, and not an answering machine, there had been no real reaction. None whatsoever. Just total silence at the other end of the line. Her years of using telephones to make awkward sales calls told her that this was not a normal reaction.
In fact it was distinctly abnormal. Lassiter's idea had had some sort of effect.
Whether it was the desired effect remained to be seen.

****

"Aye but ur we arrested or whit? Ah'm chokin' fur a drink an' ma sister hus tae let the wumman she works fur know where she is. An'

ma poor wee wife disnae keep well. Ur ye chargin' us wi' anythin' or whit?"
Reggie was returning to something approaching his old self. Jean was semi- comatose on the couch in the interview room of the police station. Phillippa Jarvie was just pleased to be safe and being looked after.
The pretty young policewoman, on duty at the door of the interview room, studiously ignored all three of them.

****

"Sarah, this is strictly between you and I, alright pet? The truth is I'm worried about this visit from our doctor friend and this supposed gun expert guy. Why does he need to come round at all, upsetting you. Frankly, I find the whole thing a bit disturbing, myself. Why can't that idiot son of mine-do please tell him I said that- just take the damn things round to Meredith's house, or his surgery, or whatever. I know Daniel's going to be there that night but, keep this under your hat. So am I. Only they don't know it yet. None of them. And I would strongly ad vise you to have that nice guy Lassiter there too. He seems very level headed. Maybe even the police. Or am I just being an old fool?"
"No you're not C.J.. But I do think the police a bit over the top though Apparently Daniel has to look out the proper licence certificates or something. You know Daniel. He never knows where anything is. Hopeless And I've already asked Tom Lassiter to be here, if he can, when they come. And I'm so pleased you want to come too. I'll phone you once I know what night it is they're coming."
"Grand. I still don't understand why they have to come at all. You know the more I'm finding out about Dr. Patrick John Meredith the more strange I find him to be. And he can't play golf for toffee!"
"Oh C.J.. That's hardly a good enough reason. Apparently, one of the guns may have won something at some time or other. A medal or something. And they need paperwork or certificates or something. Daniel told me, but I wasn't really listening, to be honest. But I'm delighted you're coming round and I'm sure Tom Lassiter will be delighted to meet you again too."
"And I him. I admit I'm none the wiser about why Meredith needs to be there at all but I've given up. You take the best of care of yourself and phone me about the arrangements. Best to your mum when you see her next. I take it Lassiter's still taking you or are you going yourself now? Because, if you need me..."
"Oh C.J. Listen to yourself. You do far too much as it is. I'll phone you. I promise."
"Oh before I go. What about that little woman Phil? Has she

phoned? Because that must be getting to you by now as well."

"No, nothing at all. I'm really very worried now. Very worried indeed."

"Well, try not to. Phone me at anytime. About anything. Day or night."

"I know. God bless."

....

"Phil. Ur the doors aw dubbed up? Gie's a hauf."

"Ye're feart "Adjie" in't ye? Ah telt ye no tae fuck aboot wi' Horner din't ah? Me an the "Plum" go back a lang wiy. But as yasual ye hid tae know better din't ye? Fuckin' wide boy. Yir jaw wis nearly wide tae. Wide fuckin' open!"

"Aye but it's no just him noo is it? Fuckin' Hagan an they posh bastarts wi' the suits an' the shooter. No' tae mention that fuckin' headcase P...

"Who?"

"That man that came here wi them fae Scotstoun. Mental he is! Fuckin' mental!"

"Oh aye that's right. Well ye met him in wan ae thae places din't ye? What the fuck did ye get tied up wi' him again fur?"

"He came lookin fur me in the bookie's wan day. Ah knew you widnae dae the drugs because ae Horner no' daein' them ony mair. Ah thought ah could make a few bob on the side. That wis a' Phil honest?"

"Horner used tae dae the drugs tae. Ye know that. Telt me wanst they nearly kilt a pal ae his an' that's why he stoapped dealin' them. Probably read that thoan auld Gambino guy in the Mafia stoapped daein' them fur somethin' like that. Know him he's ayewis oan aboot. Think's he's great. Is he deid that auld guy or whit?"

"Adjie" was not listening. "Adjie" did not care one toss whether Carlo Gambino was alive or dead. But he did care if "Adjie" Jamieson was.

....

Lassiter dried his face with the paper towel. He hated paper towels. Never seemed to dry the face right. Patting his unruly mop of hair into place, he adjusted the comfortable leather jacket and opened the toilet door just in time to catch the entrance. And it was quite an entrance. No other word for it. A stage entrance. But a very impressive one!

Big, bluff Tony Pearson towered above the little man by his side. Crombie was a sight to behold. Crombie was wearing a "Crombie". An immaculately tailored Crombie overcoat, complete with flower in the lapel buttonhole. A spotless white shirt with cutaway collar and a perfectly knotted silk tie. In his right hand was a bag obviously holding a recent purchase from one of Glasgow's best known gent's outfitters. A gray Homburg hat completed the image.

A tiny little man, the face was that of a Mafiosa or or an ex professional fighter. Maybe even a booth fighter. The broken nose and ancient blue, gray facial scar tissue spoke for itself. This was a man who had lived, and lived a long time. He sat down. He did not remove the hat. He smiled, but only at Gil. Lassiter joined them at the table.

"Mr. Crombie? Good of you to come."

"Mr. Lassiter. Mr. Lassiter I'm here to help an old friend. I mean no disrespect son, but that is the only reason. That and because I knew, liked and respected Tommy Gallagher. And his family. When this meeting is over I will deny ever having told you this. But I will tell you now. Tommy Gallagher was certainly murdered. And not outside that pub. He was attacked outside the pub certainly. But he was murdered in the hospital. I think I know why now.

This is in strictest confidence, Mr. Lassiter, but from what my friend Gil has told me , you may also just be getting very close as to why as well. Maybe even to something else. By whom!"

"Just Lassiter, please Mr. Crombie. Lassiter's fine."

"In deference to my great age and wisdom, I would ask that you continue to address me as Mr. Crombie, Lassiter."

The cultured speaking voice and dead pan expression had Lassiter fooled. Eventually the old man's face creased in a friendly grin. He extended a tiny right hand.

"Nice to meet you Lassiter. Bill Crombie. They know what I drink in here. I'm lucky to be still alive, never mind still working. And drinking"

Lassiter admired the little man's style. You didn't get to his age, and mix with the people he had done without being very, very clever. Luck had nothing to do with it.

END CHAPTER

CHAPTER THIRTY TWO

FAMILY TALKS AND SNAPS

"Turner was of the old school. There were weapons used in those days too you know. Of course there were. People have always been vicious. Down through the centuries, that's never changed. And never will. I put it down purely and simply to the way life was then. People did more manual work, and were more naturally fit because they did so. If they were lucky enough to be healthy that is. Nowadays they have to train, go to gyms and so on. Nothing wrong with that.

Turner was naturally tough though. Fit, hard as nails. And he was a sneaky, dirty fighter. By God, could he handle himself."

"Look as if you could yourself, if you don't mind me saying."

"It's been known Lassiter. It's been known. Anyway after the war there was a lot of money to be made out of scrap metal and Turner proceeded to do just that. The opposition was dealt with Turner's way, and very soon he had none to deal with. He employed only the normally unemployable. Villains, cuthroats and so on and soon no one would cross him. The rest you know."

"Gil tells me you knew him well and most of those who worked for him. Did you ever come across two brothers called Meredith. This is pure guesswork incidentally. One of them eventually married his daughter."

"Let's say I knew him as much as I wanted to. We were hardly friends Lassiter. The name Meredith means nothing. But over the years I met him for a variety of reasons. And as he was never alone I did meet some of those he kept closest to him. Those he trusted most, and there weren't too many of them let me tell you. There were two brothers later on I think. By this time he was very wealthy and pseudo respectable, the way they all eventually try to be. I understand friend Horner's having a go at it just now. He never volounteered information, but the older one had a nickname, or initials or something, as I recall. Something Turner called him by when speaking to him. Algy or something like that. Ended in a "Gee" sound at any rate. I remember that much"

"Adjie", Reggie anything like that?"

"Could have been I suppose. Long time ago Lassiter. Sometimes whisky's very helpful where memory's concerned."

Gil grinned and motioned Tony Pearson in the direction of the bar.

"Any chance it was P.J.?"

"Now that sounds very close. P.J. yes. I think it might have been something like that."

"What age? About the age I am now? Gangster type?"

"No, no Lassiter. That's why I remember him so well. This one was very well dressed, well spoken and about the same age as myself at the time. No, maybe a few years younger. I told you Turner was trying to change his image by this time. The brother-if brother he was- was younger though. Younger, smaller and more unstable looking if you know what I mean. A bloody nutter in other words. Smarmy, dangerous type."

"Fucking hell Gil. He's just described James and Dr. Patrick John Meredith."

"Possibly, Tommy boy, possibly. But what does Patrick John become when he signs his prescriptons?"

"P.J. And it would be the same on something else wouldn't it? And what might that be?"
"A death certificate kid. A death certificate!
Gil spoke the words very softly, but to Lassiter it sounded very loud. Very loud indeed!
Crombie coughed loudly and sarcastically to remind them all he was still there.
"There was something else that surprised me about that meeting. It was a change in Turner's manner. A subtle change, but a change nevertheless. He treated these two differently from his other gang members. More respect or something. Particularly the older one. Almost as an equal, or maybe even more than that. Like he was already relinquishing some of his power to this guy. When I'd met him before he simply gave orders. With these two it was more like consultation. Asking their opinion. That sort of thing."
"Maybe just starting to feel his age?" suggested Lassiter.
"Or his mortality and vulnerability. That was the impression I got." said Crombie pointedly pushing his empty glass ever so slightly across the beer stained table.

****

"You're going to have to be very careful. We don't know whether they really do know anything or whether it's all still supposition. See what you can find out and let James know. No, on second thoughts, don't let James know. He's liable to do something stupid. Only Ellen or myself. The timing for this has to be spot on. Fucking guns! You're a fool Daniel. A bloody fool! Still she seems to have accepted the rubbish about the gun collector. Unstable bitch. Something will have to be done about her."
He put the phone down and sat staring at at his doctor's appointment's diary.
At the other end Daniel Taylor also replaced the receiver. His hands shook uncontrollably. His mind raced back thirty odd years to the hospital and his orders from the man in the white doctor's coat and the sudden interruption from the nurse.
"Dr. Meredith. Could you spare a moment?" she'd said softly.
That was before he'd gone into Gallagher's private room alone. If only he'd stood up to him then. If only!

****

Hegarty gave Reggie and Phillippa the long stare followed by the interminable silence. It usually worked. It certainly did on Reggie's wife Jean.
"It was a' their idea mister, ah mean officer. Ah jist did whit they telt me tae dae honest. It must huv been her idea. He's no' goat the bluddy brains."

She pointed at Phillippa and Reggie in turn. The events of the last few days had taken their toll on both of them. Reggie looked terrified and mystified in equal proportions. Phillippa just terrified. They were both well aware that they could now be in severe trouble with the law.

"Right you tell me everything. Now. Or else the key will be thrown away and that's a promise."

Phillippa did most of the talking as it had indeed been all her idea.

"She always said she saw him going into Mr. Gallagher's hospital room alone. She always said that. It never changed."

"I take it you're referring to Mr. Daniel Taylor?"

"Yes. Well him first. Then the doctor. It was just a bit of a joke. Because he wasn't nice to me and said cruel things to me when I was working for him and that nice Mrs. Taylor. Honest Mr. Hegarty. And then the money really DID start to go in the box number and I thought, well.... I suppose it was alright to keep it."

"Do you know how many years I could organise for you? Blackmail?"

"Oh no Mr. Hegarty. I'd die if I went to prison."

"You've got that bloody right. Fancy that idea?"

"I've told you everything. Honest."

....

"Hello Danny? Tommy Lassiter. Before YOU decided to become a public enemy did you ever meet the one before you? Ally Turner? Or more importantly. Any of his team?"

"Awright Tommy ma' man? Wan or two ae them. But ah didnae know them or anythin' like that. Apart fae that wee shit Morton who done ma faither. But he wisnae really anythin' tae dae wi' them. Just poncin' aff he's uncle's name. Great uncle he wis really. They were a' a loat aulder than us. Bad auld bastards tae ah heard. How?"

"I want you and your pal Horner to have a look at some old photos Gil's going to dig up. P.J. too if she doesn't mind. And Maggie and Andy Lynch."

"Fuck's sake Tam. Ye'd be better organisin' another wan ae yir meetin's in that "Grapes" place An we're no' pals Horner an' me. Cut that shite oot!"

"Joking Danny. Just a joke. And I've already arranged it incidentally."

"Whit?"

"Another meeting in the "Grapes" Once Gil digs these photos up I'll let you all know."

"Smart bastard in't ye?"

****

The tape that Lassiter had asked Maggie to doctor slightly and then play to some doctors, amongst others, had an immediate effect. Phone calls were made, and family conferences organised, almost immediately. P.J. Jeffries was forewarned that she would receive a strange phone call from a strange woman referring to the Gallagher case. Hopefully this would draw some reaction from either of her senior partners and an admission they had received a similar call. Highly unlikely Lassiter thought, but remotely possible. Lassiter was unaware one of them had already done so to P.J. Maggie was asked to look out for a reaction of any kind from James Meredith. Gil and Lassiter of course would monitor any reaction from Daniel Taylor. Gil was of the of the opinion that there wasn't a great deal of point in watching out for strange behaviour in Taylor's case, as strange behaviour was the norm for him.
"Bloody old cynic." observed Lassiter searching his leather jacket draped over one of the office chairs, for his cigarettes.
"You haven't worked here as long as I have. And they're on the floor undeneath the desk, by the way. See if Tony Pearson's under there when you're down there. I haven't seen him come back from the "Grapes" yet. Always a bad sign."
Lassiter chuckled drily and reached underneath the desk for his cigarettes.
Tony Pearson was not in the "Grapes" for once and Gil knew it. Pearson had spent all morning doing the legwork he had been asked to do. First of all at Glasgow's Mitchell Library, and then in Glasgow's South Side showing the photographs he had collected there to some old , but still fairly dangerous inhabitants of the area.

****

Pearson, Gil and Lassiter sat at Gil's desk the photographs in front of them.
"By God you'd swear it was the boy wonder himself. He's improved over the years has C.J. Taylor." said Lassiter reaching for his coffee. "He looks like a more dangerous Daniel."
"Look a little bit closer at the younger man behind him talking to the barmaid." said Pearson, "the one next to Turner."
"It bloody is! It's James Meredith." said Gil.
"Then the one you're looking at, isn't C.J. Taylor. It's Doctor Patrick John Meredith or P.J. as he was known then. Apparently he was known for his arrogance even then. And his violence. The hair's a lot shorter, but that's who it is according to at least two people who have good reason to remember him. A real bad bastard according to them."
"Bloody hell. Are you sure it's him Tony?" said Lassiter groping across the table for his cigarettes.

"Not really. Would you be?"

END CHAPTER

CHAPTER THIRTY THREE

DOCTOR'S ORDERS

"But you've always been as fit as a fiddle C.J., what with you're golf and everything. Are you sure you're alright?"
"Now don't fuss Sarah. It's only for tests. Bloody doctors. Got to justify their existence sometimes. I'm perfectly alright , honestly. Probably something I've eaten. But the dizzy turn seemed to concern them. Must have blacked out because I came to on the pavement, with a very concerned James Meredith standing over me. Enough to make anyone's blood pressure shoot up that."
"Now stop joking C.J. and do what you're told for once. The doctor knows best. I've heard high blood pressure can be very dangerous unless properly treated. Hypertension they call it nowadays. Is it very high, did Dr. Meredith say? Just because we don't see eye to eye, doesn't mean he doesn't know what he's talking about"
"Well he put that thing round my arm and tut tutted at his little machine so I suppose HE thought it was. Apparently it can be caused by all sorts of other illnesses too, and that's what they want to check first of all. So I'm phoning to let you know I'm in the hospital at the moment. Be in for a couple of days apparently. Complete rest and complete tests, according to this very pretty young nurse standing next to me, who's enough to raise any male's blood pressure."
"We'll come round straight away."
"You'll do no such thing. You're not well yourself yet. And besides I'm not allowed any visitors for a day or so yet, or so they say. Just till they check me out."
"Can I speak to the nurse?"
"Stop fussing Sarah. I'm perfectly alright. The only reason I'm phoning to let you know in the first place, is because I said I'd be there when Meredith and his firearms chappie come round. Now it looks as if I might not be. When is it anyway?"
"He just phoned Daniel. Must have been about you being in hospital. Why didn't HE tell me. I'll never figure him out. Day after tomorrow apparently. The chap's coming home from wherever he is at present, tomorrow night."
"Right. I think I'll still be in here. Phone Lassiter and make sure you've definitely got company when they come. Because I'm going to do it now anyway. I've got his number keyed into this mobile somewhere."
" He and Daniel don't really get on C.J.. They never have. I hope...."

"Do it Sarah. I know my son. Believe me. Your peace of mind is paramount in all this. Bloody guns in the house. Fool! Phone Lassiter. I'm going to do it as soon as you and I stop talking. My son is a an inconsiderate fool for even letting all this upset you in the first place. Maybe he's trying to be less so and that's why he didn't tell you I was in here. Hope so. Phone Lassiter now. Put your ailing old father-in-law's mind at rest. Promise?"
"Alright. But I'm sure you're over reacting. Honestly."
"Am I? Maybe it's Dr. Patrick John Meredith who's over reacting. Maybe I don't need to be in hospital at all. Still, no option now. I've just been handed one of those very attractive and revealing backless gowns. And something very sinister looking has just been wheeled up to the foot of the bed."
Sarah chuckled in spite of her herself. C.J. could be so funny. Just like him to be thinking of her instead of himself.
"Alright. We'll get something organised. I promise. You keep well and let us know the instant we're allowed in to see you. Promise?"
"The moment they let me out expect to see me on your doorstep. Don't worry about that my dear."
Sarah put the phone down and dialled Lassiter's number.

****

" I told you. He's a very strange man. Never grown up. Likes to be associated with dangerous things, and dangerous people. A fringe risk taker. Like that in the newspaper industry too. Danger by association. That sort of thing. A thrill seeker. Bloody tosser, in other words. Didn't surprise me in the slightest when he told me he had two shotguns in the house. Without the appropriate paperwork of course. Typical. Didn't say they were valuable though."
"Well that was Sarah on the phone. I know where I have to be the day after tomorrow to make sure the guns are removed. Taylor really is an inconsiderate bastard. After all Sarah's been going through of late he sells the bloody things to the doctor she suspects of negligence at best, and God knows what else in her father's death, and then invites him round for tea and shotguns. Fucking idiot!"
"You're not wrong there, Tommy my son. And that's being kind to him."
"What about you Gil? Want to be there? Old C.J. was supposed to be there for support but he's in the hospital for tests apparently. He phoned me too."
"Can't Tommy boy. I promised Horner I'd meet him. Maybe Danny?"
" No thanks. Nobody seems to know where Danny is right now anyway. Not Maggie , or even P.J., apparently. Hope he's alright."
"He'll be alright. Hope whoever he's gone to see is."
Lassiter chuckled drily and said thoughtfully
"Looks like just Sarah and me then."

"Looks like it. Don't be getting any romantic ideas. You'll have company. Her husband, a doctor who may also be a criminal, and an unknown third person who may or may not be a firearms expert. Oh, and two shotguns thrown in for good measure. Good luck Tommy boy."

"Thanks Gil. You've been a tower of strength."

"Always glad to help."

Lassiter replaced the receiver and reached absent mindedly for his cigarettes. He thought briefly about enlisting Hegarty's help and then dismissed the idea. Not yet. Not yet. Still too many pieces missing from the jigsaw.

****

He heard his son's voice in the corridor before the sleeping tablets had time to have the desired effect.

"I don't care what claptrap you told my wife. He's my father and if he's unwell I'm going in to see him."

"But Mr. Taylor your father's perfectly alright. He's just been given something to make him sleep that's all. Please be reasonable. The doctor..."

The door opened and his son burst through it.

"Dad. Sarah phoned me back and she was very upset. They said I couldn't see you and......"

"Daniel, Daniel. It's alright nurse. He's a headstrong boy. Always has been. Why don't you ever do what I tell you son? I'm still awake nurse. Give us a couple of minutes alone nurse, will you please? And then I promise I'll do as you ask. Sit down Daniel. Sit down."

"Dad? What happened. They said you passed out or something. The doctor..."

"Never mind the doctor. I want you to listen carefully to what I'm going to tell you and this time you must do exactly as I say. Clear?"

"Clear."

"This won't be easy but you must follow instructions for once. Lives depend on it, your's included."

Father and son were alone as they had been thirty years or so previously. Prior to the arrangement!

****

"She hasn't seen you before and as she certainly won't see you again, it really doesn't matter who you say you are. As far as she's concerned you're merely there to remove the shotguns after verifying that they are indeed valuable, and in good working order, prior to purchase by your client. And obvously you must be satisfied that is the case. A test must be carried out to enable you to do that, so therefore you must remove them to allow you to carry out such a test. Simple. The unfortunate Mrs. Taylor is of course as yet unaware that this test may well be carried out in her drawing room, but then life's full of little surprises is it not?"

END CHAPTER

CHAPTER THIRTY FOUR

HOUSE CALLS

" I know I'm asking a lot Patricia, but if you wouldn't mind it would be of tremendous assistance. My husband's workload, in addition to my own, would be just a little too much and it's only for the next couple of days until he gets back from this damned conference. He only found out last night. I know it's short notice but between the two of us we'll get through it. I can count on you then?"

"Of course Ellen. I'll come through later and you can give me all the details."

"Splendid. See you later."

P.J. Jeffries replaced the handset on the internal telephone and sighed. She could have done without additional cases at the moment, but she knew where she stood. Ellen had put it in the form of a request but in reality it wasn't that at all. As a junior partner she was simply expected to comply. Damn!

****

"He's asleep Dr. Campbell. His son arrived earlier unannounced and demanded to see him, just after I had given him the sleeping tablets you suggested . So I did allow them five minutes or so together, if that's alright."

"Of course it was nurse. He'll be o.k. I'm quite sure of that. But I still want to have a closer look at him over the next day or so. We don't know as much as we should do about hypertension, so I want to check him over thoroughly tomorrow. Eliminate some of the more serious possibilities. I met him at a function not so long ago you know. Charming chap. Not so impressive lying in a hospital bed though. Funny how illness can change one's appearance. I'll look him over in the morning. Good night nurse.

"Good night doctor."

****

"Hello?"

"Good evening Mrs. Taylor. Ellen Meredith here. I'm sorry to bother you but Doctor Jeffries did ask me to ring you on her behalf. She's on a rather urgent house call at present. She had intended to drop in on you just for a chat and bring some more of your tablets at the same time. However my husband's in Birmingham and it's putting a bit of extra pressure on Patricia and myself at present. I spoke to both of them earlier today and I understand from my husband that he's calling to see your husband on Wednesday evening in any case. I'd forgotten all about that. Would it be alright if he brought your medication then? According to our calculations, you should still have sufficient to do until then. Is that correct? Because if it's not, I'll come round now and bring it."
"No, no Doctor Meredith. You're perfectly correct. I've still got some left. Enough for a couple of days at least."
"That's fine then. Doctor Jeffries just asked me to check. And you've been better generally? These things can take some time before you feel any real improvement in your health. But you will. I'm sure of that ."
"I hope so. I still feel very stressed at times."
"We'll have to do something about that then. Won't we? Well good evening Mrs. Taylor. My husband will call on you on Wednesday as planned. He'll be there to take good care of you then. That I am sure of. Good evening and thank you."
Sarah put the phone down and wondered why every time she spoke to that woman she ended up wishing she hadn't.

****

Hegarty arrived at Lassiter's flat, very slightly the worse for wear, around ten p.m. on the Monday night.
"This had better be good old son. I've had a long day, and it seems like a week. The Chief Super wants to know why the interest in people who appear to be perfectly respectable, not to mention professional. Always problemmma.., problemmaatic....buggar it Lassiter, bloody difficult is what I'm trying to say. You know what I mean. Possibility of allegations of police and newspaper harassment. That kind of thing. Have you got something? Is that why you wanted to see me? Because if you haven't I've got a couple of pints waiting for me."
"Maybe. Maybe. It's still all very loose. Disjointed. But if the connection to the hospital between all these people is indeed a dodgy connection, then we might very well be in business. Even more so if the connection is not just as straightforward as I first thought it might be. Still very much a connection but looked at from a different viewpoint. Either way I need more time, and I want the police to stand back for a while longer. People have to be allowed to incriminate themselves here. Otherwise they'll disappear back into

their safe little thirty year hidey holes. And I think Sarah and her mother deseve more than that. The police have to accept some responsibility here. What do you say?"
"Fine by me. But the Chief Superintendent is a very different matter."
"He doesn't need to know. For more than one reason."
Hegarty wasn't drunk enough to miss the thoughtful manner in which Lassiter made that last statement.

"Maggie? Lassiter. Can you come round some time tomorrow? I need to ask you some things about your new employers. And about your job in general. Information mostly. About metals. Value. That sort of thing. Metal seems to keep popping up in people's lives in this thing. Either worked with it, made their money supplying it, or delivered it. And a man thirty years ago who bought and sold scrap. A lot of people with one thing in common. And one man who may have been killed because of it."
"Never knew anybody that desperate for a sale."

Lassiter chuckled in spite of the gravity of the situation.

"I'll drop in tomorrow around ten. I've got a customer near you anyway."
"Thanks Maggie? Any word from Danny incidentally?"
"I know where he is. I'll tell you tomorrow."

****

From the very beginning there had been a great deal about the Gallagher case that Lassiter had found disturbing. The fact that he knew almost everyone involved personally, was the first thing. More importantly the people involved all seemed to know each other. He found that even more disturbing, almost alarming. And why were non events like Reggie and his sister of such importance to so many people. People who normally would have nothing to do with the Reggies of this world. Or even the Phillippas. And how come she ended up just happening to be employed by Sarah and her charming husband. Especially when she seemed to know so much about the removal of hospital drips , and the arrival at the very same hospital ward, minutes earlier, of her employer of some thirty odd years later. It all bothered him a great deal. So he decided to put a stop to that by finding out the answers. And Lassiter was very single minded when he decided on anything.

****

" The police let all three of them go without any charges being

pressed for anything. More to do with their time than interrogate two drunks, and a failed blackmailer was what Hegarty said. But he was slightly more interested in her than the two piss artists , I know that. Apparently the Chief Superintendent insisted he let all three go. Can't think why. That devious bitch knows something."
"Thanks Gil. How did you get on with Horner?"
"Oh Johnny boy's alright in his own way, you know. His really violent stuff is all behind him now. Got people to handle that, if he needs them. Got people to find out things for him too. Things that you and I maybe wouldn't find out. That's what it was all about."
"Great. Let me know. Now Phillippa Jarvie?"
"According to what Sarah told me about when she first started her, her husband - the boy wonder himself- was very much against it for some reason. Never got on with her."
"How come she got the job then? He never listens to what Sarah wants."
"Now that bothered me too. Apparently Sarah enlisted old C.J.'s help again. C.J. insisted and D.T. relented. Does anything his daddy tells him to. Sarah liked- likes I think is more appropriate-her and she got the job. End of story."
"And Sarah still has no idea of her whereabouts?"
"Not as far as I know."
"Good. Keep it that way. Tell your new pal Horner to keep a very close eye on all three. One , or possibly all three , is connected to somebody very dangerous and it's not Horner. That I do know."
"Told you. He's mellowed. A pussycat now."
"Yeah. So I heard, and then saw. Remember?" Lassiter put the phone down and held on to the sarcasm. Still an awful lot of things to find out about an awful lot of people.

****

"Lassiter, I'.m a cop and a bloody good one at that. We never forget a face. Course I remember him. And a bad bastard he was too. Heard talk of a brother too, though I never saw or had anything to do with him. Are you sure that it's the same guy. I've never seen this Meredith."
"But he was the doctor who was in attendance at the Gallagher wounding?"
"I told you. I was only a beat cop then. Stuck me outside to keep the ghouls back. I wasn't important enough to be dealing with doctors and the like. I remember the barman though. And the older guy in that photo. Had dealings with him a couple of times. But that was a good five years-maybe more- before the Gallagher incident. Had a nickname or initials or something. Certainly didn't call himself Meredith. Most of them had nicknames back then. And he certainly wasn't doctor material. Surgeon, maybe, cause he sure could open

people up. But family doctor? Never!"
"This other guy. The one at the bar. Is that the brother? The younger one talking to the barmaid."
"I told you. I never had any dealings with the brother."
"Well that's got us nowhere fast."
"Glad to be of no service. Now hold on. I'm not the only old cop in the city. Somebody'll remember these two. But be very careful Lassiter. If you're wrong about all this and go around upsetting perfectly respectable, professional people the Chief Super will descend on you from a great height. Come to think of it! Come on. Let's wake the old bastard up. He's still a bloody good cop!

****

"Morning Lassiter. By God you look rough. Got a new girlfriend?"
"Sod off Maggie. You're too early. I've haven't had my caffeine or nicotine fix yet. And yes I did have a late night as a matter of fact. With a Chief Superintendent no less."
"You're the newspaper man. Must be a story for the tabloids there. The journalist and the Chief Superintendent. Make headlines everywhere."
"Buggar off! No, don't. Make yourself useful and stick the kettle on. I'm going into the bathroom. Haven't had my morning cough yet, never mind morning coffee."
"You're utterly disgusting Lassiter. Hurry up. I don't have much time. I've to meet with James Meredith on the other side of the city in less than an hour."
Lassiter halted at the door and gave her one of his looks.
"Right. Two ticks."

END CHAPTER

CHAPTER THIRTY FIVE

THE BONES KNIT AND THE JIGSAW STARTS TO FIT

Lassiter sat on the old sofa in the nursing home, and dealt with it the way he had dealt with everything all his life. Head on. It was the only way he knew how. No frills and to the point. Both Sarah and her mother sat staring straight ahead. Only Theresa spoke.

"God bless you Tommy son. You've done everything we asked of you. Now maybe my Tommy can rest easy."

It was only then they both started to cry.

"I'm very, very sorry. There was no easy way to tell you. No softer way. I'm very, very sorry."

Lassiter left the room and Sarah and her mother to their grief.

****

"Lassiter? Gil. Phone me. This is incredible stuff. And I mean incredible! It must be fucking true. Because I'm getting the same story from Horner and Hagan.

Lassiter replayed the message on his answering service over and over. The problem was when he followed the instructions on it he ended up talking to Gil's answering machine. If it was the same incredible stuff that Hegarty and Chief Superintendent Bradford had advanced as a possibility, he had the bastard. And what Maggie had told him only re-inforced the theory.

****

Phil Jamieson spoke to Lassiter in the untidy cellar after asking Malky to look after the bar for a couple of minutes.

"Aye. An aulder man. Looked like a doactor or lawyer or sumthin'. Real well dressed an' that. Reggie was fuckin' terrified ae him. Ah thought at first it wis because he thought he wis fae the Social. But the strange thing wis when he met him, an' the guy telt us he'd nuthin' tae dae wi' the Social the wee bastard wis still terrified. Mair feart somehow."

"And you're sure that's what he said. The older man I mean? The first time he came in?"

"Aye. Said he used tae know wee Reggie's mither. Years ago like"

"Where's your brother just now/"

"Ah don't know. Honest. Ah huvnae seen him since last night. An' that's the God's honest. Horner warned me tae tell ye the truth aboot anythin' ye asked me."

"It better fucking be. Let Horner know if he turns up again. Might do him a favour."

****

Crombie and Gil sat in the same dingy pub in the South Side where Crombie had first met Lassiter.

"It's possible, I suppose." Crombie pushed the empty whisky glass across the table in Gil's direction. "Turner never mentioned having any other children to the press. But then nobody ever asked. The

daughter never mentioned anything like that. But then she never mentioned having a father much, either."
"It would maybe give someone a motive to get rid of Gallagher wouldn't it?"
"Remember something son. In Glasgow there doesn't need to be much of a motive sometimes. Life's cheap in some parts of this city. Nothing changes much. Maybe you're getting carried away with youself."
"I bloody hope so."
"You worry too much son. Give them all time. They'll screw it all up. Again! That Lassiter's a shrewd one though. They hadn't reckoned on someone like him. You go where he goes. Take my word for it.. You'll always be one step ahead."

****

"It would certainly explain a lot Lassiter. It's Sarah I'm worried about. I've never understood how such a charming man could have such an obnoxious son. I mean you and Daniel Taylor go way back. Could you? Understand it I mean?"
"I only met the father recently but I know exactly what you mean P.J. It takes a bit of getting your head round. Unless you accept Danny and Horner's- and now even the Chief Superintendent's, no less- possible version of events. Maybe the biggest thing he's guilty of is being a pain in the arse."
"No maybe's about that. And you're sure Sarah's agreed to go through with this?"
"Don't try and stop her P.J. Remember it's her father who was murdered all those years ago. Keep Danny under control for me."
"I might not be able to Lassiter."
"You're a bloody doctor. Give him a sleeping pill, or seduce him or something, but keep him occupied. It needs to be just Sarah and I there. Or it won't work."
"You're advising professional misconduct Lassiter. But the second option's not. I'll do my best."
"Succeed. The jigsaws nearly finished and I don't need Danny or anybody else overturning the bloody table now.

****

"My father? Still pretty weak I'm afraid. But they've allowed him home just the same . Complete rest. No exertion or undue excitement. Thanks for asking Lassiter. It gave us both a bit of a jolt I can tell you. But Dr. Campbell says he should be o.k."
"That's grand Daniel. Sarah thinks the world of him I know. And you're quite sure you don't mind me being there tomorrow night when Meredith and his pal come to take those guns away. Only

Sarah asked me and....."
"No, funnily enough it's something my father was quite insistent about too. Don't know why. But he was getting a bit uptight about it and that's the last thing he needs right now. Paddy John and the other guy should be here by eight o'clock he said. So if you arrive any time before that."
"Thanks Daniel."
"How's the Gallagher thing coming along. I'm afraid I haven't been here much of late what with other business, then my father. Haven't been on top of things as I normally would be. Right Gil?"
"What? Oh right Daniel. Oh we've struggled on without you. Not really got anywhere though have we Tommy boy?"
"Not making much headway at all, at the moment, Daniel."
"Excellent. What I mean is that you haven't missed me too much. That's what I meant. Well, I'm off. I won't be in tomorrow at all. But I'll see you tomorrow night Lassiter?"
"Definitely, Daniel. Most definitely."
Taylor picked up his briefcase and left the main office of The Glasgow Voice.

▪▪

"Right maestro. Shoot. Tell me what you've got and I'll tell you what I know."
"Right" said Lassiter leaning across the desk in Taylor's office and stifling a yawn. "Keep the coffee coming. It's going to be a long night. I started with the premise that most people are refreshingly and boringly normal. But the biggest mistake most people make there is in thinking that people don't change. Of course we change. We evolve over the years, the centuries. A leopard can't change it's spots. Bollocks! Just look at us. You, me, P.J.-a stunning example-, Maggie even Johnny Horner for God's sake. So what I'm saying is, I took nothing for granted. Allow for people changing, and you can look at everything from a different angle."
"Two words. Danny Hagan."
"Fuck you. The exception to prove the rule. Let's think of it from a different angle. Children are not carbon copies of their parents. Not clones. Can you think of a bigger example of that than Taylor? But I'll come back to that. Now to the thing that puzzled me in all this from the beginning. The importance of Reggie and his sister to so many people, and how Phillippa Jarvie knew the correct buttons to press with Daniel Taylor and the hospital thing. The answer is she didn't. She saw a film once and then decided to take a chance. Refreshingly normal. But where did she get the cunning nature from? Her brother used to have it as well, but he's changed over the years too. We've established their mother was a decent enough, hard

working single girl. That led me to wonder about the father. Nobody seemed to know anything about him. And who was this older man who came looking for Reggie and told Phil Jamieson he was an old friend of Reggie's mother. He terrified Reggie and another, slightly younger man terrified Reggie's sister. And then they were taken away somewhere and really terrified for three days. Why? Why Gil? Somebody had something very important to hide."

"The Merediths?"

"Almost certainly. It was certainly one of the Merediths who visited the Jarvies when they were locked up in Reggie's house. The Scotstoun team told the police that much. And she confirmed it when interviewed by them. But there's someone else involved here. Gut feeling."

"Ellen Meredith?"

"Now that one's really got me confused. She's even got Hegarty in two minds. Over the years there's never been one whiff of scandal. Any link to her father. He left her money sure, but any father would do that. But there's something else. And for that I'm going to go back to what Theresa Gallagher said she heard her husband mention, and what Andy Lynch also said he mentoned in the pub. She said he spoke about death certificates and he said he spoke about guns and medals. Was he in that pub to meet someone? Who was the older man sitting in the pub by himself? According to Lynch, the other guy and Gallagher appeared not to know each other. How do we know they didn't. We don't. Nor did anyone ever bother to find out."

"A lot of guesswork here Tommy boy."

"A lot of possibilities too Gil. What more do you know about metal, Gil? We know that a lot of people have made a lot of money out of it. Take scrap metal for openers. Turner made a lot of money out of that side of it. All major building contracts also involve huge amounts of metal as we already know. Structural steel, re-inforcing rods, heavy metal plates, metal sheeting, roofing, scaffolding, and we haven't even thought about fencing, grilles, or the semi-precious stuff for decoration. Copper piping, aluminium and stainless steel, brass. The list goes on and on. Consider this. Major work was going on at a major hospital at that time."

"Fucking hell kid! And all the Merediths were in and out of there on a regular basis. You just might be on to something here. And Gallagher delivered metal to the same hospital. We've got to find some link though."

"Hold on. Not as simple as that. Almost everyone we know was connected to that hospital. P.J. Jeffries worked there too. Even that little shit Reggie. And I'm willing to bet your friend Horner would have something to do with any fiddle that might be available."

"He'd be younger then. A lot younger."

"So would P.J. and Reggie. And there's always some sort of fiddle

going on. Don't forget Horner and P.J. Jeffries were pretty close at that time too maybe. And people involved in drugs are really very close. And then of course we have a metals magnate and his failure of a son."
"You've only stuck them in because the son stole your girlfriend. Besides I don't know if he was a metals magnate at that time. Taylor's father."
"My point exactly. Find out when he started to make all his money."
"Anybody you've left out?"
"One or two. One or two. Your little friend Crombie's a colourful character isn't he? Knew a lot of strange people back then. Bet he still does too. The older man?"
"Oh fuck off Lassiter! Now you're getting ridiculous."
"It pays sometimes. Coffee time! I told you we were in for a long night. I still haven't told you what Maggie had to say. And you haven't told me about Hagan and Horner."
"This is getting interesting."

END CHAPTER

CHAPTER THIRTY- SIX

CERTIFIABLE

Gil placed the well used coffee pot in the centre of Taylor's desk and slid Lassiter's mug over to him.
"You start, " he said, "because I want to hear what you've got to say first. I don't think you're going to like what I've got to tell you, and I'm not going to take the chance of you fucking off like some avenging angel before I know all the facts." He removed his spectacles and rubbed tired eyes with thumb and middle finger. Lassiter gave him one of his looks before pouring his own coffee.
"Right. Maggie Hagan is one very clever lady. She knows a lot about most things, and virtually everything there is to know about metal. The strange thing is she doesn't seem to know an awful lot about her new employers."
"Meredith Metals?"
"Oh she knows the firm. I'm talking about Meredith. And she knows even less about Taylor. Strange that don't you think. She's been in that game for years. You'd have thought...."
"Might have an answer for you there. Only might, mind you."
"Well anyway. It was Maggie who started me off on the hospital track. Not from the Gallagher death angle. From the money angle. And something else. With it being for a hospital, and all with sorts of government and health board involvement, every scrap of metal-no pun intended-used there would need proper documentation. For obvious reasons. Was it all? I don't know, and I'm quite sure you

don't. The point I'm making is that I'd never thought of anything like that. And perhaps the police didn't either. Everything was much looser back then wasn't it?"
"Including most of the people I knew. You for one. Go on."
"Well it started me thinking about greased palms, and sticky fingers, and contracts up for grabs. And how it might be just important enough for someone to look the other way. And keep doing it. Even when someone got killed for some reason connected to it all. A place meant to keep people alive responsible , in some very obscure way, for someone's death. What do you think?"
"But you've no proof. All supposition."
"Granted. Now we really come to the "what if" stuff. What if the older man in the pub that night was the same older man who came to the Jamiesons pub looking for Reggie all those years later. Maybe the two pub appearances by this older man are connected in some way. According to reports that night-and this is documented fact because I'm quoting from Crombie's newspaper- "MR. GALLAGHER'S FAMILY DOCTOR HAPPENED TO BE CLOSE BY AND WAS QUICKLY AT THE SCENE." Why was he close by Gil? And how did they contact him? No mobile phones in those days. How quickly is quickly? Instantly?"
"Bloody good point kid. Must admit I never picked up on that. Stupid of me."
"Especially when you gave me the damn clipping in the first place."
"Must have missed it."
Lassiter gave him another look and then grinned a tired grin
"Nobody's perfect. Right, something else. On Theresa Gallagher's own admission she only THOUGHT she heard her husband talking about death certificates. Sounded like it, but she wasn't certain. Could she have overheard him saying something else? And maybe he wasn't talking about "guns and medals." Maybe he was admittedly , bearing in mind the gun thing at Sarah's tomorrow night, but maybe it's got fuck all to do with guns and medals."
"Well what then?"
"Your turn Gil. Your turn."
"Right. But you've got to realise that what I've got to say at the end of all this is coming from someone who is still, technically at any rate, a suspect in both our eyes. We discount nobody, although personally all my bets lie at the Meredith door. Providing there really is a case to answer in the first place. About the hospital, I mean"
"Right."

"According to both Danny Hagan and Horner, P.J. Jeffries told them something. I believe she may also have told Maggie recently too, although I don't know that. She seems to think there was another child in the Turner family. A male. Apparently one or two things Ellen Meredith said when they were both a good deal younger, hinted at that. When younger she would tell people-long before she had the split with Turner senior- that her father was the least of their worries. When her big brother came out of hospital he would look after her. P.J.'d be about twelve or so at this time. Years later when they were both doctors and she HAD made the break from her father P.J. apparently made the mistake of mentioning her family to her and she was instructed never to mention either of "those two" ever again."
"Maybe she was referring to her mother."
"Perhaps. But it's unlikely she would refer to her mother as "him" is it? Apparently the words were something like "he's ten times worse than my father ever was." Neither Horner or Danny had ever met this brother. Nor had P.J."
"Sometimes lonely children invent older brothers or sisters."
"True. But it's unusual to be still disowning them when you're a respectable, qualified doctor in your late thirties."
"Point taken. Point very much taken."

****

It was a cold thing. When they started to interfere with any of his plans it was not what he had heard others describe as red hot rage that took hold of him. He was always calm. Cold, calculating, maybe even serene. It would all be dealt with tomorrow. It was always the same. When something had to be done properly he had to deal with it himself.
The diary had had the usual calming effect. He returned it to the safe and sat alone in the dark.

Tomorrow.

****

"According to Hegarty and the Chief Constable, if the Merediths are the people behind all this, it's principally down to this brother nobody wants to talk about. And it's not as simple as turning our attentions to James Meredith. For a start he's not-if we can believe anything they have to say- her brother but his. And secondly he's too young. The man we're maybe looking for is older. By a fair bit. That leaves us with his brother, the doctor."
"Now wait a minute Tommy boy. He's married to Ellen Meredith. Don't tell me you're talking incest here."
"Nothing surprises me any more. Disgusts and sickens me , yes. Surprises me no. All that shit aside, who says they're married anyway. Maybe they just share a home like millions of other

respectable siblings. It's a very normal, common occurrence. Happening all over the world. According to P.J. they're very seldom together anyway. If he's not away somewhere, she is. The reason they took her on as junior partner in the first place."
"I'd need to check first of all. It would certainly explain some things. The death certificate theory. The thing about " guns and medals" given where you're going tomorrow night. The older man in the pub that night and the one looking for Reggie. The family doctor's timely appearance. But what have Reggie, and his wife and sister got to do with it all?"
"I haven't the faintest idea. Have you? If not stick the kettle on."
"The simplest thing you've said all day. And what's the boy wonder got to do with it also?"
"Fuck off. I'm going out for a walk to get more fags. Be back in five."
"Make it ten. I'm finding it hard keeping up with all this."
"You and me both Gil. You and me both."

....

"Twenty Benson please pal. King Size please. Ta."
"Sales of those have dropped. Along with every other fag in the shop."
" Good. Do I get a discount then?"
"Bloody street traders. Cheap booze, cheap fags, cheap tobacco. Na, you don't get a discount but I do give a certificate saying they'll kill you with more quality. Quality tobacco see. Tried and tested. Not that reject stuff they sell on the street. Are you alright pal?"

Lassiter stared at the shopkeeper. Fucking hell! You stupid bastard Lassiter!

That might be it!
"I'm fine thanks pal. Just remembered something. That's all. Thanks a lot. Hope business picks up for you. I mean that. I really do.

****

"Listen to me Horner. He's getting close. You know where he's going to be tomorrow night. He'll be alone. Be there. No fucking excuses. He's out for fags at the moment. I know him. Knight in shining, fucking armour. To protect the damsel in "stress." There won't be any cops, if I know Lassiter. Be there. And not alone. I'll meet you there."

Gil put the phone down.

END CHAPTER

CHAPTER THIRTY SEVEN

CERTIFIED

"Gil, you and I both know only too well what it was like back then. Glasow was not a clever place to be for lots of people, for lots of reasons. We were up and down to England like fucking yo-yos. A lot of guys stayed down there and made their lives down there. Just as many didn't. Can you get Tony on this. I know it's a lot. Most of it probably meaningless. Certificates is what I need for these names. Birth, marriage, death if any. Licences for guns, dogs, televisions. Sick lines if they make a bloody difference. I mean it. There's something we're missing. A connection somewhere."

"Right Tommy boy. Oh Daniel Taylor phoned earlier when you were out for fags. Just wanted to make sure you'd be there tomorrow night. Apparently Sarah wants you there, and so does old C.J. the father. He's still not too clever, the old boy apparently. Still well enough to realise that his son shouldn't be left alone anywhere with loaded guns anyway. This expert guy will need to check everythings in working order. And paperwork and so on, It probably means he'll need to fire a couple of rounds somehere apparently. Talking of rounds, that's where Tony'll be right now. The Grapes."

"Get him back. Why didn't you tell me Taylor had phoned when I got back earlier?"

"Forgot. What's Pearson supposed to be looking for?"

"People's fathers and mothers. And brothers and sisters."

"Is he allowed to know why?"

"Doesn't need to. But some bastard's not who they claim to be. And I'm beginning to get an inkling who. And more importantly why."

Lassiter didn't notice the almost imperceptible way Gil's eyes narrowed ever so slightly. He'd need to be on top of his game tomorrow night. Lassiter was like a Jack Russell with this.

****

Hagan was alone this time. Immaculately dressed as always , he stood like a sore thumb from the rest of the customers in Phil Jamieson's pub. Those who knew who he was, cleared a path for him through the lunchtime crowd. Those who didn't, were soon told to do so by those who did.

"Nae team wi' ye Danny?" Phil Jamieson said nervously his eyes darting to the front and side door of his pub. "Mr. Horner's no in."

"Ah'm no' lookin' fur Mr. "fuckin" Horner P.J. ma man. Huv ye' no' heard? We've kissed an' made up. The noo onywiys. Naw, Ah'm lookin' fur that daft brither ae yours. The wan that hid tae git a bit

ae paper that says he' no' daft. Mind that P.J.? Ah think that actually proves ye UR daft masel. Ah've goat a wee message fur him. See if onythin' happens tae ma pal Tommy Lassiter, or that tosser Taylor's braw wee wife wife in the next day or so, Ah'll be back so Ah wull. An' Ah'll bring ma ain fuckin' company wi' me! Wid ye tell 'im that fur me P.J.? Wid ye dae that fur me? Brithers ur supposed tae look eftir wan anither. Ta. See ye later P.J. ma' man. Ah'll decide who needs sortit oot in a' this shite! See ye!"
"No' if Ah see you fuckin furst ye'll no" Phil Jamieson muttered to himself under his breath to Hagan's immaculately dressed, retreating back.

****

Phillippa Jarvie was not happy about it, but there wasn't a thing she could do about it. She had to remain under police supervision and report to the lady probation officer once a week for the foreseeable future. Hegarty had made that very plain. He had also made it very plain that it wasn't his choice, but that of the Chief Constable himself. She was also instructed to have no contact whatsoever with any member of the Taylor household. She was not to return to her own home, but to stay with her brother and his wife until further notice. What Hegarty didn't know-but she did immediately she was so instructed-was that that meant she would be greatly out of pocket to feed their habit. Reggie and Jean were of course delighted with the arrangement. .
What none of the three of them knew was why. But the police and one other person did.

Tony Pearson of The Glasgow Voice was just about to find out also.

And of course that meant so also would Gil and Lassiter.

....

"Adjie" Jamieson slid from the back seat of the Jaguar and ran uptairs to his bedsit clutching the holdall with the expensive clothes inside. They were his size exactly and so were the exprensive brown brogues. They were also brand new, along with the tweed sports jacket and expensive slacks. The last words from the driver of the Jaguar rang in his ears as he locked his front door and dumped the holdall in his hallway.
"I will pick you up at seven p.m. tomorrow night. Be ready and be clean shaven. That thing looks filthy. So, the moustache and beard off, and the new clothes on. Shave tomorrow night. Not before. I want you to be as presentable as is possible for you. And keep your

bloody mouth shut at all times. All you have to do is look the part. A gunsmith. Not a bloody blacksmith. Clear?"
"Adjie" who knew very well never to argue with this man, had nodded furiously and scurried upstairs.

****

"Ur ye sure?" said the Wee Man taking another swig from the wine bottle.

"Ah'm fuckin' tellin ye. That's no' Mr. Horner's motor. It's that ither wan that's the same. The wan we seen before. Look it's no' him that's drivin it. Fuck's sake Wee Man! It's that auld doactor fae the Health Centre. The wan that nearly goat us lifted yon day. Mind Wee Man? He's wife works there tae. She's a doactor tae. Widnae gie you ony mair ae thae uppers ye waanted. Said ye were in a bad nuff state a'readys. Mind? Ye telt 'im ye'd open he's jaw. An' he wis phonin' fur the polis when we fucked off. D'ye mind him noo? Looks a wee bit different, wi' thae specs an' that. Must need them fur drivin."

"Oh fuck aye. So it is. Auld bastart!"

"Whit's he daein drappin' "Adjie" aff? How dae they know wan anither?"

"Fucked if Ah know Gallie!"

....

Phillippa Jarvie stared at Hegarty. Then she stared at Lassiter, Tony Pearson and her brother in turn. As usual Reggie was in a state of intoxication , albeit fairly mild. By his standards at any rate.
"She never mentioned his name. Just said he was an English gentleman. A travelling salesman or something. A professional man anyway. Why? Is he still alive or something? Doe he have money for us or something?"
Hegarty ignored the last two questions, and continued shuffling the paperwork spread out on his desk before him. After some time spent staring at her , he spoke.
"I'm asking the questions here. Did she refer to him as an English gentleman? Or did she refer to him as a gentleman who travelled up and down to England. There's a world of difference."
"I can't remember now. Never really listened much when my mother

used to talk about him."
"Ah did." said Reggie suddenly. "It wis wan ae the times youse lot lifted me fur kerryin' a blade when Ah wis younger. She said sumthin' tae me when Ah goat oot the cells. Gie'd me a skelp oan the ear an' told me sumthin' he'd said tae her waanst."
"And what was that Reggie?"
"Never kerry a weapon unless ye're prepared to yase it." He'se words she said. She said he'd been born in Glesga but he'd hid tae go doon tae England, fur some reason or ither."
"Thanks Reggie. I mean that."

And Lassiter did mean it. Every word of it.

****

"Right you know where he'll be. And you know what time. He's getting very, very close to unravelling all this. There must be no slip-ups. Everything has to go like clockwork."
"Whit aboot Hagan? Don't tell me he knows fuck all aboot this. Lassiter's he's pal. He must know. If that bammy bastard gets there furst, afore ah dae....."
"Hagan's got bottle. No question. But he'd need more than bottle for this. Have you ever thought why he and Lassiter admire each other so much? They're both loners. Loose cannons to a certain extent. And that Johnny, my friend, is their Achilles heel. Or heels to be precise."
"Whit?"
"Never mind. Be there on time."
Gil replaced the receiver on the telephone in his flat and Horner the mobile phone in the pocket of his camel haired overcoat.
The Jaguar moved silently into gear and joined the traffic outside Phil Jamieson's pub.

****

"Ah'm tellin' ye Maggie. Adjie's chinged. Lassiter husnae chinged a' that much, but Adjie's definitely chinged. Ah don't know 'im any mair. An' ah've never trusted that bastard Horner. Ask P.J."
"Danny. We've all changed. Lassiter too. Maybe not so much. But Lassiter too. You're the only one who hasn't. Now shut up a minute and listen. Lassiter's on to something here. I don't know if he's told anybody else but he's on to something. And it concerns you, and me, and P.J. here because I think both of our bosses are in it up to their bloody necks. All the Merediths maybe.. He 's been asking me all sorts of funny questions about my job. and my car and James Meredith."
"Well me too, to a certain extent. About why Patrick Meredith spends so much time in England. And how long I've known his wife and

does she have a temper like his. And the weirdest one of all. Do I think they look alike? He's not drinking again is he?"

Both Maggie and Danny burst out laughing.

"We'd a' know it if the Tommy boy wis back oan the swally. The whale ae Glesga wid know it. Right, here's whit we dae."

****

"Whit you daein in here ya wee tosser? Ah'm sick fuckin barrin' ye, an' that wee midget that's alang wi' ye. Gaun! Get tae fuck afore ah slap the pair o' ye'se!"

"We'll no' be a minute Phil. Honest. We jist came in tae gie Mr. Horner a message. An' you an' a'. It's aboot "Adjie". We heard ye'se wur lookin fur 'im. Me an' the Wee Man seen 'im. He's back. In he's ain hoose ah mean. Mebbe YOU know Phil. But ah thought Mr. Horner...."

"Mr. Horner disnae speak tae the likes ae youse. He's no' here onywiys. Here. There a boattle ae scud. Noo fuck off an' git blootered, an' gie ma heid peace. Gaun noo!

"Cheers Phil. He wis wae that auld doactor fae the Health Centre. In he's big motor."

"Wi' who? Here. C'mere back here a minute you!"

****

Dawson took another draw of his roll up cigarette and stared cooly across the desk at Rankin.

"Why tell me this? I could have you charged along with them. And they will be charged eventually. Fucking bank on it. You didn't need to come here. Why?"

"Well. I never liked the old bastard. Never trusted him. Still don't"

"You can look after yourself."

" YOU fucking bank on that. Na'. I owed you one. You played the game wi' me. I'm returning the favour. We're square."

"Thanks. Watch you're back. He might be an old bastard but he's a dangerous old bastard."

"So am Ah. An' ah.m no' auld."

Dawson laughed.

"Neither am I. Behave yourself Rankin and we probably won't see each other again."

They nodded acknowledgement to each other's fitness. Rankin left Dawson's office.

****

Lassiter sat alone in his flat. He just had to be that way sometimes. There were times when he neither wanted nor needed people. They got in the way. He checked his watch before closing the blinds and sitting in the dark. He wasn't meeting Gil in the "Grapes" till ten p.m. so that gave him almost four hours alone to think. He could have done with more. There were still so many things that didn't sit easily with the Meredith theory. Too many.

****

Chief Superintendent Bradford had spent the entire afternoon in solitude also. People got in his way too. Bradford did not tolerate people getting in his way. There was only one way to deal with that. Either he moved a little. Or they did. A lot and permanently.
He switched his computer off and opened his wall safe.

****

The phone rang just as Lassiter was about to leave the flat on his way to meet Gil. It was P.J. Jeffries.
"Lassiter? P.J. You're going to the Taylor's tomorrow night? I'm with Maggie at the moment. Danny's gone walkabout again. Complete with angry facial expression and no explanation. Not to mention axe. What the hell's going on Lassiter? I can't take much more of this. I'm sure he muttered something about the Taylors earlier on."
"Fuck."
"And I had a strange call from Dr. Campbell at the hospital. He's an old friend, and he was very concerned about C.J. Taylor leaving hospital before all his test results came back, and he had a chance to study them. Bill Campbell seems to think he may be a lot sicker than he thinks he is. He's met him before and couldn't get over the change in him. Says he hardly knew him. What is that bastard Taylor doing to his family?"
"I don't know P.J. But I do know this. Maybe all this has absolutely nothing to do with him. Maybe. Don't worry about Danny. Worry for the person he's looking for. Thanks for letting me know. I've got to go out now to meet Gil. Anything else turns up leave a message."

****

"Do Paddy John? Do? You will do nothing. Come now Paddy John. Surely you can manage that? After all you've managed it for the last thirty odd years. Just carry on doing it, or your brother –in- law will

have something to say on the matter.
You will keep your appointments tomorrow as arranged. Everything as normal. I will attend to all other matters. You really should pay more attention to your own wellbeing. Physician heal thyself!"
The phone went down with a soft click. He was left alone in the surgery. There wasn't a great deal of arrogance about his manner now.

****

Lassiter decided to leave the car and walk to the "The Grapes." Not because he felt like a drink, although he often did still, but because he always thought better when walking. There was still a great deal about all this that made no sense to him. He had the type of mind that took one issue at a time and dissected it. Tonight he decided on death certificates, guns and medals
and what they might really mean to this case. The chat with Maggie had been invaluable in that respect. Could that really be the explanation for what people thought they'd heard Gallagher say?
Perhaps Gil and the others knew the answer but didn't know they knew it.

END CHAPTER

CHAPTER THIRTY EIGHT

DEAD CERT

"The Grapes" was situated very near the offices of "The Glasgow Voice" and it was that fact, and that fact alone, that saved Gil from the wrath of Danny Hagan that night. Lassiter recognised the purposeful Hagan swagger from a distance as he, Lassiter, strolled towards the newspaper's main entrance. He also recognised the hand in the left hand pocket of the smart gaberdine overcoat. Lassiter had the time warp feeling again.
"Where the fuck are you headed?"
"Stiy oot it Tommy boy! Stiy tae fuck right oot it! Ah mean it Tam. Ye know whit Ah'm like."
"It' a good fucking job I know it, or you would have just made the biggest mistake of your life. Thank fuck I met you. I don't think this has really got all that much to do with with Daniel Taylor."
"Who said ah wis eftir that fuckin eejit? Naw, naw son, it's yir fuckin' pal Gil AH'M eftir. Fuckin' Gil! "Adjie!" "Adjie" Gilmour. That's who ah'm eftir noo!"
Lassiter came back out of the time warp and into the jigsaw again. Fucking hell!
"Come on pal, there's a coffee stall over there. We have to talk. We have to Danny!

"Tam. Listen tae me. Ye've been away fae this dump too fuckin' long. Too long son. This fuckin' place is worse noo than it ever wis. Wee shits runnin' aboot wi' blades bigger than themsels'! Blade ye fur the price ae a joint. Ye're oot ae touch Tam. An' that bastart "Adjie"'s gonnae let ye go tae a meetin' yirsel' wi' these Meredith fuckers , whoever they ur? Yirsel? Withoot back-up? Wi' two sets ae faimilies that might huv topped some poor bastart thirty odd years ago? Fucks sake Tam. We were a' muckers thegither."
"That was thirty odd years ago too, Danny. Things change. Who told you all this anyway?"
"P.J. and Maggie. They wur worried aboot ye. WE huvnae chinged. No' us."
He blamed the cold night and the smoking, but Lassiter could feel something very close to a lump in his throat..
"Tell them I thank them both for it. Danny, if you want to do me the biggest favour you've ever done me, go home to both of them now. Please? I'll be fine. I've got something I have to do tonight. Make sense of all this"
"Ye sure?"
"Positive."
"Look eftir that wee Sarah bird the morra night. Wee cracker. Ayewis wis. See ye Tam."
"See ye Danny. An' Danny. What I said about P.J. and Maggie. I meant it. You too. Crazy bastard!
"Fuck off Lassiter, or Ah'll use the aixe oan you!"
"See you Danny. And thanks."
"See ye , Tam."

****

....

Lassiter entered "The Grapes" and acknowledged Gil's presence. Waving in his direction, he lifted his right hand to his mouth to enquire if anyone required a re-fill. Gil waved back to indicate he didn't, but it didn't surprise him that both Tony Pearson and Crombie did. What did surprise him was Maggie's presence and the presence of the other man. The young, and very fit looking younger man casually, but relatively expensively dressed, seated beside her. A toyboy?
"You're a lucky man." Lassiter said to Gil placing the drinks on the table at the rear of the lounge. "Hello Maggie. I'm Lassiter by the way." he said extending a hand by way of introduction to the boyfriend or whoever he was.
"Rankin" said the other quietly. HE didn't extend HIS hand

"How so, kid?" enquired Gil.
"Tell you tomorrow." He wasn't about to say anything till he found out who this Rankin guy was

****

"Shut up Danny. Sit down and shut up. Give me that stupid bloody thing. You know you weren't going to use it on Gil or "Adjie" or whatever you want to call him now, anyway. I know you. It would have broken your heart to do something like that. Why don't you just grow up? Because if you don't you might just ruin everything. Maggie's not here. She's gone to see Lassiter and the others. Lassiter didn't know she would be there, so how could he tell you. Bloody paranoid, that's what you are."
"Somebuddy's paranoid P.J.. And they huv been fur the last thurty fuckin' years, hen. An' she might be mixin' wi' 'im right fuckin' noo."
"Lassiter's there Danny."
"Aye, right enuff. Tam's there, right enuff."

....

"I owed a guy a favour. A cop. An' that's the only reason I'm here. His boss got him to ring me back and tell me how I could settle the score. They know I'm ex-army and asked me to speak to your pal here, or you if I could get you. Don't worry. I've spoken to him. Hope you do the bastards." Rankin nodded curtly and left the pub before Lassiter got the chance to return the nod.
"Nice guy." said Lassiter sarcastically, staring at Rankin's retreating back.
"Wait till you hear who he is and what he had to tell us. You might like him a bit more." answered Gil.
Lassiter drew his chair closer to the table.

****

"Right, tomorrow about seven or so then. Thanks for ringing Ellen. She wants to speak to you Sarah. I think it's about those bloody pills you swallow like sweets." Daniel Taylor handed the phone to his wife and returned his gaze to the wide screen television.
"Hello."
"Hello Mrs. Taylor." Was it her imagination, or was there always a degree of something approaching menace in the doctor's tone. "Just to confirm what I told you previously. My husband will attend to you tomorrow evening. Two birds with one stone sort of thing" The voice was soft but the little laugh was strange. "I've given him strict instructions. About your treatment that is."
This time Sarah thought the laugh sounded slightly hysterical.

****

"You didn't tell Danny you were coming here to meet us? Shit! Keep an eye on the door Gil. And your back to the fucking wall."
"How could I ? Gil phoned after he'd left. Shut up Lassiter. I know how to handle Danny. And so does he." Maggie jerked a thumb in Gil's direction.
"Admire your faith in me Maggie. There was a time. Might be interesting to see nowadays." Gil had a strange look in his eyes that even the horn rims couldn't hide.
"Grow up , the pair of you. Right Gil. What have you got?"
"It's more what Tony's got. Right star crime fighter. If you can put the drink down long enough."
"Right Lassiter." Tony Pearson was back to being a journalist. And he was a good one. "The guy who just left? Quite important Rankin. More important who his father is. I met them both today."
"Shoot."
"Quite appropriate that word, as it happens. Guns and medals?"
"Eh?"
"Rankin senior was employed by old "Scrap" Turner too at one time. Said he remembers this P.J. guy. A real vicious bastard. Obsessed with knives and guns. He didn't work for Turner for long, but he remembers this guy and the fact that when he did, everyone else was afraid of him. He noticed even Turner was wary of him. Consulted him more than the others."
"Told you." said little Crombie suddenly raising his whisky to his lips. He still had the Homburg hat on and his Crombie overcoat. They were obviously trademarks.
"But that's not all. Young Rankin went into the army on the advice of his father. God knows why as it didn't seem to suit either of them. Particularly the army. Artillery. Apparently he was more involved in the maitenance of guns than firing them, although he was a crack shot.. Scrap value there, you see. Old habits die hard. Did you know that the bigger guns have a leaded brass content. Used as bearings for swivelling the buggars or something."
"So?"
"Commonly referred to as "gunmetal". "Gun metal?" "Gun , medal?" Worth a thought."
"Fucking hell!" said Lassiter thoughtfully.
"Told you." said Maggie quietly.

....

"Adjie" Jamieson only answered the door to his brother, because he was his brother, and even then only because he had telephoned him first to tell him he was coming. And coming alone. Even at that he was obviously nervous. Only other peoples lives were unimportant to "Adjie". His own was very important.

"Right "Adjie". The fuckin' truth. Whit's a' this goat tae dae wi' a wee shite like Reggie, he's ugly sister an' an auld doactor wi' a Jaguar like Horner's"
"Right. Ah'm only tellin' ye this because it's jist us two. Nae further. Goat it?"
"Fuck's sake "Adjie." Ye're ma wee bree. Who Ah'm Ah gonnae tell?
"Right. Sit yir erse doon. Naw, pour us a hauf furst."
Phil Jamieson poured his brother a very generous measure of whisky from the bottle in the kitchen and carried it through to him, switching on the small tape recorder in his pocket as he did so.

****

"Did you let Rankin's father see that photograph? The one in the pub with the young Meredith or whatever he was calling himself back then ? The one with the brother in it."
"I did and he's a bit confused about that. Thinks it's the same guy but couldn't really swear to it."
"Why?"
"Well his eyesight's failing a bit now. And he only met him once or twice anyway. Wearing the gear he wore in the scrapyard. Complete with cap or hard hat. The guy in the photograph's all dickied up. So is his brother. But he did remember something else about else the guy he knew. He was highly intelligent. Well read. Had to attend hospital on a regular basis for something or other according to Rankin's father. Mental problems?"
"Perhaps. But maybe we should look at that differently too. Maybe he was attending hospital for a different reason altogether. Maybe-if he was very clever- he was just clever enough to be training or learning something. Like how to be a nurse? Or maybe even a doctor! Things were very different back then. If a working class boy -or girl for that matter- was going to get anywhere , big sacrifices had to be made. Work and study were equally important. People literally had to work all through their education."
"You're right Lassiter." said Crombie. "I had to. But more so my cousin. He's dead now. Became a criminal lawyer eventually. And a very good one at that. But I remember him working as a labourer, and in a bakery. And studying, and going to night school."
"And now the bad news. There is no birth certificate or record anywhere of Turner having a son."
"Means nothing. Doesn't mean he didn't have one. Or more than one. Things like that weren't spoken about in those days. Affairs. That sort of thing." said Maggie. The mood was infectious. They seemed to be getting somewhere. "Might have had a son. A son who managed to become a doctor. Maybe even inspired his sister to do the same."

"Then why did she disown her father? And the brother you say might have inspired her? No. We're still missing a hell of a lot here. Pity. The doctor thing would tie in very neatly with Gallagher talking about death certificates. And Meredith's interest in guns and knives. Tomorrow's visit to the Taylor's certainly shows an interest in guns. Going all the way back to a very dangerous young man who worked in a scrapyard. Possibly his father's scrapyard." Lassiter leaned back in his seat and searched in his pocket for his cigarettes.
"Maybe not. You've made me remember something Lassiter. Remember our talk the other morning. If you look at all this from a different angle...."
"Oh I remember Maggie. I remember it very well. Think about everything that Tony's just told us too. We're getting there."
"You're a bit of a twisted buggar Lassiter. But I love you for it. I'm going home to check something. Phone me later?"
"Bank on it Maggie. Bank on it!
Lassiter smiled an enigmatic smile as Maggie made for the pub door. Nobody gets that look just because they've just found their cigarettes thought Gil.
This was going to have to be timed to perfection. He had to know what Horner had found out. And he had to know before Lassiter, Maggie or Danny Hagan. Most of all Hagan!

END CHAPTER

CHAPTER THIRTY NINE

DEAD CENTRE

"He who pays the salary rang-or rather got Sarah to ring- to give us the glad tidings he's not well and won't be anywhere near the place today, thankfully, but will be tomorrow, if he's well enough. Never been well enough. He needs an update on the Gallagher situation. Apparently he's wanted on television again. Fucked if I can understand why. Knows nothing about anything. But he'll definitely still be well enough apparently, to play host to you tonight."
"Everybody knows something Gil. And he'll know a lot more tonight. Sarah sound o.k.?"
"Surprisingly chipper. Must be the thought of seeing her old flame again tonight Tommy boy."
"Fuck off , Gil. Sarah is in for one hell of a shock when I get there . No way round it I'm afraid. It's the way it's got to be."
"Why do I get the impression there's something you're not telling me? And not going to."
"Possibly because there is, and I'm not."

****

Alone in his garishly decorated home Horner sat in his dressing gown listening to "Adjie" Jamieson's distinctive voice describe how he had been selling all sorts of thing for years without either Horner's, or even
his own brother's knowledge or permission. And selling Horner down the river at that, because he had been doing it on behalf of someone else.
Horner carefully took the small tape from the cheap plastic tape recorder. Mass produced he could buy another in any supermarket. He was going to have to do it with a damaged right hand, though.
He sat in his expensive armchair , blood dripping through his fingers onto the equally expensive carpet. He didn't stop squeezing until the tape recorder was totally crushed in his vice-like grip.
The cold fury was back. After a makeshift bandaging job, Horner opened the wall safe and took out the gun

****

.

"What was Maggie on about last night?" Gil looked thoughtful as he stirred his coffee.
"Maggie Hagan is a very clever lady. There isn't a thing she doesn't know about the job she does. She really is very knowledgeable about the metals game. What she doesn't know a great deal about, is the man who employs her. Or men to be precise." Lassiter looked even more thoughtful as he answered.
"And P.J Jeffries?"
"Almost the exact same answer. Except in her case it's men and one woman. Somebody pulled a very large string to get Maggie Hagan that very attractive position at Meredith Metals. No one in their right mind would refuse a package like that. But it's not the state of Maggie Hagan's mind we're concerned with here Gil, is it? Somebody's mind certainly, but it's not Maggie's."
"Did she phone you this morning?"
"Yes."
And that was when Lassiter suddenly decided he need cigarettes and had to go out.
It gave Gil the moment alone he had been waiting for to make the phone call.

.

****

"Thanks Tony. You're sure about all this? Documented fact? All of it?"

"Stand on me Lassiter. All of it. I can understand the police not

connecting any of this all those years ago. What they thought was a run of the mill unprovoked assault was anything but. Ten a penny in those days."
"Complacency. Never take anything for granted Tony. Gives people room for manouevre."
"When are you going to give this to Gil?"
"Depends. I'm having to do a lot of thinking about an awful lot of things at the moment."
"Don't take too long Lassiter. You can't go into this alone."
"Who can't?"

****

At the precise moment Lassiter re-entered Taylor's office to resume his conversation with Gil, a number of very significant events were taking place elsewhere in the city. One doctor was regretting the ill-advised issuing of drugs to certain people to keep other people in their accustomed state of apathy, and also the hasty issuing of certification, and two of the city's major crime figures were now on a collision course. The most significant of all these events was taking place elsewhere in very different parts of Glasgow.
Two people were shaving, prior to their visit to the Taylor home that evening

.

****

"You say Pearson gave you this? I told you he was brilliant."
"Well Pearson and your little pal Crombie together apparently. Explains the importance of Reggie and his sister. Reggie and Phillippa? Still can't get my head round those two names. P.G. Wodehouse names. From Maryhill?"
"That's probably where Jess got them from. Lived in a fantasy world seemingly. Bloody hell Lassiter. So their real name according to this is Turner. But according to everything we know about the father he was younger. A salesman from down south. The mystery brother?

Turner's son?"
"Starting to look like it. But who is he Gil?"
"Got to be Meredith. The older man in two pubs. But wait a minute. There's thirty odd years to account for here. That won't work, He'd be positively ancient by now, if not dead."
"You're not thinking straight Gil. The average age of the drinkers in the pub that night-including Andy the barman-would be about eighteen or nineteen. Cast your mind back to how YOU thought then. Somebody of twenty-five or so was pretty old to you and I then. Gallagher himself was only thirty seven and I remember thinking of him as a really old guy. It's all relative Gil. And it would now appear that the answer to this bloody thing hinges on a relative."
"Or relatives Tommy boy. Plural. Must be Meredith!"
"He certainly keeps popping up every where. Certificates. Access to drugs. Hospital involvement. And now the possibility that he just might be be both father and son to known criminals. Fuck's sake Gil. I think we're really on to something here!"
Lassiter decided to keep what Maggie had told him that morning to himself for a little while longer. Maybe even till the next day.
Given that that there was to be a next day for him in the first place.

****

"Sarah? How are you my dear?"
"C.J.? You sound wonderful! Back to your old self almost. You've obviously been following doctor's orders. I can't get over the change. Your voice sounds as strong as ever."
"Oh it'll take more than team of doctors , with their forecasts of doom, to get rid of an old fool like me Sarah my dear. I feel wonderful as a matter of fact. Better than ever actually. Maybe I did need a rest. And according to Ellen Meredith my blood pressure's spot on now. Good for a man my age at any rate, if there is anybody else as old as that. I think they'll need to shoot me. Now listen. I'm going to be there tonight after all. Don't tell Daniel, Lassiter or most important of all, any of the Merediths. Tell nobody Sarah. I've been worried about you and now I'm going to be there make sure this goes alright. Promise? I feel responsible for all this mess somehow. That fool of a son of mine. I'll be there to take care of you. I swear it. Now promise me you'll tell nobody. Including that nice Mr. Lassiter."
"I promise C.J. You're an angel!"
"Do you get old angels? Any I've seen in books are very young. No, no my dear. I'm just a father-in-law trying to do what he's supposed to. See you tonight"
Sarah put the phone down and started to hum a little tune to herself. She hadn't had a good secret to keep to herself since she

was a little girl.
And then her life, or most of it, had all started to go horribly, terribly wrong.

****

Chief Superintendent Bradford listened intently to what Hegarty was saying. It was his great strength. He firmly believed it was often more important to listen than to talk although there was admittedly a time for both. Pearson and Crombie also said nothing. Both were paid to report and write. They also knew when to shut up. Stroking at the little moustache almost nervously he finally spoke.
"Good God. How on earth was all this missed?"
"Or ignored." said Hegarty
"Who, other than Lassiter, knows about this?" This time he spoke directly to Tony Pearson.
"No one as far as I'm aware. But there will be other people. Count on that. Thankfully most of them will not know or care about the importance of that knowledge. Reggie and his sister obviously don't know. But Lassiter does."
"Well I'll tell you what's not going to happen. He's not going in there like John Wayne or ,God forbid , Charlie Bronson to look good in front of his old girlfriend. Not on my patch." Bradford switched on the intercom on his desk.
"Just a minute sir, please," said Hegarty, "could I suggest something here.?"

****

Lassiter left Gil at four p.m. He needed at least a couple of hours to himself again. Before leaving "The Voice" he phoned Sarah to tell her he'd be there at seven as planned. He was really worried about the effect tonight would have on her. He was slightly relieved to hear her sounding fairly cheerful as Gil had said earlier. This was not going to be easy from here on in.. For either of them.
Much of his plan now depended on how well he knew Glasgow and the reactions, and consequent behaviour patterns, of some people he had known thirty or so years previously. It was a big gamble . Lassiter was quite prepared to take it for a number of reasons. Now everything hinged on Hegarty and Pearson's ability to persuade the Chief Superintendent to let him.
When he got back to his flat there were two messages. The first was from Hegarty. He'd managed to swing it somehow. Lassiter neither knew nor cared how. But he knew Hegarty. He'd tell him someday. Always providing Lassiter survived the evening's events and was still around to be told.

The second was from a decidedly nervous sounding Daniel Taylor. The gist of that call was that Paddy John Meredith had sprained his back slightly, but had called to say-or rather his wife had- to say he would most definitely still be there that evening, albeit his brother or wife might have to drive him there. Someone would would have to at any rate. Probably Daniel Taylor himself.
That was the precise moment that Lassiter knew his theory was correct. He was no longer in any doubt
He hoped desperately that he had been right about everything, and everyone else. Because all that was still down to his own gut feelings.

It was all down to guts and bottle now!

END CHAPTER

CHAPTER FORTY

DEAD END

The Taylor residence was certainly impressive. It stood, on it's own, dead centre at the end of a very select, very exclusive quiet cul-de-sac. It dwarfed the surrounding structures. Typical of Taylor. Of the way the man thought. There were those of co

urse who questioned whether he ever did. Such as Gil. Lassiter had thought a lot about Gil recently. HIS thought process. Along with the others. P.J., Horner and all the rest.
Raising the collar of the leather jacket against the biting wind, he started up the gravel driveway towards the house. He wondered for the hundredth time if he had done the right thing by telling Gil what it was that Danny Hagan had told him that night at the coffee stall. Time alone would tell. And there was very little of it left.
He stepped up onto the pillared porch, which was meant to impress, but somehow failed to do so, and raised the ornate door knocker.

****

Bradford didn't speak. As usual he sat quietly behind his large desk. His instructions had been clear. All he expected from Hegarty was for him to tell him that they had been carried out. To the letter. Unfortunately for Hegarty and, as it would turn out, Lassiter he was not in a position to do that.

****

"You're in deep shit "Adjie" ma man. Mebbe Horner waants tae kill ye noo, tae. The polis might waant tae arrest ye. An' these three wi' me, well they never liked ye fae the furst time they clapped eyes oan ye. See a' these guys. They've goat nae time fur bastards like you. People like you get people like us a bad name. See there is honour amangst thieves, right enuff. An' hard cases, an' mebbes even some nut cases for a' ah know. But no' the wans you've been dealin wi'. Naw no' them. So you jist better come wi' us the noo "Adjie" son."
Hagan turned his back abruptly and swaggered out of the flat, leaving the three salesmen types he'd brought with him to do the rest.
He went downstairs and climbed into the front passenger seat of Maggie's new Jaguar. Behind the wheel a very nervous Maggie was still fighting the urge to throw up as she waited for the salesman types and "Adjie"

....

The plan was not going to work. Hagan! The bastard had been causing him nothing but trouble for all those years. He and his entire fucking, family. His drunken sot of a father, sanctimonious old cow of a mother, whore of a sister. And him. Posturing, swaggering throwback. It might have been acceptable if he had been a peer. Someone of intelligence. Instead of a ten a penny, would be Glasgow hard case. A street fighter. A common or garden hoodlum!
His name had ceased to be amongst the names that had to be accepted and tolerated .
It was now added to very near the top of those who had to be disposed of.
And it would begin tonight! Like all who thought they could be hard and self sufficient, his weaknesses were there for all to see and exploit. They could always be found with those who meant the most to them! And he knew who meant the most to Hagan. Fool!

****

At first P.J. assumed it was one of the Meredith's Jaguars parked next to her Mondeo in the surgery car park. Then the rear door opened and she saw Horner's camel haired overcoat. At the same time Phil Jamieson emerged from the bushes behind her.
"Hello hen." Horner's tone was not at all pleasant. "Ah'm afraid Danny's otherwise engaged. Me an' Phil here's jist gonnae take ye fur a wee run in ma motor. That awright wi' ye? Disnae really matter much if it's no' Ye're comin' wi' us onywiy."
That was when she felt the hand go over her mouth and the hard metallic object in the small of her back.
The other man's hand pushed her roughly towards the rear seat of

the Jaguar. "Ah've goat a wee hoose call fur ye tae make doactor. But no' tae worry. Ye're no' gaun anywhere ye've no' been before. Ah think ye need tae see a doactor, or mebbe's two."
Horner's voice sounded very different from the last time they'd met. This time he really did look and sound like a gangster.

****

"Oh hello James. Glad I caught you. I didn't know if you'd still be in the office. It's Maggie. Maggie Hagan. I've just landed this superb new account would you believe. It's a dripping roast. Honestly. Massive, massive potential. Obviously I thought you'd want to know."
"Maggie, I really shouldn't be here at the moment. Something's just cropped up, but of course I'm delighted for you. I'll let C.J. know as soon as I see him and you can tell me all about it later. As a matter of fact I may just see him later tonight. Sorry if I sound pre-occupied. I don't mean to. But this matter that's cropped up needs my immediate attention. Congratulations my dear Maggie. I'll need to keep my eye on you. Be taking my job soon.. See you tomorrow."
Maggie switched of the mobile and returned to the waiting Jaguar. As usual Lassiter had been right. Meredith never even asked the name of the new customer. And his voice had been strangely distant. And something else. Nervous?

How did Lassiter always seem to know these things beforehand?

****

When she opened the door and smiled the thirty odd year old, shy smile that first knocked him for six all those years ago, Lassiter felt sickened with himself. Why the fuck did life have to be such a bastard?
"Hello Sarah."
"Hello Tom. Thank you so much for coming. I'll never forget this night and your agreeing to come immediately I asked you."
"Oh shit!" thought Lassiter.

****

Gally took another swig out of the wine bottle and passed it to the Wee Man.
"Turn 'im ower Gallie. He's fuckin' bevvied. He's mebbe's goat a boattle or sumthin' in he's jaicket poacket."
Gally toe poked tentatively at the inert form lying on the grass in the public park. The man didn't move.
"Gie's a haun ya wee bastart."

Together they rolled it over onto it's back
"Fuck's sake Wee Man. Zat no' "Adjie? Wi'oot he's moustache?"
"Aye, an w;'oot hauf he's fuckin' throat!"
If "Adjie" Jamieson had cut himself shaving, it had been a very deep cut.
He was very, very dead!

.

****

Only a slight change in planning had been called for. The end result had been the same.
"Excellent. Let me be the first to compliment on you on never having lost your touch. It must have come as a great shock to the low life piece of scum. Never had any time for that sewer rat. I do hope you made it very clear to him as to why it was happening, and whose orders you were following, when you did it.
I've always thought corpses should be clean shaven in any case. I'll pick you up in an hour."
He couldn't resist the final entry in the diary before returning it to the wall safe and switching off the mobile phone. He hated the things but he had to admit they had their uses.

****

"Shut the fuck up "Adjie." Just shut the fuck up. Noo ah know why ye wurnae ther that night in the boozer. Ye're a two faced lyin' bastart! How could ye let Tam Lassiter go there himsel' the night. You an' that bastard Horner huv been runnin' bits ae Glesga fur years."
"If you'd let me speak Danny..."
"Don't fuckin' Danny me. You an' Horner wan wee bit here, thae Meredith bastarts anither wee bit there. But Tam Lassiter wis too clever fur yese baith. He's goat it a' sussed. You're comin' wi' us tae git a' this sortit oot. Tell me where Horner is the noo."
"I'm going to tell you something Hagan I should have told you upwards of thirty years ago. You're a bloody half-wit! Now fuck off!"
Even Hagan was taken aback by the ferocity with which Gil said it.

****

It was obvious to P.J now. She and Danny, and very probably Lassiter and all the others, had made a very bad error of judgement

with regard to Johnny Horner. This man was very clever. That much was evident as soon as he told Phil Jamieson to stop the Jaguar in front of what was a very familiar house to her.
It was also obvious when he took the sawn-off shotgun from the boot of the Jag., that he was extremely dangerous.

****

"Now if you're prepared to listen to him , Danny, we might just get all this sorted out. Gil is now a respected newspaperman. Not a teenage hoodlum called "Adjie." I didn't know it myself until very recently. Lassiter trusts him for God's sake and he's the one who is in danger of getting his bloody head blown off tonight"
"Thanks Maggie. Now sit on your fucking arse Danny, and listen. Yes, Johnny Horner is what he is, and yes, we have had an uncomfortably close business relationship for any number of reasons over the past years. But his business is not mine and vice versa. I'm a newspaperman and he's a fucking gangster. Forgive me if I'm upsetting you old pal but what exactly do YOU class yourself as? He didn't even know who I really was, until very recently. A bit like yourself again, eh Danny? He gives me and my newspaper information at times. And I him. A very common occurence in the media world my friend."
Danny still looked far from totally convinced. Convinced enough however to motion the three salesmen types to take a backstep for the moment. The one who looked like an accountant appeared disappointed. Only he knew the reason why. Maybe Gil didn't show enough fear. On the contary , Gil didn't show any. The accountant disappeared into Maggie's small kitchen to see if she had any whisky. There wasn't. He looked even more disappointed and came back in. Danny glared at him to sit down. He did.
"All settled are we? Good. Then I'll explain some things to you as I know you meant well, Danny me old mucker. You see the problem with Lassiter is, he's a dogged bastard. And dogged bastards upset people. He's nearly solved this case. Maybe I'm wrong and he's totally solved it. But just to be on the safe side I've always had a little contingency plan. A plan B Danny."
Hagan looked grateful for the explanation. He'd always known the importance of secondary plans. He'd used them often enough.

****

Bradford stroked the little moustache thoughtfully, inspected the new information Hegarty had placed on his desk once more, and finally looked up.
"By God this had better work or you and I won't. Ever again. Right.

Set it up! I want that house totally blocked off."
"Shouldn't be too difficult sir. He lives in a dead end."
If Hegarty had intended any black humour, neither man acknowledged it.

END CHAPTER

CHAPTER FORTY ONE

LAST WORDS AND FIRST STEPS

"Sarah, we don't have much time. Where is your husband?"
"Lassiter? What's wrong? You look different. Has something happened? To Daniel I mean? Is he alright?"
"That remains to be seen. But as far as I'm aware he's alright at present. Where the hell is he?"
"At the chemists , I think. And then to his father's he said. He'll definitely be here. He's got to be."
"And so does someone else. Sit down. You're going to need every ounce of the guts I know you have. There is no easy way to tell you this. But I'm going to. Because you asked me to. And for your mother too. Sarah, I know who killed your dad. And I also know why. You've been very wrong in your judgement about who you can trust and who you can't in all this. But that's to your credit. The last thing you want to do is blame yourself. No one would wish to be able to follow the thought patterns of a homicidal maniac. Much less two!"
"Lassiter. My mother and I asked you to find out who killed my father. Have you done that?"
"Yes."
"Thank you. I'll be able to handle it. God bless you Tom. Go ahead."
"He's going to have to, unless this goes like fucking clockwork."

....

"So you see Danny, far from being suspicious of my relationship with Horner, you should be grateful. Right at this moment he should be making sure that someone's plans for P.J, and later Maggie, do not come to fruition. Would you like to come with me now and make sure that he has managed to do that? Believe me you have no axe to grind with Johnny Horner. Pardon the pun. You too Maggie. I want

you with us. Do you think we could manage without the sales executives for the time being Danny? They might get in our way."
Hagan grinned and nodded dismissively to the accountant type and his two friends.
"You're the man "Adjie." Thanks boays. It wis me that hud it erse fur elbow. Ah'll gie ye'se a bell. This is fuckin' personal noo. Me an "Adjie"'ll handle it fae here."
The salesmen types made for the door. Gil gave Maggie a resigned shrug at the use of his old nickname.

****

The expressions on Sarah's face had changed from anguish and horror, through total disbelief and finally to rage. She raced towards the gun cabinet upstairs in the hall to search for the key in the drawer beneath. Lassiter made no move to stop her.
"Don't be bloody stupid Sarah. Do you really want them to get away with this scot free? Again? Why do you think I came so early? I wanted you to know exactly what happened. And how they're going to be made to pay. Anyway, you know they're not loaded. And never will be, if I've got anything to do with it. Now come here and stop crying. These bastards have no idea what they're walking into. What time is it? We've still got about forty five minutes or so. Time your husband was back. You see I got that all wrong too. About him and his father."
"Bastard!"
Lassiter genuinely did not know who she was referring to. She had a few to choose from. It might even have been him.

****

Before leaving his office, Bradford took his personal diary from the wall safe and studied the list of names for the last time. It had been a long list. He had learned early in his life in the force not to assume that the obviously guilty were guilty of anything at all. Other than being in the wrong place at the wrong time perhaps. When a highly intelligent criminal was also aware of that fact the police had very real problems. And physcopaths were highly intelligent people.
He began scoring out names with the old fashioned, gold plated fountain pen.

He knew he had to hurry. There was very little time now.

****

Horner sat in the doctor's seat the shotgun pointed lazily in their

general direction.
"Dangerous fuckin' things these. Ah've heard ae them bein' used oan some caper or ither, an' then disappearin' tae be used somewhere's else. Oan anither joab like. A' the weans ur runnin' aboot wi' them noo. Thae junkies yase them a' the time ah hear . Niver yased tae be as many aboot back in the sixties. But they wur ayeways there. Some crazy bastard wis aye prepared tae yase them. Wisn't he doactor? Ah heard there's two kickin' aboot the noo that's goat a wee history tae them. An' somebuddy needs them back. It's personal wi' me ye see. An auld pal ae mine's gaun tae see aboot it the night. Imagine us two in ma motor wi' three doactors Phil? An' a wee man that runs he's ain metals company. We'll be awright but.
Least we should be a'right if this fucker disnae go aff unexpected like."
She didn't know whether it was fear or hysteria, but P.J. Jeffries had to stop herself from giggling.

****

"There is and always has been a link to the medical profession in this case. Meredith was your family's G.P. all those years ago. It's perfectly understandable why you didn't like the man then, and still don't. Nobody likes him. At least I haven't come across anyone. But that doesn't mean he went around the city of Glasgow dispensing with patients by using the business end of a knife all those years ago . We had to find some sort of a link to the criminal world. We did that once we discovered who Ellen Meredith's father was. And what business he made his money from. Some of it, anyway. They both worked in the same hospital where a major rebuilding contract at that time involved the use of massive amounts of metal. Enter Meredith Metals. No one seemed to question the astonishing speed with which James Meredith's company mushroomed, or the massive amount of business from the hospital contract placed with his company and then sub contracted. Business that should have been put out to tender but wasn't. Doctor Patrick John Meredith attended to that somehow or other. God knows how he managed it but manage it he did. How much time have we got?". Lassiter glanced up at the expensive carriage clock on the Taylor mantelpiece.
"Right, still got almost half an hour."
"What if they're early?"
"If they are, the full explanation will have to wait. Now this is where it get's really tricky, so bear with me please. I'd never have found all this out without my old friends. And Gil's. He knows some people I don't. Ready? First of all let me say that I believe your husband is a very disturbed man. For a number of reasons. However that doesn't mean he's guilty of too much either, other than looking after his

father's interests. And being a spineless prat. But I knew that thirty years ago. And so did you deep down. Who was responsible after all, for the involvement of certain people in your life? Such as the Merediths, knowing full well that you didn't trust either of them. Not to mention putting your mother into a nursing home almost wholly owned by good old Paddy John and Ellen Meredith. And a golfing buddy of their slimy brother. But the worst thing he did to you was to let you think he cared about you. And some other people did that too. People like Phillippa Jarvie. The scheming little bitch is still alive and well, incidentally, but I wouldn't concern yourself too much about that. What I would ask you to concern yourself with is something Gil's pal Tony Pearson discovered. And something my pal Danny Hagan always knew, but managed to unintentionally forget. It's about the Jarvies mother and father. Who she was and who he is. Yes IS! And he's on his way here now. I'm going to nail this bastard this time for you."

END CHAPTER

CHAPTER FORTY TWO

CLOSING WORDS

"The city was different for us all back then" said Hegarty to Bradford from the front seat of the Chief Constable's offical Mercedes, as it made it's way through the outskirts of Glasgow heading for the Taylor residence. Bradford nodded immersed in his own thoughts from the rear seat. This had to go right. Too much at stake.
"The old razor gangs were a thing of the past, and we had a new breed of thug to contend with. The territorial gangsters. Some of the bigger gangs were huge. And vicious bastards they were too. Very common to be killed, or at the very least seriously damaged, just for being in the wrong pub or dance hall. For no reason other than not being known well enough."
"Or too well known." commented Bradford. "I remember good old Frankie Vaughan coming here to try and talk some sense into the lot of them. Remember that Jim.?"
That was why Hegarty had always been able to get along with his superior. He really HAD been a working policeman. It was at that moment that the two smaller police vehicles containing Dawson and his crew of , ready for anything, boys overtook them. Dawson tipped his temple casually if slightly insubordinately. Hegarty laughed. The Chief Constable didn't Timing! Timing!

....

"Phillippa and Reggie Jarvies' mother was called Jessie and took various jobs in pubs and hotels and so on. She did her best to bring them both up. Life was not easy in Maryhill. Especially for a single mother. Well, single most of the time , would be more exact Not in the sixties. Unfortunately neither of them inherited their mother's easygoing nature. But they did inherit her habit of inheriting "things." Things that didn't belong to them In addition to that habit Reggie , in particular, was one vicious little shit when younger. It's now obvious where he got that from. Wonder where it went. Because he's a sorry individual now ."

"That's the brother she spoke about?" Sarah was now listening intently. She owed it to Lassiter for doing what she'd asked him to. More than ever she realised she'd never stopped loving him.

"The same little shit. Bad little bastard then. But I suppose he eventually realised he wasn't in the same league as some people. You see Reggie knew all along who was responsible for your dad's death. Oh yes he knew alright. What he didn't know, until very recently, was that one of the guys who scared him so much was his own father. His and Phillippa's. So don't you be too hard on yourself about trusting her and others. Most of the people involved in this only had one or two pieces of the jigsaw. You had none at all. Pearson and old Crombie made a hell of a lot of the pieces fit. That photograph Tony dug up is the key to it all. You see he's in it. And so's she. The barmaid. The barmaid is Jessie Jarvie. Reggie and Phillippa's mother. Danny Hagan confirmed that when I showed him the photograph. He was raised in the same Maryhill street as Reggie. And he remembers his old Irish mother telling him to stay away from Reggie. In case he turned out like his father. Who nobody ever seemed to meet incidentally. But Danny's old mother obviously had at some stage in her life. Did I hear a car?"

"No" said Sarah looking out the window "Ellen Meredith did say seven-thirty at the earliest. It's still only ten past."

"The guns are important too but not greatly. They are important because they are valuable , yes, but that's not why he wants them back. Yes, back. They were valuable back in the late fifties when he and old "Scrap" Turner stole them from a farmhouse in Aberdeenshire. A farmhouse where a very wealthy old couple had their throats cut. Never caught the intruders. Never tied it in with what happened to your father almost ten years later either. No the reason he want's to be here personally, and not your normal doctor, is because of you and me Sarah. We're a threat to him now. He's coming here to kill us both!"

"Any decent coffee? I'm sorry but the last cup was crap."

Sarah giggled nervously, and ruffled his hair as she passed. She was still absolutely terrified but the anger somehow dwarfed the terror.

"Still nuts Lassiter. After all these years. That's why I asked Gil to get your help. That and the other thing."

"What other thing?"

"I'll tell you later. If we're both still alive!"

■■

"Keep your mouth shut both of you. Only I speak here. YOU, in particular, or I swear I'll kill your father as well as your wife. You in the back seat just keep your mind on the job ahead of you. If you fuck this up I'll kill you as well. Be sure of that.
Excuse me officer, any chance of us getting through here? Only, I'm a doctor on an urgent call. This man's wife needs urgent attention. This is an acquaintance from the golf club in the back seat. We were having a social evening, when Mr. Taylor came into my golf club seeking my assistance. I wasn't drinking incidentally. Never do when I'm working next morning. Be happy to take a breath test. But please be as quick as you possibly can."
"Not necessary sir. My own wife is a patient at your practice. Visits your good lady wife on a regular basis. Just go through, when the car in front of you allows you. Lovely cars these Jaguars. Always wanted one myself. Maybe some day."
"You will I'm quite sure. With a helpful attitude like yours, I'm sure you'll go far."
Dawson smiled respectfully and gave the roof of the Jaguar a respectful pat to signal for the driver to proceed.
"I think it's a bogus call out anyway sir. Still we have to double check everything these days."
"We live in very dangerous times officer. Very dangerous times indeed. Thank you for your assistance."
The last of three Jaguar cars on their way to Taylor's house moved through the temporary roadblock. The other two had already arrived and had moved into position at the rear of the house. Next to the Chief Constable's Mercedes.

****

"When this is all over I'm charging the whole fucking lot of them Tom. Offensive weapons, threatening behaviour, kidnapping. I'll give them mean streets of bloody Glasgow. Lassiter and his sidekick, too. Withholding information from the police....
"Now settle down gaffer. They haven't really done anything much. Apart from Don Corleone there, and his old pal the mad axeman that is. And in their own daft way all THEY were trying to do was help out a couple of old pals solve a murder case that we couldn't. And still can't, until Lassiter and that very brave young lady in there see this through."
"She's not young. She's fifty if..."
"Oh give youself a break Bernie. That's just because you and I are a

couple of old farts who don't know our arses from our elbows any more. Lassiter's just proved it."
"Not yet he hasn't. And that's insubordination. I'll add that to the list of things I have to see about when this is all over."
"In that case I hope your team get's fucking thrashed at the weekend."
"Now hold on. You just went over the score Hegarty."
They both laughed the way only policemen could laugh.

....

Daniel Taylor came into the lounge first, looking very agitated.
"Paddy John and the expert chap are just on their way in. They've got to get some things from the boot of the car first."
"No they're not." said Lassiter.
"Oh hello Lassiter. Glad you could make it. Sorry, what was that you said? How's business"
Lassiter had risen from the couch, and now moved over to stand in front of Taylor.
"I said, no they're not. But never mind that. You asked how's business. Well, I know it's not really about business tonight Daniel, but if I could just have a quick word."
This time the head butt came with such ferocious force it it instantly broke Daniel Taylor's nose and knocked him out cold.
Sarah had to stop Lassiter from having a kick at him, for good measure, as he lay on flat out on the carpet.

....

"Oh let's ask the question anyway Mr. Horner."
"Don't be daft hen. Nae chance thae polis wid let us anywhere near that place."
A very strange look came into Patricia Jeffries M.D's eyes and she spoke in a dialect she hadn't used for over thirty years.
"But we cannae leave them in there themsels, Plum. They might get fuckin' slaughtered."
Horner's sudden burst of laughter echoed in the enclosed space of the rear seat of his Jaguar.
"Awright P.J. Ah'll go ower tae the ither motor an' git the team. You go ower an' ask yir question."
At that precise moment they both were catapulted back over thirty years of their lives. And it felt good.
Just for an instant, P.J. missed being that hoodlum girl of all those years ago.

....

Bradford was a pragmatist. He now knew who was responsible for Thomas Gallagher's death in that hospital all those years ago. He had Lassiter to thank for that. He therefore also now knew who wasn't responsible. They were collectively responsible for a great number of other things over the years perhaps, but certainly not the Gallagher killing. And on the other hand, they HAD been of assistance to Strathclyde police in a number of ways. Perhaps they still could be. He had already taken a great risk in allowing Lassiter to confront the killer, or killers as the case may be, on his own, in order to prove his still unbelievable point. Lassiter deserved to get all the assistance at his disposal. And these people were offering their assistance.

"Bernie, he's in there on his own with no backup. You and I have to stay out here in Taylor's garage-cum- study to hear the proof over that intercom thing over there that his wife has left switched on. We've agreed we can't have the place swarming with officers just yet. Give them that key to the games room his wife gave us. You've got the weapons of mass destruction, Hagan and Horner were carrying."

"Never heard of pool cues Tom? Those two could probably commit GBH with the fucking chalk. I'll let the newspaper guy in there though. He's a regular visitor."

"There's an intercom in there as well." said Gil. "Why aren't you in there? It leads straight onto the hall."

"The sound might carry. Too close. The gun cabinet's upstairs in the hallway. Only you Gilmour. Get your arse in there now. If it get's really nasty when they do arrive, it's anybody's game. I mean that. I'll overlook anything that needs overlooking later. Those are two very brave people in there."

"Corroborating evidence. Who fucking needs it?" growled Hegarty.

"I do." said Bradford. "And so does the law. And you. And Lassiter. There won't be any cock-ups this time. Timing. Timing. The moment we hear it Dawson and his boys come out the woodwork. Butch and Sundance here might be needed beforehand. Dawson's team are good but we might need substitutes before the first team arrives. If you see what I mean. If Lassiter's correct about all this we are dealing with very, very dangerous people here. Sorry to disillusion you lot. But you are not in the same league. And definitely no women. Clear?"

"You don't follow football by any chance do you Chief Constable?" enquired Maggie Hagan sweetly. "Women can play a bit too, I think you'll find. Isn't that so P.J.? I seem to remember you played a bit when we were young. Looking back I wasn't bad myself. If you're letting them in, you're letting us in. Chauvinism was very common back in the sixties, wasn't it?. As was incompetence."

"Ouch!" said Bradford.

"Fuck!" said Hegarty.

Bradford had no intention of letting them in. But that didn't mean he had no intention of letting them ALL loose, if the situation called for it. He might have to. He might need everybody. Anything could go down in there.

****

"Here they come. I'll do the talking." said Lassiter rising from the sofa at the sound of footsteps in the hall. Daniel Taylor now lay moaning and clutching his broken nose.
"Is that you doctor? In here. Mr. Taylor needs attention now too. His nose started bleeding suddenly. Quickly, please"
"What's happened here?" The voice was familiar. And so was the face of the man standing behind him in the hallway.
"You tell me. You're the fucking doctor. You've played that part before haven't you? Pretty well too. Nearly as well as you played numerous other parts. Are their many of you in acting circles? Physcopaths I mean. Because you're little friend behind you. He's a pretty good actor too."
"Oh dear me Mr. Lassiter. I think we'll just have cut this a little short. I tend to rush things a little these days. Must be my age. Blood pressure's been playing me up lately. Did you hear?"
"Oh yes I heard. But what I didn't hear was the truth. The patient in the hospital did have high blood pressure. But then he's had it all his life. No fucking wonder. I would too, if I had a son like that. Nice touch that. You're neglecting your duty doctor. I really feel that nose may be broken. But then how the fuck would you know? You're no fucking doctor. But you WERE a half-arsed nurse of sorts at one time. Don't you think it's time you stopped shielding your face with that ridiculously large hood. Pretty pointless now. Your little friend's not bothering to. Nice to see you again. You're nearly as good an actor as he is Congratulations. Still getting enough drink bought for you?"

****

Dawson's familiar voice crackled metallically over the police radio. Amazingly, he still sounded calm
"We woul appear to have a problem here Chief."
"Nature?"
"Nature of a fucking sniper taking officers down from an old, abandoned Ford Transit in the supermarket car park, across the street. Two officers down. Repeat two down. Leg shots only. The bastard's good. He's firing through the rear door hinge as far as we can see at the moment. Can't really get a clear view. Get a helicopter or something here."
"Tom. Get in there and stop that fucking lunatic now. I don't care how you do it. Now get out the car! I mean it. Use what it takes.

But I want them alive. All of them. Out the car! Now!"
And with that the Chief Constable's driver hit the accelerator and the Merc. careered across Taylor's immaculate front lawn making full use of sirens , blue lights and anything else he could think of.

****

His reaction to the events outside suddenly brought it home to Lassiter. He was quite, quite mad. Both he and Sarah were in deep, deep shit. And the other one behind him was laughing also, as though nothing had happened!
"Dear me. What's this neighbourhood coming to? No place for anyone to live this!"
And Lassiter knew he meant every word he said! Especially he and Sarah were concerned

****

.
"Take ma' word for it. That's who it'll be." said Horner. "Must be. You only learn to shoot like that in two places. Polis and army. It's that tosser fae the Scotstoun team. Wan ae them onwiy."
"But he told Dawson..."
"I wish you fuckers were jist as fuckin' gullible, when ah'm lyin' tae yese. Dawson wis set up win't he? You'se lot should know a' aboot that shoun't yese? Youse are fuckin' experts!"
Hagan started to laugh. Hegarty started to curse. Then he started to think. He entered Taylor's garage and pressed the intercom.
"Lassiter? Jim Hegarty. You'd better let me speak to him. They've only left me here. His plan appears to have worked. Tell him to let Sarah come out, and I'll come in in her place. It's a sad fact of life. But he'll have better bargaining power with me. A serving police officer. Daniel Taylor knows that. So far he hasn't killed any law officers. Only leg shots. Ask him if he'll speak to me. There's no one else out here. Tell him to send his friend out to see if you like. There are two spare cars here. C.I.D. cars. But the officers who drove them here both left with the Chief Constable. Tell him to check."
Lassiter stared cooly at them both and then at Daniel Taylor. He didn't speak. Taylor did.
"He's right you know. All the stops are always pulled out to save a police officer's life. She's nothing by comparison. Listen to what he's saying. Please. You don't have to kill us all. If..."
"Shut up you. You make me sick to my stomach. Lassiter you go with my friend to the back door and see. With any luck she'll still be alive when you come back."
Lassiter knew that he had taken two men at the same time before. But those two men hadn't had three boning knives in their

possession at the time. He led the way to the back door.
"If he's telling the truth, let him in. But she's going nowhere. I have plans for her. I have plans for all of them. I might make them all kill each other. That might be fun ."
That was when Taylor started being sick on the expensive carpet.

****

"Whoever he is, he started firing the moment the Jaguar disappeared, and we started to dismantle the road block. He's good alright. Both officers got it in virtually the same place. Same leg too." Dawson took a final draw from his roll up and flicked it away. He looked ready for anything. Bradford was going to use that.
"What's he doing here?" He pointed to Phil Jamieson.
"Says Horner sent him. To tell us he thinks it's Rankin. Must be fit. Got here before you."
"No way. Horner must have known beforehand, and dropped him off nearby. He wasn't at Taylor's house."
"Aye Ah wis. Fucked off eftir we goat there."
"Well you can repeat the performance now. This is police business."
"Nae chance. Ma brither goat his throat opened by wan ae these bastarts. That makes it ma business. There's a wiy up the back ae that supermarket. Oan tae the roof. Yese'll see better fae there. Ah'm sick breakin' in tae that joint. Fuckin' dawdle."
"Dawson, get up there. See if you can get a clear shot. But that's all, for the moment. Do you hear me? Just see. Nothing else. Clear. You'll have to let him show you how to get up there."
"Right."
Jamieson and Dawson made off down the street, using parked vehicles for cover, till out of range.

****

"Two Jaguars. Both empty. And him."
"My,my Inspector Hegarty. Jaguars, no less? Paying the C.I.D. too much money obviously."

"They were escorts for the Chief Constable. But they all had to go as you obviously heard. Something very major going down elsewhere. But I believe you know about that already."
"I really don't know what's happening to this area at all. All down to poor policing if you ask me. What do you think Lassiter?"
"You really don't want to know what I think. About anything. Especially you."

"Now, now Mr. Lassiter. That's no way to talk to a well respected pillar of the community."
"No. But it'll do for you won't it?."

****

Rankin knew he was going to die that night. Rankin didn't care. He'd stopped caring much about anything after being drummed out of the army. But he did care that his father didn't die that night. He'd believed him when he told him that his father certainly would die, if HE didn't do as he was told. What he didn't believe was that that he could trust him. Fuck! What a mess.
Maybe, with a bit of luck, that Lassiter guy might just get lucky. Rankin had had the makings of a good soldier at one time. A remarkable marksman, he'd definitely showed promise. But promises can be broken. And so can concentration. If Rankin had not been drummed out of the army so quickly, he might have learned more. About the importance of reconnoitre before any mission. And the importance of the surprise element. The Ford Transit had been abandoned at the side door of the warehouse of the grubby old fashioned supermarket, now one of the downmarket, bargain hunter concerns. Everybody had had the opportunity to move the Transit. No one ever had. Rankin's problem, although he didn't know it, was that it was parked too close to the emergency exit door of the supermarket. And the roof. But Rankin had other concerns.
The sound of whirling rotor blades announced the arrival of the police helicopter. And the police marksmen.

****

"Right Lassiter. I'm always interested in myself. Tell me about myself. Because it's never going any further than this room. None of you are. I know that much. What I haven't yet decided is the method. I'll think about that as you tell me how you came to be in such a dangerous position, through your constant prying into my affairs."
"Good a place to start as any. Your affairs. You swept a young chambermaid off her feet when you were still fairly young, and fathered two children. They were in and out of your life with amazing regularity later on, only they didn't know it. They knew you, but they didn't know who you were. You would enjoy that I'm sure. You enjoy destroying families don't you? Is that because your own turned their back on you? Father and sister? So you were determined to be more respected than her, and more feared than him. But to be cleverer than them both too. Very important that. Very important. Because they both told you something when you were younger. That you might be different from them. Your father was a career criminal. Very

violent, very dangerous. So were you. But the difference was this. Your father was bad. On occasion very bad.
You were mad! Quite mad! And not on occasion. On a permament basis!"
"Carry on. That last statement just decided how you will die. But do go on. We should have time. The police should be occupied for quite some time yet I believe."
"Let me go to your medical "career" First nursing. You were quite capable at that. You studied hard at night school. Through that you gained a number of things. And a number of connections. You were employed for a time as a trainee male nurse in a mental institution. Some dangerous people in these places. But you were more dangerous than any of them. You knew it. The authorities didn't. Complacency again, you see. You got friendly with one of these slightly less dangerous patients, and introduced him to your father when he was released. Enter the Meredith connection. James All of your lives have been connected ever since. The Turners and the Merediths. Through marriage, through business, through the medical profession. And through murder. But not all of you are guilty of involvement in that. I honestly believe only you and the odd little bastard behind you knew the whole truth about that. And I don't think even he knew everything. How could he?"

END CHAPTER

CHAPTER FORTY THREE

THE BODY OF THE HALL

Rankin knew the arrival of the helicopter meant it was only a matter of time. It depended how long he could hold them off . He knew they would be able to pick him off easily now. He had no chance with any shot from above.

The helicopter was above and ahead of him. But there was now also someone above and directly behind him. Dawson dropped the smoke bomb from the roof, just as Phil Jamieson burst through the emergency exit door with the "SUPERSAVER" bargain claw hammer above his head and , more importantly, right above Rankin's. Above him Dawson took steady aim with the Mauser.
"Seen "Dirty Harry" have you?"

****

Lassiter's mind was working overtime. The hood had been thrown back and he had felt Sarah's body stiffen next to his, He clutched her hand in his. To stare at him too much could provoke him too early. It also made Lassiter physically sick to look at him. He could not begin to imagine what was going through Sarah's mind. Even Taylor's. It would appear he was in as much danger as they were. What the fuck were they dealing with here? He changed his approach.

"There are quite a number of things I do not understand here. Perhaps you could help me out ?"

"All that meddling and you don't know all the answers yet? Ask anyway. I might tell you before I kill you. On the other hand I might not."

" "Adjie" Jamieson? Why did he have to die?"

"He was one of my mistakes. Oh yes, I have made a few along the way. Another mental aberration. I'm referring to him when I use that expression. Another mental patient. Oh he was ruthless and cunning alright. He served his purpose a couple of times. But he also served himself a couple of times. A low life. He deserved a low death. The man behind me has proved more dependable over the years. If a trifle squeamish on occasion. Not tonight though, in case I give you any false hope. Wouldn't want to do that. No mustn't do that."

"And you're children? No feelings for either of them?" He smiled and spat out the reply

"Of course. Utter revulsion."

"You're a fucking reptile!"

Lassiter knew he had gone too far. He lunged towards him with the the glittering blade and the glittering, hate-filled eyes just as the intercom from the games room came on.

"Hello? Gil here Are you both alright? The door was open. Anybody in? I need to speak to Daniel. There's a very serious incident just down the road."

It was nothing to the serious incident that then began in the Taylors' luxurious front lounge.

For a man of his age the speed was astonishing. Lassiter would certainly have been dead if Daniel Taylor hadn't caught his ankle as he lunged forward, the wicked, razor-sharp blade held above his head. Reaching down with other hand he pulled Taylor to his feet by the hair. The action was performed in one fluid, continuous movement. The next one obviously was going to involve the drawing of the blade across Taylor's throat. The problem he had with that movement, was that Danny Hagan and Johnny Horner had just arrived at his rear via the upstairs landing window. The one Lassiter had told Sarah to make sure she left open. The one right next to the gun cabinet, the contents of which the "doctor" had supposedly come to inspect. Horner clubbed the smaller man in the hallway across the temple with the heavy wrench from Taylor's garage and Hagan contented himself with holding Hegarty's police issue revolver at the

base of the "doctor's" skull.
"Move a fuckin' muscle Meredith ya bastard an' yir brains are a' ower the fuckin' carpet!"
"Thank fuck! Both of you!" said Lassiter. And then, slightly more calmly. "It's not Meredith incidentally. And I'm sure you recognize the other little bastard. Don't you? Hope you haven't killed him Plum. The only reason I say that is that the police need him alive. Other than that I couldn't give a toss. Come on Sarah. Out of here. You too Daniel. You'll have to get that seen to. That doesn't mean I'm sorry I did it. You've got some guts after all. I would say thanks but I wouldn't mean it. Not after what you did to her. And her mother. So I'll settle for this. If ever you need my help again don't hesitate to go elsewhere. Now I believe my friend Hegarty here will accompany you. He really DOES need to talk to you. I don't. Now, I have a lot of friends I really do want to talk to. Hello Gil, girls. You ladies will have to keep a very watchful eye on me tonight. I can't remember when I last wanted a fucking drink so much."
"Just remember why you wanted to stop so much."
"Maggie, I've said it before, you make everything sound so simple. Come on Sarah, P.J.. Gil, would you take Butch and Sundance over there. Your nerves up to driving your Jaguar Maggie?"
"I'm not sure Lassiter. I don't know if I....."
"You'll get over it. One thing's for sure. He'll never sit in it again. Will you C.J.? You're still in good shape for your age. That should give you all the more time to rot somewhere. Wish I could watch. And you Andy. You'll probably have a lot longer. You can relax a bit now, Danny. Here comes John Wayne and the Seventh Cavalry."
Dawson came in at a crouch , Mauser clutched straight out in both hands. Bradford followed looking very concerned and then very relieved. Then what seemed like the entire Strathclyde Police Force .
"I'm taking MY back-up for a drink now if that's all right with you Chief Superintendent."
"Course it is Lassiter. Before you go. Is that bastard dead?" Bradford pointed to Andy Lynch's inert body stretched out in the hallway.
"Unfortunately, not."
"There's a great you still have to explain Lassiter."
"You'd better fucking believe it. This is not over yet. Not by a long chalk. Come on Sarah. Let's go troops!"

END CHAPTER

CHAPTER FORTY-FOUR

COMMENCING TALKDOWN

"Right Lassiter. Explanation time. First of all, let me offer my sincere thanks to you and everyone else who helped you sort out this bloody mess and help us catch this fucking monster. And his little sidekick. I mean that. Particularly Mrs. Taylor. Very brave lady that."

"Sarah's got more guts than the rest of us put together. I'm sure you'll understand why she wants nothing to do with that name anymore. Not that it was ever his real name anyway. It was Turner. Ellen Turner did have a brother. And he did spend a lot of his youth in physciatric care as a child. First as a patient and later on in life as an enthusiastic trainee nurse. His father looked after him financially, but other than that had very little time for him. He spotted something in his illegitimate son that disturbed him a great deal. Turner was used to people being afraid of him. This boy wasn't. Afraid of him, I mean. Never at any time in his life. Old Turner lavished all his attention on his daughter. All his life he doted on her. All HER life she loathed him. She had no fear of him either. She knew he would never harm a hair on her head. But she WAS afraid of this decidedly odd, violent half-brother. I never did get the length of discovering who HIS mother was."

"Amazing resemblance between him and the real doctor guy. Meredith."

"Purely co-incidental that. And used very cleverly over the years to great effect for mutual benefit. But it was purely co-incidence, as I understand. You may discover something there. But I doubt it. Ellen Meredith and her husband are guilty of concealing a great deal of things over the years however. Like THEIR son for starters. And how they would consider doing virtually anything for sufficient money. And also how, way back thirty-odd years or so ago, all their paths crossed once more, and they hit on a method of doing just that. You see Doctor Patrick John Meredith had a brother too. And he wasn't exactly an angel either. But he knew a bit about the metals industry by that time. The legitimate metals industry. Well it was before THEY started fucking about with certain areas of it. I'd never have uncovered most of this without the help of a lot of people Chief Superintendent. Maybe none of it. Not your average upright citizens some of them, admittedly. But last time I looked none of them were homicidal. Horses for courses. I'd ask you take that into account when dealing with them. They are real friends of mine. I think you'd agree they proved that last night. All of them."

Bradford gave Lassiter, Hegarty and Gil his official Chief Constable stare. Then he nodded and gave Lassiter his full attention.

"It's a long story and will take a bit of time. Any decent coffee? And I think I'll need more fags."

Hegarty grinned and went to the door of Bradford's office to pass on Lassiter's requirements.

****

"They met at university. Apart from

medicine they had something else in common. He was very arrogant, and obviously heading straight to the top of his profession. She was arrogant enough to decide there and then that she was going with him. She decided to become preganant by him. And then he'd feel committed to her which ,oddly enough for someone like him, he did But ready to appear back in her life was someone who really did need committed. And never had been. This information was supplied to me by my friend PJ., or Doctor Patricia Jeffries as she's better known nowadays. P.J. had also had a difficult youth and Ellen Meredith sympathised with her struggle to become a doctor. Ellen Meredith was not without some feelings for others. At any rate she confided some things to her that are important in this case. Whether some of it was by accident, or not, is unimportant. The fact is she did. And that's how I first discovered that Turner had a son. And that in his youth the same son had associated with Patrick John Meredith's younger brother James. Where Paddy John Meredith was arrogant, his younger brother was wayward. A would be gangster. Only a would be, however. Never really tough enough. But he knew some people who were. He too was slightly unhinged. Unstable. Turner junior could use people like that. In the late sixties and early seventies the young people in Glasgow, like everywhere else at the time, had a very free and easy attitude to sex. Life was for living. Live fast. Because maybe a lot of them weren't going to live too long. So they indulged in a lot of sex. What they had scant knowledge of was contraception. When Turner heard he may have fathered twins to a barmaid he disappeared down south with the younger Meredith in tow. He wasn't prepared to take any responsibility for that slut and her brats. But later on he would take on the responsibility for other peoples's children. He had no choice there. But that move made sense. He had two reasons for doing this. One of them was business. And the other because of who he had killed. And that's when his real children came back to haunt him and life started to get just a little bit difficult for him. And very, very dangerous for some people who knew him. Or thought they did.

Because her brother had been present the night Thomas Gallagher was attacked outside the pub, Phillippa Jarvie knew first hand that he had nothing to do with the assault. Reggie had never lied to his sister and vice versa. They were very close. Still are. When she discovered years later of Daniel Taylor's presence the night Gallagher was hospitalised, the opportunity arose to perhaps make some money from her hated employer and she could scarcely believe her luck when she did. All because of a film she'd seen. What neither of them ever knew was why. Or who thought it worthwhile to make sure she kept her mouth shut. Turner knew that Gallagher had to die that night. And it WAS because of money. But not money owed to young Morton, the blossoming moneylender.

Gallagher didn't owe any money to anybody. But he did know something about certificates. Hospital certificates. Now this is where I started to get everything wrong so I don't blame anyone else for doing the same. This is very important because it blew my theory away completely. But thanks to Maggie Hagan, and strangely enough the younger Meredith brother's metals firm, it gave me another theory. The right one. And it started me thinking along totally different lines. Driver's lines! And remember Gallagher was a driver by profession. My coffee's nearly finished Jim."

"You must have hollow legs. Thank God it's not still bloody vodka you're on. Chief?"

Bradford nodded assent to coffee as Lassiter reached into each pocket in turn of his leather jacket for his cigarettes.

"Now it starts to involve the young barman Andy Lynch. And why his hearing wasn't so good that night. Or his memory thirty years later. But he certainly did everything else right thirty odd years ago. Just as Turner or C.J. Taylor or whatever the bastard was calling himself by that time told him to."

Lassiter lit his cigarette, and lifted his mug of coffee.

****

Doctor Campbell nodded to the pretty nurse and then to the capable looking policeman on duty outside the locked room where they were holding Andy Lynch.

"He should be alright by morning. However that was a very substantial blow to the side of the head he took. The officer here will make sure nobody gets through that door if you're called away for any reason. The drip stays in till morning. I'll check on him then.. No visitors whatsoever officer. Only this nurse here to be allowed in to check on his condition at any time. Very dangerous man as I undertand it. That is why he is so heavily sedated. But then you know all this already."

The police officer nodded.

****

"Before I go on," said Lassiter, "I take it it goes without saying that these two bastards are being securely held well away from each other?"

"Lynch is under twenty-four hour police guard in hospital. You've got your pal Horner to blame for that. He needed medical attention I think you'll agree. You were there. You saw what happened."

"I bloody heard it. He did not fuck about did old Plum."

"Who/"

"Never mind. Unimportant. And the other one Chief Constable? Where is he? I believe him capable of anything. Even now."

"At the moment he should be getting ready to depart for the District Mental Health Institution or however they refer to these places nowadays, where he will remain until his trial date."
"Political fucking correctness. He's a bad bastard however you care to say it. Fucking lunatic." growled Hegarty into his oversized coffee mug. Lassiter grinned at him.
"Why don't you just use the soup tureen from the police canteen Jim? Be smaller. Easier to handle." He ignored his old pal's glare and lit his umpteenth cigarette.
"Right I'll get on with finishing what is, and always was a very complicated and very sad story for some very important people in my life. You're right Jim. He was just a bad bastard. He still IS just a bad bastard unfortunately.

.

END CHAPTER

CHAPTER FORTY FIVE

TALKDOWN AND COMEDOWN

"They know he's their father now. They've both been informed. I have no right to withold information of that nature. And nor do you Lassiter." Bradford looked more relaxed than at any time since Lassiter had first met him. "It was all going to come out now in any case."
"Nor would I," said Lassiter. "What was their reaction? They're a strange pair at the best of times."
"And that's exactly how I would describe their reaction. Phillippa Jarvie seemed almost proud somehow. The daughter of some sort of celebrity or something. Reggie too. Or maybe it was the shock of seeing him sober for once. I don't know. But he had a very strange look in his eyes. I think it was mainly the fact that he wasn't drunk, and pretty smartly dressed for a change. But something else. The fear had gone. As if he'd suddenly become somebody again."
"He has. He'll live off this story for the rest of his life. Her too. Anyway I am about to tell you the real reason why Thomas Gallagher was killed. It does indeed involve doctors and certificates and hospitals. And most importantly of all. Metal! This is where the information supplied by Maggie Hagan was so important. The brain can play tricks on you because of what the eyes and ears tell it. And if the information is wrong, so is the conclusion it reaches. Or mistaken at any rate. Here we go."

****

"You're not the same policeman. The one I saw earlier." The pretty young nurse going in to check on the restrained Andy Lynch was being extremely careful, just as Doctor Campbell had told her to be.
"Naw, hen. There's mair than wan polisman in Glesga. Same as nurses ah bet. An' doactors. Even visitors tae the hoaspital. Bet ye thae nurses ur a' different when their shift chinges tae."
She laughed at him, and herself for being stupid, and allowed him to open the room door. Wasn't she going off duty herself at six and hadn't that old Doctor Meredith just started duty instead of that other good looking young Doctor
O' Connor? Pity that.

****

"Both the Meredith brothers were, are and for all I know, probably always will be criminals. What they're not-certainly in this case at any rate- are murderers. And neither is Ellen Meredith. There are only two. C.J. Taylor and Andy Lynch. Some of the other people I know in Glasgow admittedly may have come pretty close at times. You've met some of them. But Glasgow's always been like that."
"Too fucking right." muttered Hegarty. Bradford merely nodded his head in assent.
"Right. Turner/ Taylor, as I'll call him for the moment, and young Meredith between them both knew about metals from way back, and they were both pretty good salesmen. And Turner had money, because his sister didn't want to know too much about her father's money at that time. But her fucking husband did. And that's where it all started. In the early days of their involvement in metals, Taylor and James Meredith simply set about terrifying the existing oppositon by various means. That changed with the passing of the years and they started to employ more conventional methods. Like blackmail, extortion, fraud and simply forcing other people out of business. Run of the mill stuff." Bradford smiled behind the folder about Meredith Metals he was pretending to read.
"And here's where Doctor Patrick John Meredith makes his arrogant reappearance . Does he remind you of someone incidentally? Someone a good deal younger. I'll come back to that. As you know the new hospital was under construction back then. A dripping roast for metal firms if they got the contracts. Or "A" metal firm, if that particular metal firm landed the contract in it's entirety. That firm was –you've guessed it- Meredith Metals and who was the driving force behind that? Patrick John Meredith's younger brother and more importantly his brother-in-law, one C.J. Taylor, as he was now calling himself. I don't know how he swung it but Doctor Patrick John Meredith did. Along with something else. His wife's opinion of both his and her brother had also changed dramatically by now, once she

saw a seemingly endless supply of money on the horizon. Life had started to chip away at her scruples. And what did Thomas Gallagher have to do with all this? I had no idea till Maggie Hagan started me thinking along different lines. Lines? That's quite funny. Driver's lines were what eventually got Thomas Gallagher killed. Quite good that."
Hegarty had started to look very puzzled. And Bradford was too, but he wasn't going to show it.

****

"Ah'm tellin' ye. Somethin' big's goin' doon an' neither even me nor Hagan knows whit it is. That big eejit Malky's been left in charge ae the Jamieson pub. Nae bastard knows whaur Jamieson is. An' the polis should huv kept Reggie an' that queer sister ae his in the jile, cos they've fucked off an' a."
"You're sure. Them too?" Horner's agitation was rubbing off on Gil. "Surely to God Taylor's not still calling the shots. He's capable of trying. We know that."
"Let Lassiter know."
"YOU let me know as soon as you hear anything. Danny too.
"Nae bother. Watch your step. An a' thae lassies tae. P.J. should be a'right wi' Hagan aboot. Maggie tae. Whit aboot Mrs. Taylor. Whaurs she it?"
"Fucking Hell!" said Gil out loud. "I think she's on the way to see her mother nursing home by herself. That fucking prat she married is still in hospital himself. Meet me at the nursing home Plum. And bring Danny and the girls."
Gil put the phone down and smiled across the desk at Sarah.
"Let's go Sarah. What will be, will be."

....

"All this business about things Gallagher said about "death certificates" and "guns and medals" really had me fucked up for a while." Lassiter was now looking fairly relaxed about things having had sufficient caffeine and nicotine in his bloodstream for the present. "They made some sort of sense but not sufficient. Then Maggie Hagan unwittingly made me realise that he hadn't referred to either. Gallagher had actually been talking about things "metal" as opposed to things "medical". Nor had he been talking about guns as such. There's a morning DJ does a spot about misheard lyrics. Give it a listen sometime, both of you. You see what Theresa Gallagher had actually heard her husband talking about on the phone to someone, was not death certificates. What he had actually said was "TEST CERTICATES." Metals documentation, in other words. And

when Andy Lynch's statement of thirty odd years ago stated Gallagher mentioned "guns and medals", that was a complete red herring. Must have been C.J.'s idea. No, what he really was referring to was "gunmetal"
"Eh?" said Hegarty. "What the fuck's that then?"
"It's a type of leaded brass alternative or something apparently. Used in bearings for heavy artillery and the like. But that's not so important at the moment. Similar fraud on the army at some time, probably. It's this "test certificates" business. Taylor and James Meredith were obviously supplying sub standard, or even scrap, metal to the hospital. Instead of the prime, properly certificated Grade A stuff they should have been supplying. Criminal. Now do you see where I'm heading?
An awful lot of money involved. No mere driver was going to be allowed to fuck it all up."

Bradford narrowed his eyes and moved forward in his chair.

****

Gil kept his eyes firmly on the huge artic. headed south with it's load of structural steel beams, joists, channels and the like.
"I'm staying well back from that bastard," he said half to himself and half to Sarah in the passenger seat. She didn't answer.
"And that's all she said? You're sure it was her?"
"Oh it was Phillippa alright. We spoke often enough. I'd know her voice anywhere. And no she didn't say where she was phoning from. I've told you Gil."
"Tell me again."
"She said. "I'm really sorry for all you've gone through Miss Sarah. You were good to me."
"And that was it?"
"Yes, Then she just hung up."
"Fucking hell!"

He turned into the nursing home driveway.

****

"When I asked you earlier if Daniel Taylor reminded you of anyone I was probably being unfair to both of you. I've spent more time in his company. And his father's"
"It couldn't have been easy for you in there with Taylor and Lynch." said Bradford. "Any of you."
"That's my point. C.J. Taylor is not Daniel Taylor's father. He's his uncle. Or half-uncle or whatever you want to call him. Patrick John Meredith M.D. is Daniel's real father. And Ellen Meredith his mother.

JAMES Meredith is also his uncle therefore. God help them all. The arrogance? The ignorant behaviour? And the reason for all those years of deception is really quite simple. Nothing criminal there. Sarah would have had nothing to do with him if she'd known who his real father was. Theresa Gallagher would never have allowed it. Bad enough that they bore a physical resemblance. C.J. Taylor and Meredith I mean."
"For fuck's sake, Lassiter. Why?" broke in Hegarty.
"Because it was very important to Taylor, C.J. Taylor that is, that he had a reason to be close to her. To get her to trust and confide in him. He had to know that she didn't know, or even suspect, anything."
"Fuck's sake Lassiter. You know how to break off relationships in style." grunted Hegarty . "Most of us just settle for giving the fucking ring back."
Even Lassiter and Bradford had to laugh at that one.

****

"Good evening officer. Doctor Patrick John Meredith. I'm filling in for the doctor you met earlier. Dr. Campbell? And I believe you know Nurse Bryce. Is that correct? These two gentlemen with me are hospital employees. Porters. There's a bed in that room that we must have. A spare one I might add. Not the one containing your suspect. We're not that short of beds. But we are short. Could we remove the vacant bed please? By all means come in with us. In fact I would prefer it if you did. Thank you so much. I know the Chief Constable personally. I'll mention your assistance to him Constable.... Crawford? Thank you so much Constable Crawford. No after you. I insist."
Constable Crawford was glad to help. He liked to help. So helpful he failed to notice Reggie remove the drip and Phil Jamieson the cap from the base of the inverted drip bag as he bent down to help in freeing the legs of the two beds which had somehow become entangled.
"Thank you so much Constable Crawford. Yes, if you could just pull the door behind you. That's it. I think we'd better let Mr. Lynch sleep hadn't we? And thanks once more for your assistance. Who knows. You may just have saved somebody's life tonight. I'll be sure to mention you to the Chief Constable when next I see him. You're a fine officer. Good man. Good evening again. Nurse would you check the patients drips are still secure every half hour or so? Because it could be life threatening if they're not. Thank you. "

****

"It was Rankin and the involvement of the Scotstoun team that first

made me think there might be something odd about Andy Lynch. When I met Rankin supposedly for the first time in the "Grapes" that night with Gil, Tony Pearson and the others I knew I'd seen him somewhere before and later I remembered where. The night Gil and I met Lynch in that Clydebank pub Rankin had sent Lynch a drink over. I also found it odd that someone from Drumchapel would have a Clydebank pub for his local. And Scotstoun is very near to Clydebank. Drumchapel is also of course, only in the other direction. However it did register that Lynch and Rankin seemed to be pretty friendly. And both Hagan and Horner knew him well also. That at least put him on the fringes of Glasgow's sixties gang element. And now he was mixing with the Merediths and the C.J. Taylors of this world at their golf club. Co-incidence? Maybe, but it made me think. And where was he the night Gallagher got attacked? Behind the bar in the very pub where Gallagher was last seen. If Hagan and his back-up boys-and girl, hadn't attacked Gallagher, and Reggie and the Morton crew were too busy running out the back door, who did that leave? Hagan? No. He and the rest were too busy wrecking a pub. The police found Gallagher lying badly injured outside the cellar door of the pub. Why the cellar door? Why there? I had a theory about that. And the little shit proved me right when he appeared at Sarah's with her "doting father-in-law ". I think I'm ready for some food now Tom. Your canteen up to much?" Lassiter rubbed his eyes with both hands.
"I'll get something sent up" said Bradford.

****

C.J. was very sure of two things. One , that he would be released without charge as Lynch would be too terrified to give evidence against him. He had money for his lawyer-the best criminal lawyer anywhere-to get him completely vindicated. And then he would attend to every last fucking one of them. Lassiter last. And that spineless bitch he had still had the hots for after thirty years. They would be last.
He giggled to himself alone in the back seat of the blacked out Range Rover heading for the district mental health institution. The handcuffs infuriated him. Didn't they realise who he was? He liked the sirens and the blue flashing lights from the police escort though. SOMEONE knew how important he was. That much was evident.

****

"Tell your mother to try her best with all this Sarah. You're very

lucky really you know, no matter how much pain you've had to suffer. Not every one has parents they can be proud of. I hope you'll be able to see that someday. Lassiter's a clever guy. He'll get everything right eventually. He's got someone you can trust in there. Danny Hagan. Danny and Maggie will drive you back " Gil had a strange, faraway look in his eyes behind the horn rims.
"Where are you going Gil? You don't look well. Are you alright?"
"Got something to do kid. Press business. Pressing, press business. Good eh? Still a newspaperman you know."
"Be carefull Gil. You don't look well. Are you alright for driving?"
"Just tired kid. Old and tired. See you later kid. Tell Lassiter to watch his back now the show's over. Tell him the real "Adjie" said that. He'll know what I mean."
Gil put the car in gear and headed for his final meeting with Daniel Taylor. They still had a story to put to bed. He was glad Pearson had phoned him that afternoon with the news. It made things a bit simpler. Not much. But, a bit.

****

Lassiter felt refreshed after the break for food and the second cigarette.
"When you find yourself in a dodgy situation with possible trouble at both exit doors it makes sense to sit where you are doesn't it? Unless what? Unless a friend offers you sanctuary somewhere else. Even safer. And that's exactly what happened to Tommy Gallagher that night. A friendly barman ushered him into the pub cellar until everything blew over. And then drew a friendly knife across his throat from behind, before pushing him outside the emergency exit door. Nobody ever looked for any blood inside the cellar. Danny and the others were too busy wrecking and thieving to worry about a "terrified" barman who'd locked himself in a cellar to escape them. It was only years later- some thirty - odd to be -exact- that Danny remarked to me that it wasn't really Andy Lynch's style. A coward he was not. A "bit of a fuckin' nutter" was how Danny described him to me. One worth the watching. And that meant something coming from Danny Hagan. Now whether C.J. Taylor was also in that cellar that night or not is immaterial. It's got his mark all over it. His style. His motive. His total lack of any kind of compassion. It runs in the family. Where the Jarvies only inherited their father's lack of compassion and vicious streak the other two got the lot. They inherited the one thing from their father the other two didn't. His brains. And if you don't move very quickly on this, they might just go on to use them for the next decade or so."

"Fuck's sake Lassiter what are you trying to tell us now. More of them? He's got more fucking offspring than go to Parkhead every Saturday."
Lassiter had never heard Bradford swear. He found it amusing for some reason. Hegarty obviously didn't. He'd also thought it was all over.
Lassiter decided not to tell them the rest. For the moment at any rate.

END CHAPTER

CHAPTER FORTY SIX

TO THE END OF THE ROAD

"Who are you talking about now? It can't be any of your old street friends, be cause none of them HAVE any brains do they?"
"I'm sure Dr. Jeffries and Maggie Hagan would be over the moon with your assessment of their intellect Chief Superintendent."
"You said it was a man Lassiter. Or men anyway. I'm not deaf."
" I don't think I did Chief Constable, but alright. Have it your way. But don't think for one minute that Horner, Hagan and yes, even Reggie and Phil Jamieson, are withot brains as you put it. You don't stay alive in their way of life for as long as they have without them. "Adjie" Jamieson couldn't have had too many admittedly. Look what happened to him. The drink may have eventually got to Reggie, but he was never stupid either. Besides it was Danny Hagan's brilliant memory for the old days that got us the Lynch connection. And who Jessie Jarvie's husband or whatever she called him, really was. And Horner's contribution. Some of the smartest people I know are experts at appearing stupid. Or gentle and harmless. There's one on his way to a secure unit now. How long did he get away with it?"
Bradford suddenly took an interest in shuffling the documents on his desk. Lassiter could teach him a thing or two and he knew it
"Right we're on the home stretch now and..."
Suddenly Hegarty burst back into Bradford's office from the incident where he'd gone to check things a few minutes previously.
"Forget everything. Some bastard's just topped Andy Lynch. In the hospital maybe. He's fucking dead anyway. Car's waiting to take us there."
"Listen to me Bradford. Send someone else. They want you with Lynch to take your fucking mind off Taylor. Trust me on this. Get in touch with the vehicle moving Taylor. Something is going down . Even bigger than before."

****

"I knew and he always knew it could come out of the past to haunt him at any time. All in all he seemed to cope with it pretty well. Lived with it. He'd had these turns before. That was why I was so mystified by his sudden recovery. I can understand it now Makes sense now after what you've just told me Patricia. I've got to go. There's a fatality at the hospital. Nothing unusual I know, but this one shouldn't have happened For a number of reasons. The police have just lost a very important material witness and murder suspect. And maybe me a very important job."

"Thanks Bill. Don't worry. It's not you're fault you're caught up in this. There are still some very dangerous people involved here, according to a friend of mine. Really dangerous."

P.J. Jeffries put the phone down on Dr. Bill Campbell and his puzzlement as to why C.J. Taylor had got better so quickly and why Andy Lynch so dead so quickly.

****

"It's perfectly alright nurse really. These are two very close friends of mine. Is it all right if they stay? They haven't seen my mother in years. Maggie and Danny Hagan they're called. They're going to run me back home when visiting's over. I'm still on a lot of medication and can't drive. No don't worry about Danny. He always keeps his coat on. I take it you won't mind if he nips in and out for a smoke now and then. There may be other visitors later. Thank you."

"Certainly Mrs. Taylor. You're mum's a lot brighter today incidentally. I'll bring tea through shortly."

Maggie and Sarah gave the nurse their brightest smiles. Danny Hagan didn't. Nor did he give her his coat and axe.

****

"Hagan and his sister are with Sarah at the nursing home. Rankin's still banged up isn't he? But his three mates aren't. Where the fuck are they Jim?"

"It's alright Lassiter. We hauled them back in so Rankin would have company before he gets life."

"It's more than Lynch or Jamieson have got. Assuming Lynch also did Jamieson, that leaves Phil and Reggie still on the loose. Reggie's sister who is decidedly odd, and all the Merediths. And Horner and all the scum he knows. That all?"

"You might not even be close Chief Superintendent. You're certainly far out on one or two of them. At the very least."

"You're far out Lassiter. Always have been."

"Thanks Jim. Now go back to sleep. This definitely the road they woul take?"

"If it isn't, somebody's dead for giving me the wrong in formation"

Bradford was in a foul mood now. "Again! It's happened again" he kept muttering.
"Let's hope I haven't got the wrong information" Lassiter spoke to his reflection in the rain speckled back seat window.
The Chief Constables Mercedes was really shifting now. Ten minutes or so. Timing! Timing! And this time it had to be spot on! It fucking had to be!
Alone in the back seat Lassiter seemed infuriatingly relaxed about the whole thing. He knew something about timing also.

****

"On no account must any member of the public approach this man. He is very highly dangerous and was en route, under police supervision, to be held under maximum security, awaiting trial.. He was due to appear in court on at least one murder charge and the suspicion of others. He was also due to be charged with the attempted murder of a number of people in premises at......"

Daniel Taylor switched off the portable television in the hospital ward. Taylor was a very bad patient, as all the nursing staff already knew. He too was still under police supervision and awaiting charges being levelled for conspiracy, illegal firearms and whatever else the police could come up with. Lassiter had offered to help the police in any way he could there. Taylor, being Taylor however, had already convinced himself he would beat any charges. Daniel Taylor had inherited his real father's arrogance and, to a lesser extent-much lesser- C.J. Taylor's callousness. He would blame his uncle James- Meredith-, his wife or if nothing else was working his mother and father. Most of it was their fault anyway. They made him do it after all. And after all it was C.J. Taylor who'd pulled Gallagher's drips out when the nurses all thought he was the real Dr. Meredith that night. In a way you couldn't blame him really. There was a lot of money at stake. A lot of money. Sufficient to pay somebody to engineer his escape from a police escort taking him to a high security prison. In some respects Taylor still admired C.J. Until he remembered the eyes that that was. And his laugh. Especially the laugh. How the fuck had he done it? Escape like that?
"Switch that back on sir. The lives of fellow police officers are at stake here."
It was not a request from the officer at his bedside and the "sir" was heavy with sarcasm
"That man tried to kill me."
"And a number of other people also as I remember it. Including your wife. Thing is, I might finish the job if you don't fucking switch it back on. "Sir"

Dawson looked like he meant it. Dawson did.

****

"Police are interviewing the driver of the articulated vehicle at present and at the very least there will be charges concerning the unsafe nature of the load of metal he was responsible for. What is of prime concern at the moment is that both the vehicle concerned, and even the metal itself, are the property of Meredith Metals a company almost wholly owned by the escaped prisoner . The load spillage caused a temporary diversion to be...."

The nursing staff in Theresa Gallagher's nursing home tried not to look at the very tough looking man , with one hand in the left hand pocket of his smart overcoat, who had suddenly joined them as they watched television in the room set aside for smokers and television watchers. Nor did they pass comment on his unasked for statement.

"Gaun yirsel' Maggie! That wis ma wee sister that done that!"

Suddenly Danny Hagan was the only person left in the smoking room. He wouldn't be for long

****

.

Lassiter flipped the mobile phone shut and gave his dry laugh after Sarah's frenzied phone call from her mother's nursing home. He had a mental picture of the chaos Danny had caused at the quiet little home for the sick and elderly.. The arrival of armed police would certainly have brightened old Theresa's night up. Theresa would like Danny. At least he now knew they were all safe. He wondered briefly if Danny had surrendered his axe yet.

Fucking nutter, Hagan!

****

"Listen hen, ah mean doactor. It wisnae as if ye'se knew aboot the murders an' that. Ye'se wur intae a fiddle big time, aye. But that's a' Who wisnae in thae days? That right P.J.? Ye'se wur a' feart fae him. Goat that? Even that eejit boay ae yours. Yir man's a stuffed shirt an' a crook right enuff but he's no' a killer. He's jist proved it tae the polis. Him an'a"

Horner nodded in James Meredith's direction who was sitting beside him in the front seat of Horner's Jaguar parked outside the Western infirmary in Glasgow's rough Anderston - cum - Partick area. "An' whit he disnae know, wherever the fuck he is, is that that wee shite Lynch isnae deid. Never needed drips in in the furst place. But

Lassiter waanted somebuddy tae think he did so he could git tae him. Somebuddy that wid go tae Jamieson an' wee Reggie tae feenish the joab again. Same kind ae trick thoan C.J. Taylor dun wi' yir man in the hoaspital wi' the blood pressure an' that. The doctor didnae know it wisnae Taylor in there sick. An' they two baith know better than tae cross me again! Ah think Phil might still think ah'd sumthin' tae dae wi' openin' he's brither's throat. That WIS Lynch an' Taylor. But ah cannae tell Phil that. Ye need tae keep some ae them in their place."
He reminded Ellen Meredith a lot of her long dead father. A career criminal. But somehow he didn't seem so bad any more. Not really. Maybe she should have tried....
She shook herself out of it and took P.J.'s arm as they got out of the car, to go into the hospital.

****

Dawson was looking at his watch too often. He was obviously waiting for someone to arrive. Or for something to happen. Either way it really disturbed Daniel Taylor. He got the same vibes from Dawson as he did from Lassiter, Gil and a number of other people. That they actively disliked him or even worse. Under normal circumstances it pleased him to annoy people. But not in Dawson or Lassiter's case. They were liable to do something about it. So he was relieved when Dawson spoke.
"Change of shift soon. I don't like the smell in hospital wards. But I really hate the fucking smell in this one. Funny it seems to be worse in your room "sir". Ah good that'll be your other visitors I think."
Taylor looked up expecting the little tap on the room door to perhaps be a family member or maybe a nurse.
An unlikely duo entered and he was suddenly very frightened again.
"Hello Daniel" said Gil in a tone of voice Taylor had never heard him use before. Very, very menacing.

"I've got someone with me. Couldn't keep her away as a matter of fact."
"There are drips and drips Mr. Taylor." came a terrifyingly familiar voice from behind the half-open door. Phillippa Jarvie entered the room.
"Right, I'll be off then." said Dawson cheerfully.

END CHAPTER

CHAPTER FORTY SEVEN

THE LAST DANCE

Lassiter had to sit alone , preferably in semi or even total darkness when he needed to think. Sometimes he would play some of his favourite music from his large and varied record collection. Sometimes not. Tonight it was not. His flat was in total darkness now as he wrestled with the last piece of the jigsaw. Because he knew if he did not find it, and find it now, he may as well not have bothered with finding the first piece. This was very far from over. And he had a matter of hours to press home the final piece. The press! Bradford had used them , and the media in general, with great skill over the last thirty six hours or so. As far as the general public was concerned another man had died in the same hospital as Thomas Gallagher had some thirty years earlier. The name had not been disclosed, but Glasgow's reading and viewing public knew that both the suspects in the Gallagher case had escaped justice. One dead. The other at large after a daring escape from police custody. The television images of the hijacked police Range Rover, with the blacked out windows, and wide open doors, had been flashed all over Scotland. Inept police had allowed persons unknown to stage a road spillage and force the police vehicle to a halt. An extremely violent and dangerous physcopath was once more at large. And one marginally less so had been allowed to die in hospital Also under police guard! Glasgow's underworld knew the the names however. They knew C.J. Taylor had escaped and that Andy Lynch was dead.

Glasgow's underworld could not have been more wrong. Andy Lynch was still very much alive and C.J. Taylor still very much locked up! The press had been extremely careful with their wording. There had been no lies told. But skilful use of language had led an awful lot of people to believe that the police had screwed up yet again just as they had done some thirty years previously. They hadn't! Lassiter had called in a lot of favours to achieve that impression. The way people used words told a lot. Lassiter had spent the last half hour or so trying to remember exactly the words Theresa Gallagher had used when describing her two visitors to the nursing home that day. At the time when he had thought one of them may have been Horner, he had shown her a photograph of him which she had shaken her head at negatively and vigorously. She had described them both however. One scary, one older. Not old. Older!

Suddenly it became quite important that "Adjie" Jamieson was Phil Jamieson's slightly younger brother. Older. Not "OLD" C.J Taylor, Patrick John Meredith, Crombie. They could all now be referred to as old. The visitor with the scary man had merely been "older"

Lassiter was starting to get somwhere. She'd also described her not so scary vistor as well dressed. Well dressed and older. The field narrowed again.

****

"Right. Ah've goat folk tae see later. Ur ye awright Phil? Look son ah know "Adjie" wis yir brother an' that, but see whit happened? It wis bound tae happen tae him sooner or later. The wiy he wis kerryin' oan. Fuck's sake, ye telt 'im yirsel often enough din't ye? But ah know he wis faimily right enuff, an' ah'm sorry fur ye. Ah'll gie ye a phone the morra, or drap in tae see ye. Thanks fur the photie ae the three ae us gaun tae that weddin' By fuck we a' look smart in it right enuff. Dressed up like tailor's fucking dummies. Even you. Only kiddin' son. Jist tryin' tae cheer ye up a bit. Lassiter says tae tell ye that you an' that wee shit Reggie done a rare joab at the hospital. Wi' Meredith ah mean. Everbuddy thinks Lynch is deid."
"If ah'd hud ma wiy he wid be. Didnae know ye wur sentimental Mr. Horner Waantin' a photie ah mean?"
"No' sentimental Phil. Jist gettin' auld Phil. Auld an' daft son. An' careful!

****

Sarah stared at the telephone receiver in total disbelief . The woman had to be mad. Or was she trying to drive Sarah mad? Did she think for one moment that Sarah could stomach being in the same room as her. Especially now that she knew who her father was? And her brother. And then she said the one thing that could have made any difference.
"It was Mr. Lassiter's idea that I phone you."
"What do you want Phillippa?"
"To tell you that I never meant to harm you. I..."
"Right. You've told me."
"You were good to me Miss Sarah. Like an angel. I'm going to pay you back."
The line went dead and suddenly Sarah realised that there had not been a hint of malice in Phillippa Jarvie's words. Quite the reverse in fact. Sadness. Regret. But not a hint of malice.

****

Lassiter still sat alone in the darkness. He'd known him a lot of years now. But so much of it they'd spent in different places. Did they REALLY know each other nowadays? Had they ever , come to that? Or Danny Hagan? Did he know HIM any more? When he thought about it he only really knew more about himself now, and his feelings for Sarah. And he now knew who had killed Thomas Gallagher of course. He knew about the two physcopaths Taylor and Lynch. And he thought he knew who Taylor's real sons were by now. And if he was right, these two were even more dangerous than

their father. They too knew how to appear to be relatively harmless. . Maybe even better at it. And they weren't old. Only older. And smartly dressed. That eliminated a few people right away. Like Hegarty and Gil. Or did it?
Lassiter really did believe in practising the sermon he preached. Trust no one. He remembered what Tony Pearson had told him not to broadcast. If Gil really hated Taylor so much then why hadn't he taken the opportunity to ruin him over the Phillippa's half-arsed attempt at blackmail? Could there be things concerning Gil himself, from thirty years previously, he didn't want investigated . And the photograph of them both at some press do or other. Pritchard dishevelled and half pissed. Gil without glasses and looking sober and handsome. And very elegantly attired!

****

He looked at himself one last time in the mirror, and was satisfied that the new suit was up to standard. Like his others. Couldnae let them a' see him lookin' inferior tae Horner. Horner jist THOUGHT he knew how tae dress. Too fuckin' flash but. Hagan really did know how to dress. Everybuddy said it aboot him. Ayewis hid knew how tae dress. Plum hid never been in the same league as him. Fur onythin' Fightin', weemin' you name it. Hagan wis yer man!
"Right P.J. Ah'.m ready tae go tae that poofs pub they a' drink in. It'll suit some ae them that's fur sure. Mind ye Horner's no' jist as bad as ah hid him doon fur. Done the business fur Lassiter an' that's a fact. No sae sure aboot that bastard "Adjie" any mair right enuff. Fuckin' Taylor done mair than him that night. The young wan ah mean. The newspaper eeejit."
"Danny. He didn't do that for any other reason than the fact he was staring death in the face. Not for his wife. Not for Lassiter, not for you or anybody else. For himself. Why do you always admire the wrong people. And , more importantly, trust the wrong people. You were right about Lassiter though. I'll give you that. Clever AND tough. Watch out Hagan, I might just leave you for him."
"No dae him much good bein' clever and tough if he's deid an' a'."
"Oh grow up Hagan. Right, I'm ready tough guy."

....

It was a different coldness he was experiencing now. It terrified and paralysed him with it's intensity. It came with the realisation that he had been outhought and out-manoeuvred. He wasn't going to get out of this bastard cell. Ever. Lassiter! Lassiter!
For the first time in his life C.J. Taylor was experiencing it. The starkness of it had a numbing effect.
Unadulterated terror. Was this how they had felt? His victims?
Alone in his cell, C.J. Taylor sat down on the hard bed. And alone

in the cell C.J. Taylor started to cry. And then scream.

They weren't going to help him! Oh fuck!

****

Lassiter picked Sarah up a couple of hours before leaving for the final meeting in the "Grapes". His normal facial expression was that of a man slightly tired of life and it's pitfalls. He did not look that way tonight. Determined, forceful yes. But something else. Happy. Lassiter had the final piece of the jigsaw. He now knew who had helped Taylor and Lynch escape justice for so long. His lone visit to Theresa Gallagher's nursing home, with only a photograph cut from The Glasgow Voice for company, earlier, had confirmed his theory that no way did their thirty year criminal activities go unchecked without someone's help. Somebody with clout. Someone who knew how to use the press, and the media in general, with practised ease. And he'd just done it again. And had been doing for the last thirty-six hours or so. That was why Lassiter had told no one of his suspicions for so long. No one!

Including the press and the police. Especially them!.

He wasn't letting anyone close to the jigsaw board now. Not till the big picture was there for all to see and the lid very firmly on the box.

....

"Do you remember Sarah? I have no idea why it all happened that way but it did. It was a gang thing. A culture. No matter where you went at that time they had a reputation for it. Down South. Up North. It didn't matter. They would grudgingly admit that the Glasgow boys- and girls- knew how to do it. Dress, I mean. Remember? And dress well. We spent a lot of money on clothes."

"When did you get out of the habit Lassiter? Just joking. I like your old leather jacket. Suits you. What's all this about , Tom? And why is everybody invited to the "Grapes?"

"Because by pure co-incidence , organised by myself and other people of course and actually entirely unco-incidental, the "Grapes" are having a good old fashioned sixties/ seventies night tonight . And all our friends are going to be there. In a time warp. Together with somebody who's nobody's friend. But quite definitely warped."

"Lassiter, I think I just want to forget. Put it behind us. We deserve..."

"Sarah, this case is not closed. Your father's murderers are behind bars and that is where they'll probably both die, if I've got anything to do with it. But there are still others involved. The architects of all this.. People I believe to be even more callous and dangerous. And I've got a confession to make. What I said about Reggie and Phillippa Jarvie being C.J. Taylor's children? There now seems to be

something of a problem with that. He did indeed have two children by good old Jessie from Maryhill. But they were both male. Reggie and Phillippa Jarvie did indeed grow up with Jessie and latterly, and very occasionally, Taylor in Maryhill as their children, but they weren't. They were twin brother and sister yes. Taylor's children no."
"But why did you tell everyone..."
"Because that's what I was told at the time. They are quite plainly someone's beloved twins but they're not Taylor's. And I now know whose. Remember the drunken nurse? Nobody would believe her story about dark deeds concerning drips removed from dying patients, when she drank the way she did. Then why bother listening to her tales concerning two doctors who sanctioned the swapping of two children for another two. Just because the supposedly adoring father didn't want the first two. Because one of them happened to be a girl. And he didn't like girls. Well not enough to admit to having fathered one at any rate. The old nurse was dead on. In both instances."

****

Bradford was more relaxed than Hegarty or anyone else had seen him for weeks. It was all over bar the shouting. As the song said the only way now was up. Or something like that. Two particularly brutal murderers safely under lock and key, and he was more than happy to take the plaudits undoubtedly on their way for his sterling work. Take the Commisioner's mind off that stupid bitch from Greater Manchester, or wherever the fuck she was from who'd been getting all the applause recently. Women had no right to be Chief Constables anyway. Especially when she outranked him. Of course he had had to keep that opinion very much to himself. Not politically correct in this day and age.
Hegarty did not think it advantageous to his own career to voice his opinion on that score. Nor to remind Bradford that so far everything had been more or less down to Tom Lassiter and HIS sterling work.

****

Horner looked at Lassiter with his best Carlo Gambino stare.
"D'ye mean tae say ah've kerried this fuckin' daft photie aboot a' day, an' took the shape oot ae a good coat jist fur ye tae tell me..."
"I'm really sorry Johnny. I know it wasn't Phil Jamieson now. But the age group fitted and I thought it might be worth checking. Give him my apologies. For everything."
"Disnae know it wis fur you onywiy. Thinks ah've went saft. My Goad there the Kinks oan! C'moan Maggie. Gie's a wee birl roon the

flair."
Lassiter leaned back in the comfortable chair in the private function room upstairs in the "Grapes", The private function itself was in full swing and the sixties/early seventies music was strangely apt for the confrontation that undoubtedly lay ahead of him that night. Closure at last. He watched Horner and Maggie disappear into the middle of the crowd thronging the small dance floor. Horner was basically a good enough guy really. Pity about his lifestyle. And his coat. He could always buy another. The young was DJ first rate. Knew the age group and the era. He'd done his homework. And he was young too. Too young to remember any of the stuff that he was now playing. It didn't surprise Lassiter that he seemed to really like most of the music he had been asked to play. The music had been different class then. Everything had.
Even Hagan looked more relaxed tonight, sitting across the table from Lassiter with P.J. He and Horner had even been laughing together earlier over some thirty year old escapades. Good. Lassiter needed them like that. Especially Hagan until he finally confronted him with it all. Old pals my arse! Things were undoubtedly goiing to get very nasty later.
All Lassiter had told Hegarty was that they were going to going to come face to face with the people who had really taken over the fair city of Glasgow when Ellen Meredith's father , old "Scrap" Turner, had eventually shuffled off his mortal coil. And although he had the right men in C.J. Taylor and Lynch for the Gallagher murder there was an even bigger fish. Or "fishes" as he had put it. It was very important that Bradford and Dawson both be there. He didn't really care if they brought the entire Strathclyde Police Force but it might make it more difficult to stay out of sight until they got the signal. The one only Hegarty knew.

****

Hegarty didn't look uncomfortable but Bradford did. He also looked faintly ridiculous out of uniform. In public Bradford was never out of uniform but he was tonight. And it didn't suit him. Nobody else in the downstairs public bar of the "Grapes" took a blind bit of notice of the two off duty postal workers sitting quietly in the corner, but Bradford still felt very uncomfortable. Dawson and his team looked the part certainly as assorted plumbers, scaffolders electricians and so on. Bradford just looked like a Chief Superintendent dressed as a postal worker.
"Relax Norrie for God's sake. Nobody in here will recognise you without the diced bunnet with the silver decorations, and the jacket with the pips. And you're not the only guy in Glasgow with a moustache." said Hegarty out the side of his mouth. A difficult feat,

as he was taking a swig of his pint at the same time
"It's different for you and the others. Your face hasn't been in every newspaper and on every television set in Glasgow. Especially recently."
"Your's may have been, granted. But not wearing tinted specs and a woolen tammy." Hegarty chuckled. He was enjoying Bradford's discomfort.
"Lassiter better have a good reason for all this fancy dress crap."
"He always has had before. For everything" said Hegarty thoughtfully, hoping Bradford didn't notice the sideways glance he had given his superior.

Bradford sat in stony silence.

****

Lassiter sat alone at the table as the others danced. He was not a dancer. Never had been. He watched Maggie Hagan, now dancing with her brother. Why had she done it? Lied to protect him for all those years. Maggie was no criminal. Neither was she easily frightened. Hagan had no idea that Lassiter knew now. Why the fuck had she done it?

****

"And that's how it all happened. Ellen Meredith and her prat of a husband helped cover it up all those years once more. The swapping of those children in the maternity unit of the hospital. Just because some important bastard wanted twin boys instead of a boy and a girl. So C.J. Taylor, who didn't want any family anyway, terrified Jessie into settling for dear little Reggie and Phillippa, instead of his own twin boys. I'm surprised he even let her have them. And she did her best with them knowing all along they weren't her own. Says a lot for her. She didn't have any choice in the matter admittedly, but it still says a lot for her. So you see Sarah maybe Phillippa Jarvie has a point. She's not Taylor's daughter after all. But God help her she thinks she is now. Think about this? Would she have phoned you to apologise if she was? Doubt it. No feelings you see. Feelings don't exist in the Taylor make-up. Well not any one else's at any rate. Would you agree? Maybe she's just never had a break. Until you gave her one. Fuck knows about her twin brother though. Never could take to that little shit!"
"Maybe he just never had a break?" Sarah gave an ironic little smile. "And who told you all this? It's all true? What's wrong now?"
"Oh nothing. I was just thinking about what you said about that little shite Reggie. Maybe you've got a point there. And yes it is all true. Stack of bibles. But it was very important to three people that no

one found out. You're going to find out who they are tonight. And then you and Theresa can really try and put this behind you."
Sarah Taylor knew for certain then that she loved an old ex-drunk who only seemed to posses one old, worn leather jacket

And a king-sized heart.

****

Lassiter hadn't wanted to face up to it at first, but there were too many things now forcing him to. The main one was Danny's deep distrust of Gil. No. More than distrust now. Dislike. They had been very close at one time in their lives. At the root of it all was Hagan's inability to change. Gil had obviously changed a great deal. Danny had not. Could not. Why? His loyalty , and old fashioned gang mentality had started to give Lassiter some sleepless nights recently. He had very suddenly turned against his old right hand man. But only after he'd been re-united with him. What was all that about? Lassiter knew that that same old loyalty would ensure his silence about whatever it was. But all that was going to change. And change before the night was out. Hagan would be forced into it. When the main guests arrived. The gentlemen of the press. Followed by the gentlemen of Strathclyde police.

Strangely enough, the one man he wasn't too worried about was Johnny Horner. That would probably have been a disappointment to Horner, Lassiter was quite sure. Anyway "Plum" was in his own time warp. " Last Timing" it away in the company of Mick and the rest of The Stones. But he was worried about something else. He'd just seen three familiar faces arriving at the door of the private function suite. An accountant type and two salesmen types. And they had tickets. Danny had his back-up now. Bloody hell!

Lassiter barely had time to note THEIR arrival when Gil, Tony Pritchard and a very small man in a Homburg hat, and an immaculately tailored Crombie style overcoat, appeared behind them.

Lassiter waved the newspaper contingent over to the table in the furthest corner of the lounge which the bar staff had reserved for his press guests.

But not before he checked where Hagan had got to. And Hagan was now deeply involved in conversation with the three men who looked like salesmen, but were anything but.

****

Lassiter had always had the ability to sit in a company of people, take full part in that company of people with regard to idle conversation, but with his thoughts elsewhere. His mind raced constantly. It was no doubt impolite, if not a major character flaw, but he couldn't help it and it worked for him. He could also give people his undivided attention when required. He was very good at that too. So maybe it was a major asset. Flexibility. At the moment his mind was in overdrive. And his memory. For the umpteenth time that night he had to remind himself of the police presence downstairs. And his signal for them later. Which was why he'd arranged with the DJ, the bar staff, and anyone else who needed to know, the importance of his instructions being followed to the letter. Or the lyrics to be precise. And to make sure they suddenly blasted out in the downstairs bar. He was now in the hands of the the pub's sound system. And so were an awful lot of perfectly innocent sixties fanatics. That he could not help but it still troubled him greatly.

"You know, when this is all over I'm never coming back here."

"Glasgow."

"Possibly. But I know I won't be able to stay away. No, I'm talking about this fucking pub. I've hated it since the day and hour I first set foot in it. Never a real pub Glasgow pub in the first place."

"Well, you should know Lassiter."

"Why did you cover up for him for so long Maggie?"

"He fooled me too Lassiter."

"Not as much as me."

"Much as I detest what he and the Saville Row team over there have been up to all these years to try to take over from old "Scrap", I swear I didn't know Lassiter. Do you believe me?"

"If I didn't Maggie you wouldn't be going home tonight. Believe that. You still haven't answered my question."

"He asked me to help him. I didn't really know what with. Even back then, when we were all young he was different from the others.

"What do you mean back then. When the DJ stops for his break I want you, Sarah, and PJ to disappear to the ladies. Only you don't go to the ladies. You go downstairs and you go home. Understood?" Maggie nodded. This was the Lassiter of old talking.

"That serious?"

"That fucking serious. And incidentally you're spot on about the city. Just wrong about the street."

Maggie stared back at Lassiter. Why did he always have to talk in riddles?

****

"'Member that wan Lassiter? The Pretty Things? Thoan singer hud longer hair than the Stones. Mind?"

"Will you do me a favour Johnny? A big favour. Something's going down later and it doesn't involve you. When you see the three girls

excusing themselves to go the ladies at the break, go with them."
"Eh?"
"Not to the fucking ladies Johnny. I've told them to get out of here. Just like I'm telling you now."
"An' huv Hagan toss his aixe at ma back oan the wiy oot. Nae chance. Ah'm no' turnin' ma back oan anybuddy Lassiter."
"He won't do that. Don't you worry about that. Too much on his mind. And you don't really think anyone in here tonight could be carrying weapons tonight. Other than one or two policemen downstairs that is. Dawson for one. And he'll either shoot you in the leg -he's excellent at that- or Hegarty will shoot you in the arm. And then Bradford will give you twenty years. Now what do you say Plum?"
"Stoap ca'in me that. Ah'm a respectable gangster noo. Follyin' lassies tae the toilet! Like bein' back in the auld Barraland fur a quick swig oot their cairry-oot. But seein' as ye pit it like that. That Dawson's no right in the fuckin' heid by the way. He's liable tae shoot somebuddy right enough."
Lassiter grinned. He'd grown to quite like this hoodlum.
"You're not wrong there, Plum. Sorry. Couldn't resist it. You go downstairs and then you go home. O.K. The police won't stop you."
"That'll make a fuckin' chinge."
Lassiter grinned again. The tension was easing slightly with each one of his friends he was getting out of the way. Hagan was the major problem now. As he had been all along, if only Lassiter had been able to see it. The glaringly obvious, yet still undetectable problem. He had lied about his reasons for not trusting Gil, so had he told Lassiter the truth about the events leading up to the Gallagher murder in the first place?

END CHAPTER

FINAL CHAPTER

CHAPTER FORTY EIGHT

"GRAPES" PRESSINGS

"Gil, Tony. Give me your hat and coat Bill, and I'll put them behind the bar for you. It's going to get very warm in here. You're all looking exceptionally smart for men of our profession, I must say. Let me get you all drinks first, and then we can talk. Thank fuck we can all relax a bit now, eh?"
"He'll give you his coat. But I don't think I've seen him without his hat in twenty years or more. That right Bill? Bill's Homburg. A legend. He buy's a new one from time to time, of course. But other than that I'd bet he sleeps with it on." Gil looked relaxed, Tony Pearson ever so slightly pissed, and Bill Crombie very,very out of place. And time, come to that. Even for the sixties atmosphere the

staff and customers were doing such a grand job of generating.
"Gil. We have to talk later. All three of us. There's something still not sitting right with me in all this. Maybe you lot can steer me in the right direction. You came in the side way like I asked? Good. It's about good old Danny boy. Don't look now, but he's up at the bar and he's got the three salesmen of the month for company again. Who are these bastards and what the fuck has he invited them here for?"
Without looking round, Gil muttered something to Pearson who sobered up rapidly.

"The ones who pulled the shotgun stunt in the Jamieson pub?"

"None other. And I don't think they're here to dance ."

Lassiter looked at the three men as Tony Pearson stooped to inform old Crombie of whatever it was that Gil had just said to him. And Bill Crombie's reaction let Lassiter know that he had been right all along. Or recently at any rate. The late arrivals were dangerous. Very dangerous indeed, judging by Crombie's reaction. The police were downstairs certainly, but he and all the others were upstairs. And it was getting close to the time where all the cards or pieces of the jigsaw had to be placed on the table.

****

Lassiter whispered something to Sarah in passing as he walked over to Hagan and his entourage at the bar.
"That's my boy," said Gil softly to Pritchard and Crombie as they all sat down in the semi circular bench seat at the rear but facing the bar. "Go for it, Tommy kid"
Pritchard's eyes narrowed and Crombie's face took on a more watchful look. He was suddenly deeply interested. And he hadn't been when he came in.

****

"Awright Tommy boy?"
"No I'm not fucking alright. Why? That's all I want to know. Why? Have you got any idea, any conception, of how much I trusted you, and now it comes to this. All because you refuse to change.
To grow up. Despite your sister asking you, your woman, old and dear friends. You're a loser Danny. And tell him to take that look off his face, before I fucking knock it off. You're bespectacled friend there. I'm not that old and he doesn't impress me one bit. Not one

fucking bit. Now let me tell YOU something. I knew you'd try some of this shit. The police are downstairs. And they're armed some of them. Think about it."
Lassiter turned his back abruptly on Hagan and the rest and walked back over to Gil and the newsmen
"Gaun yirsel Tommy boy! Oor time's comin" said Hagan quietly.

.

"He's got balls Danny. I'll give you that. Let's see if he's still got them at the end of the night." said the accountant type thoughtfully. His companions said nothing.

****

Lassiter deposited Crombie's Crombie coat behind the bar with a nonchalant wink to the barmaid and headed back across the crowded dance floor to where Sarah sat alone in a fairly secluded corner. The press could wait. Sarah could not. His nonchalance was an act. A sham. Bradford's words from the last two occasions that they had been in each other's company on very dangerous occasions , rang like an alarm bell in his mind. Timing! Timing!
"When Maggie and the others leave so do you Sarah."
"I'm not leaving you on your own Lassiter."
"Sarah , you are. And that's that. And stop staring at Hagan and his boys. That's the last thing they need. Or me come to that. . There's still a lot more to this than there would appear on the surface. CJ and Lynch are certainly the killers. No doubt about that. But there are other people just as responsible for your dad's death. And they're in this pub at the moment. And they're not getting out. Not till I say so. And then we can finally put this to bed. Once and for all. You see someone's been leading us all up the garden path right from the start in this case. About silly little Reggie, and his equally silly sister. And about the Merediths too, by and large. And Horner and the Jamiesons. Everything. And they made very clever use of the media and myself, and the police to do it. And they very nearly got away with it too. Would have done if it hadn't been for one office junior or whatever they call them now. Trainee journalist she is really. And a very good one at that. She put two and two together and believe it or not came up with four. Or three to be precise."
"I could kill you when you do that Lassiter. Bloody riddles"
"You'd better be quick. Or patient. I believe there might well be a queue.
"I'll tell you this much though because I don't have the time for the rest. The fact that your husband is and always has been a randy, two-timing bastard and that you had the audacity to throw me over because of him, is the key to it all. That, and the fact that Jill, the girl who works at "The Voice", remembers her job interview almost

word for word. And the two people who interviewed her for the position. Neither of them being your dear husband. And guess what? She's a fabulous investigative journalist in the making
She's been working solely for you and I since you asked for my help. The campaign against Hagan was just what he wanted really. Too obvious. Seeming victimisation. Got the public on his side to some extent. Took their mind off the real issue. Just as he wanted all along."
Lassiter sat alone as the DJ drew ever nearer to the end of his first set. He really was very good. Very professional, with a feel for music that was written and performed when he was very young, if even born. You couldn't be taught that. It was a gift. A talent.
"Ladies and gentlemen. I don't want to , but they tell me I have to. Take a break that is. It has been a real privelige to play some of these sounds. Well, all of them really. This is class .Real class. So I'm heading for the break with three continuous. The Small Faces and "All or Nothing", Creedence Clearwater Revival and "Bad Moon Rising" closing with Arthur Conley "Sweet Soul Music". See you all after the break."
Lassiter waited for meltdown

****

Downstairs Bradford checked his watch for the fifteenth time in as many minutes. The strain was showing. Hegarty looked at his long time boss as though really seeing him for the first time. Lassiter had been right about him too. Just as he had been about everything else. Was the bastard ever wrong about anything? He sincerely hoped not. For both their sakes.

****

Lassiter stared intently at each of them in turn. Horner first, then Maggie and P.J. Jeffries, Gil, Pearson and the finally the strange little man Crombie. Quite a collection. And then you had Hagan and HIS very strange friends. He was very,very glad of the police presence downstairs. Because the instant he lit the blue touch paper for this lot, anything could go down. Anything. He eventually turned back to Sarah. She had to know. Everything. It was her right. And his obligation. She might be left disillusioned again. But that was better than dead. She had to know before she left. And there was now very little time.
"Let's take our drinks over to the corner Sarah while it's quiet because it's not going to stay that way. That's for sure. And I'm not talking about the music either."
As he passed Gil and and the other two gentlemen of the press he

laid a hand on Gil's shoulder.
"Give me ten minutes. Here'a menu, if any of you feel like eating later. Very probably indigestible in any case. Keep your eye firmly on Hagan and his business conglomerate over there for me. This thing has always been about Hagan really. From the off."
"No problem kid."

****

"Tell me something before I tell you what I know. And can prove. I know she only met him once but I value her opinion. What did she think of him?"
"Instant dislike. Strong dislike."
"And the other one?"
"She liked him. Said she saw a lot of you in him. I think she felt a bit sorry for him too."
"Good old Theresa. Never wrong about people."

****

"Noo shut the fuck up and listen tae me. Ah'm the wan that knows him. He knows sumthin'. An' when Lassiter knows sumthin', he's fuckin' dangerous. He wis ayewis a sneaky fighter. Jist when ye thought he wis fucked, he'd stick his haun oot tae ye, smile and yase the other haun tae hit ye wi' a fuckin' ashtray or sumthin'. An' a boot in the crutch oan the wiy doon fur good measure tae. He knows sumthin', awright. We might huv tae chinge things. We should huv sorted him when we hud the chance. Bastard!"

****

"You can't blame Maggie for this. She genuinely thought he had changed or was trying to, at the very least. When Danny Hagan was not charged with anything over your father's murder, other than mobbing and rioting and possession of a very offensive weapon, she believed her brother. There ensued a thirty year campaign by the media to right this dreadful wrong. As far as they and the police were concerned-or some of the police at any rate- Hagan did it. And look what happened. The real killers escaped justice for the same thirty years or so. But what also happened was that it took people's minds off all the other usual Glasow nonsense that had been going on both before and after your dad's murder. Including some very important events that had taken place at a Glasgow hospital. And I'm sorry Sarah , I'm not talking about your father's murder here. I'm not even talking about all the bribery and corruption with regard to contracts that resulted in that murder. I'm talking about two children being exchanged for two other children by a drunken nurse who just happened to be friendly, if slightly older, with the other drunken nurse who years later discovered something funny with regard to your father's life saving drips. And why are these children all so important? And more importantly, why were they exchanged in the first place? Let's take the second point first. They were exchanged for no other reason than that one of the fathers didn't like girls, and the other one didn't like anybody . As simple as that. One of these fathers went on to organise your dad's murder along with another physcopath, while the other-the one who wanted only male children-went on to become the undisputed orchestrator of crime in the city for the next thirty years. Talk about sins of the father? That bastard made Capone look soft hearted."

"Who?"

"Well, I..."

"Haw Sarah. Ah've no' hud a dance aff you yit. Mind ah've booked ye fur the start ae the second hauf."

Horner stood behind Sarah , slightly the worse for wear. Lassiter shook his head both in resignation and negation.

"I thought you had a prior engagement later. Oh for God's sake Sarah. Give him his dance then. Make it quick. And don't worry. It's not him. You're probably safer with him than anyone else in here right now. Including me. Remember our deal Johnny. Later? About the ladies room?"

"Oh aye, right. Ah'll be the talk ae Glesga fur weeks."

"And don't tell me you won't love every minute of that."

Somehow it made Lassiter feel a lot better to know Sarah would be with Horner before it started to get nasty. And somehow he also knew that Horner was going to keep the deal they'd made. He just knew it somehow.

****

When Dawson leaned across the table to steal one of Hegarty's cigarettes two things happened. One, he annoyed Hegarty who hated bad manners, and two he annoyed Bradford who could see the butt of the Mauser protruding from his inside pocket.

"For fuck sake Dawson. How may times do I have to tell you. You're not bloody Charles Bronson. He's better looking than you."

Hegarty chuckled and took one of his own cigarettes. A pipe smoker, he did enjoy the odd cigarette.
"Charles fucking Manson's better looking than Dawson. And probably better natured. Now listen Dawson. Lassiter is going to give us a signal. The only way he can do it from up there is this. When..."

****

"Maggie always knew that he didn't go to the pub that night because of his father. What she never knew was why. Believe me none of it was her fault. She could have prevented nothing. Trust me on that Sarah. I know Maggie. There is no badness in her. Unlike him."
"I think what amazes me most about you've just told me, is the fact that he fooled you Lassiter."
"Along with a lot of other people Sarah. The media campaign to incriminate Hagan was really a godsend to him. There was some very emotive language used , and all that that achieved was to divert people's attention from the real issues. The hospital incidents and the real reason for your father's murder. I'm sorry. Very sorry. And yes, I'm sorry to say he did have me fooled. I'm sorry about that more than anything. People are blind sometimes where old friends are concerned. Have blind spots at any rate."
"Lassiter you fool. Do you think I, of all people, haven't realised that now. Everything time I think of that bastard C.J., I cringe. It terrifies me. No it's just that you're more cynical than me. More street-wise. But you got him in the end didn't you? As soon as I can I'm going to divorce Daniel and marry you. You don't have any say in the matter."
"How about "fucking hell?" Sorry, but it's the best I can come up with at the moment. And I haven't got him yet. Or them, to be precise!"

****

Lassiter had to pass Hagan and his back-up as he made his way up to speak to the young DJ to organise the signal.
"Why are you still here Danny? You've had your last warning. They're downstairs and some of them are armed. And none of you are, or you wouldn't be in here. I know the bouncers, remember? Anything you want to tell me before I get the show on the road?"
"Just this Tommy boy. You're right enuff. We're no tooled up. But how dae ye know naebuddy else is? A loat ae people in here in't thur? An' they didnae a' come in the wiy we did. Best ae luck pal."
As he made his way up to where the young DJ was checking his equipment he realised that it was still the best he could come up

with.
"Fucking hell!"

****

All three of them were content to take a back seat , both figuratively and literally , and watch Hagan swagger across the floor and content himself with merely LOOKING dangerous for the time being. The older, more experienced man watched Lassiter intently for some time before he spoke very quietly yet very firmly.
"There's no doubt he knows something. And Danny knows it. But you have to stay alive before knowing something will do you any good. Those two little toerags who can't wait to be gangsters. What were their names? The two little shits who discovered that other useless shit "Adjie" Jamieson's body? They'd kill him for a fiver. Organise it."
The two younger men nodded. They knew better than to question a word he said. The last time they'd dared to, Jamieson was dead exactly one hour later. They had never dared to question him again. They had been very, very fortunate to get away with it all for so long. Amongst many other things, like looking like harmless professional people. And being anything but.

....

Maggie and then P.J. both hugged Sarah in turn. They both knew that Lassiter had only ever been in love with one woman. And now she had eventually made the right choice and asked his hand in marriage. Maggie exhaled a steady stream of smoke from her cigarette and chuckled.
"Go for it girl. You know you'll never, ever be able to understand him of course? I tried for long enough, and then just gave up. It was the same with Gil. Of the two I would say he was even more difficult to understand. Lassiter just liked to drink. Gil liked to drink, and then fight. Lassiter was just as good at that. But he didn't go looking for it. Gil did. Back then at any rate. You'll gather I wasn't very good at choosing who to go out with. I always seemed to fall for Danny's friends. And they ALL had to be able to fight. Part of the job requirement.. Just look at his three guests tonight for God's sake. Bloody fool that he is. Lassiter knows everything there is to know about it all now. Animals." Maggie's years of playing a part helped mask the unutterable sadness she felt inside now. She had to get away before she broke down. She was going to need a lot of help coping with this.
"No fool like an old fool" said P.J. staring across the hall. She still looked stunned. How much had he told her? Anything? Sarah said nothing more. She was learning from Lassiter already. P.J. was looking at Hagan's friends. Sarah was studying Hagan. The man's

body language exuded danger as he crossed the dance floor. Hagan knew it and enjoyed doing it. The little half-smile was no smile at all. What it was really saying to people was. Hope you know who I am. Heard of me, have you? She was terrified for Lassiter. Absolutely terrified

****

Lassiter handed the three requests that he wanted played later to the DJ and awaited his reaction. At that exact moment Gil handed the menu Lassiter had given him earlier to Crombie and awaited HIS reaction. They were miles apart.

****

"No problem. Will do Mr. Lassiter. I don't think they all quite fit in with the era though do they? I mean..." said the young DJ after checking to make sure he had all three as instructed earlier. Much earlier

"Just play the fuckers son. Just play them. And at that time."

****

"Lassiter's got big trouble" said Bill Crombie handing the menu over to Tony Pearson who hadn't seen it yet.

"He's seen right through the Hagan thing." He turned to Gil.

"Told you he was one clever bastard. Wish he really worked for us."

****

.

"For fuck's sake Hagan. Gie yirsel a break. Ye're even makin' me nervous."

"That's the fuckin' idea Plum. That's the fuckin' idea. An' when it dis start tae go doon you stiy the fuck oot it. Hear me? Eftir a' ah've done fur the bastard. Goin tae that daft fuckin' meetin's wi' him tae make sure he wis awright. Bastard! Back seat fur you. Hear me."

"Don't fuckin' threaten me Hagan."

"Ah'm no threatenin' ye. A word tae the wise that's a'. A word tae the wise. Fuckin' eejit reporter. He's been away fae me too long. He's forgoat some things aboot me. Needs remindin'"

Horner stared long and hard at Hagan and finally realised he was not joking. He nodded abruptly and walked away giving Hagan's back-up a wide berth as he did so. It was not his fight. "Fuck it!"

And he had already promised Lassiter he wasn't going to be there anyway. Nothing more. Clear conscience. "Yir on yir tod Lassiter! Best ae luck wi' yir auld pal. Thank fuck it's no' me!"

****

"You just press that button there. The green one. And the music from upstairs comes through to the bar. Bags the first dance mind." Betty was sixty if she was a day. But she was a damned good barmaid. And she knew better than to upset Strathclyde Police. She knew Hegarty and she'd seen this one on telly. Must be to do with that murderer that escaped on his way to the loony bin.
"He's never in here is he , Mother o' God?"
"No Betty. He's not here. Wherever he is right now he's definitely not in here. Thanks luv. Buy the girls a drink later. On me." Bradford smiled his media smile.
"Providin' we're still fucking alive." muttered Hegarty under his breath. "This could be a real bastard this one Norrie."
"But they don't have a Dawson Jim."
Hegarty stared across the crowded bar and nodded grimly. " How do you know? That Hagan bastard's capable of anything About half an hour yet? That right?"
"That's right. Timing, Jim. Timing. Critical."
"Hope to fuck none of us end up critical."
They both grinned. Police humour.

****

Lassiter knew Hagan better than Hagan knew Lassiter. He had known all along that Danny would not risk starting anything while his sister and his lover were still in the "Grapes." The same could not be said of the other three. They had no such inhibitions. Their brand of violence had no time for such drawbacks. They would react when the time was right for reacting, regardless of who might be there. For there to be a reaction however, there first had to be a reason to react in the first place. And it was getting very, very close to the time where he would provide them with that.

****

Hagan watched as Horner collected his camel hair from the impromptu cloak room. And was astonished to hear him ask for Maggie's, P.J.'s and Lassiter's good looking woman's as well. Like every one else involved in this he had stopped thinking of her as Daniel Taylor's wife long ago. She was Lassiter's woman. That much was obvious more so by her attitude to him than his to her. He'd always been an odd fucker that way. Still, that was his problem. The fact that all four were obviously about to leave, meant only one thing to Hagan. With the exception of Lassiter's bint they were all doing as he had told them earlier. They must have persuaded her too. Or else it had been him. It didn't matter one fiddler's fuck. They were all going. He could now do exactly as he pleased. And what Lassiter was afraid he would. Always had been too soft when it came down to the nitty gritty shit, Lassiter It had never been one of Hagan's failings. Nor the other three.

****

"Promise me."
"I've already promised you Sarah. I'll be as careful as is humanly possible. But they have to be provoked. And they have to know who's provoking them. Do they think for one minute I believe they came in here empty handed? Any of them? I remember Glasgow dance hall tricks too. Their chosen weapons of mass destuction are in here alright. All of them. The fact that they've all been searched and nothing found means exactly that. Nothing. All it takes is for one or two of those inebriated grandmothers or spinsters up there twisting the night away to have been asked beforehand, and they'd have smuggled in a fucking truckload of armaments. Why do Glasgow women do these things for Glasgow gangsters? They've always done it. Since the sixties at any rate."
"I didn't. And I wouldn't."

"That's only because I never asked you." Sarah had to think hard about that one. Would she? If he'd asked? She honestly didn't know the answer to that one.
"Now get out of here. With the others. They're waiting. And Horner's just fucking bammy enough to be reconsidering. Get him out of here. And tell the other two girls thanks from me. I love them both. Jealous?"
"Not in the slightest."
"Fucking charming!"
"Don't get killed. Please."
"Get out of here. And tell Horner too. And make sure Hagan sees you all leaving. Alright?"
Sarah nodded still terrified for him. She gave him a childish peck on the cheek and hurried away without looking back. She'd kill herself if anything happened to this man. She knew the answer to THAT question if anyone ever asked.

....

Tony, the DJ, had been slightly puzzled by the bits of paper Lassiter had originally scribbled the requests on. But he'd searched all three out, and brought them as instructed. Unrelated and different from some of the stuff that was going down so well with the crowd up to now. But he had learned right from the start never to try to figure out the request spots. They only meant something to the person who requested them. And those who had been told to listen out for them. Or not as the case may be. After all everybody liked a surprise didn't they? And Lassiter was the man paying.

Lassiter, on the other hand, was out to make sure somebody else did. It might be thirty years late. But they were going to pay alright.

But what he did know for sure was they wouldn't like his surprises. Any of them.

****

"Are you sure gentlemen? Nothing to eat at all? The night's young and if you're going to enjoy it, you're better on a full stomach is what I always say. And it's all on Mr. Lassiter. You're quite sure?"

"I don't really give a shit what you always say. Mr. Lassiter is...."

"Please excuse Mr. Crombie my dear. He's not feeling too well. I think it's all the noise. And the heat. I'll explain to Mr. Lassiter later on. Thanks very much for you're concern, Please take a tip in any case. You're an excellent waitress. Please."

Cheryl stuck the fiver in the half pint glass along with the other smaller tips and flashing her brightest smile , went back to the serving hatch.

"Heat and bloody noise? Don't know how he can hear much with that stupid bloody hat on his stupid old head. Or hear anything. Old fool. Too bloody old to be in here anyway." she said to the girl who was making up the meal orders.

They both glanced over to the table where Gil, Crombie and Tony Pearson were deep in conversation. The strain was beginning to tell on the pressmen. Certainly on Crombie, at any rate.

Even Gil looked slightly more agitated than normal to Lassiter who was now approaching their table on his way over to give Hagan his last warning.

"Five minutes Gil. I'll be back in five. Have you had a look at the menu?"

Lassiter couldn't get used to seeing Gil and Pritchard in suits. And , more importantly, looking very smart in those suits into the bargain. It was a real scoop that one. Worth a press release on it's own.

"O.K. kid. Five minutes."

****

"You will be aware by now that the police are downstairs and I for one want to walk out of this place. Listen carefully to me. I don't give a shit for your reputation. I know you will already have arranged whatever you've arranged with regard to your shotguns, or baseball bats and pool cues, or heat seeking fucking missiles or what ever. If you too want to remain alive do exactly as I say. Not what Hagan's already told you. Understand?"

The accountant type stared hard at Lassiter before an almost imperceptible blink of the eyes behind the spectacles gave notice that he was at least willing to listen to him.

"Right. What is going to happen now is this."

****

They sat across the table staring directly into each other's hate filled eyes. Lassiter spoke first.

"I trusted you. And because I trusted you I made the mistake of trusting other people you told me it was alright to trust."

"You're fuckin' problem."

"Old Turner always knew that you were the real rising star. CJ was too emotionally unstable, and too pointlessly vicious maybe, to be trusted with the keys to the kingdom. Evil enough sure, but not rational enough. Really good criminals need to be dispassionate. Not physcopathic. Quite prepared to kill when the occasion demands it But never to let emotions get in the way of good business. Or lunacy. Why did you let me think you're father was dead now? You didn't go to that pub that night because of your father. That wouldn't have been good business. Not when the situation was being taken care of any way. Right so far?"

"Get fuckin' oan wi' it Lassiter. Because ye've no' goat much fuckin' time left. Whit ye lookin' at them fur? It's me ye're dealin wi. Ah'm the wan ye know."

"Or thought I did. Alright. The best way to deflect attention from oneself sometimes is to attract it. By doing something slightly different. Not expected. To be close to something maybe, but obviously not part of it. You're an ace at that. Learned that one from your father. Now let's turn to your father for a moment. A pillar of society him. Gave his own children away, just because he hated girls. Only liked boys. Maybe something Freudian there. Steady now. Settle down. Once I finish the story, I've got some nice music to calm you down. Wouldn't do to start anything just yet. That way you'd never know how much I really knew. Maybe told somebody else. Maybe already have. Never thought of that did you? Very remiss of you. According to the papers and the police, one Danny Hagan went to that particular pub that night to avenge a wrong done to his father. Not so. Anybody who knew or knows Danny Hagan, knows he was set up for that one. Deflection again see. Just enough attention. But yet not enough for the real truth. You are a clever bastard no question about that. Now let's talk about the façade. Way of dressing, talking ,looking. Everything. You're still doing it. Even tonight. And your help at the Taylor's house that night. Stroke of genius that. Very brave. And all the time, the act. A friend. You knew them all too. All the Merediths and what they were. Crooks yes. Murderers no. Not like you. . Old Turner was right you see. CJ Taylor and his equally physcotic little friend had fucked up. And Turners real successor told you to sort it out. Right again? And you always did what he told you to do. Still doing it. Doesn't sit well sometimes does it? With you or your brother. Let's come to your brother for a minute. Because he's a clever bastard too. Visiting nursing homes. Telling old ladies his name's Horner. You've always had to keep an eye out for him haven't you? Or ON him, might be nearer the truth. That right? Yes you knew them all. Or rather the family did. Rankin and the Scotstoun team. And Rankin's father. Threatened to kill him didn't you? Indirectly at any rate. Through Taylor. But he fucked up again."

He stared at Lassiter. Gone was the tired, world weary gaze. The eyes emanated raw danger now, narrowed and glinting in the dark of the dance hall.

"What makes this easy is what you did to Sarah, Maggie and PJ. And good old Horner. I've grown to like him. Old Plum. Plum. "Grapes" We're getting a bit fruity again. Settle down you. I haven't come to you yet. Your turns coming. I want to talk to you about hospitals. And to him about nursing homes, and visits to pubs in the East End. To put the frighteners on people. Fun this isn't it? And we've got music to look forward to later. I think most people are enjoying themselves. What do you think? Seem to be anyway. I hope nothing happens to spoil it for them. That DJ's terrific. Music with a message. Says that on his card. Certainly getting the message over tonight. Memory lane stuff, eh?"

"Shut the fuck up. Whit dae ye waant?"

"Me? Nothing."

"A' this means fuck all. You cannae prove a thing. Onybuddy else that knew onythin' is either deid or gonnae be. We jist need to find wan ae them. No' a problem. He'll fuckin come tae us."

"C.J.? He'll find it difficult, as he's still banged up. Always has been. And Lynch isn't dead. Never has been either. Isn't the media marvellous? You can make people believe anything if you're clever enough. But I think you know that already don't you? Thirty years practice. You'll get thirty years too. But you won't do it. Too old now. So you'll just die inside. All of you. All the same to me."

"You'll no' see it. You'll fuckin' die in here."

"Stop doing that will you? Changing you're accent. I know a lady who's much better at it than you are. How could you do this to Maggie for all these years? She told me one night that she would do

anything for you. Idolised you most of her life. And that wasn't thirty years ago, she said that. That's why she never told anybody your little secret about the pub that night. But she told me something else that same night. Although she loved you, she was always terrified of you, and what you were capable of. Told her not to be stupid. You were sound. A good guy. Look who was the stupid one. Still, we all make mistakes. We don't all get the chance to rectify them."
"Ah'm really gonnae enjoy doin' you right in ya bastart."
"See? You're doing it again. Wait till I hear my requests will you? Not long now."

****

"You'll need to explain all this to me later. I know what you're saying but you've lost me somewhere. Or Lassiter has to be more exact."
"Did you sleep through the bloody sixties and seventies Norrie?"
"I was busy becoming a force within the force. As you should have been. Wasted talent. You're a better cop than I could ever dream of being."
"Know more about fucking music at any rate. That much is obvious. But not as much as Lassiter does. He's always been fascinated by words too. Their different meanings. Usage. That sort of thing. Who was it said that? About the pen being mightier than the sword. Lassiter believes it anyway."
"Just you hope and pray that they're both right. So they're the signals? Those three songs? Get the boys ready. Timing. Timing"
"What're you worried about? We'll see how good they are when they're up against Dawson and his crew."
"All these years. Of missing the obvious."
"The press got it all wrong too. Wrong slant."
"Or all right. Depends how you look at it."
"Fuck sake Norrie. You're turning into Lassiter."
"No chance. He's a one of you said. Remember?"

....

Reggie and his sister had come by special invitation too. Hagan's. Nobody had seen them come in. They'd arrived after Horner and the three girls had left. A lot of people had started to leave by that time so there were vacant and secluded seats at the rear of the hall. The other guests were by now too pre-occupied , not to mention inebriated to notice the two new arrivals. Lassiter had not seen them come in. But Hagan had. He had swaggered arrogantly to the gents toilet as Lassiter stood up and moved towards the little stage to give final instructions to the DJ.
"You sober?"

"Jew."

"Goat them?"

Reggie opened his coat to reveal the weapons. Hagan took the smallest of the two handguns and slipped it into the inside pocket of his immaculately tailored suit.

"Ah jist want ye tae know sumthin' apart fae whit ye already know. See thoan night at the bus stoap when Lassiter pulled you up in front ae the ither boays. He wis the wan that wis laughin' it ye the maist. Do him Reggie. Ah know ye've no' forgoat how."

"Fuckin' watch me Danny. Ah'll get the bastard."

Hagan proceeded towards the gents. The arrogant little twist of the mouth that passed for a smile was back. He opened the cistern in the cubicle, wiped the gun with his immaculate silk handkerchief and concealed it behind the the cistern. He knew where it was if needed. But he certainly had no intention of going back for it. All he had to do now was watch Reggie. Hagan knew he was still a vicious little bastard. Hagan had never underestimated anyone. Except Lassiter.

****

"You see your father knew too much about Turner and his cronies. He knew too much about hospitals and drunken old nurses who also knew too much. Much more than he needed to know. You on the other hand didn't seem to know enough. I had to find it all out for myself. Piecemeal. About doctor's who took kickbacks, about a team of ex-soldiers prepared to help with a bit of enforcement. About why a sex obsessed newsman didn't take the opportunity to interview a very pretty trainee journalist himself. Am I making sense? What time is it? Oh a good five minutes yet. Don't want to miss my music. About an old woman in a nursing home who recognised the other man who came down to see her one day with "Adjie" Jamieson to find out how much she really knew. From a newspaper clipping I had to find myself later. A back copy of The Voice. Poor old dead "Adjie". He had to go not because of Taylor or Lynch or the Merediths or any of them. He had to go because he'd seen you again, and then later your brother. In the Jamiesons' pub What kept fucking everything up was the attention given to people like the Merediths, the Scotstoun boys, the Jamiesons, even Horner. Horner had the reputation of being the kingpin of criminal business in Glasgow, and it was you all the time. I'd always wondered about the changing thing. Or not, to be precise. How other people had seemed to progress in whatever direction they had chosen. And yet you hadn't. They were driving about in bloody Jaguars all over Glasgow. And there you were. Still where you'd always been. Only difference seemed to be that you didn't want any publicity of any kind. Still very tough, and certainly not to be provoked. But quiter. World weary and cynical."

"Right ah've fuckin' heard enough. Ah think we'll just take ye outside the noo."
"Tell him to shut his fucking mouth. He's only fit to frighten old women in nursing homes. And old drunks in pubs. But the old drunk's barman, PHIL Jamieson recognised that same clipping of your brother from the back copy. As the supposed maniac who brought the Scotstoun Team in. Now let's recap a bit. You didn't go to the pub that night because someone had told you something about your father. Your father had told you not to go to that particular pub that night.. And you always did what your father said. Am I confusing you now Tony? Gil knows what I mean. The pub thirty years ago. You were the real surprise for me. Bill sort of gave himself away. Must be his age. Had to hand the reins over some time ago. To his other son. Didn't he Gil? Like the menu? Handwritten by me. I thought you'd appreciate it. What did I write? Something about music being the food of love or some such shit? Here comes your music now. And don't move a fucking muscle any of you. Hello Danny my old pal. Nice to see you come up at the back there. With your business associates. More than he did for you thirty years ago. Gil and I have met them before. I think Gil's met them more often than me though, I'd hazard a guess. But they were never on his side at any time. He just thought they were. And don't turn round now Mr. Crombie, but I do believe your real children have joined us. You know the two you swapped with C.J. Taylor because you hated girls. Still think you're decidedly odd with regard to that. Especially for these two. "Adjie" Gilmour and Tony Pearson. The "Glasgow Voice". Very ironic. And their senile old father who thinks he's Don Corleone. What a fucking bunch Danny boy eh?"
"Fuck sake Lassiter. Get that bastard "Adjie" oot ae here before ah dae him some real damage. Ah telt ye all along it wis that bastard din't ah? Din't ah? He tried tae git me time fur years. The loat ae them. Wi' their fuckin' newspapers. Oh fuck it. Ah'm no waitin fur nae polis. Ah'm jist gonnae dae him right now. Reggie's goat a..."
"Danny, my old friend I'd be delighted if you did. But two things might happen. I might not get to hear my requests. And less importantly when Dawson charges up those stairs like Dirty "fucking" Harry he might just shoot you by mistake. And then what would I tell P.J. and Maggie. I'm not suicidal."
"Could ah fuckin' fooled me."
"Content yourself with disarming Reggie. Alright Reggie? Thanks for your help."

"Nae bother big man. Ah'm sorry aboot a' thae years ago noo.. Mebbe's ah'm growin' up. Onywiy Danny telt me it wis him that wis daein' the laughin' it me. No' you, sae much."
"Trick is, sober up Reggie. You and your sister have had a raw deal

because of these three bastards. Thanks for going to see Taylor in the hospital with this slimy bastard, Phillippa. I'll let Sarah know how much help you've been. She'll come round eventually. I hope you get some money from the press for all this. All of you. I'll help as much as I can. That goes for you too Danny. That goes without saying."
"Well don't say it. Dae it!"
"Now, now Daniel. The gentlemen of the press want to hear my requests. And so do Strathclyde Police I understand!"
Downstairs in the public bar there was complete silence as the young DJ's voice boomed suddenly from the speakers.

****

"Ladies and gentlemen. We have three tracks specially requested by our friend and patron tonight Mr. Tom Lassiter. He admits they are probably not every one's favourites, and not even strictly from the era we're dancing the night away to tonight. But they do have a special significance both for the gentlemen of the press here with us tonight, and some more friends of his downstairs. The first is by the Bee Gees. And that will be followed by Procul Harum. And regrettably, for me at any rate, the second is not the massive hit "Whiter Shade of Pale" The third I'm sure is perhaps not so well known , but fits the occasion according to Mr. Lassiter, and stands on it's own at any rate. A very fine song.
So here we go then with "Words" by the Bee Gees to be followed by the perhaps lesser known , but nevertheless quite brilliant "Homburg" by Procul Harum!
"Ye're still a fuckin' headcase Tam" said Danny Hagan with his arm round Gil/"Adjie's" neck and Reggie's gun aimed ever so casually at Tony Pearson's right temple
"And we'll finish with the third and final track. "THE VOICE" by John Farnham."

****

It was at that precise moment Dawson and his boys hit the stairs with their Mausers and Webleys.
Dawson was just crazy enough to be enjoying himself.
And the music!

THE END

www.ingramcontent.com/pod-product-compliance
Lightning Source LLC
Chambersburg PA
CBHW020613310726
48979CB00008B/1470/J

* 9 7 8 0 9 5 7 0 8 7 1 0 1 *